CONTENTS

ACKNOWLEDGEMENTS

A number of people have helped us in the preparation of this book. In particular we would like to thank Gillian Beer, Glen Cavaliero, Diana Collecott, Sirius C. Cook, Con Coroneos, Leela Gandhi, Susan Gevirtz, Pip Hurd, Lynn Knight, Sandi Russell, Perdita Schaffner, Gill Thomas and Oliver Wilkinson for their advice and kind assistance. We are grateful to the Australian Federation of University Women, Western Australia, for providing us with a special grant in 1989, and to the Australian Federation of University Women, Queensland (Audrey Jauss-Freda Freeman Fellowship). We are indebted to the pioneering research on modernist women's writing undertaken by Shari Benstock, Gillian Hanscombe and Virginia Smyers.

Permission to reproduce the following stories has been kindly granted by the following: Djuna Barnes: by The Authors' League Fund, 234 West 44th Street, New York 10036 and Historic Churches Preservation Trust, Fulham Place, London SW6 6EA as literary executors of the Estate of Djuna Barnes, for 'Katrina Silverstaff' from *A Book* (1923); Kay Boyle: by the author and the Watkins/Loomis Agency, New York, for 'Wedding Day' from *Wedding Day and Other Stories* (1930); Bryher: by Perdita Schaffner, for 'Extract' from *Contact*, 3 (c.1921); Leonora Carrington: by Virago Press and Penguin, USA for 'Pigeon, Fly!', written in French between 1937 and 1940, translated by Kathrine Talbot, from *The Seventh Horse* (1990); Emily Holmes Coleman: by Phyllis Jones as literary executor of the Estate of

vii

Emily Holmes Coleman, for 'Interlude', from *transition* (1927); Colette: by Martin Secker and Warburg Ltd., for 'The Hand' from *La Femme Cachée* (1924), translated by Matthew Ward; H.D.: by New Directions Publishing Corporation, agents for Perdita Schaffner, for 'Kora and Ka' Copyright 1930 by Hilda Doolittle; Janet Flanner: by Natalia Denesi Murray, literary executor of Janet Flanner, for 'Venetian Perspective', Copyright Natalia Denesi Murray, first published in *The New Yorker*, 25 August 1936, reprinted in *Short Stories from The New Yorker*, Gollancz (1951); Susan Glaspell: by Daphne C. Cook, literary executor, for 'A Jury of Her Peers', probably written in 1917, reprinted in *Modern American Short Stories*, edited by Edward O'Brien (1932); Frances Gregg: by the Estate of Frances Gregg, for 'Male and Female', published here for the first time; Mina Loy: by Roger L. Conover, literary executor of Mina Loy, for 'Street Sister', published here for the first time; Anaïs Nin: by Peter Owen Ltd., London, for 'Ragtime' from *Under a Glass Bell* (1944); Jean Rhys: by André Deutsch Ltd., London for 'Illusion' from *The Left Bank and Other Stories* (1927); Dorothy Richardson: by Mark Paterson and Associates on behalf of the Estate of Dorothy Richardson for 'Visitor' from *Life and Letters* (1945); May Sinclair: by the Curtis Brown Group Ltd. on behalf of the Estate of May Sinclair for 'The Token' Copyright May Sinclair from *Uncanny Stories* (1923); Stevie Smith: by Virago Press and James MacGibbon for 'The Story of a Story' from *New Savoy* (1946), reprinted in *Me Again* (1981); Gertrude Stein: by Calman Levin for the Gertrude Stein Estate, for 'Miss Furr and Miss Skeene' from *Geography and Plays*, Four Seas, Boston (1922); Virginia Woolf: by the executors of the Virginia Woolf Estate and the Hogarth Press for 'The New Dress' from *A Haunted House* (1944).

INTRODUCTION

One afternoon in September 1912 in the tea room of the British Museum, Hilda Doolittle became H.D. Or, to be more precise, one of her poems was signed in this way for the first time – not by Hilda Doolittle herself, but by Ezra Pound, her friend, former fiancé, some would say mentor. Although she was to use many different names in her writing career, she remains best known today by these enigmatic, asexual initials. Was this an act of liberation, freeing her from the name of her famous, scientific father, a name which she found comical and embarrassing? Or was it an act of appropriation – a man, another Pygmalion, imposing a new name upon a woman, marking her as his creation?[1]

The ambiguity surrounding H.D.'s name and identity is particularly intriguing here. This anthology, the first of its kind, draws together twenty-six stories by women writers of the modernist period, roughly 1890 to 1940.[2] Like their work, the women occupy a complex – even contradictory – place within literary history. 'You know that kind of woman', remarks Djuna Barnes. Yet there is no single 'kind' of modernist woman writer, as these stories demonstrate. They were written by the famous and by those whose names are hardly known; recluses and extroverts; the rich and the impoverished; novelists and poets; heterosexuals, bisexuals and lesbians, and women from different class backgrounds.[3] A number of them wrote or lived under adopted names: Bryher, Colette, George Egerton, Vernon Lee, Mina Loy, Katherine Mansfield, Jean Rhys. Some, including

H.D. and Dorothy Richardson, wrote under a number of different names – masculine, feminine and ungendered.

This was a particularly exciting and productive era for women writers, many of whom felt they had escaped from restrictive social or family structures. Just as their writing – experimental and avant-garde – challenged orthodox literary values, so many of their lives challenged traditional notions of femininity. Until recently, they were largely forgotten. And though respected – even famous – in their own day, most modernist women remain marginal figures in history compared to the modernist men (Joyce, Pound, Eliot, Conrad, Lawrence, Ford, for example). Their work deserves a wider audience.

This anthology is part of the feminist project of re-reading modernism. In this context, the re-naming of Hilda Doolittle stands as a symbol of the struggle over the meaning of women writers and their work, whether 'H.D.' is read as a feminist refusal of patriarchal identity, as a celebration of gender ambiguity, or as a mark of oppression from which the writer struggled all her life to be free.[4] Set side by side, the stories raise interesting possibilities for reading and interpreting women's place in modernism.

What were the conditions that produced these stories? For artists, this was a new period of internationalism. Many writers were expatriates, the most famous being the 'lost generation' of British and Americans in Paris between the wars, which included many of the women here.[5] This alone differentiates them from the previous generation of women writers. The conditions of expatriotism were at once liberating and alienating, and the paradox was often productive.

Widely dispersed as these writers sometimes were, complex networks existed between them – emotional and erotic on the one hand, professional and artistic on the other. Few of the women in this collection were in traditional marriage partnerships; it has been argued that this is precisely what made it possible for them to write.[6] More than half of them knew, loved, disliked or wrote about each other in an informal network which stretched from Paris to New York via London, and took in both local and expatriate women as well as men.

Behind or beside most of these women stood at least one woman, and often a man or two: this was true of Barnes, Bryher, Flanner, H.D. and Mansfield, among others. Gertrude Stein is perhaps the most famous such case. She came to Paris from the United States with her brother in 1903, and from 1910 until her death over thirty years later, she lived with Alice B. Toklas, amanuensis, lover, confidante and cook, whose support was crucial to Stein's work. Their friends and acquaintances included Winifred Bryher, the journalist Janet Flanner, Natalie Barney (whose lesbian salon was a centre for many expatriate women), Sylvia Beach and Djuna Barnes. Like Stein, Barnes was highly regarded among the expatriates in Paris: only the work of James Joyce, one of her few male friends, was considered to surpass her own.[7] The publication of her novel *Nightwood* (which T.S. Eliot accepted for Faber and for which he wrote an introduction) in 1936 was due largely to the persistence of Barnes' friend, Emily Holmes Coleman. Other women in their circle included Kay Boyle, Mary Butts and Mina Loy.

Paris was not appealing to all expatriate writers, however. For Jean Rhys, who existed on the margins of literary society, it was a place of economic and emotional exploitation. Nor was H.D. particularly comfortable there. She shared with Dorothy Richardson and Virginia Woolf an intense love of London. Dorothy Edwards, too, moved to London for a time from her native Wales. H.D.'s early friends there included May Sinclair, who described her as 'the best of the imagists' (though she was to leave imagism far behind as she went on to produce her finest work), and Richard Aldington, whom she would later marry, and with whom she established an avant-garde coterie, the 'Other Bloomsbury'.

The extensive professional networks sometimes included direct or indirect financial support. Peggy Guggenheim provided constant if frugal assistance for Barnes and others. H.D., together with several other writers here, was published by Robert McAlmon's Contact Editions in Paris.[8] McAlmon, in turn, received financial assistance from his wife, Winifred Bryher, whose wealth allowed her to support many literary interests and writers, including Mary Butts, Dorothy Richardson and Edith Sitwell.

Bryher also patronised modernist writers through her ownership of some of the literary and film magazines which proliferated in the period. A lot of these were founded and supported by women, including *The Little Review*, edited by Margaret Anderson and Jane Heap (1914–29), Harriet Monroe's *Poetry* magazine (1912–35), Dora Marsden's *The Freewoman* and *The New Freewoman* (1911–12, 1913; continued as *The Egoist*, 1914–19). New publishing ventures and bookshops, such as Sylvia Beach's famous Shakespeare and Company in Paris, also provided many opportunities for experimental writers.[9]

These personal and institutional connections were important for many writers, perhaps especially for women. Rather than a collection of separate experiments undertaken by individual geniuses (a model often used to discuss key modernist men), modernism might be more usefully thought of in terms of *cultural formations* which helped provide opportunities for individuals to write.[10] And the cultural formations of the period are much more than simply a context for the experimental writing which took place.

Developments in the new areas of psychoanalysis and film, in experimental publishing, in art and music, and in modes of living all influenced modernist writing. The period encompassed a wide range of innovative literary forms and ideas, from the decadent writing of the 1890s to the various avant-garde movements (imagism, futurism, dadaism, surrealism, etc.) and beyond. Fragmentation, uncertainty and open-endedness – challenging and transforming traditional values and forms – also characterised modernism. These strategies are noticeable in H.D.'s work. In 'Kora and Ka', fragmentation and palimpsest are used to create a disjointed sense of identity, which in turn raises interesting questions about H.D.'s ambiguous attitude to her own bisexuality. Such techniques were also important in the development of the short story which flourished in the period and in which women were particularly active.[11]

Central to these literary experiments were changes in the understanding of subjectivity. On the one hand modernist writing was responding to ideas from psychoanalysis (especially from Freud), from evolutionary theory, socialism, suffragism and other philosophical debates of the time; on the other, the writing itself *produced* new ideas and values. The fiction interacted with the material conditions under which it was produced *and* with ideas occurring in other kinds of writing, especially ideas about the construction of the self. For example, Charlotte Perkins Gilman, perhaps the most overtly political of the writers here, wrote a number of texts about gender and oppression, also exploring these issues in her fiction. 'The Yellow Wallpaper' portrays a woman driven mad when she is forbidden to work or to write after the birth of her child. She manages to write secretly, but this does not save her from hallucinations and eventual breakdown. Her madness – or hysteria – is shown to be the result of social oppression, and not something biologically determined by her sex as earlier writers would perhaps have claimed.[12] Other writers here reveal their engagement with ideas from a wide range of philosophical, fictional, political and psychoanalytical writings of the time, which enabled them to break new ground.

It is often argued that modernism explored the loss of belief in a stable, 'essential' self. Women, however, have been seen as the 'other' to man's 'one', and as mirrors to reflect the (imaginary) wholeness or unity of man. As the myth of the unified, autonomous self began to be explored and exposed *as* myth women were less likely than men to mourn its passing as they had never had the right to full participation in it in the first place.[13]

Moreover, definitions of masculinity and femininity were strongly challenged, not least by the activities of the suffrage movement. The debates around women's suffrage refocused questions about the meaning of 'woman' – was she rational? What did she want and what rights could she claim? How could she be represented – both in Parliament and in art? The shifting meanings attached to 'woman' (and, though it is not usually stated, to 'man' as well) reveal it to be a category which is culturally constructed and which changes over time, as can be seen in the different notions of motherhood – crucial to the meaning of 'woman' – portrayed in some of the stories here. For the narrator of Coleman's 'Interlude', giving birth, far from being a realisation of her 'true' nature as a woman, is a profoundly alienating experience. And in Egerton's 'The Spell of the White Elf', motherhood is posited as a social, not a biological role. Furthermore, 'woman' is a category with differences *within*; differences of class, race, age, language and so forth might be just as important as gender in the construction of a sense of self, as many of these writers recognised.

*

What did these women write about? The differences among their stories are as important as the similarities. But there are certain issues which recur, in various forms. A number of the stories look at the 'woman question'. What does it mean to be a woman, and what does being a woman *mean*? Some writers explore this question through women's relationships to work. The writing that is the work of Stevie Smith's narrator is regarded by her friends as personal gossip rather than professional output, while the denial of the right to work is a key factor in the madness suffered by Gilman's narrator. Other stories pursue this theme through portrayals of sexuality – lesbianism, bisexuality and heterosexuality.

Femininity in these stories is regarded in various ways as *constructed*, not innate. This is important in Dorothy Richardson's 'Visitor' where femininity, like the embroidery that represents it, can only come with practice; and in Frances Gregg's 'Male and Female', where heterosexuality has to be learned as well. Another view is of femininity as a masquerade – an obvious disguise whose very obviousness reveals that the 'feminine' is a construct.[14] In 'Illusion' by Jean Rhys, the feminine is expressed – and parodied – through its most obvious, superficial features: clothing and make-up. The woman in Woolf's 'The New Dress', however, has no ironic distance on femininity as a mask.

These stories also raise questions about the relationship between gender and *reading*. In Susan Glaspell's 'A Jury of Her Peers', the ability to 'read' the domestic signs enables two women to discover the truth about a murder, and to hide that information from men. Here, restrictive notions of feminine deference are appropriated to their advantage, though the larger framework of the story shows how the same notions have oppressed one woman to the point where she is driven to commit murder. Similarly, Vernon Lee's narrator 'reads' the doll of the story's title as a mode of representation which at once idealises and oppresses women.

These are often stories about *writing*. In the stories by Mary Butts and Stevie Smith, the act of writing itself is part of the plot, but it is also an issue in many of the other stories, as they explore, in their own forms and narrative methods, the different ways in which a story might be told. Motivation and causality are thrown into question in Barnes' 'Katrina Silverstaff'; in Nin's 'Ragtime', elision and fragmentation create a dream-like sense of a repressed or discarded femininity from the narrator's past returning to permeate the present. In Stein's 'Miss Furr and Miss Skeene', a story of a lesbian couple, certain words and phrases are repeated and compel the reader's attention to the act of writing; the words themselves become part of the plot. In each case, the act of telling is part of the story's meaning and is crucial to its representations of gender.

What is fascinating about these stories is the way in which questions surrounding gender and writing converge. This is striking in Mary Butts' 'The Golden Bough', whose title echoes J.G. Frazer's pioneering anthropological work (1890–1915). Setting Frazer's theme of sacrifice in London after the First World War, Butts inverts traditional roles: the man, who is the sacrifice, becomes muse to the woman. The war has changed everything, so how, the story asks, is one to be a 'woman' or a 'man' in the post-war world, and how might these shifting definitions be represented?

The Great War can be seen as a point of crisis for constructions of gender, particularly masculinity, as myths of heroism and war were subverted by the powerlessness, fear and shellshock (seen as a form of hysteria) many men experienced. Femininity also underwent changes, as women took over men's work on the home front and finally won the right to vote. War *angst* can be found in the writing of many modernist men, whether or not they were actually engaged in fighting; it also permeates much writing by women, especially by H.D., whose story 'Kora and Ka' explores gender identity, the unconscious and the relationships between those who have survived the war and those who have not.[15]

Other stories – by Barnes, Boyle, Colette, Flanner, Glaspell, Mansfield and Sinclair, for example – look at issues surrounding heterosexuality and marriage, while relationships between women – as lovers, friends, rivals, sisters, sources of support or of oppression – are examined by Colette, Glaspell, Lee and Stein, among others. All of these stories look at relationships between sexual, social and gender identity, raising questions of how narrative techniques and gender politics interact.

The twenty-six stories collected here are as diverse as the women who wrote them. They offer new and challenging ways of thinking about modernism, about writing, and about women's place in literary history.

Bronte Adams, Oxford and Trudi Tate, Cambridge
1990

NOTES

1. There are several different accounts of H.D. acquiring this name, an event which is sometimes seen as the birth of the Imagist movement in poetry. For H.D.'s version of the story, see *End to Torment*, Carcanet Press, Manchester, 1980. See also Rachel Blau DuPlessis, *H.D.: The Career of that Struggle*, pp. 6–7, Harvester Press, Brighton, 1986. DuPlessis notes that H.D. wrote under a number of different names – Delia Alton, Rhoda Peter, John Helforth, among others.

2. The dates of modernism are widely disputed. We have tried to represent a wide range of the styles of the period, and to show modernism's development in the 1940s in the stories by Dorothy Richardson and Stevie Smith.

3. With the exception of Nella Larsen, all the writers here are white. Further research may show the assumption that Black women of the period did not employ modernist strategies in their writing to be incorrect. The absence of Black women's writing is significant, both for this collection and for our understanding of modernism. See Sandi Russell's recent study of Black women writers, *Render Me My Song: African-American Women Writers from Slavery to the Present*, Pandora, London, 1990, which includes a discussion of Nella Larsen.

4. Paul Smith, 'H.D.'s Identity', *Women's Studies*, 10, 1984.

5. Shari Benstock, *Women of the Left Bank: Paris 1900–1940*, Virago, London, 1987, is a useful and detailed study of expatriate women writers in Paris.

6. Gillian Hanscombe and Virginia Smyers, *Writing for their Lives: The Modernist Women 1910–1940*, The Women's Press, London, 1987.

7. Benstock, p. 236.

8. Other Contact Editions include: Bryher, *Two Selves* (1923), Mary Butts, *Ashe of Rings* (1925), H.D., *Palimpsest* (1926), Mina Loy, *Lunar Baedecker (sic.* 1923), Gertrude Stein, *The Making of Americans* (1925). *The Contact Collection of Contemporary Writers*, ed. Robert McAlmon (1925) contained twenty pieces of writing, nine of which were by women.

9. On Sylvia Beach, see Noel Riley Fitch, *Sylvia Beach and the Lost Generation: A History of Literary Paris in the Twenties and Thirties*, Penguin, Harmondsworth, 1985. Bryher founded the film journal *Close Up* (1927–33) and owned *Life and Letters Today* (1933–50). For further discussion of the little magazines' publication of women's work, see Hanscombe and Smyers, Ch. 11.

10. Makiko Minow, 'Versions of Female Modernism', *News from Nowhere*, 7, 1989; Raymond Williams, *Culture*, pp. 60–86, Fontana, Glasgow, 1981.

11. The rise of the short story was accompanied by some alarm at the moral degeneracy of readers, for it was feared they would become incapable of reading longer fiction. This is possibly connected with the fact that it was sometimes seen as a 'feminine' form of writing. On the relationship between the short story and gender, see Mary Eagleton, 'Gender and Genre', in *Re-Reading the Short Story*, ed. Clare Hanson, Macmillan, London, 1989.

12. Gilman, *Women and Economics* (1898), *Man Made World* (1911). For a useful discussion of feminism and 'The Yellow Wallpaper', see Lynne Pearce's chapter in Sara Mills et al., *Feminist Readings, Feminists Reading*, Harvester Wheatsheaf, Hemel Hempstead, 1989.

13. Patricia Waugh, *Feminine Fictions: Revisiting the Postmodern*, Routledge, London, 1989 has an excellent discussion of women, subjectivity and modernism.

14. Joan Riviere, 'Womanliness as a Masquerade', *International Journal of Psychoanalysis*, 10, 1929; reprinted in *Formations of Fantasy*, ed. Victor Burgin, James Donald and Cora Kaplan, Methuen, London, 1986. See also Stephen Heath's essay on Riviere in the same volume.

15. On gender and the First World War, see Elaine Showalter, *The Female Malady: Women, Madness and English Culture, 1830–1980*, Virago, London, 1985; Sandra M. Gilbert and Susan Gubar, 'Soldier's Heart: Literary Men, Literary Women, and the Great War', in *No Man's Land: The Place of the Woman Writer in the Twentieth Century*, vol. 2, *Sexchanges*, Yale University Press, New Haven, 1989; Claire M. Tylee, *The Great War and Women's Consciousness: Images of Militarism and Womanhood in Women's Writings, 1914–64*, Macmillan, London, 1990. See also H.D.'s account of the First World War in *Bid Me to Live*, Virago, London, 1984.

JEAN RHYS
ILLUSION

M iss Bruce was quite an old inhabitant of the Quarter. For seven years she had lived there, in a little studio up five flights of stairs. She had painted portraits, exhibited occasionally at the Salon. She had even sold a picture sometimes – a remarkable achievement for Montparnasse, but possible, for I believe she was just clever enough and not too clever, though I am no judge of these matters.

She was a tall, thin woman, with large bones and hands and feet. One thought of her as a shining example of what character and training – British character and training – can do. After seven years in Paris she appeared utterly untouched, utterly unaffected, by anything hectic, slightly exotic or unwholesome. Going on all the time all round her were the cult of beauty and the worship of physical love: she just looked at her surroundings in her healthy, sensible way, and then dismissed them from her thoughts . . . rather like some sturdy rock with impotent blue waves washing round it.

When pretty women passed her in the streets or sat near her in restaurants – La Femme, exquisitely perfumed and painted, feline, loved – she would look appraisingly with the artist's eye, and make a suitably critical remark. She exhibited no tinge of curiosity or envy. As for the others, the *petites femmes*, anxiously consulting the mirrors of their bags, anxiously and searchingly looking round with darkened eye-lids: 'Those unfortunate people!' would say Miss Bruce. Not in a hard way, but broad-mindedly, breezily: indeed with a thoroughly gentlemanly intonation . . . These unfortunate little people!

She always wore a neat serge dress in the summer and a neat tweed costume in the winter, brown shoes with low heels and cotton stockings. When she was going to parties she put on a black gown of crêpe de chine, just well enough cut, not extravagantly pretty.

In fact Miss Bruce was an exceedingly nice woman.

She powdered her nose as a concession to Paris; the rest of her face shone, beautifully washed, in the sunlight or the electric light as the case might be, with here and there a few rather lovable freckles.

She had, of course, like most of the English and American artists in Paris, a private income – a respectably large one, I believe. She knew most people and was intimate with nobody. We had been dining and lunching together, now and then, for two years, yet I only knew the outside of Miss Bruce – the cool, sensible, tidy English outside.

*

Well, we had an appointment on a hot, sunny afternoon, and I arrived to see her about three o'clock. I was met by a very perturbed concierge.

Mademoiselle had been in bed just one day, and, suddenly, last night about eight o'clock the pain had become terrible. The *femme de ménage*, 'Mame' Pichon, who had stayed all day and she, the concierge, had consulted anxiously, had fetched a doctor and, at his recommendation, had had her conveyed to the English Hospital in an ambulance.

'She took nothing with her,' said the *femme de ménage*, a thin and voluble woman. 'Nothing at all, pauvre Mademoiselle.' If Madame – that was me – would give herself the trouble to come up to the studio, here were the keys. I followed Mme. Pichon up the stairs. I must go at once to Miss Bruce and take her some things. She must at least have nightgowns and a comb and brush.

'The keys of the wardrobe of Mademoiselle,' said Mme. Pichon insinuatingly, and with rather a queer sidelong look at me, 'are in this small drawer. Ah, les voila!'

I thanked her with a dismissing manner. Mme. Pichon was not a favourite of mine, and with firmness I watched her walk slowly to the door, try to start a conversation, and then, very reluctantly, disappear. Then I turned to the wardrobe – a big, square, solid piece of old, dark furniture, suited for the square and solid coats and skirts of Miss Bruce. Indeed, most of her furniture was big and square. Some strain in her made her value solidity and worth more than grace or fantasies. It was difficult to turn the large key, but I managed it at last.

'Good Lord!' I remarked out loud. Then, being very much surprised I sat down on a chair and said: 'Well, what a funny girl!'

For Miss Bruce's wardrobe when one opened it was a glow of colour, a riot of soft silks . . . a . . . everything that one did not expect.

In the middle, hanging in the place of honour, was an evening dress of a very beautiful shade of old gold; near it another of flame colour; of two black dresses the one was touched with silver, the other with a jaunty embroidery of emerald and blue; there were – a black and white check with a jaunty belt, a flowered crêpe de chine, positively flowered! – then a carnival costume complete with mask, then a huddle, a positive huddle of all colours, of all stuffs.

For one instant I thought of kleptomania, and dismissed the idea. Dresses for models, then? Absurd! Who would spend thousands of francs on dresses for models . . . No nightgowns here, in any case.

As I looked, hesitating, I saw in the corner a box without a lid. It contained a neat little range of smaller boxes: Rouge

Fascination; Rouge Mandarine; Rouge Andalouse; several powders; kohl for the eyelids and paint for the eyelashes – an outfit for a budding Manon Lescaut. Nothing was missing: there were scents too.

I shut the door hastily. I had no business to look or to guess. But I guessed. I knew. Whilst I opened the other half of the wardrobe and searched the shelves for nightgowns I knew it all: Miss Bruce, passing by a shop, with the perpetual hunger to be beautiful and that thirst to be loved which is the real curse of Eve, well hidden under her neat dress, more or less stifled, more or less unrecognized.

Miss Bruce had seen a dress and had suddenly thought: In that dress perhaps . . . And, immediately afterwards: Why not? And had entered the shop, and, blushing slightly, had asked the price. That had been the first time: an accident, an impulse.

The dress must have been disappointing, yet beautiful enough, becoming enough to lure her on. Then must have begun the search for *the* dress, the perfect Dress, beautiful, beautifying, possible to be worn. And lastly, the search for illusion – a craving, almost a vice, the stolen waters and the bread eaten in secret of Miss Bruce's life.

Wonderful moment! When the new dress would arrive and would emerge smiling and graceful from its tissue paper.

'Wear me, give me life,' it would seem to say to her, 'and I will do my damnedest for you!' And, first, not unskilfully, for was she not a portrait painter? Miss Bruce would put on the powder, the Rouge-Fascination, the rouge for the lips, lastly the dress – and she would gaze into the glass at a transformed self. She would sleep that night with a warm glow at her heart! No impossible thing, beauty and all that beauty brings. There close at hand, to be clutched if one dared. Somehow she never dared, next morning.

I thankfully seized a pile of nightgowns and sat down, rather miserably undecided. I knew she would hate me to have seen those dresses: Mame Pichon would tell her that I had been to the armoire. But she must have her nightgowns. I went to lock the wardrobe doors and felt a sudden, irrational pity for the beautiful things inside. I imagined them, shrugging their silken shoulders, rustling, whispering about the *anglaise* who had dared to buy them in order to condemn them to life in the dark . . . And I opened the door again.

The yellow dress appeared malevolent, slouching on its hanger; the black ones were mournful, only the little chintz frock smiled gaily, waiting for the supple body and limbs that should breathe life into it . . .

When I was allowed to see Miss Bruce a week afterwards I found her lying, clean, calm and sensible in the big ward – an appendicitis patient. They patched her up and two or three weeks later we dined together at our restaurant. At the coffee stage she said suddenly:

'I suppose you noticed my collection of frocks. Why should I not collect frocks? They fascinate me. The colour and all that. Exquisite sometimes!'

'Of course,' she added, carefully staring over my head at what appeared to me to be a very bad picture, 'I should never make such a fool of myself as to wear them . . . They ought to be worn, I suppose.'

A plump, dark girl, near us, gazed into the eyes of her dark, plump escort, and lit a cigarette with the slightly affected movements of the non-smoker.

'Not bad hands and arms, that girl!' said Miss Bruce in her gentlemanly manner.

VERNON LEE
THE DOLL

I believe that's the last bit of *bric-à-brac* I shall ever buy in my life (she said, closing the Renaissance casket) – that and the Chinese dessert set we have just been using. The passion seems to have left me utterly. And I think I can guess why. At the same time as the plates and the little coffer I bought a thing – I scarcely know whether I ought to call it a thing – which put me out of conceit with ferreting about among dead people's properties. I have often wanted to tell you about it, and stopped for fear of seeming an idiot. But it weighs upon me sometimes like a secret; so, silly or not silly, I think I should like to tell you the story. There, ring for some more logs, and put that screen before the lamp.

It was two years ago, in the autumn, at Foligno, in Umbria. I was alone at the inn, for you know my husband is too busy for my *bric-à-brac* journeys, and the friend who was to have met me fell ill and came on only later. Foligno isn't what people call an interesting place, but I liked it. There are a lot of picturesque little towns all round; and great savage mountains of pink stone, covered with ilex, where they roll faggots down into the torrent beds, within a drive. There's a full, rushing little river round one side of the walls, which are covered with ivy; and there are fifteenth-century frescoes, which I dare say you know all about. But, what of course I care for most, there are a number of fine old palaces, with gateways carved in that pink stone, and courts with pillars, and beautiful window gratings, mostly in good enough repair, for Foligno is a market town and a junction, and altogether a kind of metropolis down in the valley.

Also, and principally, I liked Foligno because I discovered a delightful curiosity-dealer. I don't mean a delightful curiosity shop, for he had nothing worth twenty francs to sell; but a delightful, enchanting old man. His Christian name was Orestes, and that was enough for me. He had a long white beard and such kind brown eyes, and beautiful hands; and he always carried an earthenware brazier under his cloak. He had taken to the curiosity business from a passion for beautiful things, and for the past of his native place, after having been a master mason. He knew all the old chronicles, lent me that of Matarazzo, and knew exactly where everything had happened for the last six hundred years. He spoke of the Trincis, who had been local despots, and of St. Angela, who is the local saint, and of the Baglionis and Cæsar Borgia and Julius II, as if he had known them; he showed me the place where St. Francis preached to the birds, and the place where Propertius – was it Propertius or Tibullus? – had had his farm; and when he accompanied me on my rambles in search of *bric-à-brac* he would stop at corners and under arches and say, 'This, you see, is where they carried off those Nuns I told you about; that's where the Cardinal was stabbed. That's the place where they razed the palace after the massacre, and passed the ploughshare through the ground and sowed salt.' And all with a vague, far-off, melancholy look, as if he lived in those days and not these. Also he helped me to get that little velvet coffer with the iron clasps, which is really one of the best things we have in the house. So I was very happy at Foligno, driving and prowling about all day, reading the chronicles Orestes lent me in the evening; and I didn't mind waiting so long for my friend who never turned up. That is to say, I was perfectly happy until within three days of my departure. And now comes the story of my strange purchase.

Orestes, with considerable shrugging of shoulders, came one morning with the information that a certain noble person of

Foligno wanted to sell me a set of Chinese plates. 'Some of them are cracked,' he said; 'but at all events you will see the inside of one of our finest palaces, with all its rooms as they used to be – nothing valuable; but I know that the signora appreciates the past wherever it has been let alone.'

The palace, by way of exception, was of the late seventeenth century, and looked like a barracks among the neat little carved Renaissance houses. It had immense lions' heads over all the windows, a gateway in which two coaches could have met, a yard where a hundred might have waited, and a colossal staircase with stucco virtues on the vaultings. There was a cobbler in the lodge and a soap factory on the ground floor, and at the end of the colonnaded court a garden with ragged yellow vines and dead sunflowers. 'Grandiose, but very coarse – almost eighteenth-century,' said Orestes as we went up the sounding, low-stepped stairs. Some of the dessert set had been placed, ready for my inspection, on a great gold console in the immense escutcheoned anteroom. I looked at it, and told them to prepare the rest for me to see the next day. The owner, a very noble person, but half ruined – I should have thought entirely ruined, judging by the state of the house – was residing in the country, and the only occupant of the palace was an old woman, just like those who raise the curtains for you at church doors.

The palace was very grand. There was a ballroom as big as a church, and a number of reception rooms, with dirty floors and eighteenth-century furniture, all tarnished and tattered, and a gala room, all yellow satin and gold, where some emperor had slept; and there were horrible racks of faded photographs on the walls, and twopenny screens, and Berlin wool cushions, attesting the existence of more modern occupants.

I let the old woman unbar one painted and gilded shutter after another, and open window after window, each filled with little greenish panes of glass, and followed her about passively, quite happy, because I was wandering among the ghosts of dead people. 'There is the library at the end here,' said the old woman, 'if the signora does not mind passing through my room and the ironing-room; it's quicker than going back by the big hall.' I nodded, and prepared to pass as quickly as possible through an untidy-looking servant's room, when I suddenly stepped back. There was a woman in 1820 costume seated opposite, quite motionless. It was a huge doll. She had a sort of Canova classic face, like the pictures of Mme. Pasta and Lady Blessington. She sat with her hands folded on her lap and stared fixedly.

'It is the first wife of the Count's grandfather,' said the old woman. 'We took her out of her closet this morning to give her a little dusting.'

The Doll was dressed to the utmost detail. She had on open-work silk stockings, with sandal shoes, and long silk embroidered mittens. The hair was merely painted, in flat bands narrowing the forehead to a triangle. There was a big hole in the back of her head, showing it was cardboard.

'Ah,' said Orestes, musingly, 'the image of the beautiful countess! I had forgotten all about it. I haven't seen it since I was a lad,' and he wiped some cobweb off the folded hands with his red handkerchief, infinitely gentle. 'She used still to be kept in her own boudoir.'

'That was before my time,' answered the housekeeper. 'I've always seen her in the wardrobe, and I've been here thirty years. Will the signora care to see the old Count's collection of medals?'

Orestes was very pensive as he accompanied me home.

'That was a very beautiful lady,' he said shyly, as we came within sight of my inn; 'I mean the first wife of the grandfather of the present Count. She died after they had been married a couple of years. The old Count, they say, went half crazy. He had the Doll made from a picture, and kept it in the poor lady's room, and spent several hours in it every day with her. But he ended by marrying a woman he had in the house, a launderess, by whom he had had a daughter.'

'What a curious story!' I said, and thought no more about it.

But the Doll returned to my thoughts, she and her folded hands, and wide open eyes, and the fact of her husband's having ended by marrying the launderess. And the next day, when we returned to the palace to see the complete set of old Chinese plates, I suddenly experienced an odd wish to see the Doll once more. I took advantage of Orestes, and the old woman, and the Count's lawyer being busy deciding whether a certain dish cover which my maid had dropped, had or had not been previously chipped, to slip off and make my way to the ironing-room.

The Doll was still there, sure enough, and they hadn't found time to dust her yet. Her white satin frock, with little ruches at the hem, and her short bodice, had turned grey with engrained dirt; and her black fringed kerchief was almost red. The poor white silk mittens and white silk stockings were, on the other hand, almost black. A newspaper had fallen from an adjacent table on to her knees, or been thrown there by someone, and she looked as if she were holding it. It came home to me then that the clothes which she wore were the real clothes of her poor dead original. And when I found on the table a dusty, unkempt wig, with straight bands in front and an elaborate jug handle of curls behind, I knew at once that it was made of the poor lady's real hair.

'It is very well made,' I said shyly, when the old woman, of course, came creaking after me.

She had no thought except that of humouring whatever caprice might bring her a tip. So she smirked horribly, and, to show me that the image was really worthy of my attention, she proceeded in a ghastly way to bend the articulated arms, and to cross one leg over the other beneath the white satin skirt.

'Please, please, don't do that!' I cried to the old witch. But one of the poor feet, in its sandalled shoe, continued dangling and wagging dreadfully.

I was afraid lest my maid should find me staring at the Doll. I felt I couldn't stand my maid's remarks about her. So, though fascinated by the fixed dark stare in her Canova goddess or Ingres Madonna face, I tore myself away and returned to the inspection of the dessert set.

I don't know what the Doll had done to me; but I found that I was thinking of her all day long. It was as if I had just made a new acquaintance of a painfully interesting kind, rushed into a sudden friendship with a woman whose secret I had surprised, as sometimes happens, by some mere accident. For I somehow knew everything about her, and the first items of information which I gained from Orestes – I ought to say that I was irresistibly impelled to talk about her with him – did not enlighten me in the least, but merely confirmed what I was aware of.

The Doll – for I made no distinction between the portrait and the original – had been married straight out of the convent, and, during her brief wedded life, been kept secluded from the world by her husband's mad love for her, so that she had remained a mere shy, proud, inexperienced child.

Had she loved him? She did not tell me that at once. But gradually I became aware that in a deep, inarticulate way she had really cared for him more than he cared for her. She did not know what answer to make to his easy, overflowing, garrulous, demonstrative affection; he could not be silent about his love for two minutes, and she could never find a word to express hers, painfully though she longed to do so. Not that he wanted it; he was a brilliant, will-less, lyrical sort of person, who knew nothing of the feelings of others and cared only to welter and dissolve in his own. In those two years of ecstatic, talkative, all-absorbing love for her he not only forswore all society and utterly neglected his affairs, but he never made an attempt to

11

train this raw young creature into a companion, or showed any curiosity as to whether his idol might have a mind or a character of her own. This indifference she explained by her own stupid, inconceivable incapacity for expressing her feelings; how should he guess at her longing to know, to understand, when she could not even tell him how much she loved him? At last the spell seemed broken: the words and the power of saying them came; but it was on her death-bed. The poor young creature died in child-birth, scarcely more than a child herself.

There now! I knew even you would think it all silliness. I know what people are — what we all are — how impossible it is ever *really* to make others feel in the same way as ourselves about anything. Do you suppose I could have ever told all this about the Doll to my husband? Yet I tell him everything about myself; and I know he would have been quite kind and respectful. It was silly of me ever to embark on the story of the Doll with any one; it ought to have remained a secret between me and Orestes. *He*, I really think, would have understood all about the poor lady's feelings, or known it already as well as I. Well, having begun, I must go on, I suppose.

I knew all about the Doll when she was alive — I mean about the lady — and I got to know, in the same way, all about her after she was dead. Only I don't think I'll tell you. *Basta*: the husband had the Doll made, and dressed it in her clothes, and placed it in her boudoir, where not a thing was moved from how it had been at the moment of her death. He allowed no one to go in, and cleaned and dusted it all himself, and spent hours every day weeping and moaning before the Doll. Then, gradually, he began to look at his collection of medals, and to resume his rides; but he never went into society, and never neglected spending an hour in the boudoir with the Doll. Then came the business with the launderess. And then he sent the Doll into a wardrobe? Oh no; he wasn't that sort of man. He was an idealizing, sentimental, feeble sort of person, and the amour with the launderess grew up quite gradually in the shadow of the inconsolable passion for the wife. He would never have married another woman of his own rank, given *her* son a stepmother (the son was sent to a distant school and went to the bad); and when he *did* marry the launderess it was almost in his dotage, and because she and the priests bullied him so fearfully about legitimating that other child. He went on paying visits to the Doll for a long time, while the launderess idyll went on quite peaceably. Then, as he grew old and lazy, he went less often; other people were sent to dust the Doll, and finally she was not dusted at all. Then he died, having quarrelled with his son and got to live like a feeble old boor, mostly in the kitchen. The son – the Doll's son – having gone to the bad, married a rich widow. It was she who refurnished the boudoir and sent the Doll away. But the daughter of the launderess, the illegitimate child, who had become a kind of housekeeper in her half-brother's palace, nourished a lingering regard for the Doll, partly because the old Count had made such a fuss about it, partly because it must have cost a lot of money, and partly because the lady had been a *real* lady. So when the boudoir was refurnished she emptied out a closet and put the Doll to live there; and she occasionally had it brought out to be dusted.

Well, while all these things were being borne in upon me there came a telegram saying my friend was not coming on to Foligno, and asking me to meet her at Perugia. The little Renaissance coffer had been sent to London; Orestes and my maid and myself had carefully packed every one of the Chinese plates and fruit dishes in baskets of hay. I had ordered a set of the 'Archivio Storico' as a parting gift for dear old Orestes – I could never have dreamed of offering him money, or cravat pins, or things like that – and there was no excuse for staying one hour more at Foligno. Also I had got into low spirits of late – I suppose we poor women cannot stay alone six days in an inn, even with *bric-à-brac* and chronicles and devoted maids – and I knew I should not get better till I was out of the place. Still I found it difficult, nay, impossible, to go. I will confess it outright: I couldn't abandon the Doll. I couldn't leave her, with the hole in her poor cardboard head, with the Ingres Madonna features gathering dust in that filthy old woman's ironing-room. It was just impossible. Still go I must. So I sent for Orestes. I knew exactly what I wanted; but it seemed impossible, and I was afraid, somehow, of asking him. I gathered up my courage, and, as if it were the most natural thing in the world, I said –

'Dear Signor Oreste, I want you to help me to make one last purchase. I want the Count to sell me the – the portrait of his grandmother; I mean the Doll.'

I had prepared a speech to the effect that Orestes would easily understand that a life-size figure so completely dressed in the original costume of a past epoch would soon possess the highest historical interest, etc. But I felt that I neither needed nor ventured to say any of it. Orestes, who was seated opposite me at table – he would only accept a glass of wine and a morsel of bread, although I had asked him to share my hotel dinner – Orestes nodded slowly, then opened his eyes out wide, and seemed to frame the whole of me in them. It wasn't surprise. He was weighing me and my offer.

'Would it be very difficult?' I asked. 'I should have thought that the Count— 'The Count,' answered Orestes drily, 'would sell his soul, if he had one, let alone his grandmother, for the price of a new trotting pony.'

Then I understood.

'Signor Oreste,' I replied, feeling like a child under the dear old man's glance, 'we have not known one another long, so I cannot expect you to trust me yet in many things. Perhaps also buying furniture out of dead people's houses to stick it in one's own is not a great recommendation of one's character. But I want to tell you that I am an honest woman according to my lights, and I want you to trust me in this matter.'

14

Orestes bowed. 'I will try and induce the Count to sell you the Doll,' he said.

I had her sent in a closed carriage to the house of Orestes. He had, behind his shop, a garden which extended into a little vineyard, whence you could see the circle of great Umbrian mountains; and on this I had had my eye.

'Signor Oreste,' I said, 'will you be very kind, and have some faggots – I have seen some beautiful faggots of myrtle and bay in your kitchen – brought out into the vineyard; and may I pluck some of your chrysanthemums?' I added.

We stacked the faggots at the end of the vineyard, and placed the Doll in the midst of them, and the chrysanthemums on her knees. She sat there in her white satin Empire frock, which, in the bright November sunshine, seemed white once more, and sparkling. Her black fixed eyes stared as if in wonder on the yellow vines and reddening peach trees, the sparkling dewy grass of the vineyard, upon the blue morning sunshine, the misty blue amphitheatre of mountains all round.

Orestes stuck a match and slowly lit a pine cone with it; when the cone was blazing he handed it silently to me. The dry bay and myrtle blazed up crackling, with a fresh resinous odour; the Doll was veiled in flame and smoke. In a few seconds the flame sank, the smouldering faggots crumbled. The Doll was gone. Only, where she had been, there remained in the embers something small and shiny. Orestes raked it out and handed it to me. It was a wedding ring of old-fashioned shape, which had been hidden under the silk mitten. 'Keep it, signora,' said Orestes; 'you have put an end to her sorrows.'

MARY BUTTS
THE GOLDEN BOUGH

S he stood by the door at the party. The man who had brought
her did not speak. He left her and crossed the room. She sat
down on a plain, small chair. He came back, and sat carefully
beside her. It occurred to her he might be drunk. He laid a finger
on her wrist. Very unwillingly she attended to him.

Then he said: 'It's a poor show. Shall we go?' Then: 'What is
it like outside?'

It was in London, and late in February. She felt the year-
stream winding about the streets. Solid, vibrating, it ebbed at
morning, but by three in the afternoon it rose, lapped up the
steps of the houses till the rooms brimmed, always moving,
moving its huge stream.

The man who had brought her was like a dipper filled at
midnight with that black water. The room she looked into was
under the sea. The people were not fish.

He had only said: '*What is it like outside?*'

She had come to London to join this life from a coast-town
where there was a pier sticking out into the sea. A wounded
officer had told her about the life in studios, and at the end of
his conversation she had taken the paste combs out of her hair,
and prepared a new attack upon the world.

The bubble of her fancies lolled out of her brain. Now the
man beside her had suggested that she should see what he saw.
She seized and popped him inside her bubble, a neat black
mannikin, and looked out into the room.

In the centre was a girl like a rag doll who was called Lois.

She gathered up her lovers like an innocent mother who has born devils and not sons. Anne had talked to the man about herself.

The man who had brought her had told her about the loss of his virginity, as though it had not been his, and something that had happened to him in the war, and then something neurotic. The pits of Lois' eyes were dark. Anne sat against the wall, a fair, gilt idol, conscious that it has not yet been worshipped and blackened, and smeared with scent and blood.

Lois was passed from hand to hand, bounced and sprawled, till a young man came and moved her away to dance. She was between his arms, a barrel of bright silk on sturdy legs – Anne saw his spine draw up, and his shoulders pass sideways with the least spring. His chin was up over Lois' head, his feet were together, he moved in a small pattern in which all variety was included. Lois followed him, and slowly abandoned herself, her legs flying, her face on his breast.

She was not asked to dance.

His hair was laid over his skull like a black wing.

Outside the brown night was waiting. It would receive her later, exhausted with envy and desire.

Her bubble contracted round her peering skull. She drew back into the wall, and pulled a slow face.

There was the man who had brought her. When the music began again, she forced him to dance. He was so drunk that he fell down immediately, and lay looking up. Two of his friends dragged him into another room. A dull, ugly boy came and sat beside her. She talked to him occasionally. An hour passed. A very young girl fetched him.

The man who was giving the party began to turn out the lights. One was left, closed up in a blue cap. The semi-mystery made it easier and duller.

A knot of men pulled Lois about. One of them burned her

arm with the stump of a cigarette. 'It won't do,' said the man who was giving the party, and pushed him away.

Anne rubbed her back against the wall, a nerve thrilling. She noticed later that she did not understand what it was all about. Yet she remembered with contempt the past simplicity of the pier, and the cinema, and the wounded young men migrating with their secrets.

Later she got up, and went to look for the man who had brought her. He was on his host's bed among the overcoats, arguing about the nature of reality.

'There is,' he said, 'absolute beauty and absolute truth, which man, by reason of certain elements in his nature is conscious of, and separate from. Both these equals are equal. So that he can live neither with, or without, absolute beauty and absolute truth.'

'I have never heard of that sort of truth and beauty. Some little thing goes wrong, and you forget about it, and years after you can't face a crowd, or go into an empty room.'

'And that is because you wanted your grandmother for wife.'

'What is there in this that accounts for the disproportionate nature of one's pain?'

The room was nearly dark. The unshaded mantle had been broken by a passing head. Its thread tried to whiten in the whistling flame. A man got up off the floor, and sat on the bed, and turned out one of his pockets counting:

'I'll tell you a thing. One does not see half of what is happening round one. There's a trick, though, by which you can. Bang a door at midnight, you'll hear the noise break up the quiet and let something through. Pull up the bathroom plug at the same hour. Go through quick into a dark room to the window. You'll see skeleton birds crossing the white sky.'

'That's funnier than absolute.'

'Not more interesting than physics.'

18

'Their observation leads you to conclude that anything may mean anything.'

That was the man who had brought her. They had thrown their overcoats on him, and he spoke over a wall. Over him the gas whistled, and lit the deadly staring face. The young man she had seen dancing had come in and began to lift the coats off him as he looked for his own.

'It's a bloody world. Let's be rude to it.'

She moved out a little on the floor, and he trod on her hand. She hid it in her dress and looked up at him. He did not see her, but Steevens sat up and asked her if she wanted to go home. They went out together.

'Have you enjoyed yourself?'

'I can't say that I have.'

'Why not?'

'You are all such dreadful people.'

'Why?'

'You drink and you pretend you are in love with those girls, and you believe in ghosts.'

'You are not used to the idea of people moving about and watching themselves try new combinations.'

'What is it all about?'

'I knew you would ask that. I rather agree that it's a question. As a matter of fact, I think it has got to a time when a little death would do our set good. No, I don't mean another war, rather a ceremonial blood-letting. A ritual death. Not another suicide. Besides, an old order's changing, we must inaugurate. I haven't got my eye on a victim yet . . . What are you interrupting for? You can stand sexual talk, why not this?'

'How do you know I like it?'

He grinned. 'You little seaside hack. If you want to learn the catch-words, you'd better talk to me.'

She trotted along sullen beside him.

*

She went to Lois' flat and watched her. Lois sat on the floor and cleaned a pair of grey shoes. Their surface brushed pale and dark like the light on fields. She powdered, rubbed and blew.

'Whose are they?'

'Leo's, the boy I dance with.'

'I saw him at the party.'

'We were blind and they burnt my arm. They're a thick lot, but he's all right.'

Lois sat back on her heels, a shoe in each hand. She clapped them and dropped them.

'Some girl has got to darn his socks. He won't be dressed when he comes in because he's resting his good clothes. I collect the pawn tickets.' She took two pounds out of her stocking. 'Nobody knows you have it there. Would you mind popping round the corner and getting these out?'

'Certainly.'

He was drinking his tea in a girl's dressing gown and a pair of cotton pants.

She looked curiously into the milky, hollow chest.

'You are a friend of Steevens, aren't you?'

'Steevens? Oh yes. We were in the same asylum. Our families put us in. We got ourselves out.'

'It was the war, I suppose?'

'Not at all. That was the excuse.'

'How did you get out?'

'Our mothers came to visit us, and when they'd seen them they took our word for it we were sane. It takes ten mad boys to make one old mother.'

'Are you all right now?'

'No.'

'Surely Steevens is all right – '

'That's where he gets you. Once a month we go on a blind together, and at the end of it we write a letter to God. Shut up, Lois.'

' – Once you start, you don't sleep at night.'

'I do with you, when it's a waste of time. But don't let Steevens take you in. He has an idea and he makes faces at it, and when you see his faces, you'll be surprised. We practise them together. Do you dance?'

'Of course.'

'That's something like real life. You'd tell me to read a Russian novel, but I know what I like.'

'I think everyone should read them because they're psychologically absolutely real.'

'You haven't seen our letter to God. That's the stuff.'

'You believe in God then?'

'God. I'd spit in His face. Do you?'

'I think he's the enlarged idea one had of one's father and mother.'

'What, those people! Lois, come here, Lois. It isn't fair. She's laying a trap for me. She's doing it on purpose. She says they're doing it all over again. I really should be mad if I thought that.'

'She's only being clever.'

They drew away from Anne.

Steevens' advice had been very dull, and very difficult and it did not work. But she was afraid of him. At his orders she martyred herself.

'I'm sure I didn't mean to say anything against your religion.'

'There, Leo, and you mustn't be rude.'

'There I was ragging. Let's dance. No, my weakness is for owls, and they're impotent.'

They danced. She minded her steps till she forgot, and stared up in his face, and he stared over her head.

She went back to Steevens, who said:

'I am sorry I behaved so badly that night. I should not have got drunk and left you alone. How did you get along – ?'

'Perfectly. Who is the boy who can dance, Lois' friend?'

'Leo Pollard.'

'Has he been mad?'

'That's what he says about himself.'

'Were you in hospital together?'

'I was never really there.'

'What sort of a person is he?'

'Charming, in spite of his little artistic stunts.'

'I heard you talking about beauty the other night, but perhaps you don't remember.'

'I have no objection to a universal arch. Boys like Leo are a decoration, a jewel, a cap-feather. One retrims you know. Life's always preening herself up with one of them.'

'What is Lois?'

'The sound shoes that will see more than one of us to our journey's end.' He turned her wrist between his fingers and thumb. 'It is amusing to see how you get it all off by heart. Now look.'

She was squatting in a mist where there were stones and white grass. It was unvaried and colourless, without the sound of water running, or settling, or wind. There were stones. She passed into a large dusty room.

He had only pinched her wrist and told her that she was inexperienced, while her experience had not been of his kind, but that suited to a lady-animal and no more.

She remembered his face under the whistling gas. He dropped her wrist. She looked round his dark, red room.

She went constantly to Lois' flat. Leo showed her his seven cigarette holders, in seven colours, for each day of the week. He also taught her to dance. Alternately she saw Steevens, and endured him for practice in what she must do in the world.

In May, Lois took her out into the country with Leo, because it was good for him to be in the air.

One day they came to a wood. Outside it there was a tree. They hurried to it through the sun. A grass road ran through the wood up to a hill with a bare cap. A red animal ran along

22

the branch. They told Lois its name, and she did not listen. They lay down in the wood.

'Why do they paint aspidistras in a window-frame instead of a bacchante running from the hounds of spring?'

'People say the bacchante does not represent pure form.'

Then Leo read them his poems, and when he had done he said:

'I shall write next a hymn on Anne's virginity. I don't doubt it's only mental, but it's good enough.'

She did not hear. She had selected that he liked bacchantes, and that was plain sailing, the old formula in the new world.

She saw that they were neither in London, nor on any esplanade and that this was something like something real at last. Up or down her hair did not matter. It would take itself up and down in its time. Something like bark peeled off her, she felt herself white and cool like a peeled stick. She did not remember to remember anything. She forgot. Then a thin wire of active hate passed from her to the boy. He would have to admire her, who had so loved dark, tender girls. It was pleasant. She could now do what she liked, it did not matter. There was something exactly right for her to do. It was coming.

Lois went away to gather sticks for the fire. Anne looked at the tree.

'Lift me up on your shoulders, Leo, and I'll climb it.' He lifted her up. She wound her skirts tight round her knees, and mounted one after another the huge arms. She dropped a leaf into his hair. He looked up and away, and began to throw sticks at his dog. The leaves filled in their net. She was shut up in a tree. There was a green room with holes in the floor, and a billiance over her head. She rested a moment. A breeze, stoppped in the breathless wood, broke through. The light filled the upper rooms. She went up them, and stepped out on to the tree-top. Above the forest the hill came over to the tree. She leaned back on the main shaft and opened her arms along two boughs, and began to sing in German, which she knew he did not understand. Presently he came out and glanced up. She hurried down hand over hand.

There was an empty six feet between the lowest branch and the ground. He came over, and she slid through his arms, and tore away.

'Come on. Let's run a race.'

They ran again and again. He left her to match himself with his dog. She was under the tree watching him. Out in the ride, he fell and cried out. She ran to him, and from another part of the wood, came Lois like a settling partridge. They turned him over, and blood was on his bare chest. A fly hurried up.

'It's his lungs,' said Lois. 'Oh, quick. There's a village over the hill.' Anne went away. At the top of the ride she saw Lois crouching, with Leo laid across her knees.

*

'What did you do?'

'I wired to his people.'

'Where was he then?'

'At Lois' flat. He could not stay there.'

'Why not?'

'It was not suitable.'

'There was Lois.'

'They sent a car and took him away. Also Lois has no money, and he needs everything.'

'He needs nothing . . . He might have been left with the girl he liked . . .'

'There, be quiet. What were you doing when it happened?'

'Running races.'

'And you forced him on and on till his lung burst. Active little animal, aren't you? It's funny you should have done it, you little green thing.'

She suffered. She looked down with empty lungs, while an enormous pain like a steel bubble rose and burst in her throat.

24

A stretch of vacant time went on after the bubble had broken, and she looked surprised at the unfamiliar torture.

'It was in a wood. Green to green. You were in a wood. They've taken him to another.'

'Who? Where?'

'His people. Don't you know where he is now? Down where his people live, a hundred miles from here. There is a house set low in wet grasses like a slug. The river sweeps past it and the trees advance on it. Blue troops of trees with great rides cut out of them. If you follow one out and up, you will see that house in an eddy of fog. It moves because the river runs so fast, and the grasses dip and the snails are in squadrons, and in winter the wind squalls in from the woods, and sinks and breathes out there.

'The stinking, wet hole! There's a plaster nymph on the lawn that sprouts ferns, a green fringe waving all the way down her back-bone. The place where pure bone turns into bright smelling leaves.'

'It is a good thing,' said Anne, 'he is so young, and a very unconscious person.'

'You're probably right. Only I've seen a dying baby and it looked wise. Even the flowers are sallow there. We'll order him red roses, bloody warriors.'

'That's a wall-flower,' she whispered.

'Have it your own way. I believe you've had everything your own way. I didn't mean to train you for that, you rotten little death-priestess . . . Since you are a priestess, you damned well behave like one. You come back here and tell me when he's dead.'

*

Lois was reading.

'*My little chérie. They've given me a fortnight to shuffle off in. The holders are for you to keep, and my kit for you to make what you can of. By the way, see Steevens has all the ties. He goes hopelessly wrong on ties. Dud cheques send on here – after I'm dead. In change for the ties, Steevens will get my poems printed. I've written a hymn on Anne's virginity.*

This is a horror; the feel of the wall here makes your nails throb, not really hard or nice and bristly and like your racoon muff. When I was in Canada. They've put me in the drawing-room – all the time I dance in and out and round about the fancy tables.

See Anne sees that hymn.

But it's all right. I'm well away now. I must tell you something. I've had an idea about God that settles it. God's always young and funny – He always has to be killed. He doesn't want anyone to believe in Him, and they hang Him up for us to have a look at death. The pretty girls cry. Lois, don't you see? This is a real idea at last. God's a young nut, and one of us, and He's killed all over again. There was Adonis.

Oh, smile at me like that. I see the treasure that has given me eyes. Lois, you are one of the pretty girls. When it's over, get blind at parties, and sing that hymn I wrote about Anne. When we're two stars together, I suppose she'll be one, too. We'll bump into her.'

She was out that night crying:

'Stand me another drink, and I'll sing. Stand me a drink.'

*

Steevens got up and tied the sash of his dressing gown, and staggered to the door. Anne came in.

'You show up like a blue light on a red stage.' He lay down again and she sat beside him.

'Do you lie here like this always with the curtains drawn?'

'And think of *fire and sleet and candlelight?* Now Leo's dead, yes.'

'But it's midsummer – '

'It won't be for ever. Then I shall get up. I shall be all right once this terrible sun is over. What have you been doing?'

She looked up at him like a dog.

'I've been writing a play about Leo, you said something ought to be done.'

'Tell me what it is about.'

'Of course it is made up. Marcus Adair, a young man about town, has lived previous to the war with a beautiful girl divorcée. When he comes back from the war his nerves are shattered. He becomes engaged to a middle-class girl, which angers his aristocratic relatives.

'Finally, on a visit to them, they induce him to neglect her for the daughter of a neighbouring squire, and she breaks it off. He returns to London, and by his dissipated life estranges himself from them completely. His fiancée meets him there in company with the divorcée. They return to the divorcée's flat, and after a long conversation with the beautiful woman about her past, the girl learns that her own outlook on life has been too narrow. Later they visit Marcus in his rooms, where he asks them both to forgive him, and shoots himself.

'Phyllis – that's the girl – induces the divorcée to return to her husband. In time Marcus' family are won over by her goodness, and together, in the old village church, they unveil a tablet to his memory.'

'Well?'

'And I've sold it to a film-company!'

'What? Sold it? Is it going to be produced?'

'Yes. They've paid me.'

'Thirty pieces of silver, I hope. Good for you, Anne. That's the stuff of immortality to give us. Or are you sharper than we think? Did you do it for revenge? But I think you're proud of it. Tell me.'

'Steevens – you must know. I can tell you now. I was in love with Leo. I had to write about him. I couldn't bear it till I had.'

He changed sides. She looked down at his back. The dark dressing gown mixed with the red sofa.

Two rings of white bones were on his ankles, and there was another round his neck. The heavy shoulders heaved up and did not sink.

'You little idiot. Green I called you. Filthy aniline dye.'

She felt she was being stoned, and began to cry. She was physically afraid.

'Go away and don't come again.'

When she got to the door she thought of something she could not remember and made another face. When she was gone, he began to cry.

'It's not for myself, it's for you, Leo, all the epiphany you've got for the fine clothes, and the fine movements, and the sensual elegance, and the silly imagination, and the pain.'

STEVIE SMITH
THE STORY OF A STORY

'I am so awfully stuck,' sighed Helen. 'You see it is a monologue, it is Bella's monologue, it is saying all the time how much she is thinking about Roland all the time, and thinking back, and remembering, and so on. It is like a squirrel in a cage, it goes round and round. And now I am stuck. Tell me, Ba, how can I come out of it to make a proper ending – ah, that is difficult.'

The two girls were having lunch together in the Winter-garden, the potted palms were languid, but underneath the palms stood out like tropic flowers the keen dark faces of the yellow-skinned business men. Everybody was drinking strong bitter coffee that was served rather cold and soon became quite cold. The yellow of the skins and the yellow of the whites of the eyes of the business men spoke of too many of these cups of coffee drunk too often.

'You do not mean to say,' said Barbara, 'that you are writing a story about Roland and Bella?'

'Well, I am trying to,' said Helen, 'but it is very difficult, but I am doing my very best.' She sighed again. Oh, how difficult it was.

'But,' said Ba, 'you know that Roland will not like that.'

'Pooh, nonsense,' said Helen, 'he told me that he would not mind. But it is so difficult, but difficult, always so difficult to write.' Helen sounded rather desperate. 'It must be right,' she said, 'quite right.'

'But Roland,' said Ba again.

Helen began to look rather dreamy. 'Human beings are very difficult,' she said. 'You know, it is like the lady in Maurice Baring, she was one of these foreign countesses he has, and she was sitting at dinner next to an English writer. "And vat is it you write about, Mr So-and-So?" she said. "Oh, people," he said, "people." "Ah, people," said the countess, "they are very difficult." '

'But Roland . . .' went on Ba.

'I do wish you would stop saying "But Roland," ' said Helen. 'I tell you Roland said to me, "Helen, I suppose you will write a story about us." And I said, "Well, perhaps I shall, but it is very difficult." "Well, do," said Roland. "write whatever you like Helen, I shan't mind." '

'Ah,' said Ba, 'he only said that to trap you.'

'No, no,' said Helen, 'he could not be so base.'

That evening Ba tidied herself and went round to see Roland and Bella. Bella was not very pleased to see her. Bella was a warm-hearted person, but this girl was rather tiresome, she was *devoted* to Roland.

'I think I ought to tell you,' said Ba, 'that Helen is writing a story about you.'

This is how the war broke out, the war that was to carry so much away with it, the personal war, the war that is so trivial and so deadly.

Bella loved Helen.

'Oh, Helen, how could you do such a thing?'

'What thing is that, Bella?'

'Why, to write a story about Roland and me.'

'Oh, that,' said Helen, 'why that is very difficult. I am so terribly stuck, you know. It is difficult.'

'But Roland . . .' said Bella.

'How is Roland?' said Helen. Helen admired Roland very much for his fine intelligence, and because this fine intelligence was of the legalistic variety, very different from Helen's.

'Roland is furious,' said Bella, 'simply furious.'

'It is so frightfully difficult,' said Helen, 'to get it exactly right.'

'He says that if you do not give him your word that you will not publish the story he will not see you again.' Bella was now in tears, she loved Helen and she loved Roland. 'It is all so difficult,' she said, 'and Ba with her student-girl devotion does not help, and this story makes it all so difficult.'

'Yes, yes,' said Helen, 'it is difficult. I am most frightfully stuck.'

'You mean you are going on,' wept Bella. 'Oh Helen, how can you?'

'Well, that is just it, I do not know that I can. But,' said Helen, 'I shall try.'

'But Roland says . . .'

'Pooh, *that*. He cannot be so stupid.'

The two friends walked together across Hyde Park to Hyde Park Corner. Coming down the long grass path between the trees towards the statue of the great Achilles, Helen saw a horse drawing a cart full of leaves and bushes. 'Oh look, Bella, look,' she said. The horse had broken into a gallop, he drew the cart swiftly after him. He was a tall heavy animal, dappled grey and white, his long flaxen hair flew in the wind behind him, the long pale hair streamed on the gale that was blowing up between the April trees.

'What is it,' said Bella, who was in the middle of saying something about Roland. 'Well, what is it?'

'That horse,' said Helen.

'How can you look at a horse at such a moment? You want it both ways,' said Bella.

Helen looked at Bella and laughed. 'It is the moment to look at a horse.'

*

She went home and went on with the story. It was building up slowly, it was not so bad now, it was coming right.

When she had finished it she took it round to Lopez, who was also a writer. Lopez was a very clever quick girl, she had a brilliant quick eye for people, conversations, and situations. She read the story right through without stopping. 'It is very good, Helen,' she said, and then she began to laugh.

When Helen had gone Lopez rang up all the friends, and the friends of the friends, the people who knew Lopez and who knew Helen, and who knew Bella and Roland, and even those who knew the devoted girl Ba.

'Look,' said Lopez, 'Helen has written a most amusing story about Roland and Bella. It is very amusing, exactly right, you know.'

Everybody was very pleased, and the soft laughter ran along the ground like fire.

Cold and ferocious, Roland heard about it, coldly ferociously he sent messages to Helen. Bella came running, bringing the ferocious messages. 'Pentheus, ruler of this Theban land, I come from Kithairon where never melts the larding snow . . .' Yes, it was like the Greek messengers who have the story in their mouths to tell it all. 'Where never melts the larding snow,' that was surely the cold Roland, so ferocious now and cold.

'He says,' cried Bella, 'that he will never see you again if you do not give him your word that never shall the story be published.'

'Pooh,' said Helen, 'we have heard about that. Very well then, I shall never see Roland again.' But she, too, began to cry. 'It is so easy,' she said, 'to close a door.'

'But he says,' went on Bella, 'that he will have his solicitor write to you, that he will have his secretary ring you up, that if the story is published he will at once bring a libel action against you.'

'It is so difficult to get these stories right,' said Helen, her thoughts moving off from Roland to the dear story that was now at last so right, so truly beautiful.

Bella shook her ferociously. 'Listen, Helen, he will bring a legal action.'

Helen began to cry more desperately and to wring her hands. 'He cannot be so base, indeed it is not possible, he cannot.' But now through the thoughts of the beautiful story, so right, so beautiful, broke the knowledge of the cold and ferocious Roland, that was now standing with a drawn sword.

'Ah, ah, ah,' sobbed Helen.

Bella put her arms round her. 'It is no good,' she said, 'no one and nobody has ever got the better of Roland.'

'But I love Roland,' said Helen, 'and I love you, and I even love the student girl Ba, and I love my story.'

'You want it both ways,' said Bella.

'There is no harm in this story,' wept Helen, 'and he is condemning it unseen. He has not seen it, it is soft and beautiful, not malicious, there is no harm in it and he is destroying it.'

'Roland,' said Bella, 'is a very subtle person, he is this important and subtle character.'

'For all that,' said Helen, 'he does not understand, he does not understand one thing, or know one thing to know it properly. He is this legalistic person.'

'He is the finest QC of them all,' said Bella.

'He knows nothing,' said Helen, and at once her thoughts passed from the benign and the happy, to the furtive, the careful, the purposeful and the defensive.

'You are childish about this story,' said Bella.

'You shall see that I am not.'

'What are you thinking of now?' said Bella, watching Helen and watching the ferocious intent expression on her face.

'I am thinking of Baron Friedrich von Hügel,' said Helen.

'Eh, who might he be, and what are you thinking about him?'

'I am thinking of what he said.'

'And what did he say?'

Helen screwed up her face and spat out the words, the terrible judging words. 'He said, "Nothing can be more certain than that great mental powers can be accompanied by emptiness or depravity of heart." He was thinking of Roland, be sure of it.'

Helen went home and knelt down and prayed, 'Oh, God,' et cetera. She was a Christian of the neo-Platonic school. She prayed that she might do the right thing about the story. This matter that had been so trivial was now running deep, deep and devilish swift. It was time to pray. She prayed that all might come right between herself and Roland and her dear friend, Bella. She knelt for a long time thinking, but it did not seem the right thing to do to suppress the story because of the threat of legal action and for the fear of it. But she knew that Roland could have no idea of this, he could have no idea of Helen but the idea that she was a friend of Bella's, a rattle, a literary girl, a desperate character, a person of no right sense or decency. 'But I will go on with it,' said Helen, and she began to cry again, and said, 'It will be the death of me.' For now the human feelings were running very swiftly indeed, and on the black surface of the hurrying water was the foam fleck of hatred and contempt.

She did not see Roland because she would not give him her word. Driven by Bella, whose one thought was that the story should not be published, because of the trouble that would follow, Helen cried, 'I will give my word in contempt, using his own weapon, for my word shall mean as much as his word meant when he said, "Write about us, write what you like, I shall not mind."'

Bella felt that her heart would break, the violence and the obstinacy of Roland and Helen would break it quite in two.

'He denies that he ever said such a thing.'

'But Bella, you heard him. You are coming out of the bathroom carrying the goldfish. You heard him, you told me that you heard him.'

'I heard him say, "Go ahead, write what you like," but it was a threat.'

Helen began to choke. 'It was no threat, he spoke most friendly, very open he was, he was treating me as a friend, he was anxious that it should be right.' She sighed and smiled and gave Bella a hug. 'It was difficult, but now it is right.'

She did not see Roland, but still she saw her dear friend, Bella. But always Bella was telling her of the affair, *Roland versus Helen*, and how the situation lay, and what Roland had said only yesterday, and what the part was that the girl Ba was playing.

The weeks went by, the story was now accepted and to be published. Nobody had seen the story as it now was, worked upon and altered with cunning and furtiveness and care and ferocity, it was now a different story, hedged and pared from legal action, but as good as it had ever been, good, shining bright, true, beautiful, but pared from legal action.

Helen prayed that the story might come safely through. The friends said that Roland would not bring an action, that he would not do it, that he was playing a game of bluff to frighten Helen, to make her withdraw the story.

But now Helen had the thought that she was dealing with a maniac, *a person who would go to all lengths*.

The danger of the situation and the care for it made her grow thin, and every time that she saw Bella the harsh cruel words of Roland were repeated, and what Ba had said was repeated, and all of it again, and again; and then again.

'Ba says that it is a good thing that she has done informing against you,' said Bella, 'for in this way the story will not be published, and everybody's feelings will be spared.'

'But the feelings and truth of the story will not be spared,' said Helen, and a bitter look came across her face. 'That does not matter I suppose?'

Bella tore on, 'Roland was saying only yesterday, "Helen will have to write a story to say how the story was not published," and he laughed then and said, "Helen must be taught a lesson," and he said, "Now that she has learnt her lesson I am willing to see her again." '

Helen put her head on the tablecloth of the restaurant where they were having lunch and wept, and she said: 'I wish Roland was dead.'

*

It was now Good Friday. Restlessly, sadly, Helen moved about the wide empty garden. The sun shone down through the fine ash trees and the lawn was bright green after the heavy rain. What a terrible day Good Friday is as the hour of twelve o'clock draws near. Her Aunt was at ante-communion, her sister at the mass of the pre-sanctified, but Helen would not go to church because she had said, 'I wish he was dead.' She went into the garden to fetch the book that she liked to read on Good Fridays and read:

> *The third hour's deafened with the cry*
> *Of crucify Him, crucify.*
> *So goes the vote, nor ask them why,*
> *Live Barabbas and let God die.*
> *But there is wit in wrath and they will try*
> *A Hail more cruel than their crucify.*
> *For while in sport he wears a spiteful crown,*
> *The serious showers along his decent face run slowly*
>   *down.*

She thought of the crucifixion that was now at twelve o'clock taking place, and she thought that she, in her hatred of Roland and her contempt for him (because of the violence of the law that he threatened to use) had a part among the crucifiers, and she wept and hid her face, kneeling against the cold bark of the fine ash tree. 'The cruelties of past centuries are in our bones,' she cried, 'and we wish to ignore the sufferings of Christ, for we have too much of a hand in them. Oh I do not wish Roland dead, but what is the use to love him and to love my dear Bella? They will not receive it and the door is now closed. But even now,' she said, 'if I withdraw the story, and give my word that neither here nor in America – (for it was not only British Rights that Roland was asking her to give up) – shall the story be published, nor after his death, will that door be opened again and shall I be received? Oh, no, no' – Helen screamed and twisted and beat her head against the cold ash tree bark – 'I cannot do this, and if I did never could it be the same between us, for it would be the act of a slave person, and no good thing.' And she knelt at the foot of the fine ash tree and prayed, 'Come, peace of God,' et cetera.

She went into the house and fetched out her writing pad and wrote to Bella: 'Dearest Bella, I think we had better not see each other for a bit. I like to think agreeably of you and Roland and even Ba, but I cannot do this now while I am seeing you, so we had better not see each other.' She paused and then went on, 'We can think of each other in the past as if we were dead.' Helen's face brightened at this idea, 'Yes, as if we were dead. So with love to you and Roland and Ba.'

When she had written her letter she thought, 'One must pay out everything, but it is not happy.' She thought of Bella's beautiful house and the beautiful pictures that Roland had collected, especially there was such a beautiful picture in the hall, the Elsheimer, ah, that was it, *it was the gem of his collection*. Helen wept to think that never again would she see her dear friends, Roland and Bella, in love and friendship, and never again would she see the beautiful house, the Elsheimer, the trees in the shady garden or the goldfish swimming in their square glass tank. She thought that she must pay out everything and she supposed that the Grünewald prints that Roland had lent her must now also be given back.

*

She fell asleep in the garden and dreamt that she was standing up in court accused of treachery, blasphemy, theft and conduct prejudicial to discipline. Roland was cross-examining her:

'Do you think it is immoral to write about people?'

'No no, it is very difficult.' She held out her hands to Bella and Roland, but they turned from her.

'You go into houses under cover of friendship and steal away the words that are spoken.'

'Oh, it is difficult, so difficult, one cannot remember them, the words run away; when most one wants the word, it is gone.'

'You do not think it is immoral to write about people?'

'It is a spiritual truth, it is that.'

The dream-girl breaks down under cross-examination by the cold and ferocious Roland. She is cross, lost and indistinct.

'The story is beautiful and truthful,' she cries. 'It is a spiritual truth.'

The girl cries and stammers and reads from a book that she draws from her pocket, 'Spiritual things are spirtually discerned, the carnal mind cannot know the things of the spirit.' She weeps and stammers, 'Of the Idea of the Good there is nothing that can be spoken directly.' The dream-girl glances furiously upon the Judge, the Counsels for Defence and Prosecution, upon the tightly packed friends, who have come to see what is going on. She reads again. 'Let those be silent about the beauty of noble conduct who have never cared for such things, nor let those speak of the splendour of virtue who have never known the face of justice or temperance.'

There was now a mighty uproar in the court, but the dream-girl cries out high above the clamour, stuttering and stammering and weeping bitterly, and still reading from her book, 'Such things may be known by those who have eyes to see, the rest it would fill with contempt in a manner by no means pleasing, or with a lofty and vain presumption, as though they had learnt something grand.'

'He that hath yores to yore,' said the Judge, 'let him yore.' And he pronounced the sentence, 'You are to be taken to the place from whence you came . . .' The police constable and the wardress in the dock beside her took hold of her.

*

On the Tuesday after Easter there was a letter from Bella. 'How could you lump me with Ba?' she wrote.

Helen sat in her office, here were the proofs of the story come by post for correction. How fresh and remote it read, *there was no harm in it*.

Her employer, who was a publisher, came into the room where she was sitting. 'What's the matter, Helen?' he said, seeing the tears running down her cheeks.

She told him the story of the story.

'Look here, Helen,' said the employer, 'just you cut them right out, publish the story, tell him to go to hell.' Then he said, 'I am afraid the editor will have to be told.'

The moment, which had been so smiling when the employer first spoke, now showed its teeth. 'Of course, I don't expect he'll mind,' he said. But mind he would, thought Helen.

She took the bath towel from the drawer in her desk and held it in front of her face. 'The law of libel,' she said in a low faint voice, 'is something that one does not care to think about.' She pressed the towel against her face. 'It is everything that there is of tyranny and prevention.'

'Yes, yes,' said the employer, and walking over to the mantelpiece he pinched the dead lilac flowers that were hanging down from the jam jar, 'Yes.'

Helen wrote to the editor to tell him. He regretted that in the circumstances he could not publish the story.

When Helen got the editor's letter she wrapped the raincoat that Bella had given her tightly about her and walked along the rain swept avenue that led to the park. She sat by the bright pink peony flowers and she thought that her thoughts were murderous, for the combination of anger and impotence is murderous, and this time it was no longer Good Friday and the soft feeling of repentance and sorrow did not come to drive out the hatred. The rain fell like spears upon the dark green leaves of the peony plants and the lake water at a distance lay open to their thrust. It was not enough to know that the door against Roland and Bella was now locked tight, she must forget that there had ever been such people, or a door that was open to be shut. But how long would it take to forget, ah, how long, ah, that would be a long time.

MINA LOY
STREET SISTER

B eing that uncircumscribed entity, an infinitarian, tradition-less, almost conditionless, I have been privileged, but so seldom, to slip over the psychological frontier of that unvisited region where those others withhold the confidences of their deprivation, and see the light that lingers in the shadow of mankind.

This happened to me once when, on the draughtiest stretch in Paris, a bitter wind blew me towards a blank wall. While regaining my breath I became aware that something had fallen to the ground, and in the arresting manner of living things detected in unusual relationship to the inanimate, a few belated stragglers had drawn up to peer at it. Sharing all inquisitiveness, I stayed there in spite of the immediate sensation of the lower half of my body forming one block with the icy pavement; the misshapen and half-deflated heap that stirred upon it had lifted a head, and was making swimming motions along the ground with its arms. It was saying something. It was saying this: 'How can I lie at ease in my bed without first having smoothed my sheets?'

A woman, with the perpetual re-iteration of the deranged, was stroking the frozen stone with her stiffened hands. I pulled her up and gave her some money. 'Get something hot – HOT,' I shouted against the blast, for she did not at once understand and I hurried off on my way home. When I looked back she was staggering dangerously on her brittle legs. Wondering if it were possible for her, even when able to pay, to get anything to eat, I slowed down. There were, as so often in France, even too many low-class little cafe restaurants along the Boulevard and tonight all empty. But I saw how she came bundling out of them, one after another, she was so filthy, almost before she got in.

In that absent-minded way I have of finding myself identified with other people's problems, I proposed I should go along with her to present a stronger front. Now I could see her face – it was like an empty rough country road, cracked all over with that shrinkage damp clay undergoes in the process of freezing, and the unclean rheumy icicles, dripping from the corners of her eyes, would have appeared – had one failed to remember the prehistoric descent of dirt or to compare all rheum to the inoffensive drip from other machines such as the panting sweating engines of propellors – appalling. Her eyes, as I looked into them were totally unoccupied, for whoever had once looked out of them, having been too long rebuffed by the world of the exterior, had drawn in so far they had lost focus, yet still she had an undeniable beauty – the heroic stamp of a life that has dared to survive a total opposition.

Swept by the curve of the wind along the deserted perspective of lately planted trees awaving, together we entered the last restaurant. 'Will you please serve this friend of mine some supper,' I ordered. But the waiter, although himself of a moronic lowliness, refused. 'So this is the way La France treats its aged grandmothers,' I hooted. And he shooed us out. This common defeat established us on the footing of absolute equality which seemed to warm her, for as we debated intimately on what was to be done, she became steadier on her legs. 'If you can walk,' I decided, 'I know what we will do. Go to the place where I buy my cigarettes. I doubt if they will want to lose my custom.' Then I noticed something quite queer. The half-delirious dead-eyed wreck I picked up had vanished, and a perfectly normal human being, with light in her friendly eyes, laid a hand on my arm. 'But, my dear,' she said, 'do you think you had better? I hate you to have unpleasantness on my account.'

KAY BOYLE
WEDDING DAY

The red carpet that was to spurt like a haemorrhage from pillar to post was stacked in the corner. The mother was shouting down the stairway that the wedding cake be held aloft and not bowed like a venerable into the servants' entrance. Oh, the wedding cake. No one paid any attention to the three magnificent tiers of it. It passed into the pantry, tied in festoons of waxed paper, with its beard lying white as hoarfrost on its bosom.

This was the last lunch and they came in with their buttonholes drooping with violets and sat sadly down, sat down to eat. They sat at the table in such a way that she flew into a rage and asked them to sit up please to sit up as if they were eating at the same table as if they were of the same flesh and blood not odd people at a lunch counter. Every bouquet that arrived, blossoming forth from its gilded or from its pure white basket, softened the sharp edge of her tongue.

'Have you decided to give your daughter the copper saucepans?' he said.

At this the mother collapsed. She deflated in her chair and pecked feebly at the limp portions of strawberries that remained on her plate. But a drop too much of that black arrogance she had inherited and could not down said No, a thousand times on every note of the scale. NO, she said. The pride of the kitchen to be scratched, burned, buttered, and dimmed. At the thought of them her heart swelled in an agony of sorrow. She was an old woman, fine arrogant old lady that she was, and the saucepans hung in the kitchen like six bull's-eyes coldly reflecting her thin face with its faded topknot of hair. Not a bite had been cooked in them for twenty years. NO swelled in her heart, brimmed in her eyes, until the two could have killed her in her chair.

'Don't cry,' he said to her. He pointed his finger directly at her nose so that when she looked at him with dignity her eyes wavered and crossed. She sat looking proudly at him, erect as a needle staring through its one open eye.

'Don't,' he said.

A thunderous NO now stormed at them, a bitter, hard, a childish no. A whimpering no. Your father prized them highly. Your father, he prized them highly, she said.

Suddenly she turned upon her daughter.

'Your brother is looking for some trouble to make,' she said grimly. 'You see that, don't you? Don't you see that he is trying to make trouble between you and your young man?'

The three of them stared into one another's faces, and a look of bewilderment came upon the old lady's face. Why she was bewildered, she did not know. She knew quite well what she was about, but her son looked at her even more sharply, and he said:

'Who was it that wanted this wedding?'

'Certainly not I,' said the old lady, and these words echoed what was in each one's mouth.

'I certainly did not want this wedding,' the old lady repeated with emphasis, when she saw she had not been contradicted. 'Your sister's choice has appalled me.'

'Enough!' shouted her son. 'No one can question that, my sister's choice!'

The roast beef made them kin again, and they sat watching the mother almost lovingly as she sliced the thin scarlet ribbons of it into the platter. It was a beautiful roast, and it had scarcely been cooked at all. The son kept snatching bits of it away, and she heaped their plates full of them.

'I'm carvin' and carvin',' she was whimpering, 'and I don't get anything to eat myself. Haven't ye had enough?' she said. She looked plaintively at them, her lip trembling as she looked into their faces.

'I'm going to take it under the table,' said her son, 'and snarl at anyone who comes near.'

At this the brother and sister burst into laughter which rocked them back and forth and flushed them to the roots of their light hair. At the end he tossed his napkin over the glass bells of the chandelier and his sister followed him out of the room. Out they went to face the spring before the wedding, and their mother stood at the window praying that this occasion at least pass off with dignity, with her heart not in her mouth but beating away in peace in its own bosom.

Here then was April holding them up, stabbing their hearts with hawthorn, scalping them with a flexible blade of wind. Here went their yellow manes up in the air, turning them shaggy as lions. The Seine had turned around in the wind and in tufts and scallops was leaping directly away from Saint-Cloud. The clouds were cracking and splitting up like a glacier; down the sky were they shifting and sliding, and the two with their heads bare were walking straight into the heart of the floe.

'It isn't too late,' he said. 'I mean it isn't too late.'

The sun was an imposition, an imposition, for they were another race stamping an easy trail through the wilderness of Paris, possessed of the same people, but of themselves like another race. No one else could by lifting of the head only be starting life over again, and it was a wonder the whole city of Paris did not hold its breath for them, for if anyone could have begun a new race, it was these two. Therefore, in their young days they should have been saddled and strapped with necessity so that they could not have escaped. Paris was their responsibility. No one else had the same delight, no one else put foot to pavement in such a way. With their yellow heads back they were stamping a new trail, but in such ignorance, for they had no idea of it.

And who was there to tell them, for the trees they had come to in the woods gave them no sign. They were alone in the little train that ran on rails through the dead brush under the boughs and snapped around corners so smartly that it flicked them from side to side.

'It isn't too late yet, you know,' he said.

At this moment they laughed. Here were their teeth alike in size as well as the arrogance that had put the proud arch in their noses. Wallop and wallop went the little train through the woods, cracking like castanets the knuckles of their behinds.

When the train stopped, these two descended, stroked the sleek pussy willows, scratched them between the ears and watched the seals awhile skipping and leaping for ripples of fish in the spring light. 'What I mean is,' he said, 'that I don't, I don't consider it too late.'

Into a little boat they got and in a minute he had rowed her out to the middle of the pond. She sat buttoned up very tightly in her white furs. The brisk little wind was spanking the waters back and forth and the end of her nose was turning pink. But he, on the contrary, had thrown off his coat, thrown it to the bottom of the boat with his feet on it, and as he rowed he pressed the fresh mud of the spring that had clustered on his soles into every seam and pocket of it. Back and forth went his arms, back and forth, with the little yellow hairs on them standing up in the wind.

'What a day for a wedding,' he said.

As he spoke there was a sudden disturbance among the birds on the bank, and the swans streamed out after them in steady pursuit, necking and bowing after the boat with their smooth coats ruffling up in the wind. Around the boat gathered the swans, peering curiously at the new race, lifting their flat heads at an angle to fix the beaks of the new race in their scarlet eyes.

Down, down could the brother and sister see into the very depths of the pond. Down under the tough black paddling feet of the swans and below their slick wet bellies could be seen the caverns of the pond with flowers blooming under the water. Every reed was podded with clear bright bubbles of light closely strung, and the fish were waving under them like little flags, deep but clear in the water. Over them was the sky set like a tomb, the strange unearthly sky that might at any moment crack into spring.

'It isn't too late,' he said.

A slow rain had begun to fall, and the fruit blossoms on the banks were immediately bruised black with it. The rain was falling, it was running steadily down their cheeks, and they looked with glowing eyes at each other's faces. Everywhere, everywhere there were other countries to go to. And how were they to get from the boat with the chains that were on them, how uproot the willowing trees from their hearts, how strike the irons of spring that shackled them? What shame and shame that scorched a burning pathway to their dressing rooms! Their hearts were mourning for every Paris night and its half-hours before lunch when two straws crossed on the round table top on the marble anywhere meant I had a drink here and went on.

'What a day for a wedding,' he said as they came wearily, wearily up the street, dragging their feet through the spring afternoon.

They found their mother upon her knees in the hallway, tying white satin bows under the chins of the potted plants. As they passed she was staring a cactus grimly in the eye. Before she turned to them she let fall one last reproving look upon the silver platter by the entry door. Once she had turned her back, her son kicked it smartly down the hall, and without a word of protest she pursued it. She was convinced as she halted it and stepped firmly on the silver tray that this outburst presaged a thousand mishaps that were yet to come.

But in peace the guests arrived, one after another and two by two, leaving their cards upon the platter and hastening forward to press their hostess' hand. The army was handsomely represented, and finally down the drawing room came the bride on the arm of her brother who was giving her away to the groom. With such a gesture he gave her away, and it was evident that she had no thought for her satin dress, nor for the fine lace that was hanging down the back of it. Not a thought for the music did she have, nor a word for the reverend except yes and no. This was the end, the end, they thought. She turned her face to her brother and suddenly their hearts fled together and sobbed like ringdoves in their bosoms. This was the end, the end, the end, this was the end.

Down the room their feet fled in various ways, seeking an escape. To the edge of the carpet fled her feet, returned and followed reluctantly upon her brother's heels. Every piped note of the organ insisted that she go on. It isn't too late, he said. Too late, too late. The ring was given, the book was closed. The desolate, the barren sky continued to fling down dripping handfuls of fresh rain.

Like a Continental gentleman he slapped his thighs, exchanged jokes with the other gentlemen, and in his bitterest moments his eyes traversed the heads of the company and exchanged salute with hers. Her feet were fleeing in a hundred ways throughout the rooms, fluttering from the punch bowl to her bedroom and back again, and her powder puff fell from her bosom and was kicked by the dancers like a chrysanthemum around the floor. Over the rooms she danced, paused at the punch table, her feet like white butterflies escaping by a miracle the destructive feet of whatever partner held her in his arms.

The punch it was that daintily and unerringly picked out her brother's steps and made him dance, that took his joints and swung and limbered them, divined the presence of his antagonism and sent him jigging. He danced with the silver platter of cards held high and perilous, and as he danced from room to room he scattered the cards about him – a handful of army officers here, a handful of deep-bosomed matrons strewn across one shoulder. The greater part of the American colony fluttered behind the piano as the mother, in triumph on the arm of the General, danced lightly by. Her face was averted from the mesh of his entangling beard, but in her heart she was rejoicing. If this were all she had to fear, she hummed: the cards could be gathered up, no glass had yet been broken. Up and down the winding roads, over the black cascades and the fountains, over the decks of the sardine boats that were barging quietly in the hemp of the Chinese rugs she danced. The punch had turned her veins to water and she felt her knee rapping sharply against the General's as she skipped. In triumph in his elderly arms, she sped away. What a real success, what a *real* success! Over the Oriental prayer rugs, through the Persian forests of hemp, away and away.

VIRGINIA WOOLF
THE NEW DRESS

Mabel had her first serious suspicion that something was wrong as she took her cloak off and Mrs. Barnet, while handing her the mirror and touching the brushes and thus drawing her attention, perhaps rather markedly, to all the appliances for tidying and improving hair, complexion, clothes, which existed on the dressing table, confirmed the suspicion – that it was not right, not quite right, which growing stronger as she went upstairs and springing at her, with conviction as she greeted Clarissa Dalloway, she went straight to the far end of the room, to a shaded corner where a looking-glass hung and looked. No! It was not *right*. And at once the misery which she always tried to hide, the profound dissatisfaction – the sense she had had, ever since she was a child, of being inferior to other people – set upon her, relentlessly, remorselessly, with an intensity which she could not beat off, as she would when she woke at night at home, by reading Borrow or Scott; for oh these men, oh these women, all were thinking – 'What's Mabel wearing? What a fright she looks! What a hideous new dress!' – their eyelids flickering as they came up and then their lids shutting rather tight. It was her own appalling inadequacy; her cowardice: her mean, water-sprinkled blood that depressed her. And at once the whole of the room where, for ever so many hours, she had planned with the little dressmaker how it was to go, seemed sordid, repulsive: and her own drawing-room so shabby, and herself, going out, puffed up with vanity as she touched the letters on the hall table and said: 'How dull!' to show off – all this now seemed unutterably silly, paltry, and provincial. All this had been absolutely destroyed, shown up, exploded, the moment she came into Mrs. Dalloway's drawing-room.

What she had thought that evening when, sitting over the teacups, Mrs. Dalloway's invitation came, was that, of course, she could not be fashionable. It was absurd to pretend it even – fashion meant cut, meant style, meant thirty guineas at least – but why not be original? Why not be herself, anyhow? And, getting up, she had taken that old fashion book of her mother's, a Paris fashion book of the time of the Empire, and had thought how much prettier, more dignified, and more womanly they were then, and so set herself – oh, it was foolish – trying to be like them, pluming herself in fact, upon being modest and old-fashioned, and very charming, giving herself up, no doubt about it, to an orgy of self-love, which deserved to be chastised, and so rigged herself out like this.

But she dared not look in the glass. She could not face the whole horror – the pale yellow, idiotically old-fashioned silk dress with its long skirt and its high sleeves and its waist and all the things that looked so charming in the fashion book, but not on her, not among all these ordinary people. She felt like a dressmaker's dummy standing there, for young people to stick pins into.

'But, my dear, it's perfectly charming!' Rose Shaw said, looking her up and down with that little satirical pucker of the lips which she expected – Rose herself being dressed in the height of fashion, precisely like everybody else always.

We are all like flies trying to crawl over the edge of the saucer, Mabel thought, and repeated the phrase as if she were crossing herself, as if she were trying to find some spell to annul this pain, to make this agony endurable. Tags of Shakespeare, lines from books she had read ages ago, suddenly came to her when she was in agony, and she repeated them over and over again.

'Flies trying to crawl,' she repeated. If she could say that over often enough and make herself see the flies, she would become numb, chill, frozen, dumb. Now she could see flies crawling slowly out of a saucer of milk with their wings stuck together; and she strained and strained (standing in front of the looking-glass, listening to Rose Shaw) to make herself see Rose Shaw and all the other people there as flies, trying to hoist themselves out of something, or into something, meagre, insignificant, toiling flies. But she could not see them like that, not other people. She saw herself like that – she was a fly, but the others were dragonflies, butterflies, beautiful insects, dancing, fluttering, skimming, while she alone dragged herself up out of the saucer. (Envy and spite, the most detestable of the vices, were her chief faults.)

'I feel like some dowdy, decrepit, horribly dingy old fly,' she said, making Robert Haydon stop just to hear her say that, just to reassure herself by furbishing up a poor weak-kneed phrase and so showing how detached she was, how witty, that she did not feel in the least out of anything. And, of course, Robert Haydon answered something, quite polite, quite insincere, which she saw through instantly, and said to herself, directly he went (again from some book), 'Lies, lies lies!' For a party makes things either much more real, or much less real, she thought; she saw in a flash to the bottom of Robert Haydon's heart; she saw through everything. She saw the truth. *This* was true, this drawing-room, this self, and the other false. Miss Milan's little workroom was really terribly hot, stuffy, sordid. It smelt of clothes and cabbage cooking; and yet, when Miss Milan put the glass in her hand, and she looked at herself with the dress on, finished, an extraordinary bliss shot through her heart. Suffused with light, she sprang into existence. Rid of cares and wrinkles, what she had dreamed of herself was there – a beautiful woman. Just for a second (she had not dared look longer, Miss Milan wanted to know about the length of the skirt), there looked at

her, framed in the scrolloping mahogany, a grey-white, mysteriously smiling, charming girl, the core of herself, the soul of
herself; and it was not vanity only, not only self-love that made
her think it good, tender, and true. Miss Milan said that the
skirt could not well be longer; if anything the skirt, said Miss
Milan, puckering her forehead, considering with all her wits
about her, must be shorter; and she felt, suddenly, honestly, full
of love for Miss Milan, much, much fonder of Miss Milan than
of any one in the whole world, and could have cried for pity
that she should be crawling on the floor with her mouth full of
pins, and her face red and her eyes bulging – that one human
being should be doing this for another, and she saw them all as
human beings merely, and herself going off to her party, and
Miss Milan pulling the cover over the canary's cage, or letting
him pick a hemp-seed from between her lips, and the thought of
it, of this side of human nature and its patience and its endurance
and its being content with such miserable, scanty, sordid, little
pleasures filled her eyes with tears.

And now the whole thing had vanished. The dress, the room,
the love, the pity, the scrolloping looking-glass, and the canary's
cage – all had vanished, and here she was in a corner of Mrs.
Dalloway's drawing-room, suffering tortures, woken wide
awake to reality.

But it was all so paltry, weak-blooded, and petty-minded to
care so much at her age with two children, to be still so utterly
dependent on people's opinions and not have principles or
convictions, not to be able to say as other people did, 'There's
Shakespeare! There's death! We're all weevils in a captain's
biscuit' – or whatever it was that people did say.

She faced herself straight in the glass; she pecked at her left
shoulder; she issued out into the room, as if spears were thrown
at her yellow dress from all sides. But instead of looking fierce
or tragic, as Rose Shaw would have done – Rose would have
looked like Boadicea – she looked foolish and self-conscious,

53

and simpered like a schoolgirl and slouched across the room, positively slinking, as if she were a beaten mongrel, and looked at a picture, an engraving. As if one went to a party to look at a picture! Everybody knew why she did it – it was from shame, from humiliation.

'Now the fly's in the saucer,' she said to herself, 'right in the middle, and can't get out, and the milk,' she thought, rigidly staring at the picture, 'is sticking its wings together.'

'It's so old-fashioned,' she said to Charles Burt, making him stop (which by itself he hated) on his way to talk to some one else.

She meant, or she tried to make herself think that she meant, that it was the picture and not her dress, that was old-fashioned. And one word of praise, one word of affection from Charles would have made all the difference to her at the moment. If he had only said, 'Mabel, you're looking charming tonight!' it would have changed her life. But then she ought to have been truthful and direct. Charles said nothing of the kind, of course. He was malice itself. He always saw through one, especially if one were feeling particularly mean, paltry, or feeble-minded.

'Mabel's got a new dress!' he said, and the poor fly was absolutely shoved into the middle of the saucer. Really, he would like her to drown, she believed. He had no heart, no fundamental kindness, only a veneer of friendliness. Miss Milan was much more real, much kinder. If only one could feel that and stick to it, always. 'Why,' she asked herself – replying to Charles much too pertly, letting him see that she was out of temper, or 'ruffled' as he called it ('Rather ruffled?' he said and went on to laugh at her with some woman over there) – 'Why,' she asked herself, 'can't I feel one thing always, feel quite sure that Miss Milan is right, and Charles wrong and stick to it, feel sure about the canary and pity and love and not be whipped all round in a second by coming into a room full of people?' It was her odious, weak, vacillating character again, always giving at

the critical moment and not being seriously interested in con-
chology, etymology, botany, archaeology, cutting up potatoes
and watching them fructify like Mary Dennis, like Violet Searle.

Then Mrs. Holman, seeing her standing there, bore down
upon her. Of course a thing like a dress was beneath Mrs.
Holman's notice, with her family always tumbling downstairs or
having the scarlet fever. Could Mabel tell her if Elmthorpe was
ever let for August and September? Oh, it was a conversation
that bored her unutterably! – it made her furious to be treated
like a house agent or a messenger boy, to be made use of. Not
to have value, that was it, she thought, trying to grasp something
hard, something real, while she tried to answer sensibly about
the bathroom and the south aspect and the hot water to the top
of the house; and all the time she could see little bits of her
yellow dress in the round looking-glass which made them all the
size of boot-buttons or tadpoles; and it was amazing to think
how much humiliation and agony and self-loathing and effort
and passionate ups and downs of feeling were contained in a
thing the size of a threepenny bit. And what was still odder, this
thing, this Mabel Waring, was separate, quite disconnected; and
though Mrs. Holman (the black button) was leaning forward
and telling her how her eldest boy had strained his heart
running, she could see her, too, quite detached in the looking-
glass, and it was impossible that the black dot, leaning forward,
gesticulating, should make the yellow dot, sitting solitary, self-
centred, feel what the black dot was feeling, yet they pretended.

'So impossible to keep boys quiet' – that was the kind of thing
one said.

And Mrs. Holman, who could never get enough sympathy
and snatched what little there was greedily, as if it were her
right (but she deserved much more for there was her little girl
who had come down this morning with a swollen knee-joint),
took this miserable offering and looked at it suspiciously,
grudgingly, as if it were a half-penny when it ought to have been

a pound and put it away in her purse, must put up with it, mean and miserly though it was, times being hard, so very hard; and on she went, creaking, injured Mrs. Holman, about the girl with the swollen joints. Ah, it was tragic, this greed, this clamour of human beings, like a row of cormorants, barking and flapping their wings for sympathy – it was tragic, could one have felt it and not merely pretended to feel it!

But in her yellow dress tonight she could not wring out one drop more; she wanted it all, all for herself. She knew (she kept on looking into the glass, dipping into that dreadfully showing-up blue pool) that she was condemned, despised, left like this in a backwater, because of her being like this a feeble, vacillating creature; and it seemed to her that the yellow dress was a penance which she had deserved, and if she had been dressed like Rose Shaw, in lovely, clinging green with a ruffle of swansdown, she would have deserved that; and she thought that there was no escape for her – none whatever. But it was not her fault altogether, after all. It was being one of a family of ten; never having money enough, always skimping and paring; and her mother carrying great cans, and the linoleum worn on the stair edges, and one sordid little domestic tragedy after another – nothing catastrophic, the sheep farm failing, but not utterly; her eldest brother marrying beneath him but not very much – there was no romance, nothing extreme about them all. They petered out respectably in seaside resorts; every watering-place had one of her aunts even now asleep in some lodging with the front windows not quite facing the sea. That was so like them – they had to squint at things always. And she had done the same – she was just like her aunts. For all her dreams of living in India, married to some hero like Sir Henry Lawrence, some empire builder (still the sight of a native in a turban filled her with romance), she had failed utterly. She had married Hubert, with his safe, permanent underling's job in the Law Courts, and they managed tolerably in a smallish house, without proper maids, and hash when she was alone or just bread and butter, but now and then – Mrs. Holman was off, thinking her the most dried-up, unsympathetic twig she had ever met, absurdly dressed, too, and would tell every one about Mabel's fantastic appearance – now and then, thought Mabel Waring, left alone on the blue sofa, punching the cushion in order to look occupied, for she would not join Charles Burt and Rose Shaw, chattering like magpies and perhaps laughing at her by the fireplace – now and then, there did come to her delicious moments, reading the other night in bed, for instance, or down by the sea on the sand in the sun, at Easter – let her recall it – a great tuft of pale sand-grass standing all twisted like a shock of spears against the sky, which was blue like a smooth china egg, so firm, so hard, and then the melody of the waves – 'Hush, hush,' they said, and the children's shouts paddling – yes, it was a divine moment, and there she lay, she felt, in the hand of the Goddess who was the world; rather a hard-hearted, but very beautiful Goddess, a little lamb laid on the altar (one did think these silly things, and it didn't matter so long as one never said them). And also with Hubert sometimes she had quite unexpectedly – carving the mutton for Sunday lunch, for no reason, opening a letter, coming into a room – divine moments, when she said to herself (for she would never say this to anybody else), 'This is it. This has happened. This is it!' And the other way about it was equally surprising – that is, when everything was arranged – music, weather, holidays, every reason for happiness was there – then nothing happened at all. One wasn't happy. It was flat, just flat, that was all.

Her wretched self again, no doubt! She had always been a fretful, weak, unsatisfactory mother, a wobbly wife, lolling about in a kind of twilight existence with nothing very clear or very bold, or more one thing than another, like all her brothers and sisters, except perhaps Herbert – they were all the same poor water-veined creatures who did nothing. Then in the midst of this creeping, crawling life, suddenly she was on the crest of a wave. That wretched fly – where had she read the story that kept coming back into her mind about the fly and the saucer? – struggled out. Yes, she had those moments. But now that she was forty, they might come more and more seldom. By degrees she would cease to struggle any more. But that was deplorable! That was not to be endured! That made her feel ashamed of herself!

She would go to the London Library tomorrow. She would find some wonderful, helpful, astonishing book, quite by chance, a book by a clergyman, by an American no one had ever heard of; or she would walk down the Strand and drop, accidentally, into a hall where a miner was telling about the life in the pit, and suddenly she would become a new person. She would be absolutely transformed. She would wear a uniform; she would be called Sister Somebody; she would never give a thought to clothes again. And for ever after she would be perfectly clear about Charles Burt and Miss Milan and this room and that room; and it would be always, day after day, as if she were lying in the sun or carving the mutton. It would be it!

So she got up from the blue sofa, and the yellow button in the looking-glass got up too, and she waved her hand to Charles and Rose to show them she did not depend on them one scrap, and the yellow button moved out of the looking-glass, and all the spears were gathered into her breast as she walked towards Mrs. Dalloway and said 'Goodnight.'

'But it's too early to go,' said Mrs. Dalloway, who was always so charming.

'I'm afraid I must,' said Mabel Waring. 'But,' she added in her weak, wobbly voice which only sounded ridiculous when she tried to strengthen it, 'I have enjoyed myself enormously.'

'I have enjoyed myself,' she said to Mr. Dalloway, whom she met on the stairs.

'Lies, lies, lies!' she said to herself, going downstairs, and

'Right in the saucer!' she said to herself as she thanked Mrs. Barnet for helping her and wrapped herself, round and round and round, in the Chinese cloak she had worn these twenty years.

DOROTHY EDWARDS
A COUNTRY HOUSE

From the day when I first met my wife she has been my first consideration always. It is only fair that I should treat her so, because she is young. When I met her she was a mere child, with black ringlets down her back and big blue eyes. She put her hair up to get married. Not that I danced attendance on her. That is nonsense. But from the very first moment I saw her I allowed all those barriers and screens that one puts up against people's curiosity to melt away. Nobody can do more than that. It takes many years to close up all the doors to your soul. And then a woman comes along, and at the first sight of her you push them all open, and you become a child again. Nobody can do more than that.

And then at the first sight of a stranger she begins talking about 'community of interests' and all that sort of thing. I must tell you we live in the country, a long way from a town, so we have no electric light. It is a disadvantage, but you must pay something for living in the country. It is a big house, too, and carrying lamps and candles from one end of it to another is hard. Not that it worries me. I have lived here since I was born. I can find my way about in the dark. But is is natural that a woman would not like it.

I had thought about it for a long time. I do not know anything about electrical engineering, but there is a stream running right down the garden; not a very small stream either. Now why not use the water for a little power-station of our own and make our own electricity?

I went up to town and called at the electricians. They would send someone down to look at it. But they could not send anyone until September. Their man was going for his holidays the next day. He would be away until September. Now I suddenly felt that there was a great hurry. I wanted it done before September. They had no one else they could send, and it would take some time if I decided to have it done. I asked them to send for the electrician. I would pay him anything he liked if he would put off his holiday. They sent for him, and he came in and listened to my proposal.

At this point I ought to describe his appearance. He was tall, about forty years old. He had blue eyes, and grey hair brushed straight up. His hair might have been simply fair, not grey. I cannot remember that now. He had almost a military appearance, only he was shy, reserved, and rather prim. His voice was at least an octave deeper than is natural in a speaking voice. He smiled as though he was amused at everyone else's amusement, only this was not contemptuous. Do not think for a moment that I regard this as a melodrama. I do not. I saw at once that he was a nice fellow, something out of the ordinary, not a villain at all.

He smiled when I asked him to put off his vacation. Nothing could be done until he had had a look at the place, and he was perfectly willing to come down that evening to see it. If it were possible to start work at once, something could perhaps be arranged. I was pleased with this, and I invited him to stay the night with us.

At five o'clock he was standing on the office steps with a very small bag, which he carried as if it were too light for him. He climbed into the car, and sat in silence during the whole long drive. When we reached the avenue of trees just before we turn in at my gate (although it was still twilight, under the trees it was quite dark, because they are so thick), he said, 'I should imagine this was very dark at night?'

61

'Yes, as black as pitch,' I said.

'It would be a good thing to have a light here. It looks dangerous.'

'No, I don't want one here,' I said. 'Nobody uses this road at night but I, and I know it in the dark. Light in the house will be enough.'

I wonder if he thought that unreasonable or not. He was silent again. We turned in at the gate. My wife came across the lawn to meet us. I do not know how to describe her. That day she had a large white panama hat and a dress with flowers on it. I said before that she had black hair and blue eyes. She is tall, too, and she still looks very young. The electrician – his name was Richardson – stood with his feet close together and bowed from the waist. I told her that I had brought him here to see if it was possible to put in electric light.

'In the house?' she said. 'That would be lovely. Is it possible at all?'

'I hope so,' said Richardson in his deep voice. I could see that she was surprised at it.

'We don't know yet,' I said; 'we must take him to see the stream.'

She came with us. The stream runs down by the side of the house, curving a little with the slope of the garden, until it joins the larger stream which flows between the garden wall and the fields. We followed it down, not going round by the paths, but jumping over flower-beds and lawns. Richardson looked all the time at the water, except once when he helped my wife across a border.

'There is enough water,' he said, 'and I suppose it is fuller than this sometimes?'

'Yes, when it rains,' said my wife. 'Sometimes it is impossible to cross the stepping-stones without getting one's shoes wet.'

Now I will tell you where the stepping-stones are. Where the stream curves most a wide gravelled path crosses it, and some high stones have been put in the water. When we came down as far as that Richardson said, 'This is the place where we could have it. We could put a small engine-house here, and the water could afterwards be carried through pipes to join the stream down below, forming a sort of triangle with the hypotenuse underground.'

I asked him if he was certain that it could be done.

'I think so,' he said seriously.

My wife smiled at him. 'I hope the building will not be ugly; it would spoil the garden.'

Richardson smiled in the amused way and answered, 'It will, but it will not be high. We must have it at least half underground, with steps to go down to it. Would it be possible to plant some thick trees round it? Yews, so long as they do not interfere with the wires.'

'Oh yes, thank you,' she said. 'I believe we could have that.'

Richardson looked about him a bit more, and he took some measurements with a tape-measure from his pocket. Then we went back to the house. At dinner I asked him where he meant to spend his holiday.

'I am not sure,' he said seriously. 'I thought perhaps the Yorkshire moors would be a good place.'

'You won't find anything better than this,' I said. 'Put off your holiday until September.'

My wife moved to the door. 'Would you have to stay here during the work?' she asked.

'Or somewhere near here, madam,' he said.

'Yes, of course, here,' she said, and walked out of the room. Richardson bowed from the waist again.

We arranged it easily. He would not put it off, but he would make this his holiday. He would bring his motorbike here and explore the country around. He could be here always when there was anything for him to do, and he considered our invitation to him to stay here more than enough compensation for the change of his plans.

Afterwards in the drawing-room he asked my wife if she was fond of music.

'That is what she *is* fond of,' I said. 'She plays the piano.'

What can anyone do with a strange man in the drawing-room but play the piano to him? She played a Chopin nocturne. Now I could watch girls dancing to Chopin's music all day, but to play Chopin to a stranger that you meet for the first time! What must he think of you? I can understand her playing even the nocturnes when she is alone. When one is alone one is in the mood for anything. But to choose to play them when she is meeting someone for the first time! That is simply wrong. Chopin's nights are like days. There is no difference, except that they are rounded off. That is nonsense. Night does not round things off. Night is a distorter. These nocturnes come of never having spent his nights alone, of spending them either in an inn or in someone else's bedroom. No! How do I know what Chopin did? But I tell you they are the result of thinking of darkness as the absence of the sun's light. It is better to think of it as a vapour rising from the depths of the earth and perhaps bringing many things with it.

But he liked it. That is, Richardson liked the nocturne. He asked her to play another. While she turned over the pages I said aloud, 'Night isn't like that. Night is a distorter.'

My wife looked into the darkness outside the window.

Richardson looked at her, then he looked at me in uncertainty. She began to play, and he, for a moment pretending to be apologetic, studied her music with concentration.

Why didn't they ask me what I meant? I could have proved it to them. In any case it was an interesting point.

She played a lot of Chopin. Then as she came from the piano she said, 'You are fond of music too. Do you play?'

'No,' he said. 'It was my great ambition to be a 'cellist, but I never learnt to play it well, and I haven't one now. It is my favourite instrument.'

'It is only the heavy father of a violin,' I said. But I said it only because all that Chopin had annoyed me. I like the 'cello very much.

'I have never liked anything better than the piano,' said my wife. 'I am sorry you do not play.'

'He sings,' I said.

He smiled with amusement.

'Do you?' she asked eagerly.

'Yes,' he said, half bowing from where he sat.

'I knew by your speaking voice,' I said. 'Please let us hear you.'

'I will bring some songs with me if you wish it,' he said. 'That is very kind of you,' and he leaned back in his chair and cut off all communication with us.

We sat in silence until my wife left us. Then we talked a little about the electric light and then went to bed.

The next day the work began. Until the small building was up and the pipes laid from it back to the stream, Richardson could do nothing more than see that the measurements were right. He carried a small black notebook, and kept looking at it and then looking up at us and saying, 'This is no work at all, you know; it is simply like a holiday.'

He brought his motorbike down, but he went for few rides. Most of the time he spent looking at the first few bricks of the building, or crossing and recrossing the stream over the stepping-stones, with no hat on, and his black notebook open in one hand, as though he were making some very serious calculations. I do not suppose he was for a moment.

As I said before, I do not regard this as a melodrama. I do not consider him a villain, but, on the contrary, a nice enough fellow, but it was irritating to me the way he wandered round in a circle looking for something to do.

In the daytime he could look after himself, but in the evening we treated him as a guest.

The second day he was here, after tea I suggested taking him for a walk. He bowed with one hand behind his back, and he kept it there afterwards. I noticed it particularly. My wife came too. We walked down the garden. Richardson, still with his hand behind his back, walking just behind her, talked to her about the work, and he said the same things over twice.

When we got to the bottom of the garden and through the door which opens on the bank of the stream she gave a cry of horror. And I will tell you why. It was because I had had the grass and weeds on the banks cut.

She turned to Richardson. 'I am so sorry,' she said. 'You should have seen this before it was cut. It was very pretty. What were those white flowers growing on the other side?'

'Hemlock,' I said. 'It had to be cut.'

'I don't see why,' she said. 'It is a pity to spoil such a beautiful place for the sake of tidiness.' She turned to him petulantly.

Now that is all nonsense. A place must be tidy. There were bulrushes and water-lilies as it was. What more must she have? A lot of weeds dripping down into the water! There is a difference between garden flowers and weeds. If you want weeds, then do not have gardens. And I suppose I am insensible to beauty because I keep the place cut and trimmed. Nonsense! Suppose my wife took off her clothes and ran about the garden like a bacchante! Perhaps I should like it very much, but I should shut her up in her room all the same.

We walked along in silence over the newly cut grass. It was yellow already with having been left uncut too long. I went first across the bridge, and my two friends who admire Chopin so much came after. We were in the cornfield now, and I will tell you what it is like. There is a little hill just opposite the bridge, and the corn grows on top of it and on its slopes. It is a very small hill, but the country around is flat, and from the top of it you can see over the trees a long distance. We began to walk up the path to the top. The corn was cut and stood up in sheaves. That is what I like.

When we reached the top Richardson took his hand from behind his back and looked around him. There is a lake a few miles away, and on either side of it the land rises and there are trees. Beyond that again is the sea. And from the hill the sea looks nearer than it is and the lake like a bay. Richardson thought it was a bay. I thought so too when I was a child.

'I did not know the sea was so near,' he said.

'It isn't near,' I answered. 'That is a lake. There are even houses in between it and the sea, only you cannot see them.'

He took a deep breath. 'You know, it is very kind of you to let me stay here. It is very beautiful. I have not seen a place I like better. I am most grateful. And the work is simply nothing. It is a real holiday.' At this point he fingered the black notebook which stuck out of his pocket.

If things had not happened as they did he might have come down often; he might have spent his week-ends here. He was not a bad sort of fellow.

He did not want to leave the hill, but my wife did not like walking about on the stubble in her thin shoes. We walked back by the path which leads between a low wall and some small fir-trees to the back of the house. I had the path made for her, because she prefers that walk.

After dinner Richardson sang. His voice was all right, deep like his speaking voice, only not so steady. She played for him, and he stood up at attention, except that, with his right arm bent stiffly at the elbow and pressed to his side, he clutched the lapel of his coat. He sang some Brahms. It was quite nice.

I went to write some letters, and afterwards I walked about in the garden. When I returned they had left the piano and were talking. He was very fond of Strauss. She had not heard the *Alpine* symphony. We were so far from everywhere here.

67

The time went on. Richardson grew more restless every day. And yet he was lethargic too. He hardly left the house and garden, and he still wandered back and forth by the work. He did not interfere with the men by giving unnecessary orders, but he still studied his notebook as though there were important calculations there. I know all this, because I watched him as if he were my brother.

My wife used to go down there to sit sometimes in the mornings. But he hardly spoke to her then. It is natural that a man would not care to talk about music and all that when the men were working in the sun. It was curious how much interest we all took in the little building and the pipes and the water, and yet when we thought of the electric light in the house, which was to be the result, all the romance was gone out of it. This is not simply my experience. It was so with my wife and Richardson too. I know by my own observation of them. The minute the building was finished we went down to see it. Nothing but a yellow brick hut with steps to go down, and an opening like the mouth of a letter-box in the wall nearest the stream.

'The water is shut off now,' said Richardson. 'We have to put a grating in it before the water comes through.'

There was a hole in the concrete floor too, and from that the pipes would lead back to the stream. The first pipe was there with a big curve in it. It was nice to see it getting on. After that they dug a ditch and put the pipes down. He helped them to dig.

Every night he sang and my wife played, but I did not always stay in the drawing-room. One night, though, I remember particularly, he sang a song by Hugo Wolf about a girl whose lover had gone, and while the men and women were binding the corn she went to the top of a hill, and the wind played with the ribbon that he had put in her hat. It was something like that; I have forgotten it. I asked him to sing it again. I suppose they were pleased that I liked something. He sang it.

An dem Hut mein Rosenband, von seiner Hand
Spielet in dem Winde.

Now I should think that the hill that she climbed in that song was like the hill in our cornfield, and the girl sat there for hours 'like one lost in a dream.'

The days passed, and everything remained the same except the work, and that went on quickly. We walked about together sometimes. One evening we went again through the door to the little river where the grass had been cut. We were going along the bank talking when we heard a splash, and there was a boy swimming in the water. I shouted to him, and told him to come out and not swim there again. His white back flashed through the water to a bush on the other side, and he began to dress behind it. When I turned back she said, 'Why did you send him away? It looked so nice.'

'He can go somewhere else to swim,' I said.

Richardson said nothing.

'He does no harm here, surely?' she said.

Bulrushes and water-lilies are not enough for her. She must have weeds and naked boys too. And do you think *she* ever bathed in a river when she was a child, and hid behind a bush when someone was coming? No, of course not. And does she think the boy wants to be seen bathing? And if he is not to be seen when he is here, he might as well go somewhere else.

We never talked about anything except the work, and he talked about music with my wife. They never said anything illuminating on the subject, though. It is a funny thing that you can spend days and weeks with a man and never mention anything but water-pipes and electricity. But, after all, you can't talk about God and Immortality to a man you hardly know. Anyhow, it is nice to see someone so much interested in his work. No. That is nonsense. He was not interested in his work. When the engine came we were enthusiastic, and he was as miserable as sin. What business has an electrician to get excited over yellow bricks and water-pipes? He was restless. He could not settle to anything. If he read a book, half the time it would be open on his knee and he looking away from it. I noticed him very particularly.

The day before everything was finished and he was to go – he was not waiting to see the light actually put in the rooms – I was chalking out a garden-bed just at the bottom of the garden by the door. It is a shady place, and I meant to plant violets there, especially white violets – not in August, of course, but it was better to get it prepared while I thought of it. I heard them coming along on the other side of the wall.

She was saying, 'Before I was married I stayed with my music master in London. He had two sons but no daughters. His wife was very fond of me. That was the happiest time of my life. One of the sons is a first violin now. I went to a symphony concert when we were in London once and saw him play. I don't know what happened to the other one.'

'Let us sit down here,' said Richardson.

I knew there was something wrong with him by his voice. I detected that at once.

I suppose they sat down on the large tree stump outside. They were silent for a moment. I suppose she was looking at the water and he was looking at her.

Then he said, beginning as though he were talking to himself, and yet apologising too, 'Please forgive me, I ought not to say it. I have never been to a place which has given me such pleasure as this. I have never noticed scenery or nature much before. When one likes a place, it is because one went to it in childhood or something of that sort. But this has been so very beautiful while I have been here. I suppose from the beginning I knew I could not come here again. It is impossible. Forgive me saying so.' His voice became deeper as he went on, I noticed that.

'Oh, but you must come here again,' she said anxiously.

'There is no one here at all, and we have so many tastes in common.'

'No,' he said; 'you think I don't mean it. I walked up and down in the garden just now and I came to a decision. At first I thought I would not speak a word to you, but afterwards I decided it would not make any great difference if I did. People do not change their lives suddenly. That is, they don't except in literature. And now I feel at peace about it. No harm at all – none. I do not mean that literature is artificial, you know, only that it is concerned with different people.'

Now what word had he spoken that a husband could not listen to? And yet we would have looked very interesting from an aeroplane or from a window in heaven.

And do you suppose she wanted to know what he was talking about?

All she said was, 'Oh, but my husband has asked you to come here himself. You must come often, and bring your songs. There is no one here to talk about music to. And I cannot go to any concerts, we are so far from everywhere.'

He was silent. They stood up, and I waited for them to come through the door. I suppose nobody could expect me to hide behind a tree so as to cause them no embarrassment. 'Excuse me, I was just passing at this moment. Please go on with your pleasant conversation.' However, they chose to go back by the other way along the bank of the stream.

We spent dinner very pleasantly. Nobody spoke a word. Richardson was not fully aware that we were in the room. He looked at the tablecloth. I did not go away to write letters after dinner. I never left the drawing-room. I suppose no one could expect me to do that. After the music we sat round the empty grate and said nothing, and we went very late to bed.

The next morning, after breakfast, I went up to the flagstaff. If you climb up the steep bank at the left of the house and walk along until you come to a narrow path with trees growing there, you come to a ledge, and the flagstaff has been put there, because it can be seen above the trees. I was standing there disentangling the rope to pull the flag up when he came up to me.

'What time are you going?' I asked, and pulled out my watch.

'At eleven,' he said.

'I suppose you think it funny that I should be putting the flag up on the day that you go?'

'I did not know you had a flagstaff,' he said. 'I suppose it can be seen even from the sea?'

'Yes.'

He was silent, and he looked across at the house.

'Where is my wife?' I asked.

'In the drawing-room, practising.'

'I hope you will send in your bill as soon as possible.'

'Oh yes,' he said. 'It will come from the firm, you know. They pay me. I wanted to walk round the cornfield before I go.'

I pulled up the flag and fastened the cord. 'I'll come with you,' I said.

We walked in silence to the top of the hill, and he stood and looked all round, at the house and at the sea. Taking leave of it, of course.

'In the village down there,' I said, 'there is a very nice girl called Agnes. She isn't pretty, but she is very nice.'

Now Agnes was the name of the girl in the song by Hugo Wolf, but I knew he would not see that. He looked at me in surprise. Then he took out his watch and said he must go. There was no need for that. If you go away on a motorbike why go exactly at eleven? He had to keep himself to a time, that is what it was. We turned to go down the hill.

'I put up the flag because it is my birthday,' I said, though that was not true.

He looked at me without listening to what I said.

When we got back to the house his motorbike was standing

outside the gate ready. He went into the house to fetch his cap, and my wife came out with him. Half-way to the gate he turned to her and thanked her. He had never experienced such pleasure in a holiday before. Then he shook hands with me and said nothing.

'Come down to see us often,' I said. 'Come whenever you like, for week-ends.'

'Oh yes,' said my wife, 'please come, and bring your music.'

He looked embarrassed. I was watching him. I knew he would be. He looked at the ground and mumbled, 'Thank you very much. Goodbye.' Then he turned and went out through the gate, and in a few minutes he drove away under the trees.

She went into the house. She thinks he will come again, call, and listen to her playing Chopin.

I went to sit down by the engine-house. The engine was working, and it throbbed noisily, while there was hardly any water in the curve of the stream. It has made a great difference to the garden. Up above the flag waved senselessly in the wind.

LEONORA CARRINGTON
PIGEON, FLY!

'There's somebody on the road. Somebody's coming to see me, someone strange, though I can only see him from afar.'

I leaned over my balcony and saw the figure getting rapidly bigger, for it was approaching at great speed. I thought it was a woman, for its long, straight hair fell down upon its horse's mane. The horse was large, with rounded, powerful bones, and it was a strange kind of pink with purple shadows the colour of ripe plums: the colour called roan in England. Of all animals, the horse is the only one who has this rosy colour.

The person on the horse was dressed in a pretty untidy manner that reminded me of the coat of a mountain sheep. On the other hand the colours were rich, almost regal, and a gold shirt was just visible between the strands of loose wool. True the shirt was full of holes and somewhat dirty when examined closely, but the general effect was impressive.

She stopped below my balcony and looked up at me.

'I have a letter which needs an immediate answer.'

The voice was a man's voice, and I found myself at a complete loss in making out the person's sex.

'Who are you?' I asked cautiously.

'I am Ferdinand, emissary of Célestin des Airlines-Drues.'

The rider's voice, very soft, was unquestionably a man's voice: a scent of heliotrope and vanilla mixed with sweat rose to my nostrils. I leaned down to him and, taking the letter from his hand, used the opportunity to look at his face, half hidden. It was a very white face, the lips painted reddish purple. The horse shook its fat neck.

'Madam,' the letter said, 'please have the great kindness to help me in my deep distress. In consequence, you will learn something much to your advantage.

'Entrust your honourable person, as well as your canvases, your brushes, and everything you need in your profession of artist to my emissary.

'I beg you, dear lady, to accept my deepest and most sorrowful respect.' Signed, 'Célestin des Airlines-Drues.'

The writing paper was heavily scented with heliotrope and decorated with several gold crowns transfixed by plumes, swords, and olive branches.

I decided to accompany Ferdinand back to his master, since the promises the letter contained interested me very much, though I'd never heard of Célestin des Airlines-Drues.

I was soon sitting on the broad hindquarters of the emissary's horse behind Ferdinand. My luggage was attached to the saddle.

We took the road to the west, a route that crossed some wild country, rich in great dark forests.

It was spring. The grey, heavy sky dropped a tepid rain; the green of the trees and fields was intense. From time to time I dozed, and on several occasions I could easily have fallen from the horse, but I hung on to Ferdinand's woolly clothes. He didn't appear to worry about me, thinking of other things, and singing 'The Sighs of the Dying Rose.'

> Its petals cold against my heart
> My hot tears could no warmth impart
> To the velvet
> Of the soft skin of My Rose
> OH MY ROSE.

These last words woke me completely, for he screamed them with excruciating brutality into my left ear.

'Idiot,' I shouted, furious.

Ferdinand laughed softly. The horse had come to a halt. We were in a huge courtyard a few hundred yards from a large house. This house, built in dark stone and of ample proportions, was so sad in appearance that I felt a keen desire to turn round and go back home. All the windows were shuttered, there wasn't a wisp of smoke from any of the chimneys, and crows were sitting here and there on the roof.

The courtyard looked as deserted as the house.

I thought that there must be a garden on the other side of the house, for I saw trees and a pale sky through a big wrought iron gate. The gate was strange, the wrought iron showed a gigantic angel sitting in a circle, its head thrown back in an anguished profile. On the right, towards the top of the circle, a little wave of water, also in wrought iron, flowed towards the Angel's face.

'Where are we?' I asked. 'Have we arrived?'

'We are at the Airlines-Drues,' Ferdinand answered after a moment's silence.

He looked at the house without turning his head. It seemed to me that he was waiting for somebody, something, or some event. He did not move. The horse stood very still, also looking straight ahead.

Suddenly bells began to ring: I've never in my life heard such a ringing of bells. The drawn-out echo hung all about us in the trees like a metallic liquid. Distraught, the crows on the roof flew off.

I was about to question my companion when a coach drawn by four black horses passed by us with the swiftness of a shadow. The carriage stopped in front of the gate, and I saw that it was a hearse, sumptuously fixed with carvings and flowers. The horses were of the same breed as the herald's, round and sleek, but these were black as muscat grapes.

The door of the house opened and four men came out carrying a coffin.

Ferdinand's horse began to whinny and the black horses replied, turning their heads towards us.

The men carrying the coffin were dressed the same way as Ferdinand, the only difference being the colour of their flowing robes: purple, black, and a very deep crimson. Their faces were very white and made up like Ferdinand's. They all had long heavy hair, badly combed, like wigs of long ago that had lain in an attic for years.

I'd hardly had time to observe all this when Ferdinand gave his horse a tap with his whip and we were plunging at full gallop headlong through an avenue, throwing up earth and stones behind us.

This journey went so quickly that I wasn't even able to look around me. But I had the impression that we were travelling through a forest. In the end, Ferdinand stopped his horse in a clearing surrounded by trees. The ground was covered by mosses and wildflowers. An armchair stood some yards from us, draped in green and mauve velvet.

'Get down, won't you,' Ferdinand said. 'Set your easel up in the shade. Are you thirsty?'

I told him I would like a drink of some sort and slid from the back of the horse. Ferdinand offered me a flask containing a very sugary liquid.

'They'll be along soon.' He went on looking into the depth of the forest. 'The sun will soon set. Put your easel along here, this is where you'll paint the portrait.'

While I was busy setting up. Ferdinand took the saddle and bridle from his horse, then lay on the ground, the horse beside him.

The sky became red, yellow, and mauve, and dusk fell. It began to rain, and large raindrops fell on me and my canvas.

'There they are,' Ferdinand suddenly called out.

Soon the clearing was full of people. These people, who were veiled, looked more or less like the men who had carried the

77

coffin. They made quite a large circle around me and the armchair. They talked together in low voices, and every now and again one laughed shrilly. There were about forty of them.

Soon a high, clear voice came from behind the circle: 'Like this, Gustave. No, no, no, my poor friend, to the left . . .'

'Who would have thought she was so heavy,' another, lower voice answered. 'And yet she wasn't fat.'

The laughter sounded like bleating sheep, and looking around me, I had the vivid impression I was surrounded by a flock of bizarre sheep dressed for a gloomy ritual.

Part of the circle moved aside, and the four men I had seen previously entered backwards, carrying the coffin.

A tall, narrow individual followed them, speaking in a high, clear voice: 'Put her beside the armchair. Have the draperies been scented?'

'Yes, Monsieur des Airlines-Drues, those were your orders.'

I looked with interest at the gentleman. I could not see his face, but I could see one of his white hands gesturing like an elephant's trunk. He wore an immense black wig, which fell in stiff curls down to his feet.

'Is the painter here?' he asked.

'Yes, sir, she's here.'

'Ah, so I see. It is very kind of you, dear lady, to honour us thus. Be welcomed.'

He came close to me and pushed aside the strands of hair hiding his face. It was indeed the face of a sheep, but covered in soft white skin. His black lips were very thin, and strangely mobile. I took his hand with a certain amount of repugnance, for it was too smooth, much too smooth.

'I've admired your work so much,' Monsieur des Airlines-Drues murmured. 'Do you think you could get a really perfect likeness?' He gestured towards the coffin, which was now open.

Two men took out the corpse of a young woman. She was beautiful and had a mass of silky black hair, but her skin was already phosphorescent, luminous, and vaguely mauve. A rather unpleasant smell wafted towards me. Monsieur des Airlines-Drues, seeing me wrinkle my nose involuntarily, gave me a charming smile of apology.

'It's so difficult,' he said, 'to part with the remains of those one has loved . . . adored. I was sure I'd have your sympathy in this matter. My wife died two weeks ago, and with this heavy, humid weather we've been having . . .' He finished the sentence by gesturing with one of his beautiful hands.

'In short, esteemed lady, please be forbearing. Now I shall go and leave you to your Art.'

I squeezed the colours from the tubes onto my palette and began to paint the portrait of Madame des Airlines-Drues.

The sheeplike individuals around me began to play pigeon, fly: 'Pigeon, fly; Sheep, fly; Angel, fly . . .'

Dusk seemed to last an interminable time. Night, which had appeared imminent, did not fall, and the dull light in the clearing remained strong enough for me to continue to work. I did not notice until later that the light imprisoned in the circle of trees came from no other source than the body of Madame des Airlines-Drues. The forest was in total darkness. I was completely absorbed in my painting and did not notice that I must have been alone with the dead woman for quite a long time.

I was pleased with the portrait, and I stepped back a few paces to see the whole composition. The face on the canvas was my own.

I couldn't believe my eyes. Yet as I looked from the model to the portrait there was no denying the truth. The more I looked at the corpse, the more striking became the resemblance of these pale features. On canvas, the face was unquestionably mine.

'The likeness is extraordinary, my compliments, dear lady.'

Monsieur des Airlines-Drues's voice came from behind my left shoulder.

'It's exactly noon now, but one isn't aware of the sun in this forest. Anyway, Art is a magic which makes the hours melt away and even days dissolve into seconds, isn't that so, dear lady? Do you think you'll be able now to finish the portrait without the model? My poor wife, you understand, has been dead three weeks. She must be pining for her well-deserved rest . . . It's not often that one has to work three weeks after one's demise.'

He laughed a little to underline his joke.

'I can offer you a pleasant and well-lit room at Airlines-Drues. Allow me, dear lady, to take you there in my carriage.'

I followed the enormous walking wig like a sleepwalker.

The studio was a big room, with a large cupboard taking up the farthest end. The room had once been luxurious, but the embroidered silk draperies were now torn and dusty, the delicately carved furniture broken, and the gilding had flaked off in places. Several large easels in the shape of swans or mermaids stood about here and there, like the skeletons of other things. Spiders had spun their webs between them, giving the room a fossilized look.

'This is Madame des Airlines-Drues's studio. This is where she died.'

I rummaged through the cupboard. A great number of clothes, wigs, and old shoes were jumbled together in great disorder. They all looked like fancy-dress costumes, and some reminded me of the circus.

'She must have played at dress up in her time alone in the studio – it's said she liked acting.'

Not the least interesting of my discoveries was a diary bound in green velvet. Her name was on the title page, the handwriting neat but curiously childish.

'Agathe des Airlines-Drues. Please respect this book, its contents are for no other eyes than those of Eleanor. Agathe des Airlines-Drues.'

I started to read.

Dear Eleanor,

How you will cry when you read this little book. I'm using patchouli to scent its pages, so that you'll remember me better. Our sharpest memories are of perfumes and smells. How you will cry! Anyway, I shall be glad. I should like you to cry a great deal.

Today is my birthday, and of course yours too. What fun to be the same age. I'd like so much to see you, but since that's not possible, I'll tell you everything in this diary – everything. (My God, If Célestin could hear me!) Marriage, of course, is a dreadful thing – but mine! My mother writes, 'I'm knitting some tiny things for you, or rather for somebody very close to you, my darling. For a little being who'll surely make his appearance soon.'

Oh, Eleanor, I'll sooner have children by one of the chairs in my studio than by Célestin. Listen! The Wedding Night (!), I lay down in the huge bed draped with acid pink curtains. After more than half an hour the door opened and I saw an apparition: an individual dressed in white feathers, with the wings of an angel. I said to myself, 'I'm surely going to die, for here is the Angel of Death.'

The angel was Célestin.

He threw off his clothes, dropping his gown of feathers to the ground. He was naked. If the feathers were white, his body was blindingly so. I think he must have painted it with some phosphorescent paint, for it shone like the moon. He wore blue stockings with red stripes.

'Am I beautiful?' he asked. 'They say I am.'

I was too fascinated to reply.

'My dear Agathe,' he continued, looking at his reflection in the mirror, 'you see you aren't among country folk anymore . . .' (They call me 'madam' here.)

He put on his feathers and wings again. I suddenly felt so cold, my teeth began to chatter. And now listen to me carefully, Eleanor. The more I looked at Célestin, the lighter he seemed to me, light as a feather. He began to walk around the room in a strange way. His feet seemed to touch the ground less and less. Then he began to glide through the door into the corridor. I got up and hastened to the door. Célestin vanished into the darkness ... his feet weren't touching the ground ... I'm absolutely sure of what I'm telling you. His wings beat very slowly ... but ...

So you see what the start of my marriage was like!

I didn't see Célestin for a week. Furthermore, I saw hardly anybody except an old servant called Gaston. He brought me things to eat, always sweet things. I lived in my studio, and I've lived here ever since. I am so sad, Eleanor, so sad that my body has become transparent, I've shed so many tears. Is it possible to dissolve into water without leaving a trace? I am so often alone that I have struck up a sort of love affair with my mirror image. But Eleanor, here's the worst of it — recently I've found it very difficult to see myself in the mirror. Yes, it's horrible, but it's true. When I look at myself, my face is all hazy. And ... I believe ... no, I'm sure, that I can see the objects in the room behind me through my body.

Now I'm crying so much I can't see the paper on which I'm writing anymore.

Every day, Eleanor, I lose myself a little more, yet I've never loved my face more. I try to paint my portrait so as to have it near me still, you understand. But ... I can't. I elude myself.

And here is another thing: the objects around me are becoming terribly clear and vivid, much more alive than I. You know, Eleanor, I'm afraid ... Listen, the chairs in this room are very old, and so is all the rest of the furniture. Last week I saw a little green bud on one of these old chairs, the kind of bud that appears on trees in the spring.

*And now ... how horrible ... it has become a leaf ...
Eleanor!*

A few days later:

*The room is full of them. All the furniture has sprouted
new green growth, many chairs have already got leaves,
small, fragile leaves of a tender green. It's ludicrous to see
such young leaves growing on such old, dusty furniture.*

*Célestin came. He didn't notice anything, but he touched
my face with those smooth hands of his ... much too
smooth ... He said, 'You will always be a child, Agathe.
Look at me. I am terribly young, aren't I?' Then he stopped
and laughed. He has a very high-pitched laugh.*

'Do you put on performances all by yourself?' he asked.

*That isn't true, Eleanor ... I only put on fancy dress to
make myself more solid, more substantial ... so as not to
... guess what I was going to say!...*

*'Agathe, when you were a little girl, did you ever play
pigeon, fly?'*

*Célestin asked me this strange question while looking
into the mirror. I replied that it was a game that very much
amused me when I was little.*

*Now the room was full of bizarre individuals dressed like
sheep. But, Eleanor, they were naked ... Their clothes
were nothing but fleece. All of them were men made up like
whores.*

'The lambs of God,' Célestin said.

*We sat down at a round table, and about twenty pairs of
hands suddenly appeared from between the strands of hair.
I noticed their nails were varnished but very dirty. The
hands were pale, greyish.*

*This was only a moment's impression, for I really had
eyes for nothing but Célestin's hands. I swear to you,*

Eleanor, that his hands were running with moisture . . . and so smooth, and their colour was strange, like mother-of-pearl. He too was looking at his hands with a secret smile.

'Pigeon, fly!' he cried, and all the hands went up in the air, waving like wings. My hands too were fluttering in the air.

'Sheep, fly!' Célestin called.

The hands trembled on the table but didn't lift.

'Angel, fly!'

So far nobody had made a mistake.

Suddenly Célestin's voice rose in a sharp cry, a terrible cry, 'CÉLESTIN, FLY!'

Eleanor, dear Eleanor, his hands . . .

At this point Agathe's journal suddenly stopped.

I turned to her portrait: the canvas was empty, I didn't dare look for my face in the mirror. I knew what I would see: my hands were so cold!

JANET FLANNER
VENETIAN PERSPECTIVE

Bertha went around Europe picking people up with her magnificent, carrying contralto. Mrs. Daphne's turn came in Venice, in front of the Grand Hotel, when a large, unknown lady in a red gown and green parasol, about to step into her gondola (the gondoliers were waiting for her, both looking tense and one ready with the boathook), turned and lifted her great arms toward the cerulean sky. 'It's yoost a dream day,' she intoned by way of introduction. The salute to nature was late Wagnerian, as was the voice. Also the pose, minus the parasol, was that of Elsa about to move off among swans. '*Ach!*' the lady added, *legato*. Her profound breasts filled, her chin drooped, she seemed to be testing her epiglottis.

She's going to sing scales, hoped Mrs. Daphne. 'It's a dream day,' she agreed after a moment, disappointed.

'Come riding wit' us,' the *récitatif* continued. 'Dot's my husband, Hans, in de boat. He has to take lots off fresh air.' Not that he's getting much, with the curtains of the *felze* drawn, thought Mrs. Daphne. All she could see beneath the black hood was a pair of white-flannel trousers, then a polite straw hat. Apparently, Hans was acknowledging the only kind of introduction he ever got.

Though she didn't ride with them then, there was no evading the Bensdorps in Venice as long as there was only one Piazza San Marco. At sundown, Bertha's voice filled it like the sundown shadows. Her contralto rolled from the door of the Basilica across to the jewelry shop under the arcade at the opposite corner. The immediate pigeons rose slightly to it, as they all rose in high flight to the midday gun, then fluttered down again singly to sit on her thumb. For Bertha was used to the centre of the stage, and the pigeons took their cue. 'I loff birds because dey sing,' she said tenderly, disentangling a squab's claws from the real-lace cuffs, the diamond bracelet, the emerald bracelet, the chain of topazes, and the petit-point handbag handle that covered her left wrist.

'Pigeons do not sing,' said Hans suddenly. It was the third time Mrs. Daphne had met him, but the first time she could recall having heard him speak. He spoke English perfectly. 'As a young man – I am old now, I am turned forty – I longed to go to Australia and ranch it, so I went to London to learn the language,' he explained. 'But I was forced to go into a bank instead.'

'V'ere you made moch money,' Bertha prompted softly. 'If you von't sing, birdie, go 'vay.'

The squab flew.

'Yes,' said Hans. 'Yes. Where I made money.'

No one spoke. In the presence of male suffering, Mrs. Daphne had learned, during her husband's final illness, to sit silent indefinitely.

'Und dot's v'y Hans loffs de open spaces so moch,' yawned Bertha. 'It vas dot Australia v'ich laid her spell on him.'

'And on which he has never yet laid his eyes, I wager,' said Mrs. Daphne to herself. Apparently, the Bensdorps had seen everything else, though. They had just come from Fulda and Goslar, with their pretty, confining baroque. Valley villages without view in the Vosges, squeezed in between overhanging mountain tops. Italian walled towns where one couldn't see out, Mediterranean islands where one couldn't get off. Majorca, Brioni. Brioni, Bertha especially recommended. Not a wild spot on it that she could remember, outside of the stone quarries; an island as nice as a polo lawn.

'Hans has got claustrophobia, dot's v'y ve eat outside,' Bertha went on as they arrived at the restaurant, where they were dining. It was in a hedged garden on a narrow canal that smelled of August. Overhead, where the vines gaped, the trellis had been sealed in with canvas. From where he sat, packed in between them in the corner, Hans had a full view of the second violinist and the wreck of someone's lobster. Prompted, Bertha ordered three lobsters and one waltz. And *scampi*. Friend octopus. *Gnocchi bolognesi. Pollo. Polli.*

'I'd better make dem chickens two,' she calculated. 'Hans only likes de v'ite meats und yoost picks.'

And *zucchini* in batter, raw artichokes in oil, *finocchi* and Gorgonzola, she shouted after the waiter. Soave in carafes, and Orvieto and Lacrima Cristi in bottles; that way they could take their choice, Bertha said, and leaned back in her small chair.

'Offen I haf starved enough. To eat good,' she mumbled later over the leg of a chicken, dark against the jewels on her hand, 'to eat good iss part off a good life. Like nature und art. Nature und art I loff so I could eat dem, too,' and she cut herself some cheese. Mrs. Daphne preferred hearing about nature. The art lay in listening to Bertha. Hans set the perfect example.

Theirs had been a pure love match, a flame kindled between two lonely Nordics in a one-room front in Soho, Bertha explained, as she drank the Tears of Christ. Hans's banking *coups* began about the same time as their love. As both matured, the one room became five in a yoost darling liddle willa at Surbiton whose ten-foot back yard was to console Hans for all of Australia. When the thousands began rolling in, Bertha moved the *ménage* to a narrow Adam house in Bloomsbury, to a Mayfair service flat, to a shallow penthouse over Hyde Park; and finally to North Street and a ducky weeny Queen Anne cottage which she gave Hans for a Christmas present – it had cost him yoost a fortune. But so cute, a reg'lar liddle doll house wid liddle green doors und a simply sveet liddle bedroom dot gafe onto de street, de soot, und de sun.

'What room does he have in all this?' Mrs. Daphne asked suddenly of the fine, florid woman whose husband loved space and had it only in her.

'I have the small dressing room on the court; it used to be the bath,' Hans answered, as if for once he had been addressed. In the night heat, the mass of broken food and unfulfilled memories, he looked as if he were being strangled by his life and his high collar. Without either, he would have been an easy-breathing little Baltic whose only malady was that he had once wanted to run a large ranch below the equator.

'My Hans has got de sveetest, most egspensive room in de house,' Bertha intoned, 'wid a genuwine Qveen Anne canopied bed like a jewel box wid fine silk curtains, thick like mist, all round it to shut out de draft und light. Not'ing is too good for my Hans.'

No one disputed her. She took up her husband's hand and kissed it. He made no move. Mrs. Daphne couldn't discover if Bertha were intoxicated on three kinds of wine or on love and energy and possession. The second violinist passed the hat for the fourth time. The waltz again started filling the deserted garden and looping its three-time over the narrow, rhythmless canal.

As Hans paid the bill, Bertha looked over his shoulder. 'It's a lot, t'ank God,' she said, her eyes caressing the final sum. 'It's enough to have paid half my troupe in de old days.' She laughed.

'My wife used to be a great star in her own opera company,' Hans said. 'Weren't you?'

He woke the two gondoliers and helped them help Bertha in. Mrs. Daphne preferred to get in last and sit in the middle seat alone. From beneath the curtained hood, Bertha sang in her magnificent muddled contralto as they traced the narrow canals. Her voice was like an extra-heavy shadow on the water and the palaces of the city. She sang verses in the four European languages Mrs. Daphne was familiar with and café choruses in three or four more she couldn't place. 'Your wife has sung all over the world, hasn't she?' she turned to ask Hans, as if Bertha were no longer present. In a way, she was not. She was gliding over some special lunar planet peopled by large women, memories, and the blare of unmuffled, cheap, male brass.

'I gather so,' said Hans politely.

'I daresay she's even sung in Australia,' Mrs. Daphne added, on the pier of the Grand Hotel. Bertha, who was only humming now, had moved inside to take possession of the lift.

'I daresay she even has,' and the little banker reddened, as if a good customer had asked him to initial a bad check. 'I'll never see Australia, though. Not now . . .'

Mrs. Daphne bent down to look at him from her blonde, perfumed height. 'No. I suppose not. Good night.' Mrs. Daphne said good night kindly, the way people say *bon voyage* or goodbye.

Without meaning to, three days later Mrs. Daphne met Bertha in the morning mob at Thomas Cook's. '*Ach*,' cried Bertha, 'my Hans has left me! Wid'out a vord except in a letter. Yoost wrote he was returning home to pack und den go foreffer. Vun first class to London, yes; like I said, I pay for it all,' she said to the ticket clerk. 'Here, take it out; my husband's left me und I can't count,' and she gave him the petit-point handbag bloated with banknotes. 'I am crying all de morning,' she said to Mrs. Daphne. 'I haf no rouge on; my heart also feels as if it had no red in it. Make haste,' she ordered the clerk.

'But it can't be ready before an hour, Madame. At Mestre.'

'I'm all packed,' she went on to Mrs. Daphne. Her bags lay like large, smooth dogs around her incongruously small feet. 'He took de night train und t'inks he gets home first, but I beat him. I'm d'ere, vaiting, v'en he opens de door, me in my clot'-of-silfer tea-gown vit' orchids und champagne und caviar – dat's all Hans really likes; he don't like v'ite meat of chicken hardly at all – und moosic. I'fe telegraphed for a string qvartette to play so I can sing to him. Und v'en he valks t'rough de pink-silk curtains, I'll be vaiting for him vit' my arms out – so!' And she stretched them magnificently in Thomas Cook's to show how they would look in London to Hans.

'Don't, Mrs. Bensdorp,' said Mrs. Daphne. 'Give Hans a chance – to come back later,' she lied. I would lie to save any human being's life, she thought. 'He'll come back – after Australia. Give him – '

'Gif him not'ing!' Bertha cried. 'He has me und dot's enough,' and she burst into unhappy laughter.

'But if he started last night, you can't – '

'I can,' contradicted Bertha. 'By aëroplane. A special plane for me I hire. Oh, I'll be afraid,' she moaned. 'I haff been afraid of not'ing in life – men, cruelty, vomen laughing, luff, starving, pretending, failure – none off dem! Yoost v'at's not on de eart' I fear. Space! Oh, de bigness; oh, de stretch; oh, de vildness of de sky; vot fear!' and she closed her eyes. 'I could only do it for my Hans.'

'Here's your bag, Madame, thank you; if you'll please count the change,' said the clerk. 'Your motorboat's waiting. You'll find your plane at Mestre.'

'Vot are you doing, a pretty vidow voman alone in dis vorld?' Bertha asked tenderly as she kissed Mrs. Daphne on both cheeks. 'Find a Hans, find one yoost like him. Vot ve big, childless vomen need is somet'ing dot needs us, to take care off, to luff; oh, to luff.' Her face bloomed with tender passion. 'Und v'en you find it,' and the hand freed of the petit point, the jeweled bracelets, the gemmed chains, the real lace, reached out like a leash to attach a dear animal, 'don't neffer let it get away.'

MAY SINCLAIR
THE TOKEN

I have only known one absolutely adorable woman, and that
was my brother's wife, Cicely Dunbar.

Sisters-in-law do not, I think, invariably adore each other,
and I am aware that my chief merit in Cicely's eyes was that I
am Donald's sister; but for me there was no question of
extraneous quality – it was all pure Cicely.

And how Donald – But then, like all the Dunbars, Donald
suffers from being Scottish, so that, if he has a feeling, he makes
it a point of honour to pretend he hasn't it. I daresay he let
himself go a bit during his courtship, when he was not, strictly
speaking, himself; but after he had once married her I think he
would have died rather than have told Cicely in so many words
that he loved her. And Cicely wanted to be told. You say she
ought to have known without telling? You don't know Donald.
You can't conceive the perverse ingenuity he could put into
hiding his affection. He has the peculiar temper – I think it's
Scottish – that delights in snubbing and fault-finding and
defeating expectation. If he knows you want him to do a thing,
that alone is reason enough with Donald for not doing it. And
my sister, who was as transparent as white crystal, was never
able to conceal a want. So that Donald could, as we said, 'have'
her at every turn.

And, then, I don't think my brother really knew how ill she
was. He didn't want to know. Besides, he was so wrapt up in
trying to finish his 'Development of Social Economics' (which,
by the way, he hasn't finished yet) that he had no eyes to see

what we all saw: that, the way her poor little heart was going, Cicely couldn't have very long to live.

Of course he understood that this was why, in those last months, they had to have separate rooms. And this in the first year of their marriage when he was still violently in love with her. I keep those two facts firmly in my mind when I try to excuse Donald; for it was the main cause of that unkindness and perversity which I find it so hard to forgive. Even now, when I think how he used to discharge it on the poor little thing, as if it had been her fault, I have to remind myself that the lamb's innocence made her a little trying.

She couldn't understand why Donald didn't want to have her with him in his library any more while he read or wrote. It seemed to her sheer cruelty to shut her out now when she was ill, seeing that, before she was ill, she had always had her chair by the fireplace, where she would sit over her book or her embroidery for hours without speaking, hardly daring to breathe lest she should interrupt him. Now was the time, she thought, when she might expect a little indulgence.

Do you suppose that Donald would give his feelings as an explanation? Not he. They were *his feelings*, and he wouldn't talk about them; and he never explained anything you didn't understand.

That – her wanting to sit with him in the library – was what they had the awful quarrel about, the day before she died; that and the paper-weight, the precious paper-weight that he wouldn't let anybody touch because George Meredith had given it him. It was a brass block, surmounted by a white alabaster Buddha painted and gilt. And it had an inscription: *To Donald Dunbar, from George Meredith. In Affectionate Regard.*

My brother was extremely attached to this paper-weight, partly, I'm afraid, because it proclaimed his intimacy with the great man. For this reason it was known in the family ironically as the Token.

It stood on Donald's writing-table at his elbow, so near the ink-pot that the white Buddha had received a splash or two. And this evening Cicely had come in to us in the library, and had annoyed Donald by staying in it when he wanted her to go. She had taken up the Token, and was cleaning it to give herself a pretext.

She died after the quarrel they had then.

It began by Donald shouting at her.

'What are you doing with that paper-weight?'

'Only getting the ink off.'

I can see her now, the darling. She had wetted the corner of her handkerchief with her little pink tongue and was rubbing the Buddha. Her hands had begun to tremble when he shouted.

'Put it down, can't you? I've told you not to touch my things.'

'*You* inked him,' she said. She was giving one last rub as he rose, threatening.

'Put – it – down.'

And, poor child, she did put it down. Indeed, she dropped it at his feet.

'Oh!' she cried out, and stooped quickly and picked it up. Her large tear-glassed eyes glanced at him, frightened.

'He isn't broken.'

'No thanks to you,' he growled.

'You beast! You know I'd die rather than break anything you care about.'

'It'll be broken some day, if you *will* come meddling.'

I couldn't bear it. I said, 'You mustn't yell at her like that. You know she can't stand it. You'll make her ill again.'

That sobered him for a moment.

'I'm sorry,' he said; but he made it sound as if he wasn't.

'If you're sorry,' she persisted, 'you might let me stay with you. I'll be as quiet as a mouse.'

'No; I don't want you – I can't work with you in the room.'

'You can work with Helen.'

'You're not Helen.'

'He only means he's not in love with *me*, dear.'

'He means I'm no use to him. I know I'm not. I can't even sit on his manuscripts and keep them down. He cares more for that damned paper-weight than he does for me.'

'Well – George Meredith gave it me.'

'And nobody gave you me. I gave myself.'

That worked up his devil again. He *had* to torment her.

'It can't have cost you much,' he said. 'And I may remind you that the paper-weight has *some* intrinsic value.'

With that he left her.

'What's he gone out for?' she asked me.

'Because he's ashamed of himself, I suppose,' I said. 'Oh, Cicely, why *will* you answer him? You know what he is.'

'No!' she said passionately – 'that's what I don't know. I never have known.'

'At least you know he's in love with you.'

'He has a queer way of showing it, then. He never does anything but stamp and shout and find fault with me – all about an old paper-weight!'

She was caressing it as she spoke, stroking the alabaster Buddha as if it had been a live thing.

'His poor Buddha. Do you think it'll break if I stroke it? Better not . . . Honestly, Helen, I'd rather die than hurt anything he really cared for. Yet look how he hurts me.'

'Some men *must* hurt the things they care for.'

'I wouldn't mind his hurting, if only I knew he cared. Helen – I'd give anything to know.'

'I think you might know.'

'I don't! I don't!'

'Well, you'll know some day.'

'Never! He won't tell me.'

'He's Scotch, my dear. It would kill him to tell you.'

'Then how'm I to know! If I died to-morrow I should die not knowing.'

And that night, not knowing, she died.

She died because she had never really known.

*

We never talked about her. It was not my brother's way. Words hurt him, to speak or to hear them.

He had become more morose than ever, but less irritable, the source of his irritation being gone. Though he plunged into work as another man might have plunged into dissipation, to drown the thought of her, you could see that he had no longer any interest in it; he no longer loved it. He attacked it with a fury that had more hate in it than love. He would spend the greater part of the day and the long evenings shut up in his library, only going out for a short walk an hour before dinner. You could see that soon all spontaneous impulses would be checked in him and he would become the creature of habit and routine.

I tried to rouse him, to shake him up out of his deadly groove; but it was no use. The first effort – for he did make efforts – exhausted him, and he sank back into it again.

But he liked to have me with him; and all the time that I could spare from my housekeeping and gardening I spent in the library. I think he didn't like to be left alone there in the place where they had the quarrel that killed her; and I noticed that the cause of it, the Token, had disappeared from his table.

And all her things, everything that could remind him of her, had been put away. It was the dead burying its dead.

Only the chair she had loved remained in its place by the side of the hearth – *her* chair, if you could call it hers when she wasn't allowed to sit in it. It was always empty, for by tacit consent we both avoided it.

We would sit there for hours at a time without speaking, while he worked and I read or sewed. I never dared to ask him whether he sometimes had, as I had, the sense of Cicely's presence there, in that room which she had so longed to enter, from which she had been so cruelly shut out. You couldn't tell what he felt or didn't feel. My brother's face was a heavy, sombre mask; his back, bent over the writing-table, a wall behind which he hid himself.

You must know that twice in my life I have more than *felt* these presences; I have seen them. This may be because I am on both sides a Highland Celt, and my mother had the same uncanny gift. I had never spoken of these appearances to Donald because he would have put it all down to what he calls my hysterical fancy. And I am sure that if he ever felt or saw anything himself he would never own it.

I ought to explain that each time the vision was premonitory of a death (in Cicely's case I had no such warning), and each time it only lasted for a second; also that, though I am certain I was wide awake each time, it is open to anybody to say I was asleep and dreamed it. The queer thing was that I was neither frightened nor surprised.

And so I was neither surprised nor frightened now, the first evening that I saw her.

It was in the early autumn twilight, about six o'clock. I was sitting in my place in front of the fireplace; Donald was in his armchair on my left, smoking a pipe, as usual, before the lamplight drove him out of doors into the dark.

I had had so strong a sense of Cicely's being there in the room that I felt nothing but a sudden sacred pang that was half joy when I looked up and saw her sitting in her chair on my right.

The phantasm was perfect and vivid, as if it had been flesh and blood. I should have thought that it was Cicely herself if I hadn't known that she was dead. She wasn't looking at me; her face was turned to Donald with that longing, wondering look it used to have, searching his face for the secret that he kept from her.

I looked at Donald. His chin was sunk a little, the pipe drooping from the corner of his mouth. He was heavy, absorbed in his smoking. It was clear that he did not see what I saw.

And whereas those other phantasms that I told you about disappeared at once, *this* lasted some little time, and always with its eyes fixed on Donald. It even lasted while Donald stirred, while he stooped forward, knocking the ashes out of his pipe against the hob, while he sighed, stretched himself, turned, and left the room. Then, as the door shut behind him, the whole figure went out suddenly – not flickering, but like a light you switch off.

I saw it again the next evening and the next, at the same time and in the same place, and with the same look turned towards Donald. And again I was sure that he did not see it. But I thought, from his uneasy sighing and stretching, that he had some sense of something there.

No; I was not frightened. I was glad. You see, I loved Cicely. I remember thinking, 'At last, at last, you poor darling, you've got in. And you can stay as long as you like now. He can't turn you away.'

The first few times I saw her just as I have said. I would look up and find the phantasm there, sitting in her chair. And it would disappear suddenly when Donald left the room. Then I knew I was alone.

But as I grew used to its presence, or perhaps as it grew used to mine and found out that I was not afraid of it, that indeed I loved to have it there, it came, I think, to trust me, so that I was made aware of all its movements. I would see it coming across the room from the doorway, making straight for its desired place, and settling in a little curled-up posture of satisfaction, appeased, as if it had expected opposition that it no longer found. Yet that it was not happy, I could still see by its look at Donald. *That* never changed. It was as uncertain of him now as she had been in her lifetime.

Up till now, the sixth or seventh time I had seen it, I had no clue to the secret of its appearance; and its movements seemed to me mysterious and without purpose. Only two things were clear: it was Donald that it came for – the instant he went it disappeared; and I never once saw it when I was alone. And always it chose this room and this hour before the lights came, when he sat doing nothing. It was clear also that he never saw it.

But that it was there with him sometimes when I was not I knew; for, more than once, things on Donald's writing-table, books or papers, would be moved out of their places, though never beyond reach; and he would ask me whether I had touched them.

'Either you lie,' he would say, 'or I'm mistaken. I could have sworn I put those notes on the *left*-hand side; and they aren't there now.'

And once – that was wonderful – I saw, yes, I *saw* her come and push the lost thing under his hand. And all he said was, 'Well, I'm – I could have sworn – '

For whether it had gained a sense of security, or whether its purpose was now finally fixed, it began to move regularly about the room, and its movements had evidently a reason and an aim.

It was looking for something.

One evening we were all there in our places, Donald silent in his chair and I in mine, and it seated in its attitude of wonder and of waiting, when suddenly I saw Donald looking at me.

'Helen,' he said, 'what are you staring for like that?'

I started. I had forgotten that the direction of my eyes would be bound, sooner or later, to betray me.

I heard myself stammer, 'W – w – was I staring?'

'Yes. I wish you wouldn't.'

I knew what he meant. He didn't want me to keep on looking at that chair; he didn't want to know that I was thinking of her.

I bent my head closer over my sewing, so that I no longer had the phantasm in sight.

It was then I was aware that it had risen and was crossing the hearthrug. It stopped at Donald's knees, and stood there, gazing at him with a look so intent and fixed that I could not doubt that this had some significance. I saw it put out its hand and touch him; and, though Donald sighed and shifted his position, I could tell that he had neither seen nor felt anything.

It turned to me then — and this was the first time it had given any sign that it was conscious of my presence — it turned on me a look of supplication, such supplication as I had seen on my sister's face in her lifetime, when she could do nothing with him and implored me to intercede. At the same time three words formed themselves in my brain with a sudden, quick impulsion, as if I had heard them cried.

'Speak to him — speak to him!'

I knew now what it wanted. It was trying to make itself seen by him, to make itself felt, and it was in anguish at finding that it could not. It knew then that I saw it, and the idea had come to it that it could make use of me to get through to him. I think I must have guessed even then what it had come for.

I said, 'You asked me what I was staring at, and I lied. I was looking at Cicely's chair.'

I saw him wince at the name.

'Because,' I went on, 'I don't know how *you* feel, but I always feel as if she were there.'

He said nothing; but he got up, as though to shake off the oppression of the memory I had evoked, and stood leaning on the chimney-piece with his back to me.

The phantasm retreated to its place, where it kept its eyes fixed on him as before.

I was determined to break down his defences, to make him say something it might hear, give some sign that it would understand.

'Donald, do you think it's a good thing, a *kind* thing, never to talk about her?'

'Kind? Kind to whom?'

'To yourself, first of all.'

'You can leave me out of it.'

'To me, then.'

'What's it got to do with you?' His voice was as hard and cutting as he could make it.

'Everything,' I said. 'You forget, I loved her.'

He was silent. He did at least respect my love for her.

'But that wasn't what she wanted.'

That hurt him. I could feel him stiffen under it.

'You see, Donald,' I persisted. '*I* like thinking about her.'

It was cruel of me; but I *had* to break him.

'You can think as much as you like,' he said, 'provided you stop talking.'

'All the same, it's as bad for you,' I said, 'as it is for me, not talking.'

'I don't care if it is bad for me. I *can't* talk about her, Helen. I don't want to.'

'How do you know,' I said, 'it isn't bad for *her*?'

'For *her*?'

I could see I had roused him.

'Yes. If she really is there, all the time.'

'How d'you mean, *there*?'

'Here — in this room. I tell you I can't get over that feeling that she's here.'

'Oh, feel, feel,' he said; 'but don't talk to me about it!'

And he left the room, flinging himself out in anger. And instantly her flame went out.

I thought, 'How he must have hurt her!' It was the old thing over again: I trying to break him down, to make him show her; he beating us both off, punishing us both. You see, I knew now what she had come back for: she had come back to find out whether he loved her. With a longing unquenched by death, she had come back for certainty. And now, as always, my clumsy interference had only made him more hard, more obstinate. I thought, 'If only he could see her! But as long as he beats her off he never will.'

Still, if I could once get him to believe that she was there –

I made up my mind that the next time I saw the phantasm I would tell him.

The next evening and the next its chair was empty, and I judged that it was keeping away, hurt by what it had heard the last time.

But the third evening we were hardly seated before I saw it.

It was sitting up, alert and observant, not staring at Donald as it used to, but looking round the room, as if searching for something that it missed.

'Donald,' I said, 'if I told you that Cicely is in the room now, I suppose you wouldn't believe me?'

'Is it likely?'

'No. All the same, I see her as plainly as I see you.'

The phantasm rose and moved to his side.

'She's standing close beside you.'

And now it moved and went to the writing-table. I turned and followed its movements. It slid its open hands over the table, touching everything, unmistakably feeling for something it believed to be there.

I went on. 'She's at the writing-table now. She's looking for something.'

It stood back, baffled and distressed. Then suddenly it began opening and shutting the drawers, without a sound, searching each one in turn.

I said, 'Oh, she's trying the drawers now!'

Donald stood up. He was not looking at the place where it was. He was looking hard at me, in anxiety and a sort of fright.

I suppose that was why he remained unaware of the opening and shutting of the drawers.

It continued its desperate searching.

The bottom drawer stuck fast. I saw it pull and shake it, and stand back again, baffled.

'It's locked,' I said.

'What's locked?'

'That bottom drawer.'

'Nonsense! It's nothing of the kind.'

'It is, I tell you. Give me the key. Oh, Donald, give it me!'

He shrugged his shoulders; but all the same he felt in his pockets for the key, which he gave me with a little teasing gesture, as if he humoured a child.

I unlocked the drawer, pulled it out to its full length, and there, thrust away at the back, out of sight, I found the Token.

I had not seen it since the day of Cicely's death.

'Who put it there?' I asked.

'I did.'

'Well, that's what she was looking for,' I said.

I held out the Token to him on the palm of my hand, as if it were the proof that I had seen her.

'Helen,' he said gravely, 'I think you must be ill.'

'You think so? I'm not so ill that I don't know what you put it away for,' I said. 'It was because she thought you cared for it more than you did for her.'

'You can remind me of that? There must be something very badly wrong with you, Helen,' he said.

'Perhaps. Perhaps I only want to know what *she* wanted ... You *did* care for her, Donald?'

I couldn't see the phantasm now, but I could feel it, close, close, vibrating, palpitating, as I drove him.

'Care?' he cried. 'I was mad with caring for her! And she knew it.'

'She didn't. She wouldn't be here now if she knew.'

At that he turned from me to his station by the chimney-piece. I followed him there.

'What are you going to do about it?'

'Do about it?'

'What are you going to do with this?'

I thrust the Token close towards him. He drew back, staring at it with a look of concentrated hate and loathing.

'Do with it?' he said. 'The damned thing killed her! This is what I'm going to do with it – '

He snatched it from my hand and hurled it with all his force against the bars of the grate. The Buddha fell, broken to bits, among the ashes.

Then I heard him give a short, groaning cry. He stepped forward, opening his arms, and I saw the phantasm slide between them. For a second it stood there, folded to his breast; then suddenly, before our eyes, it collapsed in a shining heap, a flicker of light on the floor, at his feet.

Then that went out too.

*

I never saw it again.

Neither did my brother. But I didn't know this till some time afterwards; for, somehow, we hadn't cared to speak about it. And in the end it was he who spoke first.

We were sitting together in that room, one evening in November, when he said, suddenly and irrelevantly:

'Helen – do you never see her now?'

'No,' I said – 'Never!'

'Do you think, then, she doesn't come?'

'Why should she?' I said. 'She found what she came for. She knows what she wanted to know.'

'And that – was what?'

'Why, that you loved her.'

His eyes had a queer, submissive, wistful look.

'You think that was why she came back?' he said.

SUSAN GLASPELL
A JURY OF HER PEERS

When Martha Hale opened the storm-door and got the north wind, she ran back for her big woollen scarf. As she hurriedly wound that round her head her eye made a scandalized sweep of her kitchen. It was no ordinary thing that called her away – it was probably farther from ordinary than anything that had ever happened in Dickson County. But her kitchen was in no shape for leaving: bread ready for mixing, half the flour sifted and half unsifted.

She hated to see things half done; but she had been at that when they stopped to get Mr. Hale, and the sheriff came in to say his wife wished Mrs. Hale would come too – adding, with a grin, that he guessed she was getting scarey and wanted another woman along. So she had dropped everything right where it was.

'Martha!' now came her husband's impatient voice. 'Don't keep folks waiting out here in the cold.'

She joined the three men and the one woman waiting for her in the sheriff's car.

After she had the robes tucked in she took another look at the woman beside her. She had met Mrs. Peters the year before, at the county fair, and the thing she remembered about her was that she didn't seem like a sheriff's wife. She was small and thin and didn't have a strong voice. Mrs. Gorman, sheriff's wife before Gorman went out and Peters came in, had a voice that seemed to be backing up the law with every word. But if Mrs. Peters didn't look like a sheriff's wife, Peters made it up in looking like a sheriff – a heavy man with a big voice, who was particularly genial with the law-abiding, as if to make it plain that he knew the difference between criminals and non-criminals. And right there it came into Mrs. Hale's mind that this man who was so lively with all of them was going to the Wrights' now as a sheriff.

'The country's not very pleasant this time of year,' Mrs. Peters at last ventured.

Mrs. Hale scarcely finished her reply, for they had gone up a little hill and could see the Wrights' place, and seeing it did not make her feel like talking. It looked very lonely this cold March morning. It had always been a lonesome-looking place. It was down in a hollow, and the poplar trees around it were lonely-looking trees. The men were looking at it and talking about what had happened. The county attorney was bending to one side, scrutinising the place as they drew up to it.

'I'm glad you came with me,' Mrs. Peters said nervously, as the two women were about to follow the men in through the kitchen door.

Even after she had her foot on the doorstep, Martha Hale had a moment of feeling she could not cross this threshold. And the reason it seemed she couldn't cross it now was because she hadn't crossed it before. Time and time again it had been in her mind, 'I ought to go over and see Minnie Foster' – she still thought of her as Minnie Foster, though for twenty years she had been Mrs. Wright. And then there was always something to do and Minnie Foster would go from her mind. But *now* she could come.

The men went over to the stove. The women stood close together by the door. Young Henderson, the county attorney, turned around and said, 'Come up to the fire, ladies.'

Mrs. Peters took a step forward, then stopped. 'I'm not – cold,' she said.

And so the two women stood by the door, at first not even so much as looking around the kitchen.

The men talked about what a good thing it was the sheriff had sent his deputy out that morning to make a fire for them, and then Sheriff Peters stepped back from the stove, unbuttoned his outer coat, and leaned his hands on the kitchen table in a way that seemed to mark the beginning of official business. 'Now, Mr. Hale,' he said in a sort of semi-official voice, 'before we move things about, you tell Mr. Henderson just what it was you saw when you came here yesterday morning.'

The county attorney was looking around the kitchen.

'By the way,' he asked, 'has anything been moved?' He turned to the sheriff. 'Are things just as you left them yesterday?'

Peters looked from cupboard to sink; to a small worn rocker a little to one side of the kitchen table.

'It's just the same.'

'Well, Mr. Hale,' said the county attorney, 'tell just what happened when you came here yesterday morning.'

Mrs. Hale, still leaning against the door, had that sinking feeling of the mother whose child is about to speak a piece. Lewis often wandered along and got things mixed up in a story. She hoped he would tell this straight and plain, and not say unnecessary things that would make it harder for Minnie Foster. He didn't begin at once, and she noticed that he looked queer, as if thinking of what he had seen here yesterday.

'Yes, Mr. Hale?' the county attorney reminded.

'Harry and I had started to town with a load of wood,' Mrs. Hale's husband began.

Harry was Mrs. Hale's oldest boy. He wasn't with them now, for the wood never got to town yesterday and he was taking it this morning, so he hadn't been home when the sheriff stopped to say he wanted Mr. Hale to come over to the Wright place and tell the county attorney his story there, where he could point it all out. With all Mrs. Hale's other emotions came the fear Harry wasn't dressed warm enough – they hadn't any of them realised how that north wind did bite.

'We come along this road,' Hale was going on, 'and as we got in sight of the house I says to Harry, "I'm goin' to see if I can't get John Wright to take a telephone." You see,' he explained to Henderson, 'unless I can get somebody to go in with me they won't come out this branch road except for a price *I* can't pay. I'd spoke to Wright about it before; but he put me off, saying folks talked too much anyway, and all he asked was peace and quiet – guess you know about how much he talked himself. But I thought maybe if I went to the house and talked about it before his wife, and said all the women-folks liked the telephones, and that in this lonesome stretch of road it would be a good thing – well, I said to Harry that that was what I was going to say – though I said at the same time that I didn't know as what his wife wanted made much difference to John . . .'

Now, there he was! – saying things he didn't need to say. Mrs. Hale tried to catch her husband's eye, but fortunately the county attorney interrupted with:

'Let's talk about that a little later, Mr. Hale. I do want to talk about that, but I'm anxious now to know just what happened when you got here.'

When he began this time, it was deliberately, as if he knew it were important.

'I didn't see or hear anything. I knocked at the door. And still it was all quiet inside. I knew they must be up – it was past eight o'clock. So I knocked again, louder, and I thought I heard somebody say, "Come in," I wasn't sure – I'm not sure yet. But I opened the door – this door,' jerking a hand toward the door by which the two women stood, 'and there, in that rocker' – pointing to it – 'sat Mrs. Wright.'

Everyone in the kitchen looked at the rocker. It came into Mrs. Hale's mind that this chair didn't look in the least like Minnie Foster – the Minnie Foster of twenty years before. It was a dingy red, with wooden rungs up the back, and the middle rung gone; the chair sagged to one side.

'How did she – look?' the county attorney was inquiring.

'Well,' said Hale, 'she looked – queer.'

'How do you mean – queer?'

He took out note-book and pencil. Mrs. Hale did not like the sight of that pencil. She kept her eye on her husband, as if to keep him from saying unnecessary things that would go into the book and make trouble.

Hale spoke guardedly: 'Well, as if she didn't know what she was going to do next. And kind of – done up.'

'How did she seem to feel about your coming?'

'Why, I don't think she minded – one way or other. She didn't pay much attention. I said, "Ho' do, Mrs. Wright. It's cold, ain't it?" And she said, "Is it?" – and went on pleatin' of her apron.'

'Well, I was surprised. She didn't ask me to come up to the stove, but just set there, not even lookin' at me. And so I said, "I want to see John."

'And then she – laughed. I guess you would call it a laugh.

'I thought of Harry and the team outside, so I said, a little sharp, "Can I see John?" "No," says she – kind of dull like. "Ain't he home?" says I. Then she looked at me. "Yes," says she, "he's home." "Then why can't I see him?" I asked her, out of patience with her now. "'Cause he's dead," says she, just as quiet and dull – and fell to pleatin' her apron. "Dead?" says I, like you do when you can't take in what you've heard.

'She just nodded her head, not getting a bit excited, but rockin' back and forth.

'"Why – where is he?" says I, not knowing *what* to say.

'She just pointed upstairs – like this' – pointing to the room above.

'I got up, with the idea of going up there myself. By this time I – didn't know what to do. I walked from there to here, then I says, "Why, what did he die of?"'

' "He died of a rope round his neck," says she; and just went on pleatin' at her apron.'

Hale stopped speaking, staring at the rocker. Nobody spoke; it was as if all were seeing the woman who had sat there the morning before.

'And what did you do then?' the attorney asked.

'I went out and called Harry. I thought I might – need help. I got Harry in, and we went upstairs.' His voice fell almost to a whisper. 'There he was – lying over the . . .'

'I think I'd rather have you go into that upstairs,' the county attorney interrupted, 'where you can point it all out. Just go on now with the rest of the story.'

'Well, my first thought was to get that rope off. It looked . . .'

He stopped; he did not say how it looked.

'But Harry, he went up to him and he said, "No, he's dead all right, and we'd better not touch anythin'." So we went downstairs.

'She was still sitting that same way. "Has anybody been notified?" I asked. "No," says she, unconcerned.

' "Who did this, Mrs. Wright?" said Harry. He said it business-like, and she stopped pleatin' at her apron. "I don't know," she says. "You don' *know*?" says Harry. "Weren't you sleepin' in the bed with him?" "Yes," says she, "but I was on the inside." "Somebody slipped a rope round his neck and strangled him, and you didn't wake up?" says Harry. "I didn't wake up," she said after him.

'We may have looked as if we didn't see how that could be, for after a minute she said, "I sleep sound."

'Harry was going to ask her more questions but I said maybe that weren't our business; maybe we ought to let her tell her story first to the coroner or the sheriff. So Harry went fast as he could over to High Road – the Rivers' place, where there's a telephone.'

'And what did she do when she knew you had gone for the coroner?'

'She moved from that chair to this one over here, and just sat there with her hands held together and looking down. I got a feeling that I ought to make some conversation, so I said I had come in to see if John wanted to put in a telephone; and at that she started to laugh, and then she stopped and looked at me – scared.'

At the sound of a moving pencil the man who was telling the story looked up.

'I dunno – maybe it wasn't scared; I wouldn't like to say it was. Soon Harry got back, and then Dr. Lloyd came, and you, Mr. Peters, and so I guess that's all I know that you don't.'

He said this with relief, moved as if relaxing. The county attorney walked to the stair door.

'I guess we'll go upstairs first – then out to the barn and around there.'

He paused and looked around the kitchen.

'You're convinced there was nothing important here?' he asked the sheriff. 'Nothing that would – point to any motive?'

The sheriff too looked all around. 'Nothing here but kitchen things,' he said, with a little laugh for the insignificance of kitchen things.

The county attorney was looking at the cupboard. He opened the upper part and looked in. After a moment he drew his hand away sticky.

'Here's a nice mess,' he said resentfully.

The two women had drawn nearer, and now the sheriff's wife spoke.

'Oh – her fruit,' she said, looking to Mrs. Hale for understanding. 'She worried about that when it turned so cold last night. She said the fire would go out and her jars might burst.'

Mrs. Peters' husband broke into a laugh.

'Well, can you beat the women! Held for murder, and worrying about her preserves!'

The young attorney set his lips.

'I guess before we're through with her she may have something more serious than preserves to worry about.'

'Oh, well,' said Mrs. Hale's husband, with good-natured superiority, 'women are used to worrying over trifles.'

The two women moved a little closer together. Neither of them spoke. The county attorney seemed to remember his manners – and think of his future.

'And yet,' said he, with the gallantry of a young politician, 'for all their worries, what would we do without the ladies?'

The women did not speak. He went to the sink to wash his hands, turned to wipe them on the roller towel, pulled it for a cleaner place.

'Dirty towels! Not much of a housekeeper, would you say, ladies?' He kicked his foot against some dirty pans under the sink.

'There's a great deal of work to be done on a farm,' said Mrs. Hale stiffly.

'To be sure. And yet' – with a little bow to her – 'I know there are some Dickson County farm-houses that do not have such roller towels.'

'Those towels get dirty awful quick. Men's hands aren't always as clean as they might be.'

'Ah, loyal to your sex, I see,' he laughed. He gave her a keen look. 'But you and Mrs. Wright were neighbours. I suppose you were friends too.'

Martha Hale shook her head.

'I've seen little enough of her of late years. I've not been in this house – it's more than a year.'

'And why was that? You didn't like her?'

'I liked her well enough,' she replied with spirit. 'Farmers'

111

wives have their hands full, Mr. Henderson. And then . . .' She looked around the kitchen.

'Yes?' he encouraged.

'It never seemed a very cheerful place,' said she, more to herself than to him.

'No,' he agreed; 'I don't think anyone would call it cheerful. I shouldn't say she had the home-making instinct.'

'Well, I don't know as Wright had, either,' she muttered.

'You mean they didn't get on very well.'

'No; I don't mean anything,' she answered, with decision. 'But I don't think a place would be any the cheerfuller for John Wright's bein' in it.'

'I'd like to talk to you about that a little later, Mrs. Hale.' He moved towards the stair door, followed by the two men.

'I suppose anything Mrs. Peters does'll be all right?' the sheriff inquired. 'She was to take in some clothes for her, you know – and a few little things. We left in such a hurry yesterday.'

The county attorney looked at the two women they were leaving alone among the kitchen things.

'Yes, Mrs. Peters,' he said, his glance resting on the woman who was not Mrs. Peters, the big farmer woman who stood behind the sheriff's wife. 'Of course Mrs. Peters is one of us,' he added in a manner of entrusting responsibility. 'And keep your eye out, Mrs. Peters, for anything that might be of use. No telling; you women might come upon a clue to the motive – and that's the thing we need.'

Mr. Hale rubbed his face in the fashion of a slow man getting ready for a pleasantry. 'But could the women know a clue if they did come upon it?' he said. Having delivered himself of this, he followed the others through the stair door.

The women stood motionless, listening to the footsteps, first upon the stairs, then in the room above them.

Then, as if releasing herself from something too strange, Mrs.

Hale began to arrange the dirty pans under the sink, which the county attorney's disdainful push of the foot had upset.

'I'd hate to have men coming into my kitchen, snooping round and criticising.'

'Of course it's no more than their duty,' said the sheriff's wife, in her timid manner.

'Duty's all right, but I guess that deputy sheriff that come out to make the fire might have got a little of this on.' She gave the roller towel a pull. 'Wish I'd thought of that sooner! Seems mean to talk about her for not having things slicked up, when she had to come away in such a hurry.'

She looked around the kitchen. Certainly it was not 'slicked up.' Her eye was held by a bucket of sugar on a low shelf. The cover was off the wooden bucket, and beside it was a paper bag – half full.

Mrs. Hale moved towards it.

'She was putting this in there,' she said to herself – slowly.

She thought of the flour in her kitchen at home – half sifted, half not sifted. She had been interrupted, and had left things half done. What had interrupted Minnie Foster? Why had that work been left half done? She made a move as if to finish it – unfinished things always bothered her, and then she saw that Mrs. Peters was watching her, and she didn't want Mrs. Peters to get that feeling she had of work begun and then – for some reason – not finished.

'It's a shame about her fruit,' she said, going to the cupboard. 'I wonder if it's all gone.'

'Here's one that's all right,' she said at last. She held it towards the light. 'This is cherries, too.' She looked again. 'I declare I believe that's the only one.'

'She'll feel awful bad, after all her hard work in the hot weather. I remember the afternoon I put up my cherries last summer.'

She put the bottle on the table, and was about to sit down in the rocker. But something kept her from sitting in that chair. She stood looking at it, seeing the woman who had sat there 'pleatin' at her apron.'

The thin voice of the sheriff's wife broke in upon her: 'I must be getting those things from the front room closet.' She opened the door into the other room, started in, stepped back. 'You coming with me, Mrs. Hale?' she asked nervously. 'You – you could help me get them.'

They were soon back. 'My!' said Mrs. Peters, dropping the things on the table and hurrying to the stove.

Mrs. Hale stood examining the clothes the woman who was being detained in town had said she wanted.

'Wright was close!' she exclaimed, holding up a shabby black skirt that bore the marks of much making over. 'I think maybe that's why she kept so much to herself. I s'pose she felt she couldn't do her part; and then, you don't enjoy things when you feel shabby. She used to wear pretty clothes and be lively – when she was Minnie Foster, one of the town girls, singing in the choir. But that – oh, that was twenty years ago.'

With a carefulness in which there was something tender, she folded the shabby clothes and piled them at one corner of the table. She looked up at Mrs. Peters, and there was something in the other woman's look that irritated her.

'She don't care,' she said to herself. 'Much difference it makes to her whether Minnie Foster had pretty clothes when she was a girl.'

Then she looked again, and she wasn't so sure; in fact, she hadn't at any time been sure about Mrs. Peters. She had that shrinking manner, and yet her eyes looked as if they could see a long way into things.

'This all you was to take in?' asked Mrs. Hale.

'No,' said the sheriff's wife; 'she said she wanted an apron. Funny thing to want,' she ventured in her nervous way, 'for there's not much to get you dirty in jail, goodness knows. But I suppose just to make her feel more natural. She said they were in the bottom drawer of this cupboard. Yes – here they are. And then her little shawl that always hung on the stair door.'

She took the small grey shawl from behind the door leading upstairs.

Suddenly Mrs. Hale took a quick step towards the other woman.

'Mrs. Peters!'

'Yes, Mrs. Hale?'

'Do you think she – did it?'

Mrs. Peters looked frightened. 'Oh, I don't know,' she said, in a voice that seemed to shrink from the subject.

'Well, I don't think she did,' affirmed Mrs. Hale. 'Asking for an apron, and her little shawl. Worryin' about her fruit.'

'Mr. Peters says . . .' Footsteps were heard in the room above; she stopped, looked up, then went on in a lowered voice: 'Mr. Peters says – it looks bad for her. Mr. Henderson is awful sarcastic in a speech, and he's going to make fun of her saying she didn't wake up.'

For a moment Mrs. Hale had no answer. Then, 'Well, I guess John Wright didn't wake up – when they was slippin' that rope under his neck,' she muttered.

'No, it's *strange*,' breathed Mrs. Peters. 'They think it was such a – funny way to kill a man.'

'That's just what Mr. Hale said,' said Mrs. Hale, in a resolutely natural voice. 'There was a gun in the house. He says that's what he can't understand.'

'Mr. Henderson said, coming out, that what was needed for the case was a motive. Something to show anger – or sudden feeling.'

'Well, I don't see any signs of anger around here,' said Mrs. Hale. 'I don't . . .'

She stopped. Her eye was caught by a dish-towel in the middle of the kitchen table. Slowly she moved towards the table. One half of it was wiped clean, the other half untidy. Her eyes made a slow, almost unwilling turn to the bucket of sugar and the half-empty bag beside it. Things begun – and not finished.

She stepped back. 'Wonder how they're finding things upstairs? I hope she had it in better shape up there. Seems kind of *sneaking*, locking her up in town and coming out here to get her own house to turn against her!'

'But, Mrs. Hale,' said the sheriff's wife, 'the law is the law.'

'I s'pose it is,' answered Mrs. Hale shortly.

She turned to the stove, saying something about that fire not being much to brag of.

'The law is the law – and a bad stove is a bad stove. How'd you like to cook on this?' with the poker pointing to the broken lining. She opened the oven door. The thought of Minnie Foster trying to bake in that oven – and the thought of her never going over to see Minnie Foster . . .

She was startled by hearing Mrs. Peters say, 'A person gets discouraged – and loses heart.'

The sheriff's wife had looked from the stove to the sink – the pail of water which had been carried in from outside. The two women stood there silent, above them the footsteps of the men who were looking for evidence against the woman who had worked in that kitchen. That look of seeing into things, of seeing through a thing to something else, was in the eyes of the sheriff's wife now. When Mrs. Hale next spoke to her, it was gently.

'Better loosen up your things, Mrs. Peters. We'll not feel them when we go out.'

Mrs. Peters went to the back of the room to hang up the fur tippet she was wearing. 'Why, she was piecing a quilt,' she exclaimed, and held up a large sewing basket piled high with quilt pieces.

Mrs. Hale spread some of the blocks on the table.

'It's log-cabin pattern,' she said, putting several of them together. 'Pretty, isn't it?'

They were so engaged with the quilt that they did not hear the footsteps on the stairs. As the stair door opened Mrs. Hale was saying, 'Do you suppose she was going to quilt it, or just knot it?'

The sheriff threw up his hands.

'They wonder whether she was going to quilt it, or just knot it!'

There was a laugh for the ways of women, a warming of hands over the stove, and then the county attorney said briskly, 'Well, let's go right out to the barn and get that cleared up.'

'I don't see as there's anything so strange,' Mrs. Hale said resentfully, after the outside door had closed on the three men – 'our taking up our time with little things while we're waiting for them to get the evidence. I don't see as it's anything to laugh about.'

'Of course they've got awful important things on their minds,' said the sheriff's wife apologetically.

They returned to an inspection of the blocks for the quilt. Mrs. Hale was looking at the fine, even sewing, preoccupied with thoughts of the woman who had done that sewing, when she heard the sheriff's wife say, in a startled tone, 'Why, look at this one.

'The sewing,' said Mrs. Peters, in a troubled way. 'All the rest of them have been so nice and even – but – this one. Why it looks as if she didn't know what she was about!'

Their eyes met – something flashed to life, passed between them; then, as if with an effort, they seemed to pull away from each other. A moment Mrs. Hale sat there, her fingers upon those stitches so unlike the rest of the sewing. Then she had pulled a knot and drawn the threads.

'Oh, what are you doing, Mrs. Hale?' asked the sheriff's wife.

'Just pulling out a stitch or two that's not sewed very good,' said Mrs. Hale mildly.

'I don't think we ought to touch things,' Mrs. Peters said.

'I'll just finish up this end,' answered Mrs. Hale.

She threaded a needle and started to replace bad sewing with good. Then in that thin, timid voice, she heard: 'Mrs. Hale!'

'Yes, Mrs. Peters?'

'What do you suppose she was so – nervous about?'

'Oh, I don't know,' said Mrs. Hale, as if dismissing a thing not important enough to spend much time on. 'I don't know as she was – nervous. I sew awful queer sometimes when I'm just tired.'

'Well, I must get these clothes wrapped. They may be through sooner than we think. I wonder where I could find a piece of paper – and string.'

'In that cupboard, maybe,' suggested Mrs. Hale.

One piece of the crazy sewing remained unripped. Mrs. Peters' back turned, Martha Hale scrutinised that piece, compared it with the dainty, accurate stitches of the other blocks. The difference was startling. Holding this block it was hard to remain quiet, as if the distracted thoughts of the woman who had perhaps turned to it to try and quiet herself were communicating themselves to her.

'Here's a bird-cage,' Mrs. Peters said. 'Did she have a bird, Mrs. Hale?'

'Why, I don't know whether she did or not.' She turned to look at the cage Mrs. Peters was holding up. 'I've not been here in so long.' She sighed. 'There was a man round last year selling canaries cheap – but I don't know as she took one. Maybe she did. She used to sing real pretty herself.'

'Seems kind of funny to think of a bird here. But she must have had one – or why would she have a cage? I wonder what happened to it.'

'I suppose maybe the cat got it,' suggested Mrs. Hale, resuming her sewing.

'No; she didn't have a cat. She's got that feeling some people have about cats – being afraid of them. When they brought her to our house yesterday, my cat got in the room, and she was real upset and asked me to take it out.'

'My sister Bessie was like that,' laughed Mrs. Hale.

The sheriff's wife did not reply. The silence made Mrs. Hale turn. Mrs. Peters was examining the bird-cage.

'Look at this door,' she said slowly. 'It's broke. One hinge has been pulled apart.'

Mrs. Hale came nearer.

'Looks as if someone must have been – rough with it.'

Again their eyes met – startled, questioning, apprehensive. For a moment neither spoke nor stirred. Then Mrs. Hale, turning away, said brusquely, 'If they're going to find any evidence, I wish they'd be about it. I don't like this place.'

'But I'm awful glad you came with me, Mrs. Hale.' Mrs. Peters put the bird-cage on the table and sat down. 'It would be lonesome for me – sitting here alone.'

'Yes, it would, wouldn't it?' agreed Mrs. Hale. She had picked up the sewing, but now it dropped to her lap, and she murmured: 'But I tell you what I *do* wish, Mrs. Peters. I wish I had come over sometimes when she was here. I wish – I had.'

'But of course you were awful busy, Mrs. Hale. Your house – and your children.'

'I could've come. I stayed away because it weren't cheerful – and that's why I ought to have come. I' – she looked around – 'I've never liked this place. Maybe because it's down in a hollow and you don't see the road. I don't know what it is, but it's a lonesome place, and always was. I wish I had come over to see Minnie Foster sometimes. I can see now . . .'

'Well, you mustn't reproach yourself. Somehow we just don't see how it is with other folks till – something comes up.'

'Not having children makes less work,' mused Mrs. Hale, 'but it makes a quiet house. And Wright out to work all day – and no company when he did come in. Did you know John Wright, Mrs. Peters?'

'Not to know him. I've seen him in town. They say he was a good man.'

'Yes – good,' conceded John Wright's neighbour grimly. 'He didn't drink, and kept his word as well as most, I guess, and paid his debts. But he was a hard man, Mrs. Peters. Just to pass the time of day with him . . .' She shivered. 'Like a raw wind that gets to the bone.' Her eye fell upon the cage on the table before her, and she added, 'I should think she would've wanted a bird!'

Suddenly she leaned forward, looking intently at the cage. 'But what do you s'pose went wrong with it?'

'I don't know,' returned Mrs. Peters; 'unless it got sick and died.'

But after she said this she reached over and swung the broken door. Both women watched it.

'You didn't know – her?' Mrs. Hale asked.

'Not till they brought her yesterday,' said the sheriff's wife.

'She – come to think of it, she was kind of like a bird herself. Real sweet and pretty, but kind of timid and – flutterly. How – she – did – change!'

Finally, as if struck with a happy thought and relieved to get back to everyday things: 'Tell you what, Mrs. Peters, why don't you take the quilt in with you? It might take up her mind.'

'Why, I think that's a real nice idea, Mrs. Hale. There couldn't possibly be any objection to that, could there? Now, just what will I take? I wonder if her patches are in here?' They turned to the sewing basket.

'Here's some red,' said Mrs. Hale, bringing out a roll of cloth. Underneath this was a box. 'Here, maybe her scissors are in here – and her things.' She held it up. 'What a pretty box! I'll warrant that was something she had a long time ago – when she was a girl.'

She held it in her hand a moment; then, with a little sigh, opened it.

120

Instantly her hand went to her nose. 'Why!'

Mrs. Peters drew nearer – then turned away.

'There's something wrapped up in this piece of silk,' faltered Mrs. Hale.

'This isn't her scissors,' said Mrs. Peters, in a shrinking voice.

Mrs. Hale raised the piece of silk. 'Oh, Mrs. Peters!' she cried. 'It's . . .'

Mrs. Peters bent closer.

'It's the bird,' she whispered.

'But, Mrs. Peters!' cried Mrs. Hale. '*Look* at it! Its *neck* – look at its neck! It's all – other side *to*.'

The sheriff's wife again bent closer.

'Somebody wrung its neck,' said she, in a voice that was slow and deep.

The eyes of the two women met – this time clung together in a look of dawning comprehension, of growing horror. Mrs. Peters looked from the dead bird to the broken door of the cage. Again their eyes met. And just then there was a sound at the outside door.

Mrs. Hale slipped the box under the quilt pieces in the basket. The county attorney and sheriff came in.

'Well, ladies,' said the attorney, as one turning from serious things to little pleasantries, 'have you decided whether she was going to quilt it or knot it?'

'We think,' said the sheriff's wife hastily, 'that she was going to knot it.'

'Well, that's very interesting, I'm sure.' He caught sight of the cage. 'Has the bird flown?'

'We think the cat got it,' said Mrs. Hale in a prosaic voice.

He was walking up and down, as if thinking something out.

'Is there a cat?' he asked absently.

Mrs. Hale shot a look up at the sheriff's wife.

'Well, not *now*,' said Mrs. Peters. 'They're superstitious, you know; they leave.'

121

The county attorney did not heed her. 'No sign at all of anyone having come in from the outside,' he said to Peters, continuing an interrupted conversation. 'Their own rope. Now let's go upstairs again and go over it, piece by piece. It would have to have been someone who knew just the . . .'

The stair door closed behind them and their voices were lost.

The two women sat motionless, not looking at each other, but as if peering into something and at the same time holding back. When they spoke now it was as if they were afraid of what they were saying, but could not help saying it.

'She liked the bird,' said Martha Hale. 'She was going to bury it in that pretty box.'

'When I was a girl,' said Mrs. Peters, under her breath, 'my kitten – there was a boy took a hatchet, and before my eyes – before I could get there . . .' She covered her face an instant. 'If they hadn't held me back I would have' – she caught herself, and finished weakly – 'hurt him.'

Then they sat without speaking or moving.

'I wonder how it would seem,' Mrs. Hale began, as if feeling her way over strange ground – 'never to have had any children around.' Her eyes made a sweep of the kitchen. 'No, Wright wouldn't like the bird – a thing that sang. She used to sing. He killed that too.'

Mrs. Peters moved. 'Of course we don't know who killed the bird.'

'I knew John Wright,' was the answer.

'It was an awful thing was done in this house that night, Mrs. Hale,' said the sheriff's wife. 'Killing a man while he slept – slipping a thing round his neck that choked the life out of him.'

Mrs. Hale's hand went to the bird-cage. 'His neck. Choked the life out of him.'

'We don't *know* who killed him,' whispered Mrs. Peters wildly. 'We don't *know*.'

Mrs. Hale had not moved. 'If there had been years and years

of nothing, then a bird to sing to you, it would be awful – still, after the bird was still.'

'I know what stillness is,' whispered Mrs. Peters. 'When we homesteaded in Dakota, and my first baby died – after he was two years old – and me with no other then . . .'

Mrs. Hale stirred. 'How soon do you suppose they'll be through looking for the evidence?'

'I know what stillness is,' repeated Mrs. Peters. Then she too pulled back. 'The law has got to punish crime, Mrs. Hale.'

'I wish you'd seen Minnie Foster when she wore a white dress with blue ribbons, and stood up there in the choir and sang.'

The picture of that girl, the thought that she had lived neighbour to her for twenty years, and had let her die for lack of life, was suddenly more than the woman could bear.

'Oh, I *wish* I'd come over here once in a while!' she cried. 'That was a crime! That was a crime! Who's going to punish *that?*'

'We mustn't – take on,' said Mrs. Peters, with a frightened look towards the stairs.

'I might 'a' *known* she needed help! I tell you, it's *queer*, Mrs. Peters. We live close together, and we live far apart. We all go through the same things – it's all just a different kind of the same thing! If it weren't – why do you and I *know* – what we know this minute?'

Seeing the jar of fruit on the table, she reached for it. 'If I was you I wouldn't *tell* her her fruit was gone! Tell her it ain't. Tell her it's all right – all of it. Here – take this in to prove it to her! She – she may never know whether it was broke or not.'

Mrs. Peters took the bottle of fruit as if glad to take it – as if touching a familiar thing, having something to do, could keep her from something else. She looked about for something to wrap the fruit in, took a petticoat from the pile of clothes she had brought from the front room, nervously started winding that round the bottle.

'My!' she began, in a high voice, 'it's a good thing the men couldn't hear us! Getting all stirred up over a little thing like a – dead canary. As if that could have anything to do with – with . . . My, wouldn't they *laugh?*'

There were footsteps on the stairs.

'Maybe they would,' muttered Mrs. Hale – 'maybe they wouldn't.'

'No, Peters,' said the county attorney, 'it's all perfectly clear, except the reason for doing it. But you know juries when it comes to women. If there was some definite thing – something to *show* – something to make a story about – a thing that would connect up with this clumsy way of doing it.'

Mrs. Hale looked at Mrs Peters. Mrs. Peters was looking at her. Quickly they looked away from one another. The outer door opened and Mr. Hale came in.

'I've nailed back that board we ripped off,' he said.

'Much obliged, Mr. Hale,' said the sheriff. 'We'll be getting along now.'

'I'm going to stay here awhile by myself,' the county attorney suddenly announced. 'You can send Frank out for me, can't you?' he asked the sheriff. 'I want to go over everything. I'm not satisfied we can't do better.'

Again, for one brief moment, the women's eyes met.

The sheriff came up to the table.

'Did you want to see what Mrs. Peters was going to take in?'

The county attorney picked up the apron. He laughed.

'Oh, I guess they're not very dangerous things the ladies have picked out.'

Mrs. Hale's hand was on the sewing basket in which the box was concealed. She felt that she ought to take her hand off the basket. She did not seem able to. She picked up one of the quilt blocks she had piled on to cover the box. She had a fear that if he took up the basket she would snatch it from him.

But he did not take it. With another laugh he turned away,

saying, 'No, Mrs. Peters doesn't need supervising. For that matter a sheriff's wife is married to the law. Ever think of it that way, Mrs. Peters?'

Mrs. Peters had turned her face away. 'Not – just that way,' she said.

'Married to the law!' chuckled Mrs. Peters' husband. He moved towards the door into the front room, and said to the county attorney, 'I just want you to come here a minute, George. We ought to take a look at these windows.'

'Oh – windows!' scoffed the county attorney.

'We'll be leaving in a second, Mr. Hale,' Mr. Peters told the farmer, as he followed the county attorney into the other room.

'Can't be leavin' too soon to suit me,' muttered Hale, and went out.

Again, for one final moment, the two women were alone in that kitchen.

Martha Hale sprang up, her hands tight together, looking at that other woman, with whom it rested. At first she could not see her eyes for the sheriff's wife had not turned back since she turned away at that suggestion of being married to the law. Slowly, unwillingly, Mrs. Peters turned her head until her eyes met the eyes of the other woman. There was a moment when they held each other in a steady, burning look in which there was no evasion nor flinching. Then Martha Hale's eyes pointed the way to the basket in which was hidden the thing that would convict the third woman – that woman who was not there, and yet who had been there with them through that hour.

For a moment Mrs. Peters did not move. And then she did it. Threw back the quilt pieces, got the box, tried to put it in her hand-bag. It was too big. Desperately she opened it, started to take the bird out. But there she broke – she could not touch the bird. She stood there helpless, foolish.

There was a sound at the door. Martha Hale snatched the box from the sheriff's wife and got it in the pocket of her big coat just as the sheriff and the county attorney came back into the kitchen.

'Well, Henry,' said the county attorney, facetiously, 'at least we found out that she was not going to quilt it. She was going to – what is it you call it, ladies?'

Mrs. Hale's hand was against the pocket of her coat.

'We call it – knot it,' was her answer.

DJUNA BARNES
KATRINA SILVERSTAFF

'We have eaten a great deal, my friend, against the day of God.' She was a fine woman, hard, magnificent, cold, Russian, married to a Jew, a doctor on the East Side.

You know that kind of woman, pale, large, with a heavy oval face.

A woman of 'material' – a lasting personality, in other words, a 'fashionable' woman, a woman who, had she lived to the age of forty odd, would have sat for long fine hours by some window, overlooking some desolate park, thinking of a beautiful but lazy means to an end.

She always wore large and stylish hats, and beneath them her mouth took on a look of pain at once proud, aristocratic and lonely.

She had studied medicine – but medicine in the interest of animals; she was a good horse doctor – an excellent surgeon on the major injuries to birds and dogs.

In fact she and her husband had met in a medical college in Russia – she had been the only woman in the class, the only one of the lot of them who smiled in a strange, hurt and sarcastic way when dissecting.

The men treated her like one of them, that is, they had no cringing mannerliness about their approach, they lost no poise before her, and tried no tricks as one might say.

The Silverstaffs had come to America, they had settled on the East Side, among 'their own people' as he would say; she never said anything when he talked like this, she sat passive, her hands

127

in her lap, but her nostrils quivered, and somewhere under the skin of her cheek something trembled.

Her husband was the typical Jewish intellectual, a man with stiff, short, greying hair, prominent intelligent and kindly eyes, rather short, rather round, always smelling of Greek salad and carbolic acid, and always intensely interested in new medical journals, theories, discoveries.

He was a little dusty, a little careless, a little timid, but always gentle.

They had been in America scarcely eight months before the first child was born, a girl, and then following on her heels a boy, and then no more children.

Katrina Silverstaff stopped having her children as abruptly as she had begun having them; something complicated had entered her mind, and where there are definite complications of the kind that she suffered, there are no more children.

'We have eaten a great deal, my friend, against the day of God,' she had said that.

She had said that one night, sitting in the dusk of their office. There was something inexpressibly funny in their sitting together in this office, with its globe of the world, its lung charts, its weighing machine, its surgical chair, and its bowl of ineffectual goldfish. Something inexpressibly funny and inexpressibly fecund, a fecundity suppressed by coldness, and a terrible determination – more terrible in that her husband Otto felt nothing of it.

He was very fond of her, and had he been a little more sensitive he would have been very glad to be proud of her. She never became confidential with him, and he never tried to overstep this, partly because he was unaware of it, and partly because he felt little need of a closer companionship.

She was a fine woman, he knew that; he never thought to question anything she did, because it was little, nor what she said, because it was less; there was an economy about her existence that simply forbade questioning. He felt in some dim way, that to criticise at all would be to stop everything.

Their life was typical of the East Side doctor's life. Patients all day for him, and the children for her, with an occasional call from someone who had a sick bird. In the evening they would sit around a table with just sufficient food, with just sufficient silver and linen, and one luxury: Katrina's glass of white wine.

Or sometimes they would go out to dine, to some kosher place, where everyone was too friendly and too ugly and too warm, and here he would talk of the day's diseases while she listened to the music and tried not to hear what her daughter was crying for.

He had always been a 'liberal,' from the first turn of the cradle. In the freedom of the people, in the betterment of conditions, he took the interest a doctor takes in seeing a wound heal.

As for Katrina Silverstaff, she never said anything about it, he never knew what she really thought, if she thought at all; it did not seem necessary for her to do or say anything, she was fine as she was, where she was. On the other hand it never occurred to him that she would not hear, with calmness at least, his long dissertations on capital.

At the opening of this story, Katrina's daughter was a little girl of ten, who was devoted to dancing, and who lay awake at nights worrying about the shape of her legs, which had already begun to swell with a dancer's muscles.

The boy was nine, thin, and wore spectacles.

And of course what happened was quite unaccountable.

A man, calling himself Castillion Rodkin, passed through one Summer, selling Carlyle's *French Revolution*. Among the houses where he had left a copy was the house of Otto Silverstaff.

Katrina had opened the door, the maid was down with the measles, and the doctor was busy with a patient, a Jew much revered for his poetry.

129

She never bought anything of peddlers, and she seldom said more than 'No, thank you.' In this case she neither said 'Thank you,' nor closed the door – instead she held it open, standing a little aside for him to pass, and, utterly astonished, he did pass, waiting behind her in the hall for orders.

'We will go into the study,' she said, 'my husband is busy.'

'I was selling Bibles last year,' he remarked, 'but they do not go down in this section.'

'Yes,' she answered, 'I see,' and she moved before him into the heavy damp parlour which was never unshuttered and which was never used. She reached up and turned on one solitary electric light.

Castillion Rodkin might have been of any nationality in the world; this was partly from having travelled in all countries, and also from a fluid temperament – little was fixed or firm in him, a necessary quality in a salesman.

Castillion Rodkin was below medium height, thin and bearded with a pale, almost white growth of hair. He was peculiarly colourless, his eyes were only a shade darker than his temples, and very restless.

She said simply, 'We must talk about religion.'

And with an awkwardness unusual to him he asked, 'Why?'

'Because,' she said in a strained voice, making a hurt gesture, 'it is so far from me.'

He did not know what to say, of course, and lifting one thin leg in its white trousers he placed it carefully over the other.

She was sitting opposite him, her head turned a little to one side, not looking at anything. 'You see,' she said presently, 'I want religion to become out of the reach of the few.'

'Become's a queer word,' he said.

'It is the only word,' she answered, and there was a slight irritation in her voice, 'because it is so irrevocably for the many.'

'Yes,' he said mechanically, and reached up to his beard, leaving his hand there under a few strands of hair.

'You see,' she went on simply, 'I can come to the point. For me, everything is a lie – I am not telling this to you because I need your help, I shall never need help,' she said, turning her eyes on his, 'understand that from the beginning – '

'Beginning,' he said in a loud voice suddenly.

'From the beginning,' she repeated calmly 'right from the very start, not help but hindrance, I need enough hindrance, a total obstacle, otherwise I cannot accomplish it.'

'Accomplish what, madame?' he asked and took his hand from under his beard.

'That is my affair, mine alone, that you must not question, it has nothing to do with you, you are only a means to an end.'

He said, 'What can I do for you?'

She smiled, a sudden smile, and under her cheek something flickered. 'You can do nothing,' she said and stood up. 'I must always do it all – yes, I shall be your mistress – wait,' she said raising her hand, and there was anger and pride in her. 'Do not intrude now by word or sign, but tomorrow you will come to me – that is enough – that is all you can do,' and in this word 'all' he felt a limit on himself that he had never known before, and he was frightened and disquieted and unhappy.

He came the next day, cringing a little, fawning, uneasy, and she would not see him – she sent word 'I do not need you yet,' and he called again the next day and learned that she was out of town, then one Sunday she was in to him.

She said quietly to him, as if she were preparing him for a great disappointment, 'I have deliberately, very deliberately, removed remorse from the forbidden fruit,' and he was abject suddenly and trembling.

'There will be no thorns for you,' she went on in a cold abrupt voice. 'You will miss that, but do not presume to show it in my presence.'

'Also my floor is not the floor on which you may crawl,' she continued, 'and I do not permit you to suffer while I am in the

131

room — and,' she added, unfastening her brooch slowly and precisely, 'I dislike all spiritual odours.'

'Are we all strange?' he whispered.

'It takes more than will to attain to madness.'

'Yes.'

Then she was silent for a while, thinking.

'I want to suffer,' he murmured, and trembled again.

'We are all gross at times, but this is not your time.'

'I could follow you into the wilderness.'

'I would not miss you.'

And it was said in a terrible forbidding voice.

'I suffer as a birthright — I want it to be something more my own than that.'

'What are you going to do?' he said.

'Does one ever destroy oneself who is utterly disinterested?'

'I don't know.'

Presently she said, 'I love my husband — I want you to know that, it doesn't matter, but I want you to know that, and that I am content with him, and quite happy — '

'Yes,' Castillion Rodkin answered and began trembling again, holding on to the sides of the bed.

'But there is something in me,' she continued, 'that is very mournful because it is being.'

He could not answer and tears came to his eyes.

'There is another thing,' she said with abrupt roughness, 'that I must insist on, that is that you will not insult me by your presence while you are in this room.'

He tried to stop his weeping now, and his body grew tense, abject.

'You see,' she continued, 'some people drink poison, some take a knife, and others drown; I take you.'

In the very early dawn, she sat up with a strange smile. 'Will you smoke?' she said, and lit him a cigarette. Then she withdrew into herself, sitting on the edge of the mahogany boards, her hands in her lap.

And there was a little ease, and a little comfort in Castillion Rodkin, and he turned, drawing up one foot, thrusting his hand beneath his beard, slowly smoking his cigarette.

'Does one regret?' he asked, and the figure of Katrina never moved, nor did she seem to hear.

'You know, you frightened me – last night,' he went on, lying on his back now and looking at the ceiling. 'I almost became something – something.'

There was a long silence.

'Shall the beasts of the field and the birds of the air forsake thee?' he said gloomily, then brightly. 'Shall any man forsake thee?'

Katrina Silverstaff remained as she was, but under her cheek something quivered.

The dawn was very near and the street lamps had gone out; a milk cart rattled across the square, and passed up a side street.

'One out of many, or only one?'

He put his cigarette out, he was beginning to breathe with difficulty, he was beginning to shiver.

'Well – '

He turned over, got up, stood on the floor.

'Is there nothing I can say?' he began, and went a little away and put his things on.

'When shall I see you again?'

And now a cold sweat broke out on him, and his chin trembled.

'Tomorrow?'

He tried to come toward her, but he found himself near the door instead.

'I'm nothing,' he said, and turned toward her, bent slightly; he wanted to kiss her feet – but nothing helped him.

'You've taken everything now, now I cannot feel, I do not

suffer – ' He tried to look at her – and succeeded finally after a long time.

He could see that she did not know he was in the room.

Then something like horror entered him, and with a soft, swift running gait he reached the door, turned the handle and was gone.

A few days later, at dusk, for his heart was the heart of a dog, he came into Katrina's street, and looked at the house.

A single length of crape, bowed, hung at the door.

From that day he began to drink heavily, he got to be quite a nuisance in the cafés, he seldom had money to pay, he was a fearless beggar, almost insolent, and once when he saw Otto Silverstaff sitting alone in a corner, with his two children, he laughed a loud laugh and burst into tears.

KATHERINE MANSFIELD
A DILL PICKLE

And then, after six years, she saw him again. He was seated at one of those little bamboo tables decorated with a Japanese vase of paper daffodils. There was a tall plate of fruit in front of him, and very carefully, in a way she recognized immediately as his 'special' way, he was peeling an orange.

He must have felt that shock of recognition in her, for he looked up and met her eyes. Incredible! He didn't know her! She smiled; he frowned. She came towards him. He closed his eyes an instant, but opening them his face lit up as though he had struck a match in a dark room. He laid down the orange and pushed back his chair, and she took her little warm hand out of her muff and gave it to him.

'Vera!' he exclaimed. 'How strange. Really, for a moment I didn't know you. Won't you sit down? You've had lunch? Won't you have some coffee?'

She hesitated, but of course she meant to.

'Yes, I'd like some coffee.' And she sat down opposite him.

'You've changed. You've changed very much,' he said, staring at her with that eager, lighted look. 'You look so well. I've never seen you look so well before.'

'Really?' She raised her veil and unbuttoned her high fur collar. 'I don't feel very well. I can't bear this weather, you know.'

'Ah, no. You hate the cold . . .'

'Loathe it.' She shuddered. 'And the worst of it is that the older one grows . . .'

135

He interrupted her. 'Excuse me,' and tapped on the table for the waitress. 'Please bring some coffee and cream.' To her: 'You are sure you won't eat anything? Some fruit, perhaps. The fruit here is very good.'

'No, thanks. Nothing.'

'Then that's settled.' And smiling just a hint too broadly he took up the orange again. 'You were saying – the older one grows – '

'The colder,' she laughed. But she was thinking how well she remembered that trick of his – the trick of interrupting her – and how it used to exasperate her six years ago. She used to feel then as though he, quite suddenly, in the middle of what she was saying, put his hand over her lips, turned from her, attended to something different, and then took his hand away, and with just the same slightly too broad smile, gave her his attention again . . . Now we are ready. That is settled.

'The colder!' He echoed her words, laughing too. 'Ah, ah. You still say the same things. And there is another thing about you that is not changed at all – your beautiful voice – your beautiful way of speaking.' Now he was very grave; he leaned towards her, and she smelled the warm, stinging scent of the orange peel. 'You have only to say one word and I would know your voice among all other voices. I don't know what it is – I've often wondered – that makes your voice such a – haunting memory . . . Do you remember that first afternoon we spent together at Kew Gardens? You were so surprised because I did not know the names of any flowers. I am still just as ignorant for all your telling me. But whenever it is very fine and warm, and I see some bright colours – it's awfully strange – I hear your voice saying: "Geranium, marigold and verbena." And I feel those three words are all I recall of some forgotten, heavenly language . . . You remember that afternoon?'

'Oh, yes, very well.' She drew a long, soft breath, as though the paper daffodils between them were almost too sweet to bear.

Yet, what had remained in her mind of that particular afternoon was an absurd scene over the tea-table. A great many people taking tea in a Chinese pagoda, and he behaving like a maniac about the wasps – waving them away, flapping at them with his straw hat, serious and infuriated out of all proportion to the occasion. How delighted the sniggering tea drinkers had been. And how she had suffered.

But now, as he spoke, that memory faded. His was the truer. Yes, it had been a wonderful afternoon, full of geranium and marigold and verbena, and – warm sunshine. Her thoughts lingered over the last two words as though she sang them.

In the warmth, as it were, another memory unfolded. She saw herself sitting on a lawn. He lay beside her, and suddenly, after a long silence, he rolled over and put his head in her lap.

'I wish,' he said, in a low, troubled voice, 'I wish that I had taken poison and were about to die – here now!'

At that moment a little girl in a white dress, holding a long, dripping white lily, dodged from behind a bush, stared at them, and dodged back again. But he did not see. She leaned over him.

'Ah, why do you say that? I could not say that.'

But he gave a kind of soft moan, and taking her hand he held it to his cheek.

'Because I know I am going to love you too much – far too much. And I shall suffer so terribly, Vera, because you never, never will love me.'

He was certainly far better looking now than he had been then. He had lost all that dreamy vagueness and indecision. Now he had the air of a man who has found his place in life, and fills it with a confidence and an assurance which was, to say the least, impressive. He must have made money, too. His clothes were admirable, and at that moment he pulled a Russian cigarette-case out of his pocket.

'Won't you smoke?'

'Yes, I will.' She hovered over them. 'They look very good.'

'I think they are. I get them made for me by a little man in St. James's Street. I don't smoke very much. I'm not like you – but when I do, they must be delicious, very fresh cigarettes. Smoking isn't a habit with me; it's a luxury – like perfume. Are you still so fond of perfumes? Ah, when I was in Russia . . .'

She broke in: 'You've really been to Russia?'

'Oh yes. I was there for over a year. Have you forgotten how we used to talk of going there?'

'No, I've not forgotten.'

He gave a strange half-laugh and leaned back in his chair. 'Isn't it curious. I have really carried out all those journeys that we planned. Yes, I have been to all those places that we talked of, and stayed in them long enough to – as you used to say – "air oneself" in them. In fact, I have spent the last three years of my life travelling all the time. Spain, Corsica, Siberia, Russia, Egypt. The only country left is China, and I mean to go there, too, when the war is over.'

As he spoke, so lightly, tapping the end of his cigarette against the ash-tray, she felt the strange beast that had slumbered so long within her bosom stir, stretch itself, yawn, prick up its ears, and suddenly bound to its feet, and fix its longing, hungry stare upon those faraway places. But all she said was, smiling gently: 'How I envy you.'

He accepted that. 'It has been,' he said, 'very wonderful – especially Russia. Russia was all that we had imagined, and far, far more. I even spent some days on a river boat on the Volga. Do you remember that boatman's song that you used to play?'

'Yes.' It began to play in her mind as she spoke.

'Do you ever play it now?'

'No, I've no piano.'

He was amazed at that. 'But what has become of your beautiful piano?'

She made a little grimace. 'Sold. Ages ago.'

'But you were so fond of music,' he wondered.

'I've no time for it now,' said she.

He let it go at that. 'That river life,' he went on, 'is something quite special. After a day or two you cannot realise that you have ever known another. And it is not necessary to know the language – the life of the boat creates a bond between you and the people that's more than sufficient. You eat with them, pass the day with them, and in the evening there is that endless singing.'

She shivered, hearing the boatman's song break out again loud and tragic, and seeing the boat floating on the darkening river with melancholy trees on either side . . . 'Yes, I should like that,' said she, stroking her muff.

'You'd like almost everything about Russian life,' he said warmly. 'It's so informal, so impulsive, so free without question. And then the peasants are so splendid. They are such human beings – yes, that is it. Even the man who drives your carriage has – has some real part in what is happening. I remember the evening a party of us, two friends of mine and the wife of one of them, went for a picnic by the Black Sea. We took supper and champagne and ate and drank on the grass. And while we were eating the coachman came up. "Have a dill pickle," he said. He wanted to share with us. That seemed to me so right, so – you know what I mean?'

And she seemed at that moment to be sitting on the grass beside the mysteriously Black Sea, black as velvet, and rippling against the banks in silent, velvet waves. She saw the carriage drawn up to one side of the road, and the little group on the grass, their faces and hands white in the moonlight. She saw the pale dress of the woman outspread and her folded parasol, lying on the grass like a huge pearl crochet-hook. Apart from them, with his supper in a cloth on his knees, sat the coachman. 'Have a dill pickle,' said he, and although she was not certain what a dill pickle was, she saw the greenish glass jar with a red chilli like a parrot's beak glimmering through. She sucked in her cheeks; the dill pickle was terribly sour . . .

'Yes, I know perfectly what you mean,' she said.

In the pause that followed they looked at each other. In the past when they had looked at each other like that they had felt such a boundless understanding between them that their souls had, as it were, put their arms round each other and dropped into the same sea, content to be drowned, like mournful lovers. But now, the surprising thing was that it was he who held back. He who said:

'What a marvellous listener you are. When you look at me with those wild eyes I feel that I could tell you things that I would never breathe to another human being.'

Was there just a hint of mockery in his voice or was it her fancy? She could not be sure.

'Before I met you,' he said, 'I had never spoken of myself to anybody. How well I remember one night, the night that I brought you the little Christmas tree, telling you all about my childhood. And of how I was so miserable that I ran away and lived under a cart in our yard for two days without being discovered. And you listened, and your eyes shone, and I felt that you had even made the little Christmas tree listen too, as in a fairy story.'

But of that evening she had remembered a little pot of caviare. It had cost seven and sixpence. He could not get over it. Think of it – a tiny jar like that costing seven and sixpence. While she ate it he watched her, delighted and shocked.

'No, really, that is eating money. You could not get seven shillings into a little pot that size. Only think of the profit they must make . . .' And he had begun some immensely complicated calculations . . . But now good-bye to the caviare. The Christmas tree was on the table, and the little boy lay under the cart with his head pillowed on the yard dog.

'The dog was called Bosun,' she cried delightedly.

But he did not follow. 'Which dog? Had you a dog? I don't remember a dog at all.'

'No, no. I mean the yard dog when you were a little boy.' He laughed and snapped the cigarette-case to.

'Was he? Do you know I had forgotten that. It seems such ages ago. I cannot believe that it is only six years. After I had recognized you today – I had to take such a leap – I had to take a leap over my whole life to get back to that time. I was such a kid then.' He drummed on the table. 'I've often thought how I must have bored you. And now I understand so perfectly why you wrote to me as you did – although at the time that letter nearly finished my life. I found it again the other day, and I couldn't help laughing as I read it. It was so clever – such a true picture of me.' He glanced up. 'You're not going?'

She had buttoned her collar again and drawn down her veil.

'Yes, I am afraid I must,' she said, and managed a smile. Now she knew that he had been mocking.

'Ah no, please,' he pleaded. 'Don't go just for a moment,' and he caught up one of her gloves from the table and clutched at it as if that would hold her. 'I see so few people to talk to nowadays, that I have turned into a sort of barbarian,' he said. 'Have I said something to hurt you?'

'Not a bit,' she lied. But as she watched him draw her glove through his fingers, gently, gently, her anger really did die down, and besides, at the moment he looked more like himself of six years ago . . .

'What I really wanted then,' he said softly, 'was to be a sort of carpet – to make myself into a sort of carpet for you to walk on so that you need not be hurt by the sharp stones and the mud that you hated so. It was nothing more positive than that – nothing more selfish. Only I did desire, eventually, to turn into a magic carpet and carry you away to all those lands you longed to see.'

As he spoke she lifted her head as though she drank some-thing; the strange beast in her bosom began to purr . . .

'I felt that you were more lonely than anybody else in the world,' he went on, 'and yet, perhaps, that you were the only person in the world who was really, truly alive. Born out of your time,' he murmured, stroking the glove, 'fated.'

Ah, God! What had she done! How had she dared to throw away her happiness like this. This was the only man who had ever understood her. Was it too late? Could it be too late? *She* was that glove that he held in his fingers . . .

'And then the fact that you had no friends and never had made friends with people. How I understood that, for neither had I. Is it just the same now?'

'Yes,' she breathed. 'Just the same. I am as alone as ever.'

'So am I,' he laughed gently, 'just the same.'

Suddenly with a quick gesture he handed her back the glove and scraped his chair on the floor. 'But what seemed to me so mysterious then is perfectly plain to me now. And to you, too, of course . . . It simply was that we were such egoists, so self-engrossed, so wrapped up in ourselves that we hadn't a corner in our hearts for anybody else. Do you know,' he cried, naïve and hearty, and dreadfully like another side of that old self again, 'I began studying a Mind System when I was in Russia, and I found that we were not peculiar at all. It's quite a well-known form of . . .'

She had gone. He sat there, thunder-struck, astounded beyond words . . . And then he asked the waitress for his bill.

'But the cream has not been touched,' he said. 'Please do not charge me for it.'

CHARLOTTE PERKINS GILMAN
THE YELLOW WALLPAPER

It is very seldom that mere ordinary people like John and myself secure ancestral halls for the summer.

A colonial mansion, a hereditary estate, I would say a haunted house, and reach the height of romantic felicity – but that would be asking too much of fate!

Still I will proudly declare that there is something queer about it.

Else, why should it be let so cheaply? And why have stood so long untenanted?

John laughs at me, of course, but one expects that in marriage.

John is practical in the extreme. He has no patience with faith, an intense horror of superstition, and he scoffs openly at any talk of things not to be felt and seen and put down in figures.

John is a physician, and *perhaps* – (I would not say it to a living soul, of course, but this is dead paper and a great relief to my mind) – *perhaps* that is one reason I do not get well faster.

You see he does not believe I am sick!

And what can one do?

If a physician of high standing, and one's own husband, assures friends and relatives that there is really nothing the matter with one but temporary nervous depression – a slight hysterical tendency – what is one to do?

My brother is also a physician, and also of high standing, and he says the same thing.

So I take phosphates or phosphites – whichever it is, and

tonics, and journeys, and air, and exercise, and am absolutely forbidden to 'work' until I am well again.

Personally, I disagree with their ideas.

Personally, I believe that congenial work, with excitement and change, would do me good.

But what is one to do?

I did write for a while in spite of them; but it *does* exhaust me a good deal – having to be so sly about it, or else meet with heavy opposition.

I sometimes fancy that in my condition if I had less opposition and more society and stimulus – but John says the very worst thing I can do is to think about my condition, and I confess it always makes me feel bad.

So I will let it alone and talk about the house.

The most beautiful place! It is quite alone, standing well back from the road, quite three miles from the village. It makes me think of English places that you read about, for there are hedges and walls and gates that lock, and lots of separate little houses for the gardeners and people.

There is a *delicious* garden! I never saw such a garden – large and shady, full of box-bordered paths, and lined with long grape-covered arbors with seats under them.

There were greenhouses, too, but they are all broken now.

There was some legal trouble, I believe, something about the heirs and coheirs; anyhow, the place has been empty for years.

That spoils my ghostliness, I am afraid, but I don't care – there is something strange about the house – I can feel it.

I even said so to John one moonlight evening, but he said what I felt was a *draught*, and shut the window.

I get unreasonably angry with John sometimes. I'm sure I never used to be so sensitive. I think it is due to this nervous condition.

But John says if I feel so, I shall neglect proper self-control; so

I take pains to control myself — before him, at least, and that makes me very tired.

I don't like our room a bit. I wanted one downstairs that opened on the piazza and had roses all over the window, and such pretty old-fashioned chintz hangings! but John would not hear of it.

He said there was only one window and not room for two beds, and no near room for him if he took another.

He is very careful and loving, and hardly lets me stir without special direction.

I have a schedule prescription for each hour in the day; he takes all care from me, and so I feel basely ungrateful not to value it more.

He said we came here solely on my account, that I was to have perfect rest and all the air I could get. 'Your exercise depends on your strength, my dear,' said he, 'and your food somewhat on your appetite; but air you can absorb all the time.' So we took the nursery at the top of the house.

It is a big, airy room, the whole floor nearly, with windows that look all ways, and air and sunshine galore. It was nursery first and then playroom and gymnasium, I should judge; for the windows are barred for little children, and there are rings and things in the walls.

The paint and paper look as if a boys' school had used it. It is stripped off — the paper — in great patches all around the head of my bed, about as far as I can reach, and in a great place on the other side of the room low down. I never saw a worse paper in my life.

One of those sprawling flamboyant patterns committing every artistic sin.

It is dull enough to confuse the eye in following, pronounced enough to constantly irritate and provoke study, and when you follow the lame uncertain curves for a little distance they suddenly commit suicide — plunge off at outrageous angles, destroy themselves in unheard of contradictions.

The color is repellent, almost revolting; a smouldering unclean yellow, strangely faded by the slow-turning sunlight.

It is a dull yet lurid orange in some places, a sickly sulphur tint in others.

No wonder the children hated it! I should hate it myself if I had to live in this room long.

There comes John, and I must put this away — he hates to have me write a word.

*

We have been here two weeks, and I haven't felt like writing before, since that first day.

I am sitting by the window now, up in this atrocious nursery, and there is nothing to hinder my writing as much as I please, save lack of strength.

John is away all day, and even some nights when his cases are serious.

I am glad my case is not serious!

But these nervous troubles are dreadfully depressing.

John does not know how much I really suffer. He knows there is no *reason* to suffer, and that satisfies him.

Of course it is only nervousness. It does weigh on me so not to do my duty in any way!

I meant to be such a help to John, such a real rest and comfort, and here I am a comparative burden already!

Nobody would believe what an effort it is to do what little I am able — to dress and entertain, and order things.

It is fortunate Mary is so good with the baby. Such a dear baby!

And yet I *cannot* be with him, it makes me so nervous.

I suppose John never was nervous in his life. He laughs at me so about this wall-paper!

At first he meant to repaper the room, but afterwards he said that I was letting it get the better of me, and that nothing was worse for a nervous patient than to give way to such fancies.

He said that after the wall-paper was changed it would be the heavy bedstead, and then the barred windows, and then that gate at the head of the stairs, and so on.

'You know the place is doing you good,' he said, 'and really, dear, I don't care to renovate the house just for a three months' rental.'

'Then do let us go downstairs,' I said, 'there are such pretty rooms there.'

Then he took me in his arms and called me a blessed little goose, and said he would go down to the cellar, if I wished, and have it whitewashed into the bargain.

But he is right enough about the beds and windows and things.

It is an airy and comfortable room as any one need wish, and, of course, I would not be so silly as to make him uncomfortable just for a whim.

I'm really getting quite fond of the big room, all but that horrid paper.

Out of one window I can see the garden, those mysterious deepshaded arbors, the riotous old-fashioned flowers, and bushes and gnarly trees.

Out of another I get a lovely view of the bay and a little private wharf belonging to the estate. There is a beautiful shaded lane that runs down there from the house. I always fancy I see people walking in these numerous paths and arbors, but John has cautioned me not to give way to fancy in the least. He says that with my imaginative power and habit of story-making, a nervous weakness like mine is sure to lead to all manner of excited fancies, and that I ought to use my will and good sense to check the tendency. So I try.

I think sometimes that if I were only well enough to write a little it would relieve the press of ideas and rest me.

But I find I get pretty tired when I try.

It is so discouraging not to have any advice and companionship about my work. When I get really well, John says we will ask Cousin Henry and Julia down for a long visit; but he says he would as soon put fireworks in my pillow-case as to let me have those stimulating people about now.

I wish I could get well faster.

But I must not think about that. This paper looks to me as if it *knew* what a vicious influence it had!

There is a recurrent spot where the pattern lolls like a broken neck and two bulbous eyes stare at you upside down.

I get positively angry with the impertinence of it and the everlastingness. Up and down and sideways they crawl, and those absurd, unblinking eyes are everywhere. There is one place where two breadths didn't match, and the eyes go all up and down the line, one a little higher than the other.

I never saw so much expression in an inanimate thing before, and we all know how much expression they have! I used to lie awake as a child and get more entertainment and terror out of blank walls and plain furniture than most children could find in a toy-store.

I remember what a kindly wink the knobs of our big, old bureau used to have, and there was one chair that always seemed like a strong friend.

I used to feel that if any of the other things looked too fierce I could always hop into that chair and be safe.

The furniture in this room is no worse than inharmonious, however, for we had to bring it all from downstairs. I suppose when this was used as a playroom they had to take the nursery things out, and no wonder! I never saw such ravages as the children have made here.

The wall-paper, as I said before, is torn off in spots, and it sticketh closer than a brother – they must have had perseverance as well as hatred.

Then the floor is scratched and gouged and splintered, the plaster itself is dug out here and there, and this great heavy bed which is all we found in the room, looks as if it had been through the wars.

But I don't mind it a bit – only the paper.

There comes John's sister. Such a dear girl as she is, and so careful of me! I must not let her find me writing.

She is a perfect and enthusiastic housekeeper, and hopes for no better profession. I verily believe she thinks it is the writing which made me sick!

But I can write when she is out, and see her a long way off from these windows.

There is one that commands the road, a lovely shaded winding road, and one that just looks off over the country. A lovely country, too, full of great elms and velvet meadows.

This wall-paper has a kind of sub-pattern in a different shade, a particularly irritating one, for you can only see it in certain lights, and not clearly then.

But in the places where it isn't faded and where the sun is just so – I can see a strange, provoking, formless sort of figure, that seems to skulk about behind that silly and conspicuous front design.

There's sister on the stairs!

*

Well, the Fourth of July is over! The people are all gone and I am tired out. John thought it might do me good to see a little company, so we just had mother and Nellie and the children down for a week.

Of course I didn't do a thing. Jennie sees to everything now.

But it tired me all the same.

John says if I don't pick up faster he shall send me to Weir Mitchell in the fall.

But I don't want to go there at all. I had a friend who was in his hands once, and she says he is just like John and my brother, only more so!

Besides, it is such an undertaking to go so far.

I don't feel as if it was worth while to turn my hand over for anything, and I'm getting dreadfully fretful and querulous.

I cry at nothing, and cry most of the time.

Of course I don't when John is here, or anybody else, but when I am alone.

And I am alone a good deal just now. John is kept in town very often by serious cases, and Jennie is good and lets me alone when I want her to.

So I walk a little in the garden or down that lovely lane, sit on the porch under the roses, and lie down up here a good deal.

I'm getting really fond of the room in spite of the wallpaper. Perhaps *because* of the wallpaper.

It dwells in my mind so!

I lie here on this great immovable bed – it is nailed down, I believe – and follow that pattern about by the hour. It is as good as gymnastics, I assure you. I start, we'll say, at the bottom, down in the corner over there where it has not been touched, and I determine for the thousandth time that I *will* follow that pointless pattern to some sort of a conclusion.

I know a little of the principle of design, and I know this thing was not arranged on any laws of radiation, or alternation, or repetition, or symmetry, or anything else that I even heard of.

It is repeated, of course, by the breadths, but not otherwise.

Looked at in one way each breadth stands alone, the bloated curves and flourishes – a kind of 'debased Romanesque' with *delirium tremens* – go waddling up and down in isolated columns of fatuity.

But, on the other hand, they connect diagonally, and the sprawling outlines run off in great slanting waves of optic horror, like a lot of wallowing seaweeds in full chase.

The whole thing goes horizontally, too, at least it seems so, and I exhaust myself in trying to distinguish the order of its going in that direction.

They have used a horizontal breadth for a frieze, and that adds wonderfully to the confusion.

There is one end of the room where it is almost intact, and there, when the crosslights fade and the low sun shines directly upon it, I can almost fancy radiation after all, – the interminable grotesques seem to form around a common centre and rush off in headlong plunges of equal distraction.

It makes me tired to follow it. I will take a nap I guess.

I don't know why I should write this.

I don't want to.

I don't feel able.

And I know John would think it absurd. But I *must* say what I feel and think in some way – it is such a relief!

But the effort is getting to be greater than the relief.

Half the time now I am awfully lazy, and lie down ever so much.

John says I mustn't lose my strength, and has me take cod liver oil and lots of tonics and things, to say nothing of ale and wine and rare meat.

Dear John! He loves me very dearly, and hates to have me sick. I tried to have a real earnest reasonable talk with him the other day, and tell him how I wish he would let me go and make a visit to Cousin Henry and Julia.

But he said I wasn't able to go, nor able to stand it after I got there; and I did not make out a very good case for myself, for I was crying before I had finished.

It is getting to be a great effort for me to think straight. Just this nervous weakness I suppose.

And dear John gathered me up in his arms, and just carried me upstairs and laid me on the bed, and sat by me and read to me till it tired my head.

151

He said I was his darling and his comfort and all he had, and that I must take care of myself for his sake, and keep well.

He says no one but myself can help me out of it, that I must use my will and self-control and not let any silly fancies run away with me.

There's one comfort, the baby is well and happy, and does not have to occupy this nursery with the horrid wallpaper.

If we had not used it, that blessed child would have! What a fortunate escape! Why, I wouldn't have a child of mine, an impressionable little thing, live in such a room for worlds.

I never thought of it before, but it is lucky that John kept me here after all, I can stand it so much easier than a baby, you see.

Of course I never mention it to them any more – I am too wise, – but I keep watch of it all the same.

There are things in that paper that nobody knows but me, or ever will.

Behind that outside pattern the dim shapes get clearer every day.

It is always the same shape, only very numerous.

And it is like a woman stooping down and creeping about behind that pattern. I don't like it a bit. I wonder – I begin to think – I wish John would take me away from here!

It is so hard to talk with John about my case, because he is so wise, and because he loves me so.

But I tried it last night.

It was moonlight. The moon shines in all around just as the sun does.

I hate to see it sometimes, it creeps so slowly, and always comes in by one window or another.

John was asleep and I hated to waken him, so I kept still and watched the moonlight on that undulating wallpaper till I felt creepy.

The faint figure behind seemed to shake the pattern, just as if she wanted to get out.

I got up softly and went to feel and see if the paper *did* move, and when I came back John was awake.

'What is it, little girl?' he said. 'Don't go walking about like that – you'll get cold.'

I thought it was a good time to talk, so I told him that I really was not gaining here, and that I wished he would take me away.

'Why darling!' said he, 'our lease will be up in three weeks, and I can't see how to leave before.

'The repairs are not done at home, and I cannot possibly leave town just now. Of course if you were in any danger, I could and would, but you really are better, dear, whether you can see it or not. I am a doctor, dear, and I know. You are gaining flesh and colour, your appetite is better, I feel really much easier about you.'

'I don't weigh a bit more,' said I, 'nor as much; and my appetite may be better in the evening when you are here, but it is worse in the morning when you are away!'

'Bless her little heart!' said he with a big hug, 'she shall be as sick as she pleases! But now let's improve the shining hours by going to sleep, and talk about it in the morning!'

'And you won't go away?' I asked gloomily.

'Why, how can I, dear? It is only three weeks more and then we will take a nice little trip of a few days while Jennie is getting the house ready. Really dear you are better!'

'Better in body perhaps – ' I began, and stopped short, for he sat up straight and looked at me with such a stern, reproachful look that I could not say another word.

'My darling,' said he, 'I beg of you, for my sake and for our child's sake, as well as for your own, that you will never for one instant let that idea enter your mind! There is nothing so dangerous, so fascinating, to a temperament like yours. It is a false and foolish fancy. Can you not trust me as a physician when I tell you so?'

So of course I said no more on that score, and we went to

sleep before long. He thought I was asleep first, but I wasn't, and lay there for hours trying to decide whether that front pattern really did move together or separately.

*

On a pattern like this, by daylight, there is a lack of sequence, a defiance of law, that is a constant irritant to a normal mind.

The colour is hideous enough, and unreliable enough, and infuriating enough, but the pattern is torturing.

You think you have mastered it, but just as you get well underway in following, it turns a back-somersault and there you are. It slaps you in the face, knocks you down, and tramples upon you. It is like a bad dream.

The outside pattern is a florid arabesque, reminding one of a fungus. If you can imagine a toadstool in joints, an interminable string of toadstools, budding and sprouting in endless convolutions – why, that is something like it.

That is, sometimes!

There is one marked peculiarity about this paper, a thing nobody seems to notice but myself, and that is that it changes as the light changes.

When the sun shoots in through the east window – I always watch for the first long, straight ray – it changes so quickly that I never can quite believe it.

That is why I watch it always.

By moonlight – the moon shines in all night when there is a moon – I wouldn't know it was the same paper.

At night in any kind of light, in twilight, candle-light, lamp-light, and worst of all by moonlight, it becomes bars! The outside pattern I mean, and the woman behind it is as plain as can be.

I didn't realise for a long time what the thing was that showed behind, that dim sub-pattern, but now I am quite sure it is a woman.

By daylight she is subdued, quiet. I fancy it is the pattern that keeps her so still. It is so puzzling. It keeps me quiet by the hour.

I lie down ever so much now. John says it is good for me, and to sleep all I can.

Indeed he started the habit by making me lie down for an hour after each meal.

It is a very bad habit I am convinced, for you see I don't sleep.

And that cultivates deceit, for I don't tell them I'm awake – O no!

The fact is I am getting a little afraid of John.

He seems very queer sometimes, and even Jennie has an inexplicable look.

It strikes me occasionally, just as a scientific hypothesis, – that perhaps it is the paper!

I have watched John when he did not know I was looking, and come into the room suddenly on the most innocent excuses, and I've caught him several times *looking at the paper!* And Jennie too. I caught Jennie with her hand on it once.

She didn't know I was in the room, and when I asked her in a quiet, a very quiet voice, with the most restrained manner possible, what she was doing with the paper – she turned around as if she had been caught stealing, and looked quite angry – asked me why I should frighten her so!

Then she said that the paper stained everything it touched, that she had found yellow smooches on all my clothes and John's, and she wished we would be more careful!

Did not that sound innocent? But I know she was studying that pattern, and I am determined that nobody shall find it out but myself!

*

Life is very much more exciting now than it used to be. You see I have something more to expect, to look forward to, to watch. I really do eat better, and am more quiet than I was.

John is so pleased to see me improve! He laughed a little the other day, and said I seemed to be flourishing in spite of my wallpaper.

I turned it off with a laugh. I had no intention of telling him it was *because* of the wallpaper – he would make fun of me. He might even want to take me away.

I don't want to leave now until I have found it out. There is a week more, and I think that will be enough.

*

I'm feeling ever so much better! I don't sleep much at night, for it is so interesting to watch developments; but I sleep a good deal in the daytime.

In the daytime it is tiresome and perplexing.

There are always new shoots on the fungus, and new shades of yellow all over it. I cannot keep count of them, though I have tried conscientiously.

It is the strangest yellow, that wallpaper! It makes me think of all the yellow things I ever saw – not beautiful ones like buttercups, but old foul, bad yellow things.

But there is something else about that paper – the smell! I noticed it the moment we came into the room, but with so much air and sun it was not bad. Now we have had a week of fog and rain, and whether the windows are open or not, the smell is here.

It creeps all over the house.

I find it hovering in the dining-room, skulking in the parlour, hiding in the hall, lying in wait for me on the stairs.

It gets into my hair.

Even when I go to ride, if I turn my head suddenly and surprise it – there is that smell!

Such a peculiar odour, too! I have spent hours in trying to analyse it, to find what it smelled like.

It is not bad – at first, and very gentle, but quite the subtlest, most enduring odour I ever met.

In this damp weather it is awful, I wake up in the night and find it hanging over me.

It used to disturb me at first. I thought seriously of burning the house – to reach the smell.

But now I am used to it. The only thing I can think of that it is like is the *colour* of the paper! A yellow smell.

There is a very funny mark on this wall, low down, near the mopboard. A streak that runs round the room. It goes behind every piece of furniture, except the bed, a long, straight, even *smooch*, as if it had been rubbed over and over.

I wonder how it was done and who did it, and what they did it for. Round and round and round – round and round and round – it makes me dizzy!

*

I really have discovered something at last.

Through watching so much at night, when it changes so, I have finally found out.

The front pattern *does* move – and no wonder! The woman behind shakes it!

Sometimes I think there are a great many women behind, and sometimes only one, and she crawls around fast, and her crawling shakes it all over.

Then in the very bright spots she keeps still, and in the very shady spots she just takes hold of the bars and shakes them hard.

And she is all the time trying to climb through. But nobody could climb through that pattern – it strangles so; I think that is why it has so many heads.

They get through, and then the pattern strangles them off and turns them upside down, and makes their eyes white!

If those heads were covered or taken off it would not be half so bad.

*

I think that woman gets out in the daytime!

And I'll tell you why – privately – I've seen her!

I can see her out of every one of my windows!

It is the same woman, I know, for she is always creeping, and most women do not creep by daylight.

I see her on that long road under the trees, creeping along, and when a carriage comes she hides under the blackberry vines.

I don't blame her a bit. It must be very humiliating to be caught creeping by daylight!

I always lock the door when I creep by daylight. I can't do it at night, for I know John would suspect something at once.

And John is so queer now, that I don't want to irritate him. I wish he would take another room! Besides, I don't want anybody to get that woman out at night but myself.

I often wonder if I could see her out of all the windows at once.

But, turn as fast as I can, I can only see out of one at one time.

And though I always see her, she *may* be able to creep faster than I can turn!

I have watched her sometimes away off in the open country, creeping as fast as a cloud shadow in a high wind.

*

If only that top pattern could be gotten off from the under one! I mean to try it, little by little.

I have found out another funny thing, but I shan't tell it this time! It does not do to trust people too much.

There are only two more days to get this paper off, and I believe John is beginning to notice. I don't like the look in his eyes.

And I heard him ask Jennie a lot of professional questions about me. She had a very good report to give.

She said I slept a good deal in the daytime.

John knows I don't sleep very well at night, for all I'm so quiet!

He asked me all sorts of questions, too, and pretended to be very loving and kind.

As if I couldn't see through him!

Still, I don't wonder he acts so, sleeping under this paper for three months.

It only interests me, but I feel sure John and Jennie are secretly affected by it.

*

Hurrah! This is the last day, but it is enough. John to stay in town over night, and won't be out until this evening.

Jennie wanted to sleep with me – the sly thing! but I told her I should undoubtedly rest better for a night all alone.

That was clever, for really I wasn't alone a bit! As soon as it was moonlight and that poor thing began to crawl and shake the pattern, I got up and ran to help her.

I pulled and she shook, I shook and she pulled, and before morning we had peeled off yards of that paper.

A strip about as high as my head and half around the room.

And then when the sun came and that awful pattern began to laugh at me, I declared I would finish it today!

We go away tomorrow, and they are moving all my furniture down again to leave things as they were before.

Jennie looked at the wall in amazement, but I told her merrily that I did it out of pure spite at the vicious thing.

She laughed and said she wouldn't mind doing it herself, but I must not get tired.

How she betrayed herself that time!

But I am here, and no person touches this paper but me, – not *alive!*

She tried to get me out of the room – it was too patent! But I said it was so quiet and empty and clean now that I believed I would lie down again and sleep all I could; and not to wake me even for dinner — I would call when I woke.

So now she is gone, and the servants are gone, and the things are gone, and there is nothing left but that great bedstead nailed down, with the canvas mattress we found on it.

We shall sleep downstairs tonight, and take the boat home tomorrow.

I quite enjoy the room, now it is bare again.

How those children did tear about here!

This bedstead is fairly gnawed!

But I must get to work.

I have locked the door and thrown the key down into the front path.

I don't want to go out, and I don't want to have anybody come in, till John comes.

I want to astonish him.

I've got a rope up here that even Jennie did not find. If that woman does get out, and tries to get away, I can tie her!

But I forgot I could not reach far without anything to stand on!

This bed will *not* move!

I tried to lift and push it until I was lame, and then I got so angry I bit off a little piece at one corner — but it hurt my teeth.

Then I peeled off all the paper I could reach standing on the floor. It sticks horribly and the pattern just enoys it! All those strangled heads and bulbous eyes and waddling fungus growths just shriek with derision!

I am getting angry enough to do something desperate. To jump out of the window would be admirable exercise, but the bars are too strong even to try.

Besides I wouldn't do it. Of course not. I know well enough that a step like that is improper and might be misconstrued.

I don't like to *look* out of the windows even – there are so many of those creeping women, and they creep so fast.

I wonder if they all come out of that wallpaper as I did?

But I am securely fastened now by my well-hidden rope – you don't get *me* out in the road there!

I suppose I shall have to get back behind the pattern when it comes night, and that is hard!

It is so pleasant to be out in this great room and creep around as I please!

I don't want to go outside. I won't, even if Jennie asks me to.

For outside you have to creep on the ground, and everything is green instead of yellow.

But here I can creep smoothly on the floor, and my shoulder just fits in the long smooch around the wall, so I cannot lose my way.

Why there's John at the door!

It is no use, young man, you can't open it!

How he does call and pound!

Now he's crying for an axe.

It would be a shame to break down that beautiful door!

'John dear!' said I in the gentlest voice, 'the key is down by the front steps, under a plantain leaf!'

That silenced him for a few moments.

Then he said – very quietly indeed, 'Open the door, my darling!'

'I can't,' said I. 'The key is down by the front door under a plantain leaf!'

And then I said it again, several times, very gently and slowly, and said it so often that he had to go and see, and he got it of course, and came in. He stopped short by the door.

'What is the matter?' he cried. 'For God's sake, what are you doing!'

I kept on creeping just the same, but I looked at him over my shoulder.

'I've got out at last,' said I, 'in spite of you and Jennie. And I've pulled off most of the paper, so you can't put me back!'

Now why should that man have fainted? But he did, and right across my path by the wall, so that I had to creep over him every time!

COLETTE
THE HAND

He had fallen asleep on his young wife's shoulder, and she proudly bore the weight of the man's head, blond, ruddy-complexioned, eyes closed. He had slipped his big arm under the small of her slim, adolescent back, and his strong hand lay on the sheet next to the young woman's right elbow. She smiled to see the man's hand emerging there, all by itself and far away from its owner. Then she let her eyes wander over the half-lit room. A veiled conch shed a light across the bed the colour of periwinkle.

'Too happy to sleep,' she thought.

Too excited also, and often surprised by her new state. It had been only two weeks since she had begun to live the scandalous life of a newlywed who tastes the joys of living with someone unknown and with whom she is in love. To meet a handsome, blond young man, recently widowed, good at tennis and rowing, to marry him a month later: her conjugal adventure had been little more than a kidnapping. So that whenever she lay awake beside her husband, like tonight, she still kept her eyes closed for a long time, then opened them again in order to savour, with astonishment, the blue of the brand-new curtains, instead of the apricot-pink through which the first light of day filtered into the room where she had slept as a little girl.

A quiver ran through the sleeping body lying next to her, and she tightened her left arm around her husband's neck with the charming authority exercised by weak creatures. He did not wake up.

'His eyelashes are so long,' she said to herself.

To herself she also praised his mouth, full, and likeable, his skin the colour of pink brick, and even his forehead, neither noble nor broad, but still smooth and unwrinkled.

Her husband's right hand, lying beside her, quivered in turn, and beneath the curve of her back she felt the right arm, on which her whole weight was resting, come to life.

'I'm so heavy . . . I wish I could get up and turn the light off. But he's sleeping so well . . .'

The arm twisted again, feebly, and she arched her back to make herself lighter.

'It's as if I were lying on some animal,' she thought.

She turned her head a little on the pillow and looked at the hand lying there next to her.

'It's so big! It really is bigger than my whole head.'

The light, flowing out from under the edge of a parasol of bluish crystal, spilled up against the hand, and made every contour of the skin apparent, exaggerating the powerful knuckles and the veins engorged by the pressure of the arm. A few red hairs, at the base of the fingers, all curved in the same direction, like ears of wheat in the wind, and the flat nails, whose ridges that nail buffer had not smoothed out, gleamed, coated with pink varnish.

'I'll tell him not to varnish his nails,' thought the young wife. 'Varnish and pink polish don't go with a hand so . . . a hand that's so . . .'

An electric jolt ran through the hand and spared the young woman from having to find the right adjective. The thumb stiffened itself out, horribly long and spatulate, and pressed tightly against the index finger, so that the hand suddenly took on a vile, apelike appearance.

'Oh!' whispered the young woman, as though faced with something slightly indecent.

The sound of a passing car pierced the silence with a shrillness that seemed luminous. The sleeping man did not wake, but the hand, offended, reared back and tensed up in the shape of a crab and waited, ready for battle. The screeching sound died down and the hand, relaxing gradually, lowered its claws, and became a pliant beast, awkwardly bent, shaken by faint jerks which resembled some sort of agony. The flat, cruel nail of the overlong thumb glistened. A curve in the little finger, which the young woman had never noticed, appeared, and the wallowing hand revealed its fleshy palm like a red belly.

'And I've kissed that hand! . . . How horrible! Haven't I ever looked at it?'

The hand, disturbed by a bad dream, appeared to respond to this startling discovery, this disgust. It regrouped its forces, opened wide, and splayed its tendons, lumps, and red fur like battle dress, then slowly drawing itself in again, grabbed a fistful of the sheet, dug into it with its curved fingers, and squeezed, squeezed with the methodical pleasure of a strangler.

'Oh!' cried the young woman.

The hand disappeared and a moment later the big arm, relieved of its burden, became a protective belt, a warm bulwark against all the terrors of night. But the next morning, when it was time for breakfast in bed – hot chocolate and toast – she saw the hand again, with its red hair and red skin, and the ghastly thumb curving out over the handle of a knife.

'Do you want this slice, darling? I'll butter it for you.'

She shuddered and felt her skin crawl on the back of her arms and down her back.

'Oh, no . . . no . . .'

Then she concealed her fear, bravely subdued herself, and, beginning her life of duplicity, of resignation, and of a lowly, delicate diplomacy, she leaned over and humbly kissed the monstrous hand.

NELLA LARSEN
SANCTUARY

On the Southern Coast, between Merton and Shawboro, there is a strip of desolation some half a mile wide and nearly ten miles long between the sea and old fields of ruined plantations. Skirting the edge of this narrow jungle is a partly grown-over road which still shows traces of furrows made by the wheels of wagons that have long since rotted away or been cut into firewood. This road is little used, now that the state has built its new highway a bit to the west and wagons are less numerous than automobiles.

In the forsaken road a man was walking swiftly. But in spite of his hurry, at every step he set down his feet with infinite care for the night was windless and the heavy silence intensified each sound; even the breaking of a twig could be plainly heard. And the man had need of caution as well as haste.

Before a lonely cottage that shrank timidly back from the road the man hesitated a moment, then struck out across the patch of green in front of it. Stepping behind a clump of bushes close to the house, he looked in through the lighted window at Annie Poole, standing at her kitchen table mixing the supper biscuits.

He was a big, black man with pale brown eyes in which there was an odd mixture of fear and amazement. The light showed streaks of grey soil on his heavy, sweating face and great hands, and on his torn clothes. In his woolly hair clung bits of dried leaves and dead grass.

He made a gesture as if to tap on the window, but turned

away to the door instead. Without knocking he opened it and went in.

*

The woman's brown gaze was immediately on him, though she did not move. She said, 'You ain't in no hurry, is you, Jim Hammer?' It wasn't, however, entirely a question.

'Ah's in trubble, Mis' Poole,' the man explained, his voice shaking, his fingers twitching.

'W'at you done done now?'

'Shot a man, Mis' Poole.'

'Trufe?' The woman seemed calm. But the word was spat out.

'Yas'm. Shot 'im.' In the man's tone was something of wonder, as if he himself could not quite believe that he had really done this thing which he affirmed.

'Daid?'

'Dunno, Mis' Poole. Dunno.'

'White man o' niggah?'

'Cain't say, Mis' Poole. White man, Ah reckons.'

Annie Poole looked at him with cold contempt. She was a tiny, withered woman – fifty perhaps – with a wrinkled face the colour of old copper, framed by a crinkly mass of white hair. But about her small figure was some quality of hardness that belied her appearance of frailty. At last she spoke, boring her sharp little eyes into those of the anxious creature before her.

'An' w'at am you lookin' foh me to do 'bout et?'

'Jes' lemme stop till dey's gone by. Hide me till dey passes. Reckon dey ain't fur off now.' His begging voice changed to a frightened whimper. 'Foh de Lawd's sake, Mis' Poole, lemme stop.'

And why, the woman inquired caustically, should she run the dangerous risk of hiding him?

'Obadiah, he'd lemme stop ef he was to home,' the man whined.

Annie Poole sighed. 'Yas,' she admitted, slowly, reluctantly, 'Ah spec' he would. Obadiah, he's too good to youall no 'count trash.' Her slight shoulders lifted in a hopeless shrug. 'Yas, Ah reckon he'd do et. Emspecial' seein how he allus set such a heap o' store by you. Cain't see w'at foh, mahse'f. Ah shuah don' see nuffin' in you but a heap o' dirt.'

But a look of irony, of cunning, of complicity passed over her face. She went on, 'Still, 'siderin' all an' all, how Obadiah's right fon' o' you, an' how white folks is white folks, Ah'm a-gwine hide you dis one time.'

Crossing the kitchen, she opened a door leading into a small bedroom, saying, 'Git yo'se'f in dat dere feather baid an' Ah'm a-gwine put de clo's on de top. Don' reckon dey'll fin' you ef dey does look foh you in mah house. An Ah don' spec' dey'll go foh to do dat. Not lessen you been keerless an' let 'em smell you out gittin' hyah.' She turned on him a withering look. 'But you allus been triflin'. Cain't do nuffin propah. An' Ah'm a-tellin' you ef dey warn't white folks an' you a po' niggah, Ah shuah wouldn't be lettin' you mess up mah feather baid dis ebenin', 'cose Ah jes' plain don' want you hyah. Ah done kep' mahse'f outen trubble all mah life. So's Obadiah.'

'Ah's powahful' 'bliged to you, Mis' Poole. You shuah am one good 'oman. De Lawd'll mos' suttinly – '

Annie Poole cut him off. 'Dis ain't no time foh all dat kin' o' fiddle-de-roll. Ah does mah duty as Ah sees et 'thout no thanks from you. Ef de Lawd had gib you a white face 'stead o'dat dere black one, Ah shuah would turn you out. Now hush yo' mouf an' git yo'se'f in. An' don' git movin' and scrunchin' undah dose covahs and git yo'se'f kotched in mah house.'

Without further comment the man did as he was told. After he had laid his soiled body and grimy garments between her snowy sheets, Annie Poole carefuly rearranged the covering and placed piles of freshly laundered linen on top. Then she gave a pat here and there, eyed the result, and finding it satisfactory, went back to her cooking.

*

Jim Hammer settled down to the racking business of waiting until the approaching danger should have passed him by. Soon savory odours seeped in to him and he realised that he was hungry. He wished that Annie Poole would bring him something to eat. Just one biscuit. But she wouldn't, he knew. Not she. She was a hard one, Obadiah's mother.

By and by he fell into a sleep from which he was dragged back by the rumbling sound of wheels in the road outside. For a second fear clutched so tightly at him that he almost leaped from the suffocating shelter of the bed in order to make some active attempt to escape the horror that his capture meant. There was a spasm at his heart, a pain so sharp, so slashing that he had to suppress an impulse to cry out. He felt himself falling. Down, down, down . . . Everything grew dim and very distant in his memory . . . Vanished . . . Came rushing back.

Outside there was silence. He strained his ears. Nothing. No footsteps. No voices. They had gone on then. Gone without even stopping to ask Annie Poole if she had seen him pass that way. A sigh of relief slipped from him. His thick lips curled in an ugly, cunning smile. It had been smart of him to think of coming to Obadiah's mother's to hide. She was an old demon, but he was safe in her house.

He lay a short while longer listening intently, and, hearing nothing, started to get up. But immediately he stopped, his yellow eyes glowing like pale flames. He had heard the unmistakable sound of men coming toward the house. Swiftly he slid back into the heavy, hot stuffiness of the bed and lay listening fearfully.

The terrifying sounds drew nearer. Slowly. Heavily. Just for a moment he thought they were not coming in – they took so long. But there was a light knock and the noise of a door being opened. His whole body went taut. His feet felt frozen, his hands clammy, his tongue like a weighted, dying thing. His pounding heart made it hard for his straining ears to hear what they were saying out there.

'Ebenin', Mistah Lowndes,' Annie Poole's voice sounded as it always did, sharp and dry.

There was no answer. Or had he missed it? With slow care he shifted his position, bringing his head nearer the edge of the bed. Still he heard nothing. What were they waiting for? Why didn't they ask about him?

Annie Poole, it seemed, was of the same mind. 'Ah don' reckon youall done traipsed 'way out hyah jes' foh yo' healf,' she hinted.

'There's bad news for you, Annie, I'm 'fraid.' The sheriff's voice was low and queer.

Jim Hammer visualised him standing out there – a tall, stooped man, his white tobacco-stained moustache drooping limply at the ends, his nose hooked and sharp, his eyes blue and cold. Bill Lowndes was a hard one too. And white.

'W'atall bad news, Mistah Lowndes?' The woman put the question quietly, directly.

'Obadiah – ' the sheriff began – hesitated – began again. 'Obadiah – ah – er he's outside, Annie. I'm 'fraid – '

'Shucks! You done missed. Obadiah, he ain't done nuffin', Mistah Lowndes. Obadiah!' she called stridently, 'Obadiah! git hyah an' splain yo'se'f.'

But Obadiah didn't answer, didn't come in. Other men came in. Came in with steps that dragged and halted. No one spoke. Not even Annie Poole. Something was laid carefully upon the floor.

'Obadiah, chile,' his mother said softly, 'Obadiah, chile.' Then, with sudden alarm, 'He ain't daid, is he? Mistah Lowndes! Obadiah, he ain't daid?'

Jim Hammer didn't catch the answer to that pleading question. A new fear was stealing over him.

'There was a to-do, Annie,' Bill Lowndes explained gently, 'at

170

the garage back o' the factory. Fellow tryin' to steal tires. Obadiah heerd a noise an' run out with two or three others. Scared the rascal all right. Fired off his gun an' run. We allow et to be Jim Hammer. Picked up his cap back there. Never was no 'count. Thievin' an' sly. But we'll git 'im, Annie. We'll git 'im.'

The man huddled in the feather bed prayed silently. 'Oh, Lawd! Ah didn't go to do et. Not Obadiah, Lawd. You knows dat. You knows et.' And into his frenzied brain came the thought that it would be better for him to get up and go out to them before Annie Poole gave him away. For he was lost now. With all his great strength he tried to get himself out of the bed. But he couldn't.

'Oh Lawd!' he moaned. 'Oh Lawd!' His thoughts were bitter and they ran through his mind like panic. He knew that it had come to pass as it said somewhere in the Bible about the wicked. The Lord had stretched out his hand and smitten him. He was paralysed. He couldn't move hand or foot. He moaned again. It was all there was left for him to do. For in the terror of this new calamity that had come upon him he had forgotten the waiting danger which was so near out there in the kitchen.

His hunters, however, didn't hear him. Bill Lowndes was saying, 'We been a-lookin' for Jim out along the old road. Figured he'd make tracks for Shawboro. You ain't noticed anybody pass this evenin', Annie?'

The reply came promptly, unwaveringly 'No, Ah ain't seen nobody pass. Not yet.'

*

Jim Hammer caught his breath.

'Well,' the sheriff concluded. 'we'll be gittin' along. Obadiah was a mighty fine boy. Ef they was all like him – . I'm sorry, Annie. Anything I c'n do let me know.'

'Thank you, Mistah Lowndes.'

With the sound of the door closing on the departing men, power to move came back to the man in the bedroom. He

171

pushed his dirt-caked feet out from the covers and rose up, but crouched down again. He wasn't cold now, but hot all over and burning. Almost he wished that Bill Lowndes and his men had taken him with them.

Annie Poole had come into the room.

It seemed a long time before Obadiah's mother spoke. When she did there were no tears, no reproaches; but there was a raging fury in her voice as she lashed out, 'Git outen mah feather baid, Jim Hammer, an' outen mah house, an' don' nevah stop thankin' yo' Jesus he done gib you dat black face.'

GERTRUDE STEIN
MISS FURR AND MISS SKEENE

Helen Furr had quite a pleasant home. Mrs. Furr was quite a pleasant woman. Mr. Furr was quite a pleasant man. Helen Furr had quite a pleasant voice a voice quite worth cultivating. She did not mind working. She worked to cultivate her voice. She did not find it gay living in the same place where she had always been living. She went to a place where some were cultivating something, voices and other things needing cultivating. She met Georgine Skeene there who was cultivating her voice which some thought was quite a pleasant one. Helen Furr and Georgine Skeene lived together then. Georgine Skeene liked travelling. Helen Furr did not care about travelling, she liked to stay in one place and be gay there. They were together then and travelled to another place and stayed there and were gay there.

They stayed there and were gay there, not very gay there, just gay there. They were both gay there, they were regularly working there both of them cultivating their voices there, they were both gay there. Georgine Skeene was gay there and she was regular, regular in being gay, regular in not being gay, regular in being a gay one who was not being gay longer than was needed to be one being quite a gay one. They were both gay then there and both working there then.

They were in a way both gay there where there were many cultivating something. They were both regular in being gay there. Helen Furr was gay there, she was gayer and gayer there and really she was just gay there, she was gayer and gayer there, that is to say she found ways of being gay there that she was using in being gay there. She was gay there, not gayer and gayer, just gay there, that is to say she was not gayer by using the things she found there that were gay things, she was gay there, always she was gay there.

They were quite regularly gay there, Helen Furr and Georgine Skeene, they were regularly gay there where they were gay. They were very regularly gay.

To be regularly gay was to do every day the gay thing that they did every day. To be regularly gay was to end every day at the same time after they had been regularly gay. They were regularly gay. They were gay every day. They ended every day in the same way, at the same time, and they had been every day regularly gay.

The voice Helen Furr was cultivating was quite a pleasant one. The voice Georgine Skeene was cultivating was, some said, a better one. The voice Helen Furr was cultivating she cultivated and it was quite completely a pleasant enough one then, a cultivated enough one then. The voice Georgine Skeene was cultivating she did not cultivate too much. She cultivated it quite some. She cultivated and she would sometime go on cultivating it and it was not then an unpleasant one, it would not be then an unpleasant one, it would be a quite richly enough cultivated one, it would be quite richly enough to be a pleasant enough one.

They were gay where there were many cultivating something. The two were gay there, were regularly gay there. Georgine Skeene would have liked to do more travelling. They did some travelling, not very much travelling, Georgine Skeene would have liked to do more travelling, Helen Furr did not care about doing travelling, she liked to stay in a place and be gay there.

They stayed in a place and were gay there, both of them stayed there, they stayed together there, they were gay there, they were regularly gay there.

They went quite often, not very often, but they did go back to where Helen Furr had a pleasant enough home and then Georgine Skeene went to a place where her brother had quite some distinction. They both went, every few years, went visiting to where Helen Furr had quite a pleasant home. Certainly Helen Furr would not find it gay to stay, she did not find it gay, she said she would not stay, she said she did not find it gay, she said she would not stay where she did not find it gay, she said she found it gay where she did stay and she did stay there where very many were cultivating something. She did stay there. She always did find it gay there.

She went to see them where she had always been living and where she did not find it gay. She had a pleasant home there, Mrs. Furr was a pleasant enough woman, Mr. Furr was a pleasant enough man, Helen told them and they were not worrying, that she did not find it gay living where she had always been living.

Georgine Skeene and Helen Furr were living where they were both cultivating their voices and they were gay there. They visited where Helen Furr had come from and then they went to where they were living where they were then regularly living.

There were some dark and heavy men there then. There were some who were not so heavy and some who were not so dark. Helen Furr and Georgine Skeene sat regularly with them. They sat regularly with the ones who were dark and heavy. They sat regularly with the ones who were not so dark. They sat regularly with the ones that were not so heavy. They sat with them regularly, sat with some of them. They went with them regularly went with them. They were regular then, they were gay then, they were where they wanted to be then where it was gay to be then, they were regularly gay then. There were men there then who were dark and heavy and they sat with them with Helen Furr and Georgine Skeene and they went with them with Miss Furr and Miss Skeene, and they went with the heavy and dark men Miss Furr and Miss Skeene went with them, and they sat with them, Miss Furr and Miss Skeene sat with them, and there were other men, some were not heavy men and they sat with Miss Furr and Miss Skeene and Miss Furr and Miss Skeene sat with them, and there were other men who were not dark men and they sat with Miss Furr and Miss Skeene and Miss Furr and Miss Skeene sat with them. Miss Furr and Miss Skeene went with them and they went with Miss Furr and Miss Skeene, some who were not heavy men, some who were not dark men. Miss Furr and Miss Skeene sat regularly, then sat with some men. Miss Furr and Miss Skeene went and there were some men with them. There were men and Miss Furr and Miss Skeene went with them, went somewhere with them, went with some of them.

Helen Furr and Georgine Skeene were regularly living where very many were living and cultivating in themselves something. Helen Furr and Georgine Skeene were living very regularly then, being very regular then in being gay then. They did then learn many ways to be gay and they were then being gay quite regular in being gay, being gay and they were learning little things, little things in ways of being gay, they were very regular then, they were learning very many little things in ways of being gay, they were being gay and using these little things they were learning to have to be gay with regularly gay with then and they were gay the same amount they had been gay. They were quite gay, they were quite regular, they were learning little things, gay little things, they were gay inside them and the same amount they had been gay, they were gay the same length of time they had been gay every day.

They were regular in being gay, they learned little things that are things in being gay, they learned many little things that are things in being gay, they were gay every day, they were regular, they were gay, they were gay the same length of time every day, they were gay, they were quite regularly gay.

Georgine Skeene went away to stay two months with her brother. Helen Furr did not go then to stay with her father and her mother. Helen Furr stayed there where they had been regularly living the two of them and she would then certainly not be lonesome, she would go on being gay. She did go on being gay. She was not any more gay but she was gay longer every day than they had been being gay when they were together being gay. She was gay then quite exactly the same way. She learned a few more little ways of being in being gay. She was quite gay and in the same way, the same way she had been gay and she was gay a little longer in the day, more of each day she was gay. She was gay longer every day than when the two of them had been being gay. She was gay quite in the way they had been gay, quite in the same way.

She was not lonesome then, she was not at all feeling any need of having Georgine Skeene. She was not astonished at this thing. She would have been a little astonished by this thing but she knew she was not astonished at anything and so she was not astonished at this thing not astonished at not feeling any need of having Georgine Skeene.

Helen Furr had quite a completely pleasant voice and it was quite well enough cultivated and she could use it and she did use it but then there was not any way of working at cultivating a completely pleasant voice when it has become a quite completely well enough cultivated one, and there was not much use in using it when one was not wanting it to be helping to make one a gay one. Helen Furr was not needing using her voice to be a gay one. She was gay then and sometimes she used her voice and she was not using it very often. It was quite completely enough cultivated and it was quite completely a pleasant one and she did not use it very often. She was then, she was quite exactly as gay as she had been, she was gay a little longer in the day than she had been.

She was gay exactly the same way. She was never tired of

being gay that way. She had learned very many little ways to use in being gay. Very many were telling about using other ways in being gay. She was gay enough, she was always gay exactly the same way, she was always learning little things to use in being gay, she was telling about using other ways in being gay, she was telling about learning other ways in being gay, she was learning other ways in being gay, she would be using other ways in being gay, she would always be gay in the same way, when Georgine Skeene was there not so long each day as when Georgine Skeene was away.

She came to using many ways in being gay, she came to use every way in being gay. She went on living where many were cultivating something and she was gay, she had used every way to be gay.

They did not live together then Helen Furr and Georgine Skeene. Helen Furr lived there the longer where they had been living regularly together. Then neither of them were living there any longer. Helen Furr was living somewhere else then and telling some about being gay and she was gay then and she was living quite regularly then. She was regularly gay then. She was quite regular in being gay then. She remembered all the little ways of being gay. She used all the little ways of being gay. She was quite regularly gay. She told many then the way of being gay, she taught very many then little ways they could use in being gay. She was living very well, she was gay then, she went on living then, she was regular in being gay, she always was living very well and was gay very well and was telling about little ways one could be learning to use in being gay, and later was telling them quite often, telling them again and again.

DOROTHY RICHARDSON
VISITOR

Because Aunt Bertha is coming, something has come into the room. Making it different. The others must be thinking of her, too, but they don't seem to notice that the room is different. Too full, although Pug is not here. She is somewhere else, getting grubby, not thinking about Aunt Bertha.

Mother and Mary and Ellen are standing up and talking. They are going. They will take it with them. Yes, It is going away. There will be plenty of room for it out in the hall. Berry follows them into the passage leading to the hall, sees, through the open garden door, the slack tennis-net waiting, alone. Running along into the hall, she sees them all standing talking at the wide-open front door. It is out in the garden now; sending in a broad blaze of sunlight. Not here in the drawing-room which is *always* waiting for people to come. Berry runs down its length and out into the conservatory. The plants and ferns don't notice her. Perhaps Aunt Bertha isn't coming after all.

Loud voices in the hall, sending away the lovely smell from her fingers that had just pinched a leaf of scented geranium. Aunt Bertha has come. Running out through the conservatory door she sees the back garden smiling to itself, looking like tomorrow. Down the steps and up the other steps and in by the back door and into the breakfast-room, to be back for a minute in the waiting for Aunt Bertha to come.

'*Sweet!*'

Dickie, in his cage, all alone. 'Sweet little Dick!' Berry runs away, to forget the pain of Dickie's loneliness, to lose the worse pain, just coming, of the thought of his nights alone under his baize cover.

The letter-cage half of the front door is bolted back as well as the other. They are all out in the porch and Berry can hear wheels creaking and scrunching on the drive. Ann bounces quickly into the hall from the back stairs, setting her cap straight. And now they are all on the steps below the porch, hiding Aunt Bertha. But Berry can imagine what Aunt Bertha has seen as she came up the drive between the high trees: the bed of shrubs in bloom in the middle of the sweep, lobelias thick all round the edge – did Aunt Bertha notice how *blue* they are? – the green lawn with the stone vases at the corners filled with calceolarias, so *bright* in the sun.

'Eh, Bertha, well, me-*dear*.' Mother's voice like when you are ill, forgetting the garden and telling Aunt Bertha she is a cripple. Berry goes down the steps and gives Ellen a little push to get between her and Pug and see what Aunt Bertha is like. Perhaps she will stop being a cripple.

Short arms stuck out, jerking from side to side. Aunt Bertha on a visit, working herself forward on the seat of a bathchair, not looking at anybody, staring in front of her with her mouth open and her chin jutted out; feeling pain. Ann and the bathchairman one on each side, not able to help because of the jerking arms. Presently she will be inside the house.

Berry wants them to push her back into the chair and trundle her away.

'Now then!' cries Aunt Bertha. She has sent up her underlip outside the other and is pressing so hard that it makes two lines, pains, one each side of her mouth. Ann and the chairman crook their arms under hers and she comes up bent forward, sticking out behind, with the hem of her dust-cloak sticking out still further. Her bent-over head comes round. A bullock in a straw hat. It does not move. But her eyes are moving. She looks at everybody in turn and smiles, and leaves off looking like a bullock.

Berry runs away, runs upstairs into the empty school-room that knows nothing about Aunt Bertha. But Berry knows. She looks at the lines turning into a smile, and looks into the brown eyes that know what was there when they were all waiting for her to come.

*

When Berry comes into the dining-room Aunt Bertha is sitting at the table with the others. Lunch is roast fowl, and wine-glasses. Aunt Bertha looks like a visitor, making a party. Someone has brought Dickie in. He is singing without stopping to breathe. So happy. No need to speak when she goes round to shake hands with Aunt Bertha, because everybody is talking louder than usual until Dickie stops.

When Aunt Bertha says anything she does not look at anybody. Her eyelids go down and the pains in her freckled white face look sharper while she thinks of what she is saying and all the same she goes on managing the things on her plate, carefully, while she is talking and you don't know who she is going to look at until the end of what she says, and then she looks suddenly at whoever it is; and smiles.

Aunt Bertha is chapel. She has chapel hair, parted and shined back into a little ball behind her head. But muslin tuckers, fresh and new, round her white neck where there are no freckles, and coming out from under the brown silk sleeves on to her hands, gently.

Berry is grown-up. Sitting in a brown silk dress with Sunday frills, managing a peach like that: letting it sit for a while in the middle of the plate being a lovely ripe peach; forgetting it and sitting up very straight, with her head turned to say something to someone quite at the other end of the table, but knowing all the time that the peach is there and presently taking up the silver knife and fork, very gently, so that they have time to shine as they move, and then doing the peeling and slicing in and out of what she is saying until at last she is saying something with the first little piece of peach standing still on the end of the fork, while she finishes what she is saying, and smiles. And then pops the piece of peach into her mouth and goes far away while someone else says something.

But Berry does not want to say bro-ther, in two words. Or live in a cottage thrown into another cottage, and make eighteen dressed dawls for a bazaar to buy a new chapel harmonium.

*

Berry sits at work, bent over it like Aunt Bertha, with a very quiet, calm face. Perhaps after a while, if she can go on feeling like this after Aunt Bertha has gone away, she will learn always to be pale and quiet and suddenly smile all over her face when she speaks. And learn to say something that is true, but not easy to say, so funnily that no one will mind. My *work*, Aunt Bertha says, and, your *work*. Important. Fancywork. No. I Know that my Redeemer liveth cannot possibly be fancywork.

She thinks of the patchwork she will be doing when Miss Webb comes back. Miss Webb calls it learning to sew. And at first it was trying to keep the cotton clean and make neat stitches without a row of little blood-dots. And now it is easy. But Miss Webb does not know anything about the look of the different little pieces out of the rag-bag in the wardrobe-room, all smelling of lavender. She does not see the far-away inside of the little lilac pieces with the small pattern, nor want to look and look into the pattern and find out why it goes so deep. She does not know that the striped pieces are horrid.

Aunt Bertha looks up. But only so far as the bunch of skeins. Her eyes see the skeins, but she is thinking about something else. Her thoughts go on while she takes a fresh thread without ever looking across. With the point of her needle she presses back a little piece of fray and makes the next stitch so that it will just hold it down. Berry wishes there were a piece of fray in her text.

But there is only to see that the thick gold silk goes into the right holes. And now Aunt Bertha is sitting back with her head on one side and her eyes screwed up to see how her work looks from a distance. And now she is going on with it, looking very stern. Lifting her head, Berry holds it on one side and screws up her eyes and sees all she has done, without looking from letter to letter: I know that my Re, looking so lovely that she cannot believe she has made it, and almost wishes she were a cripple so as to sit all day, like Aunt Bertha, having a party with her 'materials'. Different coloured silks and many needles and a little silver thimble and ornamental scissors and presently something finished and looking lovely. And then thinking of something else to make.

The text is more than half-finished, not counting the diamond-shaped fullstop at the end. Her hand goes out to pat the worked silk, but quickly comes back as she remembers: Don't handle the silks but when you're threading them. The smooth gold bands of the letters are as clean as the silk in the skeins; and brighter. Much nicer than Pug's. Pug's text is in smaller letters: God is Love. Short, like Pug. And Aunt Bertha has done most of it because Pug is nearly always somewhere else and grubby. And there are only three days before Mother's birthday. Aunt Bertha will be gone; not sitting in the breakfast-room making it like a party all the morning; not going for drives with Mother and coming back and making teatime like a party. She will be at home in the cottage thrown into another cottage.

*

Secretly, in Mother's bedroom, Mary takes the texts out of the parcel. Pug's is on the top. Small. It comes out of its wrapper and there it is, a framed picture held up by Mary. Ellen says isn't it lovely and it is lovely, lovely; the crimson letters in the chestnut-brown frame. Ellen takes down Mother's smallest picture and they hang up Pug's text, to try. Pug, hanging up on the wall for everyone to see. And now Mary's hands are on the paper covering the other text. Frightened, Berry feels. Shuts her eyes. Cannot move or speak. Sees, in her shut eyes, the big beautiful Redeemer in glossy, golden letters, and the rest not finished. But she can *remember* finishing it, and doing the diamond shape and the difficult scroll. She opens her eyes. Mary is taking off the wrapping. Away, away out on to the landing.

'Lovely,' Mary's voice. Berry runs to the other end of the landing, with the word ringing in her ears. Outside the end window she sees the climbing roses looking in at her.

'Berry!'

Where to hide? In the housemaid's cupboard, crouched, hearing her breathing tell Ann's brooms she is there, hearing Mary and Ellen go downstairs. Out of the cupboard, quickly across the landing, to look. There it is. Over the mantelpiece, the lovely golden words and the fullstop and the scroll, hanging crooked. And too high to reach. And Mother will be coming up, sent up, Mary said, alone, 'on some excuse' to find the birthday surprise.

*

'There, darling. It's quite straight now, my chick. It's a beautiful text, and you've done it very nicely, bunny-chub. Mother likes it very much indeed.'

'The fullstop is diamond-shape.'

'Yes, my darling.'

'Not round like an ordinary fullstop.'

'No, dearie, it's a beautiful fullstop.'

Mother goes on looking at the text and Berry comes quite near; to see her face while she is looking. It is sad, and a hairpin she doesn't know about is sticking out, ready to fall.

'Poor *Ber*tha!'

Berry feels a thump in her heart, and her face grows hot: stupid, stupid Mother. She only knows Aunt Bertha is a cripple. Why can't she see her, up there, in the text, on the wall? She is spoiling the text, because she can't *see*.

H.D.
KORA AND KA

There are two things mitigate against me, one is my mind, one is the lack of it. Kora brought me here. She thinks that I am overworked. I am overworked. Kora is exquisite and helpful. I follow her as a child follows its mother. But she is more to me than any mother could be to any child. She is to me what a materialised substance is to a shadow. Without substance, shadow cannot exist. I cannot exist without Kora. But I am more to Kora than a shadow. I am that sort of shadow they used to call a Ka, in Egypt. A Ka lives after the body is dead. I shall live after Helforth is dead.

I look across a space of grass that is the colour of the chiffon scarf that Kora wore last night at dinner. The grass is the colour of tea-roses. From the burnt grass, there is a slight burnt fragrance like tobacco scattered across pot-pourri. The hand of Helforth lies affectedly across the grey knee of his lounge suit. The clothed knee is a dummy knee in a window. The shod feet are brown leather lumps. They rest in the grass like amputated dead feet. The hand of Helforth lives the more markedly for this. It is a long hand, affectedly flung there, living. I, this Ka, cannot see the face of Helforth.

I feel Helforth's eyes. They are glass-grey eyes. I feel his contempt. It is the contempt of integrity, he has worked too hard. I tear, as it were, the curtain that shuts me from Helforth and I feel Helforth's eyes widen. When his eyes have sufficiently stared at that wall opposite, I will look out. At the moment, the eyes of Helforth see in detail, wooden images placed on a shelf, two cows, one painted red, the other black. His eyes are focussed there, they are not wide enough for me yet. He smiles as he notes the red cow has a bell exactly matching in its minute disproportion, those the others wear on the far hill. He sees the red cow, placed at the shuttered window, like a cuckoo out of its clock. The cows are a trifle smaller than the two on wooden platforms that the patron's small child pulls on uneven wood wheels across the flagstones. These cows, Helforth notes smiling, have been carved especially for this purpose, no doubt by the same wood-carver who cut those various plaques and plates of grape-bushes and cluster of wild-apricot, indoors. The cows relate, by this association, to the house behind Helforth, to the green and the stark white and the black and the grey of its interior. Helforth is abnormally sensitive to various interior focal planes of light.

He is sensitive to all light. His eyes widen in the blinding sunlight and the sun beats down, incandescent, on his white face. The sun will sear Helforth's face away and let me come. His eyes will go blank, staring straight into the light and mine will see. I wait for Helforth's eyes to blind out Helforth. Helforth is amused and delighted with the wooden cow and its disproportionate minute wood cow bell.

Helforth must see everything. And while his eyes run along a wire where a clematis is trained, I grow impatient. The eyes of Helforth drink in the purple of the clematis blossom and gouge out colour of the rose-clematis. The passion of the eyes of Helforth disregards me, waiting. They come to rest, then, on root-stalk of the vine that clambers up the other side of the barn wall. A straggly tendril pulses toward the passion-flower, through the weight of sunlight. The eyes of Helforth follow the twining insistence of the little tendril. It seems now they will be lost for ever in the purple star. But I know Helforth, and I wait for Helforth. His eyes drop again and rest on the spiral of the grape tendril. Then his eyes fall lower on a sheaf of vine-leaves and on one leaf. As his lids fall and as his mind discards the drug-purple of the lordly blossom, I know he knows that I am waiting. His lids droop to blacken out the heady visual memory of rose and purple, and then widen. His eyes rest on the cool young vine-leaves and I come.

*

I am most at home with Helforth in this green space. The mind of Helforth has seized on one young grape-leaf. The leaf is, just this morning, flattened as if the sun had ironed it out. It still has the tenderness of the young incurved leaves. The leaf is vertebrate. A flawless spine sends out side branches and those again break off into little veins. The flat young leaf blown sideways, insists on inference. Its underside is like the rose leaves that Helforth and Kora exclaimed over, in the smoke-amethyst rose-bowl Kora brought from her room last night, to place on their dining table. Kora had said, 'the room lacks something' and made Helforth try to guess what it was.

Last night, it was rainy in spurts. They had drawn the grey stuff curtains that Kora had brought from London with other things of her own, boxes, candlesticks and this sort of glass bowl. Helforth, looking at the glass bowl, knew, now that the bowl was set there, what it was the room lacked. So, Kora will ask a question in words, then answer it in action. She is, herself, oracle and answer. She said, as she stood, looking down at the rose-bowl, 'the light from here, is gouged out like a rainbow in a pope's amethyst . . . stand here, you'll see. The convex bulge at the base, is one huge amethyst.' But Helforth does not stand. He sees the grey-rose pulse of the silver of the leaves. Two of the leaves had bent under when Kora put the rose-stems into water. The amethyst tinted clear water in the bowl turns their under-sides, old-silver. Helforth's eyes rest on that silver. He discarded last night, as well as Kora's pope's amethyst, the cluster of blossoms. His eyes discarded the royal-red of the lordly blossom, uncurled Jacqueminot and the half-opened

Gloire de Dijon, as just now he discarded the royal purple and the king-rose of the flat wide clematis. His eyes are at rest in silver and in green and in a rotation of silver-green, green-silver.

Colour had rotated in his mind but he now discards it. If he watches colour in his mind, he will be watching . . . to watch anything at the moment is dangerous. Green has been kind. At the moment, it is the one colour that disregards him. Green does not try to snatch back at him, mitigate, suggest billow of open-curtain or red, red, red. Green is most removed from red, from memory and the mole-trap of his office in the city. If he lets go the hold that I have over Helforth, Helforth will begin the old tread wheel and the iron ferris-wheel of Helforth's fatigue will grind, across colour, odour, perception, will crush me beneath it like an iron heel, a glow-worm or just hatched moth, on grit and pebble. If Helforth lets his mind catch in rotation, even the memory of this half hour of crowded perception, his mind will jerk back to all vicissitudes. His mind trod ferris-wheel, trod old, old round of balance and account, of one, two, three, of nine plus seven makes sixteen. His mind rotated to this rhythm, ground round and round, till Helforth forgot man, men, women. Helforth forced Helforth to go on in ferris-wheel of iron circle against an iron grey sky. One day his mind, just casually set in motion, discarded all the preconceived occupations of that mind. He saw the under-manager as under layers of green water, violet-laced and the numbers on his ledger shone violet-laced, nine, six, up through transparent seaweed. Helforth told Helforth, 'you must see a doctor.'

The doctor said, 'shut your eyes, Mr. Helforth.' He did so. The doctor said, 'open your eyes, Mr. Helforth.' He did so. The doctor said, 'now is the large A, to the right or the left of the small script?' He told him. The doctor said, 'look at the small O above the circle and tell me if the twin brackets are *in* or *outside* that circle.' Helforth saw a sort of chart, placed at some distance from him. The wooden frame, on which the chart was balanced, reminded him of just such an arrangement of wood and cardboard from which he had learned his letters. Helforth said casually, 'I will learn my letters.' The doctor said, 'I asked, was the bracket *in* or *out*' and he shoved the frame thing gradually nearer. As the huge page loomed before Helforth, he felt himself grow smaller. Helforth felt himself draw away, back and back, the length of the doctor's room and out of the wall behind it. Helforth became Helforth, minute at the minimising other-end of an opera-glass. Although Helforth was miles away, projected into space, Helforth himself sat there. Helforth said tonelessly, 'I don't see anything.'

The doctor turned a page of the A, B, C, Chart, said, 'don't you even see the lines across the blank space?' Helforth did not tell the doctor what he saw.

A globe rather like the shape of the Venetian glass that Kora had set on the table last night, again reminded Helforth that man was a microbe. He saw a world like a drop of water and himself enclosed in it. It was a green world. Neither the doctor nor that Helforth, drawn graphically out, through the wall, into indeterminate space, was in it. Helforth repeated to the doctor, who seemed to be exacting some form of decisive answer, 'I see nothing.'

The doctor turned a luminous lamp-ray across the face of Helforth. As that consulting room incandescence made bar and cross-bar across Helforth's haggard countenance, Helforth felt himself returning. From behind Helforth, a ridiculous dangling full-dress Helforth (seen at the wrong end of an opera-glass) rejoined him. Helforth saw Helforth at the other end of the opera-glass, then the two adjusted into one life-size Helforth. Helforth opened his eyes. Helforth saw pursed-forward mouth, chin elegantly shaved, stubble of inconsequential grey-white moustache. The doctor's face was that of an intelligent elderly wire-haired terrier. Helforth did not like terriers, though, from time to time, he endeavoured to adjust himself to them, contemplated racially, through some friend's dog. So he endeavoured to adjust himself to this man. He saw, over the doctor's cloth shoulder, a case holding a stuffed bird and, in a corner, a cluster of speckled birds' eggs, set in brown glass.

The doctor said, 'what do you see now?' Helforth told him about the speckled eggs and the stuffed bird. The doctor said, 'nerves; you must stop work.'

*

Helforth wondered as he stood waiting for a taxi, how he could do that . . . Helforth opened his eyes, saw the barn door and the sunlight and the triangle of sunlight as it lay on the barn floor. A ray of that light had crossed, gold sun-serpent, that barn floor. Helforth sat up. He examined long hands, the palms were less brown than burnt backs. Helforth lifted his throat to guillotine of sunlight. He jerked at the open collar; let sunlight sink deeper. He rose to his feet. He thought, 'have I been sleeping?' He knew he was and knew he was not sleeping. Helforth slept, Ka watched or Ka was banished and Helforth stared out, calculating, hard-eyed. For a moment, he had been standing at a street corner, waiting for a taxi while speckled birds' eggs, in dead grass, appeared in a plate-glass window. The speckled birds' eggs were the heads of the new importation of French manikins, shaved that year and gilt or silvered over. He thought, 'how can I stop work?' Then as he stepped into the taxi, he said, 'yes, I will stop work.' He wondered how he could climb out of the ferris-wheel that had been going on for so long. He was dizzy, as he thought of that, and then abstract problem became concrete, how will I step out of this taxi? How will I manage legs, arms and how will I get at my little change-purse or manage to extract loose change from my pocket? Will it be easier to reach in for my wallet which is flat and manageable? Will the taxi man be able to change a note? He wondered if he were hungry, wondered if the taxi man would think he was drunk. He hadn't smoked for some time.

The taxi stopped with a jerk, beside a pile of wooden building-blocks. The blocks were stacked each side on the road, like neolithic stone-blocks. Beyond the double doorway of neolithic wood blocks, there was a blazing brazier. Helforth saw fire. He thought, 'I am cold.' It was, he remembered, autumn. There was a mist creeping across the brazier flame, it was incense across an altar. He thought of incense, thought of an altar. He remembered that he had left the stack of letters unstamped and wondered, in neurotic agony, if the office boy would drop them into the post-box, without looking at them. He hadn't been sure of the stamps and had intended to have the lot weighed. They were all of a bulk, the usual quarter-form, sent out to the shareholders. He remembered it was autumn because of the usual form that he had forgotten to stamp, neurotically wracked for fear the boy would just sweep the lot up into his office satchel and not see they weren't stamped.

Now John Helforth, staring at sun-serpent on barn floor, stood up. I stood up. My legs were stiff. My legs were too long. The same legs had been too long that autumn, late afternoon, cramped sideways in the taxi. I had been sitting crouched down, flung down, I now remembered, like a tailor's dummy or a rag doll. I recalled exact panic of mental calculation, how will I get out of this taxi?

I got out finally because the taxi man poked his head around and said, 'the street's up, sir, shall we wait till the traffic block this end's cleared or shall I drive round it?' Taxi drivers ask these things, lest they be maligned for extorting undue tax. The frayed edges of my mind would not then stand argument. With the frayed edges of my mind, I could not stand up 'wait' or 'go around' and watch the two naked gladiators fight the thing out. I could not any more stand, watching the contest in the blood-stained sand of my own mind's arena. I got out.

Kora said, 'hello.' I had to squint close in the town mist to see who it was. I saw chin, nose; eyes were drawn back under a dark green little sort of helmet. I remembered the hat was green because I remembered thinking her yellow fur, drawn tight across her shoulders and about her hips, made her look like a caterpillar. Or wasn't the hat green? We have arguments about it. She said it was mole-grey; she afterwards called the thing *taupe*. (She would say, 'how could you think I would wear green with that coat?') I said, 'I must pay this taxi.' She said, 'O don't. Do keep him. I've been looking for a taxi.' Kora and I got into the taxi like a pre-arranged rendez-vous. I said, 'where are you going?'

She didn't seem to know where she was going, didn't seem to care much. I could never watch again the crowded agonies of that blood-strewn arena, the thing my mind was, when I stepped out of a ferris-wheel. But I could watch someone else, wonder, now what exactly is this woman's sort of worry? Has she too forgotten to put stamps on her letters. I said, 'have you forgotten to put stamps on your letters?'

Kora answered me, as if it were the one question in the whole world she had anticipated. Kora does answer that way. She said, 'letters? I was thinking of letters.' She reached into her flat hand-bag, dragged them out. She gave me a litle bundle. 'Suppose you drop the whole lot in the river,' she said. She said, 'look at them.' I sorted out the letters, just managed to make out, in the blurred light of the taxi window, that they were addressed in the same writing. The writing was decisive, the nib was stub and the down-strokes thick. But the writing was Ninevah to me. She said, 'read out the address to me.' I said, 'I'm afraid I can't. I haven't got my glasses.' I never wear glasses but I didn't want to tell her about the doctor and I didn't want to tax my mind to read things. I said, 'if it were lighter, I could read them.'

I said that evasively, not wanting to mean anything. She said, 'I haven't had tea, I'm hungry. Can't we get out here?' We got out. I paid the taxi. We went in a half familiar little side-door, we were in the Bay-tree. Kora said, 'just this once, just this once

... dinner.' I said, 'why just this once?' Kora said, 'criminals condemned to die, have a last wish haven't they?' I said, 'yes, I think so. But why?' 'Some,' Kora said, 'ask just for a good meal.' I said, 'I can't apply anything just now.' She said, 'I . . . but it's all right since you've got hold of the letters.' I said, 'I dropped them in the box outside the door here.' I said, 'I must have done it automatically.' She said, 'that's done it.'

I avoided looking at her over fish and entrée, but watched her lap up her ice like a starved cat. I slipped mine over to her. She never even noticed, went on lapping. Over coffee, I said, 'done what?'

* * *

There are two things that mitigate against me. One is my mind, one is the lack of it. I, John Helforth, go on existing in that beam of sunlight. As I stand now, stretching, the bar of light that underlined that triangle, (sun-serpent) is exactly parallel to the threshold of the doorway. Parallels, parallels . . . are two things that travel along, equidistant, and never quite meet. Parallels? I am John Helforth, I say, yawning and I endeavour to banish, in that yawn's exaggeration, the monster I call, for lazy lack of definition, 'Ka.' Ka is far off now; Ka partook of symptom, was neurotic breakdown; Ka, it is true, led me, made me, having made me, preserved me – but yawning, I say, for what? If I, Helforth, get rapt back into this Ka thing, contemplating vine-green leaf, Helforth will be good for nothing. There is so much to be done, so much to be thought of; Kora.

Kora is everything. Without Kora, Ka would have got me. Sometimes I call Kora, Ka, or reverse the process and call Ka, Kora. I am on familiar terms with Kora, with Ka, likewise. We are, it is evident, some integral triple alliance, primordial Three-in-One. I am Kora, Kora is Helforth and Ka is shared between us. Though she repudiates affiliation with Ka, and refuses to discuss it, yet the fact remains. Ka is Kora, Kora is Ka. The waif must be shared between us.

Ka weeps, wails for attention and then must be put to sleep like any tired infant. Though Ka, unhappily it seems, in that too, like most infants, is never really tired. Ka wears me to a shred. It is I who am bone-thin. Soul is, I have proved it, octopus. Nevertheless, octopus cannot devour utterly. I am frame still, albeit, bone and sinew. I stretch arms. They are my arms. I, I am John Helforth.

I stamp feet, John Helforth's feet. Feet are no longer amputated brown lumps lying flat in burnt grass. They are my feet and the shoes are from Thornton's, Bond Street. I look at shoes, my shoes. I remember how I bought these shoes, my particular shoes. I will remember. I will to remember. For one instant, for some long or short space of time, memory was eradicated. Ka brushed across my mind, a sponge on a slate. Ka then was the shape of a drop of water, magnified to the size of a universe. Ka was a universe. In it, I swam, one microbe in a water-bead. Kora and I do not talk of this thing. Kora says, 'forget that.'

Kora tells me to forget Ka that, in London, brushed out my mind. I tell Kora to forget other things. Kora's eyes strain forward, they are too big and blue, like bruised flower texture. They are flower petal, ruined in soggy down-pour, they are no longer flower, they are not good stuff, they are not rain nor sun nor water. I hate Kora when her eyes get that poked-out, bruised look. I will not look at Kora. I say, 'the kids would stifle you, after this taste of freedom. Don't set up lurid iron bars. For God, his sake, don't set up iron bars of memory.' I will to be John Helforth, an Englishman and a normal brutal one. I will strength into my body, into my loins. I say, 'for God's sake Kora, you're crippling your integrity . . . Lot's wife. Stop thinking of the children. Anyhow, you don't really want to see them, it's (to use your own phrase) guilt-complex.' She turns on me, 'children. You never had a child.' I do not retaliate, as I well might do. There are so many things that I might say at this moment, that I don't say anything. I could concentrate everything into one word, and that word, 'Kora.' I don't even say that. I don't reach out my hand as I might do, hand sculptured, she says, of meagre metal, an Aztec (she says) or archaic edition of Rodin's somewhat bloated (she says) Hand of God. I do not say 'Kora.'

I do not say 'Kora,' for why should I? I insist on masculinity and my brutality. I drag out, perhaps, tobacco, lift up and let fall disgustedly, books on a table or upset her work-box. I deliberately do something that Helforth would not do, could not do. I become a small lout in my mother's drawing room and let resentment flare up, I remember Bob and Larry, hating each equally for their several betrayals.

I let red flares eat out my mind, red Verey light shall burn up Ka who is a jelly fish, who is a microbe, who is (a specialist all but told me) a disease. I will burn away my soul with my mind, or should I say my body? I have a right like any man, like any woman, like any other ill-begotten creature, to a body.

Who gave me this broken duality? Who gave me this curse of intimate perception? I curse Ka. I say, 'I hate you, Kora; when your eyes go poking forward, you are really ugly.' I look at Kora as she stands, looking down into the courtyard where that wretched child is pulling its wooden cow on the wooden platform, making the uneven wooden wheels vibrate, dot and tick of some wretched S.O.S. between himself and Kora. I say, 'I'd like to smash that kid and its wretched wood cow. Anyhow, I've had enough of cows for one lifetime.' I underline cow, spew out, 'cow, cow, cow, mother-love or mother-lust I call it.' I say, 'this cow passion is the disintegrating factor of modernity. I mean you and your sort keep back the world.' I say, 'mother, mother, mother,' and I say, 'Larry.'

I have meant to be robust; I have meant to smash furniture. I find myself seated on the low rush-bottomed arm-chair. I beat my hands on its sides. I say, 'everything in this damn place is rushes and wood and cow, cow, cow.' I say, 'when are we going back? I can't stay here forever.' It is her turn, at this moment, to retaliate, she does not. Then I sway. Ka is coming; there is green of a pale grape tendril. I hear a voice, it is only Kora but still I say, 'Ka shan't get me.' I regret temporary weakness, I am strong again, I say, 'rushes and reeds and cows.' I say, 'your mother complex is ugly, Kora. You look into yourself with those ugly poked-out eyes, like a beggar, in Naples, cashing-in on siphilitic scars.' I go on, I say, 'cow,' I say, 'mother, mother, mother.' Then I fling myself down, anywhere, head on the table, or head that would beat through the wooden floor to the rooms that lie beneath it, 'Larry.'

*

Kora knows, the specialist knows, everybody knows that if I had said this ten years ago, I might now be all right. Kora knows and Kora will not retaliate, at least not now, not while I beat my head actually or metaphorically on the floor . . . I look up, I am really standing in bright sunlight, finishing out a yawn with an extra gape and a gulp like a fish, all but caught on a fish-hook. I disentangle fish-hook. I see where I stand. One foot is on brown grass, the other half is shoved in, against a cottage garden border of fire-blue lobelia. Sweet-alyssum ought to be there too; who plants lobelia without sweet-alyssum? I remember my mother's garden, her drawing-room. I remember Larry. The doctor told Kora if I could have remembered sooner . . . I ask myself, who is Larry? I should never have talked to Kora. I would never have told Kora, if she had not licked up that ice, in the Bay-tree, like a starved cat. I hate suffering in animals. I used to walk round and round the squares in London, to escape children. I do not like children. I do not like cats. When Kora pushes back the second plate in the Bay-tree and said, 'yes, coffee,' I knew decisively that she was more cat than caterpillar. I said to her, 'you are more cat than caterpillar'. It was the sort of remark that, in Bob, would have been called 'whimsical.' Larry and I used to practise at Bob being 'whimsical.'

Mother could have kept Larry at home. I was too young. Larry was of course vicious to have told me, in precise detail, all that he did. It was a perverse sort of sadism. I loved Larry. I would have gone on, loving men and women if it hadn't been for Larry. How could I love anyone after Larry? My mother used to say, '*Bob* would have been too noble-minded to have regretted Larry.' Bob? But Bob went that first year, dead or alive he was equally obnoxious. He was the young 'father,' mother's favourite. I was sixteen. By the time I was ready, the war actually was over. Mother reiterated on every conceivable occasion, 'Larry is only waiting to get out there.' I don't know what mother thought 'there' was. It was so near. It was 'here' all the time with me. Larry was sent to avenge Bob, I was to be sent to avenge Larry. It was already written in Hans Anderson, a moron virgin and a pitcher. We were all virgin, moron. We were virgin, though Larry saw to it that I was not. Larry.

I, John Helforth, kick at a scrubby little border of lobelia. I hear a voice call 'Helforth'. I scowl out, under hard blue eyes. There is no Ka anywhere now visible. There is Kora standing on the uneven flag-stones, she says, 'tea is ready. What were you doing all this time here, sleeping?' I say, 'yes, Kora, sleeping.' Ka has gone off. He lives in water and I say, 'I'm going tomorrow up toward Grangettes to get you water-lilies.' Kora is looking better. Her eyes are lobelia-blue, fire-blue now in her burnt face. Her arms are the colour of the chiffon scarf that she wore last night at dinner. The hollow in her neck is as fragrant as tobacco and her flesh tastes, I tell her, of water-lilies and of pears. She says, 'water-lilies and pears . . . what a mutinous sort of salad,' and I say 'for God's sake, don't be whimsical.'

My shoes are too heavy. I must get a pair of light ones or some sort of sand-shoes. What can I get here? Kora has pulled off stockings; women always have half and half sort of things to suit any odd occasion. Her low-heeled one-strap shoes are of soft café-au-lait leather. Her ankles above them and her bare legs are just one shade lighter. She has really gone a sort of honey-colour. I wait for some sort of opening to tell her, before I forget, that she is honey-colour. I pull off an apposite spray of honey-flower that seems, telepathically, to have forestalled me. 'Honey-flower,' I say as I tickle her behind the ear, 'is a prettier word than honey-suckle.' 'Is it?' says Kora. We can argue this sort of thing out, endlessly.

She blows out electric spark of the burner and pours my tea. 'Now,' says Kora, 'you are back in London; you are having your first affair; you are happier' . . . I look at Kora; I see no wide blue of fire-blue lobelia but a camelia that has opened under the touch of Larry. I see Jean and I see Larry. I wish Kora wouldn't be so blatantly and conspicuously tactful. I know the doctor told her not to let me slip out into a sort of impersonal way of seeing. I know they told her to drag out things, to make me talk, to make me tell things. Well, I will tell things, 'Kora.'

'Darling?' 'This is not London. This is no first affair. If you are trying to get me to talk about Larry, well you will do. Larry would have withered you with a pseudo-sarcastic whimsicality as he did everyone but Jeanette. Larry did not love Jeanette, she did not love him. They clung together in a world that was made for them, a world of flickering lights and long corridors,' (I fling about my rhetoric) 'of single floating wicks in glass lamps, of music behind curtains and of wind in country gables. There was a world made for Larry, there was a world made for Jeanette' (here my breath dramatically catches) 'and it was taken from them. Kora, who took it from them? Was it you, was it me?' (I pause forensically.) '*It was our Mother.*'

This may or may not have been true. I don't think poor madre, personally, prevented wicks from floating in glass lamp bowls or wind from howling in country gables. But mother had become symbol. I should have seen it sooner. I had, in Kora's language, 'inhibited' the fact that Larry really need not have gone so early. I blamed mother for the death of Larry and I was not noble like Bob. Kora declares that I was in love with madre and that Bob taking the place of father, was my rival. Fantastic explanation yet gives us topic of conversation over our little dinners. One has to talk at dinner. Kora says my attitude is fantastic and linked up with mother-complex. I say I do not think so. I explain it lucidly, as if she herself were a complete outsider, and herself had never heard of that war. I demonstrate how, systematically, we were trained to blood-lust and hatred. We were sent out, iron-shod to quell an enemy who had made life horrible. That enemy roasted children, boiled down the fat of pregnant women to grease cannon wheels. He wore a spiked hat and carried, in one hand, a tin thunderbolt and, in the other, a specialised warrant for burning down cathedrals. He was ignorant and we were sent out, Galahad on Galahad, to quell him. His men raped nuns, cut off the hands of children, boiled down the entrails of old men, nailed Canadians against barn doors ... and all this we heard mornings with the Daily Newsgraph and evenings with the Evening Warscript. The Newsgraph and the Warscript fed out belching mothers, who belched out in return, fire and carnage in the name of Rule Britannia. I said, 'Kora, go back to London. What is the matter with you? Forget sometimes that you are a mother.'

*

Kora has a look in her eyes that means sure death. I say 'fire away, old die-hard.' There is a look in Kora's eyes that does not go with a green helmet and a caterpillar coat. It goes, she is right, with grey and with a sort of undressed leather primitive pelt or polished steel-edge aegis. I say, 'when you look like that I understand old Stamford.' Stamford was, or I suppose I should say, *is* Kora's husband. I had vaguely known Kora Morrell. I think I had seen her as one of those window-dressed brides who carry out-of-season lilies. Bob was to have been a brother-officer

199

sort of property of Stamford's at that wedding. Bob was otherwise engaged about then; even Larry was not available. I 'ghosted' for them both, soon, veritably, to take on that rôle for life.

When Larry went I, in some odd manner, went 'west' with him. It was my feet that were severed . . . a mule's intestines . . . but I must stop this. The doctor said if I could encourage the sub-conscious to break into the conscious . . . but there is a limit even to that . . .

It is Larry, at last analysis, I say, who is responsible for my mind. He shouldn't have told me about Runner 32, as they called him . . . and those others. We had some mad idea of sharing things, life, war, love finally. I didn't stop to reason nor think. I was the half of Larry. That half gone, I too went. I did what I presumed Larry would have done, if he had been left in my place. I took on the rôle of Robert, I was to go in his place. It was the only thing to do, I had not the courage to begin over on my own. I had not the heart to be debonnaire. That word had lost integrity like a worm-gnawed apple. 'Debonnaire,' 'whimsical' were words rotted at the core. Larry had been 'debonnaire' at the last, I am certain and old Robert, true to type, no doubt was no end 'whimsical.'

I never stopped to reason, to think. One does not reason, walking above a torrent on one thin plank. I did not realise that *nothing* depended on me, that a row of aunts was choros out of Hades, that the 'family' was only another name for warfare and sacrifice of the young. I did not in the least realise that it would be a sort of crime if mother ('our' mother) did not have her lilies-of-the-valley on this and that occasion. Such were my erotic orgies, lilies for my mother. There was also the birth-day and the death-day of a father and two brothers. Around these days, aunts stood like crows, waiting their turn at carrion. It was not Larry who had been picked by vultures nor was it

Robert. I began to curse Larry, to curse Bob. Because of their casual and affable 'sacrifice,' I was left, flung high and dry.

*

Kora looked at me in hatred, the lobelia-blue burnt to a fire-blue in her eyes. Then there is no fire in her eyes. She had touched me on the quick with Larry. I will do the same with her brats. Her children are at school now, I will tell her what happens to small boys at school, things that happened to me, to Larry. Her eyes are steel. I will break through Kora for I hate her. I hate all women because of mother and because of . . . Jeanette. I say, 'you don't look the least like Jeanette.'

Kora says, 'what has Jean Drier got to do with me now?' I say, 'you remember you sat there, you blew out the flame, you poured my tea. You said, "now you are back in London, you are having your first love affair." You remember you said that.' Kora says she remembers. I say, 'don't treat me like Bobby or Jo. Keep your brats out of it. I am not Bobby, look tootsie ottsie, mummy's mended your bear. I don't want your teddy-bearising of this situation.' Kora says, 'go on.' She settles down to it; she reaches for her work-box. 'I don't want this eternal prodding down, I tell you, Kora, this new sort of analysis stuff can't get round the fact of Ka. I know more than any of these nerve-specialists. How can they treat me? If any one of them had had this over-mind or other-mind or over-world experience, I would listen.' Kora says quite steadily, 'isn't your over-world as you call it, simply substitution?' I say, 'for what?' She says, 'for this world.' I say, 'you ask me, then, to accept this world? You are eternally compromising.' She is running flat elastic round the top of one of those tailored knickers. I say, 'I like your knickers, Kora. I liked Jean's but then that hardly counted. Do you know, Kora, my mother used to snatch her under-things out of the way, such things too, when she saw any of us boys coming.' Kora held up the silk tailored knickers for my inspection. 'O, John,' she said, 'the poor, poor, poor old darling.' I have not heard Kora speak that way of my mother. She looks up now, across the pile of fawn and puce and light taupe things that she's mending. 'O Johnny,' she seldom calls me Johnny, 'don't you see what a mess you make of all this? Can't you just *love* your mother?' I turn on Kora, I will spew out fire and brimstone, I say 'Larry.' 'O don't, don't, Johnny, that's over.' She says, conclusively, that the war is over. 'How can it be – when Larry?' 'You,' said Kora 'are really as bad as all the fire-eating Anglo-Indians. You go on, you go on with it. Can't you see the flowers growing and ignore the grave-yard?' 'What flowers . . .' I take the taupe bit of silk thing from her. 'Ours . . . Johnny.'

* * *

Colour has rotated in his mind but he now discards it. His eyes are at rest in silver and in green and in a rotation of silver-green, green-silver. He sees a space of long room with a low ceiling. He sees the curtains Kora had drawn, now open. He sees Kora (in a chiffon sort of robe), draw aside the curtains. He sees shadow wavering across diminished sunlight and sunlight filtering through diminished green. He sees shadow wavering slightly like fern-fronds under water. He sees that the red and blue cluster of field flowers, stamped on the chiffon that Kora has drawn on, lie here, there, across bare arm, bare shoulder, the gallant little bulge her back makes, like field flowers, flung on to a statue sprayed with water. The chiffon robe is light, rain-colour or the texture of a sprayed-out garden fountain. The flowers seem to lie along the shoulder of Kora as if she had been rolling in a meadow. I see Kora as she steps into a pool of sunlight that is stippled over with leaf-shadow. Her feet are bare. They are whiter than her legs and the strap of her shoe has left a white strap on her foot. Her bare foot is shod in a whiter sheaf of white flesh. I see that the strap on the other foot is also white.

Colour has rotated in my mind and dissociation of iron-clad

idea. My mind was bound in, bound me in a little iron car of ferris-wheel perception. I went round or seemed to go round but all the time my mind, that seemed to lift me above earth, just as inevitably swung me down, back to it. I realise the triviality of that set of perceptions, think of the quarrel we have just had, think rather of a quarrel we had long, long ago before the curtains shut out sunlight as now the curtain lets in filtration of a green diminished shadow. When Kora drew the curtain, it was drawn, dramatically, across a sun-steeped late afternoon. Now Kora opens the curtain and it is still light but (almost imperceptible difference) early evening and not late afternoon. We could not have been there together on the low couch, an hour at the outside, three quarters of an hour, maybe. In that short sector of time, the world altered, slowly, slowly life drew off . . . life drew away, turgid stream, dragging with it silt and bed-rock of grinding memory. Kora was right then. It was right to prod and jab up surface anger. Surface anger can be got at, can be demolished with a like flare of anger. Kora's anger is not like Helforth's anger, but it allays and stills it. But Kora was not really angry. On the surface, Kora tells me she was angry. She sits beside me, she says, 'must we ever be angry again, Helforth?' I say, 'Kora it's like this. If I could have had bouts of resentment, anger, hatred, all through those ten years, these great volcanic break-downs wouldn't happen.' Kora says, 'yes, Helforth. I too. If I could have hated Stamford, known what he was, if I could have loathed him, I might have loathed the children.' I take the small hand, it is clothed with a brown glove as if someone had lightly varnished it and lightly passed the brush up, toward the shoulders. I slip the chiffon from the shoulder and am half-surprised when the cluster of print-poppies and corn-flowers slips off with it. I say, 'you are a bit indecent this way. As if you had on long brown gloves and a silly little throat thing, a thing my mother used to call a "dickie" in our wash suits.' I pull back the chiffon stuff and cover the discrepancy with the print-poppies and blue corn-flowers. I take Kora's hand, almost as if I had not ever kissed it. I say quite solemnly like an apology or a pledge, 'you must think better of me. I hate the children, not because they are your children, not even because they are Stamford's. I hate them because they made you suffer.' She stares straight ahead now; a small hard little profile cuts against fern shadow and the evening afterglow as it filters through those trees. The feather clouds seem to have slipped like fish through the meshes of those trees, they lie, in light pattern, on the floor, they swim about the quaint strapped-over, bare feet like a swarm of gold-fish. The shadows are gold-fish and rose-fish, from some Japanese aquarium. I say, 'forgive me, Kora.'

Her profile is hard. Sometime, somewhere, there was a jab, a sort of slice was taken out of Kora. You feel a certain sort of tenderness was removed, as one might have one's appendix removed, on an operating table. The stability of Kora is not really stable. It is the stability of a frozen rabbit that hears the hounds not far off. She seems to be listening, to be waiting. 'But Kora, they can't ever take the children.' She does not accept me, she is looking far off. She says, 'it's odd. I would never have minded, none of it would have mattered, if I had ever loved him.' I say, 'Kora you did love him.' I say even, 'you do love him.' I feel with one last flagrant tendril that binds me to the past, that this is somehow what Larry would have said. I have forgiven Larry, now, for dying and even as I said, 'I will let Larry go,' Larry stood there near me. I feel, 'this is what Larry would have said to Jeanette.' I feel with one last fibre that binds me to that past, that I must now (having discarded Larry) be once more with him, just this once, this once, Larry. I say, 'you do really, Kora, love him.'

My eyes are filmed over. I feel, in death, only the tenderness of dismissal. Kora has done this for me. Well, Kora reconciled me to death, I, appositely, will try to reconcile her to life. Kora has told me how she loved the children, she will go back to

204

them. 'Kora, you have only to go to them.' Her arms are around me, a terrible vice clutches, presses (octopus) breath from my body. I am frightened at this very sudden turn, this octopus-like clutch of those arms below my chest, crushing breath out. I am frightened at the strength and the intensity of those small arms. They are wire and fibre, they bind close, close. I bracelet her two wrists with my hands, I do not draw off those wrists. She lets go suddenly. She slips from me, lies on the floor; the print-poppies make poppy and corn-flower pattern on her back. I am amazed to see poppies and cornflowers convulsed, shaken like field flowers under high wind or down sweep of sharp scythe. Something has been cut down, it lies gasping among those silver and rose-fish from a Japanese aquarium. 'Kora.' It is Kora lying there, gasping in her agony, among rose-fish and gold-fish that have now merged into one blur of shadow. In the shadow, the soft folds of chiffon stuff now lie still.

I stoop. I lift her up, a drowned girl from the water.

'But Kora darling, love is always like that.' I have lain her on the couch, smoothed the poppies round her, kissed her. 'But Kora darling . . .' I am puzzled. Kora has been married ten years, has twice been a mother. I cannot imagine what has hurt her. I go back to Larry. I remember what Larry said of Jeanette, 'her husband is that sort of plough-boy who lies heavy on a woman.' I didn't understand. It occurred then to me that men were like that but they were plough-boys, they precisely were not gentle-men. It had never occurred to me that such things happened among ordinary even presentable sort of people. I tried to explain, tried to keep her quiet, stop her gasping, stop her endlessly, endlessly repeating, 'it wouldn't have mattered all the hideous mutilation, if just once, just once, I had known – this.'

*

We had the padrone's niece bring the tray upstairs again. Kora explained in the sort of French we talk here, 'Monsieur is tired out,' vaguely indicating papers, profusion of books and note-books, 'writing.' My writing has been a symbol and a myth. We hold to it; I am writing. I will not have invalidism thrust on me but it is Kora does the writing. She had straightened the couch cover, flung down books there and her note-books. She has neglected the cushions, re-covered with some of her stuff from London. There was a print in the dull gold one, like a marble head in velvet. I found myself surreptitiously smoothing over that print of Kora's heavy small stone head. The heavy stone head and the various bits of marble, foot, hand and severed torso had been re-assembled. Kora had gone to bits; it seemed as if each separate bit of her, had needed re-adjustment, as if I must say over and over, to hand, to thigh, to line of tortured eye-brows, 'it's all right. Love is this.' I had not kissed her, after that first kiss of my condonation as I smoothed red poppy-heads about her. I condoned not this present lapse but the fact that, till now, she had astonishingly hidden the fact that she had not loved me. I had simply thought her proud and reserved. I remembered Jeanette saying, 'I never gave myself to anyone but Larry.' At that time, I had considered Jean infallible, a woman older even than was Larry. I had taken Jean and Larry as final court of appeal, in the sheer technique of loving, and with final severance, my own bruised being had accepted things as they were. Looking at Kora, as she sat with the circles from the lampshade, dramatically, insisting that the earring and the chin were an anomaly, I realised that, but for Larry, I might have gone on . . . not understanding anything. I realised that my odd dissociation had left me free and that the ten years were not wasted. I said, 'Kora, that jade earring doesn't go with pre-fifth Attica.'

Her hand went up to her ear. She looked at me across a space of white cloth. On the cloth, arranged out of a Flemish gallery, were two tumblers with bulbous cups, with stocky-rooted stems and solid bases. One tumbler lay at my right, one placed exactly, like the Grail, in front of Kora. 'Take, eat,' I said, and shoved the flat plaque toward her. Tonight, it held a pseudo mondaine assortment of 'town' fruit, bananas, of all things, and some oranges. I said, 'what has happened to the cherries?' and Kora answered, 'I imagine they think we like change. We had cherries last night, and we had cherries at noon.' 'I seem to disbelieve in those bananas, they strike some wrong note. It reminds me of a restaurant in Soho where I once took Jeanette after we'd seen off Larry.' Now when I say Jeanette, Larry, I am one with them, we are of one age, there are four of us here. I do not say, 'Larry' now with that back-fire of resentment. I see mother sitting far off; she should be an American mother, from the back of a magazine, sitting in a rocking chair. I say, 'I seem to be American. I see mother in a rocking chair.' Then I see Kora as something flagrant herself, out of a bright painted advertisement, as she lifts the flat plaque and calls through the open door in the sort of French we talk here, 'Hedweg, Monsieur would like again the cherries.' Hedweg comes back with cherries, a marionette pulled in on a wire. She takes the bananas, does not seem perturbed about it. She probably herself, for a change, would like bananas.

I say, 'Kora, you started some time back, before you drew the curtains, while you were running flat elastic in your knickers, to give me one of your admirable treatments.' It is as if I had flicked a little whip in her face. I had not meant to be ironical. Something in one, instinct of defence, protection, incredibly stupid habit, made that tone flick in her face. I had not meant to be ironical, had not really linked up that Kora yet with this one. Seeing her, with her half-emptied goblet, a Grail, before her, I had not thought that anything I could say would now seem incongruous to her. It seemed now that Kora had second sight but Kora had not. I expected her to see through my remarks as I myself see through them.

Ka, it appeared however, still belongs to Helforth, his personal little dragon; it seemed, with the assistance of this personal little pest, that I could see around and, as it were, through walls and into tree trunks. I could see through the wall behind Kora and I saw Kora sitting in a Florentine frame, her head encompassed with an aura of lilies. I saw Kora then just as the Kore-Persephone and I realised that I too have proper affinity with her. I see that all this turn of chin and inapposite jade earrings, belonging to this minute, to me and post-war Kora and to dead Larry. Larry was dead, dead, dead, wail O Adonis, but Larry wasn't that youth. Larry was the young Dionysus, tramped to filth with the sacrificial entrails of dead mules, likewise slain for the whole world's atonement and the horror that had so often rasped me at the thought of those Alsatian dogs that ran, for their young Saxon masters, straight into the Allies' gunfire, was appeased strangely. 'Dogs and horses, Kora,' I said 'and Larry.'

I could feel Ka across my forehead like a hand placed there. I saw the Grail, I saw Kore-Persephone, I saw goblets out of a Venetian gallery and fruit now off a Flemish platter. I saw the planes of the wall, like the perspective in Tintoretto, and I saw red fire and incense across an altar. I said, 'that day, I ran across you, Kora, I saw incense across an altar. It was one of those red braziers, you know, they melt tar in . . . You had a fur like a caterpillar. You had on a green hat.' Kora looked up, reduced now to a portrait, in a subsidiary French room, in an art gallery. With a cherry between her teeth, she had, at that moment, a somewhat blatant prettiness; now she is French. Her cheeks are brushed with rose, her eyes are French-blue, exaggerated with soft shadow. Kora says, 'it wasn't a green hat but a grey one.'

I am willing to admit, now, that it was a grey one. Admitting even that technically the hat had been green, it must have been in that mist and underground etched-in sort of city, smudged in with so dull a green smear that, for process of today's comparison, it might have been grey. I see Kora now standing, by the sooty iron railings, and a tree etched above her with metallic outline and the smoke, from beyond, mingling with the grey mist. I realise one tone, no mist can smudge out, I remember the fire embers of that brazier, as promise of a fire that had not then sprung between us. We were Kora of the Underworld and Dionysus, not yet risen. I was then Larry and those others had no place then in any living landscape. Now we are Kora and the slain God . . . risen.

FRANCES GREGG
MALE AND FEMALE

Jennie Stowski was an American, despite her odd name, which was Russian Jew in origin. Her eyes were blue and with a dark intensity of gaze that made them remarkable when her imagination was stirred by an idea, or a person. She was very slender and beautifully modelled, and bore herself with that superb arrogance that is the heritage of the North American Indian to American women. She walked, too, with a long-limbed Indian stride, from the hips, deliberately aping the carriage ascribed to royalty, in as far as she was able. Believing that no one would ever choose her as a wife, a belief which her mother had nurtured in her, she loudly acclaimed that she disliked all men and never intended to marry. There was about her, however, a touch of something both neurotic, and exotic, that made her women friends regard her with envy, suspicion and a deep-rooted, if blind, jealousy. Somehow they knew that she was not 'good', in their sense of being suppressed, nice women, but also they recognised something bold and clean and fierce that commanded their respect but, oddly enough, made them hate her more deeply. It expressed itself in their casting her always in male roles in their amateur plays, and in excluding her from their more intimate conversations. This brought her no regrets for, of all the long list of things that horrified her in life, the conversation of women alone headed the list. Their sex confidences filled her with physical nausea when they came her way; their humour was more secret and sickly, and their awful state of unfulfilled desire terrible to her. She had read Freud so

210

that, long before she had an accurate physical understanding of the mechanism of sex, she was its enemy.

Her first love was an art student, Kiah. He had just won an endowment for study abroad. This very beautiful and spectacular youth was not only affianced to her best friend, but he was just going abroad to 'become the greatest painter since Leonardo', as he modestly put it. His blague was American and only skin deep. He was a good painter and he had the guts to make himself a better one, but his head was swollen with the conquests of many ladies that his beauty brought him, and his heart swollen with pity for the many ladies who were doomed to love him fruitlessly. 'And at that,' he said magnanimously, 'it needn't be so fruitless. They can all have kids if they can support them.'

Jennie loved her friend Sheila with a tender, wild, adoring passion. Sheila was beautiful, Sheila was gifted as she, Jennie, never would be. Sheila called her 'Jane' and told her that she was unique, a Greek-throwback, too fine, too exquisite for her coarse American compatriots. They spent long hours of the night explaining to each other how different they were from their fellows, and faced dewy dawns in exaltation at their own poetic maunderings, taking the rising sun, which rose stodgily and efficiently on all other dawns, as a sign, a symbol, a confirmation of their being set apart from the world.

'If only life will spare you, my little Jane,' murmured Sheila, warm lips mouthing her friend's slightly hollow cheek, 'spare you the torment and the ecstasy of love . . . of love such as I have known.' Jennie did not recognise this, then, as a wish, on the part of a jealous female friend, that she should be left on the shelf.

'I shall never love anyone but you!' she promised fervently, and moved a little restlessly away from her friend's kisses. In their girlish love-making she preferred to be the lover, rather than the loved. Being caressed made her uncomfortable. 'I can't imagine loving a man . . . not *that* way', she added, wondering, as always, what exactly 'that way' was.

'Of course, you couldn't dear, and that is why I am taking you with me to his house over the weekend. I know that I can trust you, and mamma won't let me go alone. It will be all right if you are there. You don't need to do anything. I will lend you my Peer Gynt to read.'

'Mamma won't let me stay overnight. You know that.'

'Yes, I thought of that,' Sheila replied smoothly. 'We just won't tell her. We will say that we are going for supper, and then we will miss the last trolley and not be able to get back.' They beamed at each other.

'What shall I wear?'

'What does it matter? This is *my* party, my sweet Jane.'

Very faintly, something like rebellion was born in Jennie's breast. She had not a pretty dress of her own, but her cousin had a blue frock that she could borrow, and in which, with its simple lines and full skirt, and lovely colour, she had found herself attractive when, unbeknown to its owner, she had tried it on. She had discovered something else too. Her pretty cousin coloured her lips, and faintly blued her eyelids. Jennie had none of the paraphernalia of decoration, but there was a favourite penny sweet in a red paper that came off scarlet upon one's lips if it got moist. She procured several of these sweets and tore the paper into small squares. There was a hollow place between her young breasts where she could hide a little store of these scarlet squares if she went to this party of Sheila's.

'What *are* you thinking?' demanded Sheila, 'your eyes are like stars, almost stary, and I don't mean starry,' she ended unkindly and a little pettishly; and Jennie thought 'She doesn't really mean "stary", and tried to get a glimpse of her own eyes in the mirror that reflected a flowering pear tree silhouetted against a rosy-golden dawn, and their two small heads, like a sweet medallion. Sheila, knowing herself observed, held the pose for several minutes.

'If she only knew,' Jennie thought to herself, 'I'm really trying to see me. Sheila looks awfully yellow in this light, and I'm cold.'

'Isn't the pear tree lovely?' she said aloud, a bit lamely.

'It is not the first time that I have seen the dawn like a golden rain falling through those starred branches. Ah, that was "a dawn that came too soon." You understand me, don't you, little Jennie? I was with . . . him.'

'It was awfully near the house, wasn't it?' Jennie muttered captiously; knowing from the tone that Sheila spoke of the forbidden.

Sheila looked at her with momentary suspicion. Sometimes Jennie smiled at the wrong moment; but she was reassured by the frowning face. 'Parents sleep deeply,' she said cryptically, then gave a little trill of laughter, sweet as a bird, liquid as water. 'But now my little Jennie is all puzzled. Wait . . . wait . . . she shall have a dawn all on her own . . . some day,' she promised with a wounding lack of conviction.

'Oh, keep your old dawn,' fretted Jennie, 'Let's go to bed. There will be parents in bathrobes all over the place in another half hour.'

The two girls tiptoed and giggled and dropped hairbrushes and got themselves disarrayed of a multitude of thin lawn garments threaded through with many yards of pink and blue baby ribbon. And Jennie's last wistful thought was 'I wish I knew exactly what it was the dawn came too soon about.'

When the day came, Jennie, with her reddened lips and borrowed finery, felt pleased with herself, till she saw Sheila. Sheila had a hat with masses of small flowers, and knots and knots and knots of narrow green velvet. Her frock, of oyster coloured shantung, hung like a Greek robe, and in her hands she carried a little woven basket that she had filled with the shy, faint pink blossoms of the trailing arbutus.

'You look perfectly lovely,' said Jennie with angry sincerity.

And, 'you are wearing a very pretty frock,' accused Sheila in response.

There was nothing else to do except quarrel openly, or be silent, so, in silence, they boarded the trolley, and were carried through the streets, then through dusty lanes till they reached the crossroads; from there, Sheila led the way by a short cut across a meadow.

Hezekiah Waite had shortened his truly awful name to 'Kiah', which startled and interested people and gave him the chance of adding to the legend about himself that he was painstakingly building up. It was before the days of 'publicity', but Kiah had invented the technique of a personal publicity that was working like a dream. He had managed to get himself recognised on both sides of the Atlantic, though still – officially – a student. Painters and authors alike were agog to see what that bumptious, ridiculous, exciting and beautiful youth from the States would do next. He could paint and he had something to say; how deep, how profound, time alone would show. At the moment it was original enough to have the making of a new cult, a new school. Kiah was well launched with a number of new loves. His only anxiety was just how to be off with the old. Sheila had a strong will, but more tricky to handle was the tie of his own affection and an old fealty to Sheila. That was where Jennie came in.

As the two girls approached the house, Kiah came out to stand in the porch with a friend, another six-footer with fair hair. Their silk shirts were of pastel tints, their ties were flowing, their hips were swathed in multi-coloured scarves, and their netherlimbs were encased in white flannel. As the day advanced and fell to a cool evening Kiah and his friend added to this get up velvet jackets of soft and lustrous black.

Jennie looked at Kiah and her heart left her breast and soared on uncertain wings, above his gold curls. He was the first man to whom she had spoken as youth to youth. Now, she held back, letting Sheila with her flowery hat and little basket advance with long swathed strides.

The house sat low and squat and comfortable and established, the centre of emerald lawns, not yet burned by the tropical sun of the summer, and amid straggling patches of strawberries, thorn-spikes of raspberry canes and purple and white iris rearing their lovely heads from hearts of fern. The sun was thin and piercing, but already warm. The plum trees had white stars upon their black branches, and pear and apple were a dream of snow and rose. The grass was sprinkled with the tight, heart-purple bells of the wild hyacinth. Jennie hung back and Kiah's eyes sought hers over Sheila's head.

Kiah's mother came out, pretty as any porcelain lady. She did not like Jennie and she did not like Sheila, and was rude in a brittle, pretty, ladylike way. Jennie noted that Sheila was used to this.

Kiah's father came out and he was large and bluff and faintly bewildered between his gifted son, and his pretty wife, but he liked good-looking girls on his own account, and peered with hopeful, small, bright blue eyes over his wife's head. And he fixed his eyes upon Jennie. So Sheila turned to the six-foot fair young friend of Kiah.

'I have been talking to your mother on the phone,' Kiah's mother said to Sheila. 'We have our little motherly secrets, you know.'

Sheila smiled with set lips.

'And,' Mrs. Waite went on unkindly, 'I promised her not to let you out of my sight.'

Jennie was parked in a cool room that slipped out of doors on its own through long French windows. It was dim, with dark polished floor, a huge dark piano, and the sweet alien gold of old Venetian mirrors. The windows made a frame for Sheila

215

who was staining her fingers in the strawberry patch, between the two men, and taking huge berries dropped into her mouth, first by one and then by the other, with much laughter and pretty pretty ways. Jennie longed for some of the strawberries.

'Where is that little bluebird?' In came Kiah's father with strawberries in a huge leaf. After she had eaten them, he showed her a book of birds. Jennie thought him very good and, of course, a little silly, and much too old and rather fat, but otherwise she liked him. She knew that she could never, never like Kiah's mother, which did not matter as she was never to see her again.

Supper over, Kiah asked Jennie if she would like to see cherry blossoms in the moonlight. Jennie could hardly believe her ears. Did she want to see cherry blossoms in the moonlight, *she*! She looked at Sheila with fear and trembling but Sheila was deeply involved with her new acquisition. Ignoring their company, Sheila and the fair young man rose and floated from the room. Jennie rose and did her best to float from the room too. Her heart pounded and her sight was blurred. She ran full tilt into the lintel of the door. Kiah gazed at her with tolerant eyes.

'It's all right,' he reassured her. She was far from being the first girl who had gone blind from desire when looked upon kindly by him. 'You have stepped backwards out of Time, a Vestal Virgin, used to the spaces of the Temple. You can't get used to doors.' Which was nonsense, for Jennie had passed all her days in a three-bedroom brick box with narrow corridors and dark stairs, and was used to negotiating mean space. 'I might paint you that way. Yes, there is no doubt that you are faintly lovely . . . in this light. But no, there is too much commissioned stuff waiting me. Nothing would induce me to boast, or to blow my own horn – trust the pater for doing that – but I should just like you to know that I am the greatest painter of my generation. I feel that you should know, that it is

216

due to you. You are different, finer, more perceptive than these crude Americans. You are foreign, aren't you?'

'Only the name. My father's great-grandfather, or something was a Russian.' Jennie suppressed the Jew, and then thought better of it. Sheila knew and Sheila would tell. 'He was a Jew, terribly persecuted, and . . .' Jennie searched her mind for marvel, '. . . and poetic,' she fabricated. The man had been a shoe-maker.

'That's it, of course. Jew . . . Jew, yes, it gives you distinction. I, too, am very perceptive. They say that it accounts for the unique quality of my paintings. I have something of the almost occult insight of El Greco; indeed the critics say that I have more of it than he. But I derive more from Michelangelo and Leonardo than from the Spanish – if a genius as original as mine can be said to "derive" from anything . . .'

Jennie listened to a great deal of this for the next two hours; and it was not a minute too long. He was so beautiful, slipping, in flannels and silk, through the shadowy moonlit spaces of the soft spring night. The air was full of the faint scent of the flowering fruit trees, the moon was obligingly large, blatantly romantic. It climbed the heavens with so sweet a scintillation. Jennie was all astray. Could it be she to whom this vision of male youth was describing the wonders of his personality, genius, and beauty, as ascribed to by his friends, family, the public, and, of course, himself? When they stopped in the moonlight and she looked up at him her heart hurt with the beauty of his appearance. The overlong gold curls stood away from the broad brow, gleaming in the moonlight, like an aureole, like a halo. The eyes were dark, faintly glinting sockets. The lips were darkly infolded with an effect of grief. The words that she disregarded were a blather of vanity and nonsense.

Jennie shivered slightly.

'Cold?' Kiah asked, tenderly, protectingly.

'No, someone walked over my grave.' Jennie answered. And

indeed a grave had yawned before her. She was in love with this youth, this beautiful youth, about whom she was not in the least deceived. He did not love her, would never love her, and she would never love anyone else. He was not worth it, but she could not help herself. So spoke her shrewd, honest, knowledgable soul, while the sentimental girl that she was acted Guinevere to his Lancelot in all good faith. Being a woman she could, at one and the same time, know the truth, and believe utter nonsense, and be no whit confused or disturbed. 'We must go in. Look how small and high the moon is now. It was hanging just back of that tree when we first came out.'

They turned back through the long damp grass. 'You'll catch your death of cold,' muttered Jennie's mother from some dark recess of Jennie's brain. The house sat back, the spectral ghost of itself, the gold of window and door competing badly with the silvered night. 'Almost over, almost over, almost over,' sang Jennie's heart, lorn as a nightingale. She was conscious of something, indefinable, like a drumming of the night, or her blood, something ethereal and potent that had to do with the youth and herself, something that she knew but could not quite remember, and could never forget.

In the silent hall, under the mellow indoor light, Kiah looked down upon Jennie with tender benevolence, and no pity at all, and from sentiment, from idleness, from delicious sense of power, he lifted her cold little night-bedewed hand and kissed it. The world rocked to a standstill. The heavens opened and angels sang. Jennie could bear no more. She turned and fled up the stairs to the room that she was to share with Sheila.

Why it should have been faintly borne in upon her that Hezekiah and his mother stood in some unity, and that not a noble one, against the father, and that Hezekiah was a spoiled, silly, and unreliable young man, only the gods of women could tell.

Jennie was feeling cold, stiff, very, very sad and full of marvel, but slightly silly herself. Even young knees feel the ridges in the floor if knelt upon long enough. But having pitched headlong into her role, and being young, she had not the nerve to be ridiculous in her own eyes, cast off the pose, get up, and get herself sensibly to bed. She wished that Sheila would come and release her with dignity and honour. But Sheila did not come. The night grew colder.

Downstairs sounded colloquy. 'Does Sheila mean to stay out *all* night?' That was Mrs. Waite. 'H'm, humph, grumf.' That was Mr. Waite. 'Oh, well, mother, have a heart.' That was . . . Kiah. The name was ventured upon in the solitude of her soul where herself spied upon all her capers. 'Perhaps he's converting her.' Mr. Waite, laughing at his own joke. 'Well, clergyman or no clergyman, Englishman or no Englishman, I'm going to ring the cowbell.'

A wild jangling splintered through the night, spangling against the flowering trees, and 'Sheila . . . Sheila . . . Sheila . . .' the name was sent forth to summon back the erring girl. 'Aloysius . . . Sheila . . . Sheila . . . Aloysius.' The night took shape and Sheila and her companion approached the house, a sedate two feet of bright space between them. Goodnights were said. Jennie's vigil was over. Sheila gathered the cold little fool into her arms, warmed her hands in her warm breast, called them 'her birds'. They exchanged no confidences, asked no questions. They were cold, disappointed women whom something had taunted and evaded, and they were hiding for all they were worth. At the same time their love for each other was quite genuine, and very deep. 'Sleep in my bed,' murmured Sheila, and they slept in each other's arms.

In the morning Jennie peeped timidly over the edge of her eyelids at the situation and the actors concerned. She stared resentfully at Kiah's fair friend, Aloysius, eating hugely and with great solemnity, oblivious to everything except his food. She would not have recognized him had she met him. He had neither face, character, nor aspect.

At home, Jennie faced her mother. 'I would do anything,' she spoke ungagedly, 'for him, give him anything. He is a very great artist.' Her mother's eyes raked the vibrant young body posed in its heroics before her, and the mother's eyes sank before her child's innocent, witless gaze.

The next day, Kiah called. He and Jennie walked in the park together. He came back to the house. They sat on the great horsehair sofa together, but not side by side. She wanted him to kiss her. He made no move to do it, and Jennie wondered if she ought to be the one to suggest it, but decided not. Waves of deep childish regret surged through her. The tears were very near. They stung the back of her eyes, and tickled in her nose. She was afraid that she was going to sneeze. She fumbled in the breast of her frock. Kiah watched her with suddenly intent eyes. Oh, if she only knew a little more; if only she could read what faces said, or even understand the words of women. She dragged out the crumpled little wad of handkerchief and rubbed her nose hard. Then he laughed, a funny, choked chuckling. The atmosphere of the room changed. She was on the threshold once more. He rose and drew her up by her hands, and then – just when she thought, when she was sure that his lips would be upon hers, he caught her up in his arms, swung her off the floor, as though she had been a child, and held her high in the air against his breast. She kicked indignant feet, as affronted as she might have been ten years earlier.

'Now, I am heavy!' she cried, half laughing, half annoyed.

'S-s-sh' he warned her, 'those are the things you must not say.'

Oh bother!' Jennie answered crossly, 'there oughtn't to be things one can't say. Besides, why not?'

Kiah kissed her suddenly, roughly, with hard, vehement greed. He put her on her feet and sat down on the sofa in front of her.

He was breathing as though he had been running hard. Jennie watched him curiously, her good temper restored, waiting to see what would happen next. Kiah's fair, beautiful face flushed darkly. His small blue eyes grew smaller and full of a kind of hatred. 'It's all right for you women. You are all alike . . .' Astoundingly he was blazing with passion. His eyes queried hers furiously. He stood up. 'Damn it all, it's all right for you . . . you can – Have you never learnt? Don't you know anything? Is it ignorance or devilry? – or don't you know I – No! You don't know. Nor do I. Goodbye!' He left. Jennie was too excited and amazed to be angry. What did it mean, oh what did it mean? Something had to be done about all this. Why had such a godlike being become so ridiculous? She sat down and began to outline her campaign. There was no one to marry her. There was no one to make love to her . . . unless . . . except . . .

Among Jennie's friends there was a sweet, harmless girl called Gillian. And Gillian had a lover, Walter. The two called each other 'dear' in public, and took each other for granted, in a gentle bovine way. Something might be done there. Walter was a charming young man, rich and dark in appearance, with a pretty wit, and a fine solid mind. Jennie, brooding darkly, her pink frock wide about her, looking pretty against the shining black of the sofa, made no plans – in words – but she had decided that Walter must be hers, for a time, for a season, until at any rate, she knew as much as Sheila. It was not Walter for whom she was angling, nor was it Kiah. It was something far stranger, far more mysterious, than any single person, even a person as fantastically exquisite and desirable as Kiah. It might be 'love' that she sought, but if it was love, it was something far more incredible, more mysterious, more awe-inspiring than anything that Sheila had talked about. 'I am different,' she whispered to herself. 'I know more than these people. Why Sheila is not much more than a plant, a plant that likes the sun and turns towards it, but she doesn't know why. She doesn't

221

even know that there is something to know. But I do. I am wonderful. I know . . .' but her exaltation flagged. She knew so little. She was so little desirable. She saw herself beating her way through life, like a small ship floundering in high waves. No one would ever want her, and this mystery that she had surprised, this miracle that she surmised, how would she ever find someone to open the portal for her . . . 'Male and female created He them.' She understood. There were two, and only two might find God. That was what the world was about. They thought that they fell in love with each other, but it was something else, something different. All those people who set their hearts upon one man, one woman, why was that? She knew, and yet could not fathom the thing. Kiah, for instance, was the almost perfect way for her. The sad, infolded lips were the perfect way, but there was so much else besides in which she had no part – the quick small eyes, the plump cheeks, the slightly blobby nose that knew its way about life, the bouncy, complacent spirit – why all the man, almost, was alien to her, but some one thing, something infinitely beautiful summoned her to a secret casement where they might look upon life together. Oh, there would never be anyone else like him. He was her only chance, and she could not have him. Her own sobs startled her, and brought her mother hurrying from the passage, from where she had been an interested and apprehensive observer of all that had passed between her daughter and her quasi-lover.

Jennie later telephoned Walter to ask him to return a book she had lent him.

In the evening, Jennie folded the pink frock and put it aside like a cerement, or a winding sheet. She chose a different frock to meet Walter in. He was coming at eight o'clock. Her long, still childish arms were bare, and the frock had a low neck. Her twining, creeper-like brain had imbibed some information from the absurd episode with Kiah.

It was easier than she had supposed to get Walter to kiss her.

To be sure, afterwards, he talked to her long and boringly of the girl from whom she had stolen him, for it was a steal, and she had no intention of letting him go. She even had a sense of doing a good deed. He was young. It seemed a pity that he should be so very domesticated and settled into husband-like ways. No one was ever going to call her 'dear', and find her matter-of-course, and unexciting. She wasn't even going to be good. She might be ignorant, but Sheila should see, and so should Kiah . . .

'What's the matter?' whispered Walter, his lips against her soft, thin hair, 'Are you sorry you kissed me?'

'I didn't!' wailed Jennie.

'You did. You most certainly did. But I forgive you. Really, I'm glad. It waked me up. I think that I was drifting . . . not that I don't mean to be faithful to my girl. I do. But I think this will do us both good. I understand a lot more than you think. It's that painter fellow, isn't it?'

'Oh, Walter, I'm so unhappy.' Jennie wailed now in earnest. She was hugely surprised at being seen through, and used her tears to cover her embarrassment, and to give herself a little time to see her way.

'I certainly never saw anyone who wanted to be kissed more than you did tonight,' Walter agreed with her.

'I hate you!' raged Jennie.

'I don't see any reason for hating a fellow for telling the truth. Truth's interesting. As a matter of fact, its the most interesting thing there is. Now take your wanting me to kiss you tonight . . .'

'Oh, well, I did then!' Jennie blazed at him. 'And shut up and do it again!'

Walter drew the slight figure nearer to his own, located her mouth with the gaze of a scientist, got his stance and kissed Jennie methodically. Then he gathered up his gloves and umbrella and turned a little sadly towards the door. He looked

223

at her with troubled, beautiful eyes. 'What's all this story Sheila is telling about your not coming home one night?'

'Sheila?'

'Yes.'

'I was with her.'

'That does not surprise me a bit. I have a great understanding of women. There is more to the story. It seems you didn't sleep in your own bed that night.'

'Well what does it matter if I didn't?'

'Look, Jennie, beds are where people make love to each other, and there was the painter fellow, and that Aloysius chap . . .'

'Aloysius? Oh, him, Kiah's English friend? I don't even know what he looked like . . .'

'Jennie. You are not quite a moron. You must know what he looked like.'

'Well, I do, now. But I seem only just to be seeing him. He was long and had sort of angles, and his hair was red, not red exactly, auburn; and he had a fair skin with a lot of colour in his cheeks, but he wasn't ruddy or anything like that. When he talked he didn't bellow exactly but it was rather like the dinner gong. He wore glasses and . . .'

'All right, Jennie, all right. I believe you. You didn't sleep with Aloysius.'

'Aloysius? But of course not. I slept with Sheila, in her bed.'

'Dear me, Jennie, you must have treated that poor girl very badly.'

'Well, I like that! She's the one that is telling lies about me!'

'But, why, Jennie, why? What did you do to her? It is very pathetic when women begin lying about each other . . .'

'Oh, do go home. You make me tired. I think Sheila can look after herself well enough, without you . . .'

'You don't understand. You see, if I am to sacrifice so much to you, this kissing and all that, I want to feel that you're a good girl.'

Jennie began to laugh. The tears dried on her cheeks. 'But I don't want to be a good girl, that's just it. And I don't see what Sheila is up to.'

'Nor do I. She'd be an awful fool if she thinks that Kiah is interested in you . . .'

'But he is. He kissed me . . . you don't know what kissing is, not really . . . he kissed me, I tell you . . .'

'But my dear child, Kiah would kiss a giraffe, you must know that.'

She did. No one knew it better. 'Perhaps Sheila doesn't know it.'

'Sheila is a very clever woman. No, it's not that. Maybe she wants to marry Aloysius.'

'Aloysius? Aloysius!' Jennie's second essay of the name came with such éclat that Walter looked down at her in surprise.

'Now, Jennie,' he admonished her, 'have a heart. Give the poor fellow a chance. Don't go and make a decision about him tonight. You're not yourself . . .'

'Aloysius!' Jennie was radiant. She had found her way.

*

Aloysius Darrell was not happy in America. He was seriously thinking of getting his mother to come out and join him. He had had a technique for living – living comfortably that is – that was failing him in these new surroundings. By blind, bland, infantile cunning he had always been able to get everything done for him almost without asking. His morning peevishness, too, had been well catered to. His mother always wept at breakfast, nice wet snively weeping that did a son's heart good to hear, while she nibbled her toast, drank two huge cups of coffee, and consumed morsels of cold ham that she shaved off the solid pink and fat, with greedy parsimony. He himself always ate hugely in large, well-masticated mouthfuls, taking occasion from time to time to ring the bell and bring in their one long-suffering maid to reheat the coffee, produce a second butter knife for the one he had adroitly hidden, pull the curtains back by a fraction of an inch, or, if invention failed him, there was always the replenishing of the fire. It was essential to his digestive processes to know that Hester was certainly weeping and flouncing in the kitchen. These had been his morning tactics since he was eight, and habits are hard to break.

Habits, yes that was it. They were his habits that were now disrupting his life. They were all good habits, so he blamed the country. At home he was used to climbing out from under a huge mountain of thick, weighty blankets, missing the minute rug by his bedside, feeling about on cold polished wood for his slippers, thrusting soberly pyjamad arms into a thick dressing gown, baring his breast to the blast and, standing by his window, breathing deeply and methodically of his raw, damp fog blowing in by gobbets and wisps from his East Anglian seacoast. After that he squatted in two inches of hot water in the bottom of the bathtub, meticulously soaping his body in carefully circumscribed areas, and then sluicing off the soap in jugs and jugs of cold water. There had been a time when Hester had had to carry these jugs up the back stairs, and along the corridor to his room, and he could always ring for one more when she thought she had finished. These happy days were over since his mother had installed a bath at the Vicarage. Still a lot could be done in the way of running off the hot water before his mother got to the bath. And after that came the breakfast, tears, lovely marmalade which he ate with his eyes closed, nipping up the scraping in the dish just before his mother put out a timid hand to save it from Hester herself. After that, another ceremony, a pipe, and all was well.

It can easily be understood that Aloysius had always looked upon the morning as his best and happiest period. He was 'one of those people' he assured his friends and congregations 'who always rose to a new day, a new man, prepared to enjoy life, to make the most of anything.'

Aloysius was thirty. He was without those little amusements so easily procurable at home. He was ripe for any folly. There had been a faintly pleasant episode with Kiah's girl, but these American girls impressed him as thin-blooded and terrifically sure of themselves. He explained this to Kiah, apologising for not having made a better job for his half-night out with Sheila.

'There is a time for poetry and nature, and all that, and – ' Aloysius shuddered in retrospect, 'there is a place for love, but to my mind it is not a wintry meadow with a moon blazing out at the most inopportune moments.'

'You stayed long enough anyway, considering she was my girl.' Kiah, having laid the train, had hoped for the best.

'She wouldn't come back,' replied Aloysius simply.

Kiah's hopeful look gave way to despair. 'Then she isn't your type?'

'No. No, my dear friend. I don't like them so tall.'

'And her friend?' It occurred to him that he ought to do someone a good turn with all of Aloysius at his disposal, a man obviously full ripe for marriage. He was far-sighted and Jennie, well and soundly married for a few years, might develop into something pleasant, useful, or a genius he could claim to have discovered.

'Her friend? Did she have a friend?'

'You know, blue frock and eyes all right, once she learns to use them.'

'Oh, that one. Oh, yes.' Aloysius smiled with disarming roguishness, sideways, under his lashes. 'More my line certainly.'

'I'll give you her address,' said Kiah. Aloysius called on Jennie. He called on her again several times.

Three weeks later, Kiah called, when Aloysius was not there.

'Look at it this way,' said Kiah to Jennie, taking the line of kind brutality, 'no man in his senses would marry a girl like you, with no money, and your mother and all that, even if you were, which you are not, a really sound sex proposition. You don't know enough, and you would expect too much. Sex is an art, like everything else. You learn your trade and then come back to me. Marry old Aloysius. He will tire of you in a year or two, and then there you are, good home, good income, and enough sex education to make you a fit playmate for me. I'm an artist. I'm a busy man. I don't mean to marry Sheila but she knows her stuff a thousand times better than you do. I educated her myself. As soon as she gets over this hare-brained mania for marriage and respectability, I'll go on with her education. Sex is necessary to me as an artist.' He was suddenly arrested in full flight. Jennie had interrupted. Kiah looked at her in indignation.

'That,' Jennie was saying, 'is the first sensible word you have said — sex — and that wasn't your word, not your idea. Life knew some things even before you did — '

'Well, just let me tell you this. You will have to lose that habit of interrupting if you are thinking of marrying Aloysius.'

'I am thinking of marrying Aloysius. Though I think it's a mean thing to do, like marrying a baby. Only, of course, someone will marry him if I don't.'

'Don't be so sure that you have him.'

'Why not? He asked me two days ago. We are being married and I'm going with him to England at the end of the month.'

For the first time, something like respect dawned in Kiah's face. He spoke to her as an equal.

'I say, I didn't understand. You're ... you're ...' Words failed him. 'And Aloysius. He talked as though he hardly had noticed you.'

'You don't understand the English,' Jennie answered with superb arrogance.

'Jennie ... Jennie,' Kiah was ardent, disturbed, 'look here ... you're too fine for Aloysius. Jennie ... we could have a child. Look, a son ... Jennie, there is no one like you. I could not let myself go before, but now that you've fixed it up with old Aloysius ... Jennie ...'

228

Jennie stared at him coldly. 'Believe it or not, but I mean to be faithful to my husband.'

'Jennie,' Kiah was awestruck. 'You are the first woman who has ever refused me anything. You can't mean it?'

'Can't I just! And I'll tell you another thing. You don't know anything about sex . . . or love . . . or me . . . or anything.'

Kiah mumbled her tear-salt lips, kissed her closed eyes, caressed her wildly and indiscreetly.

'And W-w-walter knows more about making love than you do.' Jennie sobbed at him.

Kiah's arms fell away from her. 'Who the devil is Walter? I thought . . . Good God, four weeks ago you shut your mouth to be kissed . . . Say, what is this . . . No girl ever put it over on me. Four weeks ago, I would have staked my soul, you had never been kissed . . .'

'Oh!' howled Jennie, 'You haven't got a soul and I hate you. I hate Sheila too. You are stupid and cruel, both of you. I hope you marry each other. I do. It's a horrid, beastly world, and nobody knows anything about sex except me . . . and I don't know it yet. B-b-but I will. I will!'

'I'll say you will,' agreed Kiah with a look that blent awe with detestation. 'You're no woman. You're a spying spinster, that's what you are.'

Jennie giggled suddenly through her tears. 'That almost makes sense.' She scrubbed her eyes dry with a handkerchief, but she did not, this time, draw out a crumpled little wad from between her breasts, 'I suppose even you can't be a fool all the time,' she said in a small, polite voice.

Kiah mashed his hat on the back of his head, sat, teetering a moment on hands clasped upon the head of his cane, and stared at her. 'God help Aloysius!' he said at last, and left the house, and Jennie's life, forever.

BRYHER
EXTRACT

Is anything sweet as death? Spice, lily, peachflower? Is any touch flame as the lips of death, fire of light, fire of the earth?

You are the swift welcome of a body. You are the passionate Aphrodite of the poppies.

It is no use pretending; I hate it all, all of it. I want Tyre, Carthage, Athens; I want the age that has never been known in the world.

Is there anything in the world sweet as your white lips, Death?

I have loved life as no other. I have loved it as the warrior that is *life* and so throws it away. Take the light, flame, fire of my limbs but I ask at the end

'Is anything sweet save death?'

Love is a poppy. There are dreams, seeds of the poppy. Beauty is slash of bud-scarlet in the green. But you are the soul of the flower . . . you are sleep.

Must bitterness drain all the colour from the saffron leaf before you come?

I – the liar – I that pretend I would fight and love – I ask at the end

'Is anything sweet save death!'

EDITH WHARTON
ROMAN FEVER

From the table at which they had been lunching two American ladies of ripe but well-cared-for middle age moved across the lofty terrace of the Roman restaurant and, leaning on its parapet, looked first at each other, and then down on the outspread glories of the Palatine and the Forum, with the same expression of vague but benevolent approval.

As they leaned there a girlish voice echoed up gaily from the stairs leading to the court below. 'Well, come along, then,' it cried, not to them but to an invisible companion, 'and let's leave the young things to their knitting'; and a voice as fresh laughed back: 'Oh, look here, Babs, not actually knitting – ' 'Well, I mean figuratively,' rejoined the first. 'After all, we haven't left our poor parents much else to do . . .' and at that point the turn of the stairs engulfed the dialogue.

The two ladies looked at each other again, this time with a tinge of smiling embarrassment, and the smaller and paler one shook her head and coloured slightly.

'Barbara!' she murmured, sending an unheard rebuke after the mocking voice in the stairway.

The other lady, who was fuller, and higher in colour, with a small determined nose supported by vigorous black eyebrows, gave a good-humoured laugh. 'That's what our daughters think of us!'

Her companion replied by a deprecating gesture. 'Not of us individually. We must remember that. It's just the collective modern idea of Mothers. And you see – ' Half guiltily she drew

from her handsomely mounted black hand-bag a twist of
crimson silk run through by two fine knitting needles. 'One
never knows,' she murmured. 'The new system has certainly
given us a good deal of time to kill; and sometimes I get tired
just looking – even at this.' Her gesture was now addressed to
the stupendous scene at their feet.

The dark lady laughed again, and they both relapsed upon
the view, contemplating it in silence, with a sort of diffused
serenity which might have been borrowed from the spring
effulgence of the Roman skies. The luncheon-hour was long
past, and the two had their end of the vast terrace to themselves.
At its opposite extremity a few groups, detained by a lingering
look at the outspread city, were gathering up guide-books and
fumbling for tips. The last of them scattered, and the two ladies
were alone on the air-washed height.

'Well, I don't see why we shouldn't just stay here,' said Mrs.
Slade, the lady of the high colour and energetic brows. Two
derelict basketchairs stood near, and she pushed them into the
angle of the parapet, and settled herself in one, her gaze upon
the Palatine. 'After all, it's still the most beautiful view in the
world.'

'It always will be, to me,' assented her friend Mrs. Ansley,
with so slight a stress on the 'me' that Mrs. Slade, though she
noticed it, wondered if it were not merely accidental, like the
random underlinings of old-fashioned letter-writers.

'Grace Ansley was always old-fashioned,' she thought; and
added aloud, with a retrospective smile: 'It's a view we've both
been familiar with for a good many years. When we first met
here we were younger than our girls are now. You remember?'

'Oh, yes, I remember,' murmured Mrs. Ansley, with the same
undefinable stress. – 'There's that head-waiter wondering,' she
interpolated. She was evidently far less sure than her companion
of herself and of her rights in the world.

'I'll cure him of wondering,' said Mrs. Slade, stretching her hand toward a bag as discreetly opulent-looking as Mrs. Ansley's. Signing to the head-waiter, she explained that she and her friend were old lovers of Rome, and would like to spend the end of the afternoon looking down on the view – that is, if it did not disturb the service? The head-waiter, bowing over her gratuity, assured her that the ladies were most welcome, and would be still more so if they would condescend to remain for dinner. A full moon night, they would remember . . .

Mrs. Slade's black brows drew together, as though references to the moon were out-of-place and even unwelcome. But she smiled away her frown as the head-waiter retreated. 'Well, why not? We might do worse. There's no knowing, I suppose, when the girls will be back. Do you even know back from *where*? I don't!'

Mrs. Ansley again coloured slightly. 'I think those young Italian aviators we met at the Embassy invited them to fly to Tarquinia for tea. I suppose they'll want to wait and fly back by moonlight.'

'Moonlight – moonlight! What a part it still plays. Do you suppose they're as sentimental as we were?'

'I've come to the conclusion that I don't in the least know what they are,' said Mrs. Ansley. 'And perhaps we didn't know much more about each other.'

'No, perhaps we didn't.'

Her friend gave her a shy glance. 'I never should have supposed you were sentimental, Alida.'

'Well, perhaps I wasn't.' Mrs. Slade drew her lids together in retrospect; and for a few moments the two ladies, who had been intimate since childhood, reflected how little they knew each other. Each one, of course, had a label ready to attach to the other's name; Mrs. Delphin Slade, for instance, would have told herself, or any one who asked her, that Mrs. Horace Ansley, twenty-five years ago, had been exquisitely lovely – no, you wouldn't believe it, would you? . . . though, of course, still charming, distinguished . . . Well, as a girl she had been exquisite; far more beautiful than her daughter, Barbara, though certainly Babs, according to the new standards at any rate, was more effective – had more *edge*, as they say. Funny where she got it, with those two nullities as parents. Yes; Horace Ansley was – well, just the duplicate of his wife. Museum specimens of old New York. Good-looking, irreproachable, exemplary. Mrs. Slade and Mrs. Ansley had lived opposite each other – actually as well as figuratively – for years. When the drawing-room curtains in No. 20 East 73rd Street were renewed, No. 23, across the way, was always aware of it. And of all the movings, buyings, travels, anniversaries, illnesses – the tame chronical of an estimable pair. Little of it escaped Mrs. Slade. But she had grown bored with it by the time her husband made his big *coup* in Wall Street, and when they bought in upper Park Avenue had already begun to think: 'I'd rather live opposite a speak-easy for a change; at least one might see it raided.' The idea of seeing Grace raided was so amusing that (before the move) she launched it at a woman's lunch. It made a hit, and went the rounds – she sometimes wondered if it had crossed the street, and reached Mrs. Ansley. She hoped not, but didn't much mind. Those were the days when respectability was at a discount, and it did the irreproachable no harm to laugh at them a little.

A few years later, and not many months apart, both ladies lost their husbands. There was an appropriate exchange of wreaths and condolences, and a brief renewal of intimacy in the half-shadow of their mourning; and now, after another interval, they had run across each other in Rome, at the same hotel, each of them the modest appendage of a salient daughter. The similarity of their lot had again drawn them together, lending itself to mild jokes, and the mutual confession that, if in old days it must have been tiring to 'keep up' with daughters, it was now, at times, a little dull not to.

No doubt, Mrs. Slade reflected, she felt her unemployment

more than poor Grace ever would. It was a big drop from being the wife of Delphin Slade to being his widow. She had always regarded herself (with a certain conjugal pride) as his equal in social gifts, as contributing her full share to the making of the exceptional couple they were: but the difference after his death was irremediable. As the wife of the famous corporation lawyer, always with an international case or two on hand, every day brought its exciting and unexpected obligation: the impromptu entertaining of eminent colleagues from abroad, the hurried dashes on legal business to London, Paris or Rome, where the entertaining was so handsomely reciprocated; the amusement of hearing in her wake: 'What, that handsome woman with the good clothes and the eyes is Mrs. Slade – *the* Slade's wife? Really? Generally the wives of celebrities are such frumps.'

Yes; being *the* Slade's widow was a dullish business after that. In living up to such a husband all her faculties had been engaged; now she had only her daughter to live up to, for the son who seemed to have inherited his father's gifts had died suddenly in boyhood. She had fought through that agony because her husband was there, to be helped and to help; now, after the father's death, the thought of the boy had become unbearable. There was nothing left but to mother her daughter; and dear Jenny was such a perfect daughter that she needed no excessive mothering. 'Now with Babs Ansley I don't know that I *should* be so quiet,' Mrs. Slade sometimes half-enviously reflected; but Jenny, who was younger than her brilliant friend, was that rare accident, an extremely pretty girl who somehow made youth and prettiness seem as safe as their absence. It was all perplexing – and to Mrs. Slade a little boring. She wished that Jenny would fall in love – with the wrong man, even; that she might have to be watched, out-manoeuvred, rescued. And instead, it was Jenny who watched her mother, kept her out of draughts, made sure that she had taken her tonic . . .

Mrs. Ansley was much less articulate than her friend, and her mental portrait of Mrs. Slade was slighter, and drawn with fainter touches. 'Alida Slade's awfully brilliant; but not as brilliant as she thinks,' would have summed it up; though she would have added, for the enlightenment of strangers, that Mrs. Slade had been an extremely dashing girl; much more so than her daughter, who was pretty, of course, and clever in a way, but had none of her mother's – well, 'vividness,' some one had once called it. Mrs. Ansley would take up current words like this, and cite them in quotation marks, as unheard-of audacities. No; Jenny was not like her mother. Sometimes Mrs. Ansley thought Alida Slade was disappointed; on the whole she had had a sad life. Full of failures and mistakes; Mrs. Ansley had always been rather sorry for her . . .

So these two ladies visualised each other, each through the wrong end of her little telescope.

*

For a long time they continued to sit side by side without speaking. It seemed as though, to both, there was a relief in laying down their somewhat futile activities in the present of the vast Memento Mori which faced them. Mrs. Slade sat quite still, her eyes fixed on the golden slope of the Palace of the Cæsars, and after a while Mrs. Ansley ceased to fidget with her bag, and she too sank into meditation. Like many intimate friends, the two ladies had never before had occasion to be silent together, and Mrs. Ansley was slightly embarrassed by what seemed, after so many years, a new stage in their intimacy, and one with which she did not yet know how to deal.

Suddenly the air was full of that deep clangour of bells which periodically covers Rome with a roof of silver. Mrs. Slade glanced at her wrist-watch. 'Five o'clock already,' she said, as though surprised.

Mrs. Ansley suggested interrogatively: 'There's bridge at the Embassy at five.' For a long time Mrs. Slade did not answer. She appeared to be lost in contemplation, and Mrs. Ansley thought the remark had escaped her. But after a while she said, as if speaking out of a dream: 'Bridge, did you say? Not unless you want to . . . But I don't think I will, you know.'

'Oh, no,' Mrs. Ansley hastened to assure her. 'I don't care to at all. It's so lovely here; and so full of old memories, as you say.' She settled herself in her chair, and almost furtively drew forth her knitting. Mrs. Slade took sideway note of this activity, but her own beautifully cared-for hands remained motionless on her knee.

'I was just thinking,' she said slowly, 'what different things Rome stands for to each generation of travellers. To our grandmothers, Roman fever; to our mothers, sentimental dangers – how we used to be guarded! – to our daughters, no more dangers than the middle of Main Street. They don't know it – but how much they're missing!'

The long golden light was beginning to pale, and Mrs. Ansley lifted her knitting a little closer to her eyes. 'Yes; how we were guarded!'

'I always used to think,' Mrs. Slade continued, 'that our mothers had a much more difficult job than our grandmothers. When Roman fever stalked the streets it must have been comparatively easy to gather in the girls in the danger hour; but when you and I were young, with such beauty calling us, and the spice of disobedience thrown in, and no worse risk than catching cold during the cool hour after sunset, the mothers used to be put to it to keep us in – didn't they?'

She turned again toward Mrs. Ansley, but the latter had reached a delicate point in her knitting. 'One, two, three – slip two; yes, they must have been,' she assented, without looking up.

Mrs. Slade's eyes rested on her with a deepened attention. 'She can knit – in the face of *this*! How like her . . .'

Mrs. Slade leaned back, brooding, her eyes ranging from the ruins which faced her to the long green hollow of the Forum,

237

the fading glow of the church fronts beyond it, and the outlying immensity of the Colosseum. Suddenly she thought: 'It's all very well to say that our girls have done away with sentiment and moonlight. But if Babs Ansley isn't out to catch that young aviator – the one who's a Marchese – then I don't know anything. And Jenny has no chance beside her. I know that too. I wonder if that's why Grace Ansley likes the two girls to go everywhere together? My poor Jenny as a foil – !' Mrs. Slade gave a hardly audible laugh, and at the sound Mrs. Ansley dropped her knitting.

'Yes – ?'

'I – oh, nothing. I was only thinking how your Babs carries everything before her. That Campolieri boy is one of the best matches in Rome. Don't look so innocent, my dear – you know he is. And I was wondering, ever so respectfully, you understand ... wondering how two such exemplary characters as you and Horace had managed to produce anything quite so dynamic.' Mrs. Slade laughed again, with a touch of asperity.

Mrs. Ansley's hands lay inert across her needles. She looked straight out at the great accumulated wreckage of passion and splendour at her feet. But her small profile was almost expressionless. At length she said: 'I think you overrate Babs, my dear.'

Mrs. Slade's tone grew easier. 'No; I don't. I appreciate her. And perhaps envy you. Oh, my girl's perfect; if I were a chronic invalid I'd – well, I think I'd rather be in Jenny's hands. There must be times ... but there! I always wanted a brilliant daughter ... and never quite understood why I got an angel instead.'

Mrs. Ansley echoed her laugh in a faint murmur. 'Babs is an angel too.'

'Of course – of course! But she's got rainbow wings. Well, they're wandering by the sea with their young men; and here we sit ... and it all brings back the past a little too acutely.'

Mrs. Ansley had resumed her knitting. One might almost

have imagined (if one had known her less well, Mrs. Slade reflected) that, for her also, too many memories rose from the lengthening shadows of those august ruins. But no; she was simply absorbed in her work. What was there for her to worry about? She knew that Babs would almost certainly come back engaged to the extremely eligible Campolieri. 'And she'll sell the New York house, and settle down near them in Rome, and never be in their way . . . she's much too tactful. But she'll have an excellent cook, and just the right people in for bridge and cocktails . . . and a perfectly peaceful old age among her grandchildren.'

Mrs. Slade broke off this prophetic flight with a recoil of self-disgust. There was no one of whom she had less right to think unkindly than of Grace Ansley. Would she never cure herself of envying her? Perhaps she had begun too long ago.

She stood up and leaned against the parapet, filling her troubled eyes with the tranquillising magic of the hour. But instead of tranquillising her the sight seemed to increase her exasperation. Her gaze turned toward the Colosseum. Already its golden flank was drowned in purple shadow, and above it the sky curved crystal clear, without light or colour. It was the moment when afternoon and evening hang balanced in mid-heaven.

Mrs. Slade turned back and laid her hand on her friend's arm. The gesture was so abrupt that Mrs. Ansley looked up, startled.

'The sun's set. You're not afraid, my dear?'

'Afraid – '

'Of Roman fever or pneumonia? I remember how ill you were that winter. As a girl you had a very delicate throat, hadn't you?'

'Oh, we're all right up here. Down below, in the Forum, it does get deathly cold, all of a sudden . . . but not here.'

'Ah, of course you know because you had to be so careful.' Mrs. Slade turned back to the parapet. She thought: 'I must make one more effort not to hate her.' Aloud she said: 'Whenever I look at the Forum from up here, I remember that story about a great-aunt of yours, wasn't she? A dreadfully, wicked great-aunt?'

'Oh, yes; Great-aunt Harriet. The one who was supposed to have sent her young sister out to the Forum after sunset to gather a night-blooming flower for her album. All our great-aunts and grand-mothers used to have albums of dried flowers.'

Mrs. Slade nodded. 'But she really sent her because they were in love with the same man – '

'Well, that was the family tradition. They said Aunt Harriet confessed it years afterward. At any rate, the poor little sister caught the fever and died. Mother used to frighten us with the story when we were children.'

'And you frightened *me* with it, that winter when you and I were here as girls. The winter I was engaged to Delphin.'

Mrs. Ansley gave a faint laugh. 'Oh, did I? Really frightened you? I don't believe you're easily frightened.'

'Not often; but I was then. I was easily frightened because I was too happy. I wonder if you know what that means?'

'I – yes . . .' Mrs. Ansley faltered.

'Well, I suppose that was why the story of your wicked aunt made such an impression on me. And I thought: "There's no more Roman fever, but the Forum is deathly cold after sunset – especially after a hot day. And the Colosseum's even colder and damper." '

'The Colosseum – ?'

'Yes. It wasn't easy to get in, after the gates were locked for the night. Far from easy. Still, in those days it could be managed; it *was* managed, often. Lovers met there who couldn't meet elsewhere. You knew that?'

'I – I daresay. I don't remember.'

'You don't remember? You don't remember going to visit some ruins or other one evening, just after dark, and catching a

240

bad chill? You were supposed to have gone to see the moon rise. People always said that expedition was what caused your illness.'

There was a moment's silence; then Mrs. Ansley rejoined: 'Did they? It was all so long ago.'

'Yes. And you got well again — so it didn't matter. But I suppose it struck your friends — the reason given for your illness, I mean — because everybody knew you were so prudent on account of your throat, and your mother took such care of you . . . You *had* been out late sight-seeing, hadn't you, that night?'

'Perhaps I had. The most prudent girls aren't always prudent. What made you think of it now?'

Mrs. Slade seemed to have no answer ready. But after a moment she broke out: 'Because I simply can't bear it any longer!'

Mrs. Ansley lifted her head quickly. Her eyes were wide and very pale. 'Can't bear what?'

'Why — your not knowing that I've always known why you went.'

'Why I went — ?'

'Yes. You think I'm bluffing, don't you? Well, you went to meet the man I was engaged to — and I can repeat every word of the letter that took you there.'

While Mrs. Slade spoke Mrs. Ansley had risen unsteadily to her feet. Her bag, her knitting and gloves, slid in a panic-stricken heap to the ground. She looked at Mrs. Slade as though she were looking at a ghost.

'No, no — don't,' she faltered out.

'Why not? Listen, if you don't believe me. "My one darling, things can't go on like this. I must see you alone. Come to the Colosseum immediately after dark tomorrow. There will be somebody to let you in. No one whom you need fear will suspect" — but perhaps you've forgotten what the letter said?'

Mrs. Ansley met the challenge with an unexpected composure.

Steadying herself against the chair she looked at her friend, and replied: 'No; I know it by heart too.'

'And the signature? "Only *your* D.S." Was that it? I'm right, am I? That was the letter that took you out that evening after dark?'

Mrs. Ansley was still looking at her. It seemed to Mrs. Slade that a slow struggle was going on behind the voluntarily controlled mask of her small quiet face. 'I shouldn't have thought she had herself so well in hand,' Mrs. Slade reflected, almost resentfully. But at this moment Mrs. Ansley spoke. 'I don't know how you knew. I burnt that letter at once.'

'Yes; you would, naturally – you're so prudent!' The sneer was open now. 'And if you burnt the letter you're wondering how on earth I know what was in it. That's it, isn't it?'

Mrs. Slade waited, but Mrs. Ansley did not speak.

'Well, my dear, I know what was in that letter because I wrote it!'

'You wrote it?'

'Yes.'

The two women stood for a minute staring at each other in the last golden light. Then Mrs. Ansley dropped back into her chair. 'Oh,' she murmured, and covered her face with her hands.

Mrs. Slade waited nervously for another word or movement. None came, and at length she broke out: 'I horrify you.'

Mrs. Ansley's hands dropped to her knee. The face they uncovered was streaked with tears. 'I wasn't thinking of you. I was thinking – it was the only letter I ever had from him!'

'And I wrote it. Yes; I wrote it! But I was the girl he was engaged to. Did you happen to remember that?'

Mrs. Ansley's head drooped again. 'I'm not trying to excuse myself . . . I remembered . . .'

'And still you went?'

'Still I went.'

Mrs. Slade stood looking down on the small bowed figure at her side. The flame of her wrath had already sunk, and she wondered why she had ever thought there would be any satisfaction in inflicting so purposeless a wound on her friend. But she had to justify herself.

'You do understand? I'd found out – and I hated you, hated you. I knew you were in love with Delphin – and I was afraid; afraid of you, of your quiet ways, your sweetness . . . your . . . well, I wanted you out of the way, that's all. Just for a few weeks; just till I was sure of him. So in a blind fury I wrote that letter . . . I don't know why I'm telling you now.'

'I suppose,' said Mrs. Ansley slowly, 'it's because you've always gone on hating me.'

'Perhaps. Or because I wanted to get the whole thing off my mind.' She paused. 'I'm glad you destroyed the letter. Of course I never thought you'd die.'

Mrs. Ansley relapsed into silence, and Mrs. Slade, leaning above her, was conscious of a strange sense of isolation, of being cut off from the warm current of human communion. 'You think me a monster!'

'I don't know . . . It was the only letter I had, and you say he didn't write it?'

'Ah, how you care for him still!'

'I cared for that memory,' said Mrs. Ansley.

Mrs. Slade continued to look down on her. She seemed physic-ally reduced by the blow – as if, when she got up, the wind might scatter her like a puff of dust. Mrs. Slade's jealousy suddenly leapt up again at the sight. All these years the woman had been living on that letter. How she must have loved him, to treasure the mere memory of its ashes! The letter of the man her friend was engaged to. Wasn't it she who was the monster?

'You tried your best to get him away from me, didn't you? But you failed; and I kept him. That's all.'

'Yes. That's all.'

'I wish now I hadn't told you. I'd no idea you'd feel about it as you do; I thought you'd be amused. It all happened so long ago, as you say; and you must do me the justice to remember that I had no reason to think you'd ever taken it seriously. How could I, when you were married to Horace Ansley two months afterward? As soon as you could get out of bed your mother rushed you off to Florence and married you. People were rather surprised – they wondered at its being done so quickly; but I thought I knew. I had an idea you did it out of *pique* – to be able to say you'd got ahead of Delphin and me. Girls have such silly reasons for doing the most serious things. And your marrying so soon convinced me that you'd never really cared.'

'Yes. I suppose it would,' Mrs. Ansley assented.

The clear heaven overhead was emptied of all its gold. Dusk spread over it, abruptly darkening the Seven Hills. Here and there lights began to twinkle through the foliage at their feet. Steps were coming and going on the deserted terrace – waiters looking out of the doorway at the head of the stairs, then reappearing with trays and napkins and flasks of wine. Tables were moved, chairs straightened. A feeble string of electric lights flickered out. Some vases of faded flowers were carried away, and brought back replenished. A stout lady in a dust-coat suddenly appeared, asking in broken Italian if any one had seen the elastic band which held together her tattered Baedeker. She poked with her stick under the table at which she had lunched, the waiters assisting.

The corner where Mrs. Slade and Mrs. Ansley sat was still shadowy and deserted. For a long time neither of them spoke. At length Mrs. Slade began again: 'I suppose I did it as a sort of joke – '

'A joke?'

'Well, girls are ferocious sometimes, you know. Girls in love especially. And I remember laughing to myself all the evening at the idea that you were waiting around there in the dark, dodging out of sight, listening for every sound, trying to get in – Of course I was upset when I heard you were so ill afterward.'

Mrs. Ansley had not moved for a long time. But now she turned slowly toward her companion. 'But I didn't wait. He'd arranged everything. He was there. We were let in at once,' she said.

Mrs. Slade sprang up from her leaning position. 'Delphin there? They let you in? – Ah, now you're lying!' She burst out with violence.

Mrs. Ansley's voice grew clearer, and full of surprise. 'But of course he was there. Naturally he came –'

'Came? How did he know he'd find you there? You must be raving!'

Mrs. Ansley hesitated, as though reflecting. 'But I answered the letter. I told him I'd be there. So he came.'

Mrs. Slade flung her hands up to her face. 'Oh, God – you answered! I never thought of your answering . . .'

'It's odd you never thought of it, if you wrote the letter.'

'Yes. I was blind with rage.'

Mrs. Ansley rose, and drew her fur scarf about her. 'It is cold here. We'd better go . . . I'm sorry for you,' she said, as she clasped the fur about her throat.

The unexpected words sent a pang through Mrs. Slade. 'Yes; we'd better go.' She gathered up her bag and cloak. 'I don't know why you should be sorry for me,' she muttered.

Mrs. Ansley stood looking away from her toward the dusky secret mass of the Colosseum. 'Well – because I didn't have to wait that night.'

Mrs. Slade gave an unquiet laugh. 'Yes; I was beaten there. But I oughtn't to begrudge it to you, I suppose. At the end of all these years. After all, I had everything; I had him for twenty-five years. And you had nothing but that one letter that he didn't write.'

Mrs. Ansley was again silent. At length she turned toward the door of the terrace. She took a step, and turned back, facing her companion.

'I had Barbara,' she said, and began to move ahead of Mrs. Slade toward the stairway.

GEORGE EGERTON
THE SPELL OF THE WHITE ELF

Have you ever read out a joke that seemed excruciatingly funny, or repeated a line of poetry that struck you as being inexpressibly tender, and found that your listener was not as impressed as you were? I have, and so it may be that this will bore you, though it was momentous enough to me.

I had been up in Norway to receive a little legacy that fell to me, and though my summer visits were not infrequent, I had never been up there in mid-winter, at least not since I was a little child tobogganing with Hans Jörgen (Hans Jörgen Dahl is his full name), and that was long ago. We are connected. Hans Jörgen and I were both orphans, and a cousin – we called her aunt – was one of our guardians. He was her favourite; and when an uncle on my mother's side – she was Cornish born; my father, a ship captain, met her at Dartmouth – offered to take me, I think she was glad to let me go. I was a lanky girl of eleven, and Hans Jörgen and I were sweethearts. We were to be married some day, we had arranged all that, and he reminded me of it when I was going away, and gave me a silver perfume box, with a gilt crown on top, that had belonged to his mother. And later when he was going to America he came to see me first; he was a long freckled hobbledehoy, with just the same true eyes and shock head. I was, I thought, quite grown up, I had passed my 'intermediate' and was condescending as girls are. But I don't think it impressed Hans Jörgen much, for he gave me a little ring, turquoise forget-me-nots with enamelled leaves and a motto inside – a quaint old thing that belonged to

246

a sainted aunt – they keep things a long time in Norway – and said he would send for me; but of course I laughed at that. He has grown to be a great man out in Cincinnati and waits always. I wrote later and told him I thought marriage a vocation and I hadn't one for it; but Hans Jörgen took no notice, just said he'd wait. He understands waiting, I'll say that for Hans Jörgen.

I have been alone now for five years, working away, though I was left enough to keep me before. Somehow I have not the same gladness in my work of late years. Working for oneself seems a poor end even if one puts by money. But this has little or nothing to do with the white elf, has it?

Christiania is a singular city if one knows how to see under the surface, and I enjoyed my stay there greatly. The Hull boat was to sail at four-thirty and I had sent my things down early, for I was to dine at the Grand at two with a cousin, a typical Christiania man. It was a fine clear day, and Karl Johann was thronged with folks. The band was playing in the park, and pretty girls and laughing students walked up and down. Every one who is anybody may generally be seen about that time. Henrik Ibsen – if you did not know him from his portrait, you would take him to be a prosperous merchant – was going home to dine; but Björnstjerne Björnson, in town just then, with his grand leonine head, and the kind, keen eyes behind his glasses, was standing near the Storthing House with a group of politicians, probably discussing the vexed question of separate consulship. In no city does one see such characteristic odd faces and such queerly cut clothes. The streets are full of students. The farmers' sons amongst them are easily recognised by their homespun, sometimes home-made suits, their clever heads and intelligent faces; from them come the writers, and brain carriers of Norway. The Finns, too, have a distinctive type of head and a something elusive in the expression of their changeful eyes. But all, the town students, too, of easier manners and slangier tongues – all alike are going, as finances permit, to dine in

restaurant or steam-kitchen. I saw the *menu* for today posted up
outside the door of the latter as I passed – 'Rice porridge and
salt meat soup, 6d.,' and Hans Jörgen came back with a vivid
picture of childhood days, when every family in the little coast-
town where we lived had a fixed *menu* for every day of the
week; and it was quite a distinction to have meat balls on
pickled herring day, or ale soup when all the folks in town were
cooking omelettes with bacon. How he used to eat rice porridge
in those days! I can see him now put his heels together and give
his awkward bow as he said, 'Tak for Maden tante!' Well, we
are sitting in the Grand *Café* after dinner, at a little table near
the door, watching the people pass in and out. An ubiquitous
'sample-count' from Berlin is measuring his wits with a young
Norwegian merchant; he is standing green chartreuse; it pays to
be generous even for a German, when you can oust honest Leeds
cloth with German shoddy. At least so my cousin says. He
knows every one by sight, and points out all the celebrities to
me. Suddenly he bows profoundly. I look round. A tall woman
with very square shoulders, and gold-rimmed spectacles is
passing us with two gentlemen. She is English by her tailor-
made gown and little shirt-front, and noticeable anywhere.

'That lady,' says my cousin, 'is a compatriot of yours. She is a
very fine person, a very learned lady; she has been looking up
referats in the university bibliothek. Professor Sturm – he is a
good friend of me – did tell me. I forget her name; she is
married. I suppose her husband he stay at home and keep the
house!'

My cousin has just been refused by a young lady dentist, who
says she is too comfortably off to change for a small housekeeping business, so I excuse his sarcasm. We leave as the time draws
on and sleigh down to the steamer. I like the jingle of the bells,
and I feel a little sad. There is a witchery about the country that
creeps into one and works like a love-philtre, and if one has
once lived up there, one never gets it out of one's blood again. I

go on board and lean over and watch the people. The[...] good many for winter-time. The bell rings. Two sleighs dr[...] and my compatriot and her friends appear. She shakes ha[...] with them and comes leisurely up the gangway. The thought flits through me that she would cross it in just that cool way if she were facing death; it is foolish, but most of our passing thoughts are just as inconsequent. She calls down a remembrance to someone in such pretty Norwegian, much prettier than mine, and then we swing round. Handkerchiefs wave in every hand, never have I seen such persistent handkerchief-waving as at the departure of a boat in Norway. It is a national characteristic. If you live at the mouth of a fjord, and go to the market town at the head of it for your weekly supply of coffee beans, the population give you a 'send off' with fluttering kerchiefs. It is as universal as the 'Thanks.' Hans Jörgen says I am anglicised and only see the ridiculous side, forgetting the kind feelings that prompt it. I find a strange pleasure in watching the rocks peep out under the snow, the children dragging their hand-sleds along the ice. All the little bits of winter life of which I get flying glimpses as we pass, bring back scenes grown dim in the years between. There is a mist ahead; and when we pass Dröbak cuddled like a dormouse for winter's sleep I go below. A bright coal fire burns in the open grate of the stove, and the *Rollo* saloon looks very cosy. My compatriot is stretched out in a big arm-chair reading. She is sitting comfortably with one leg crossed over the other, in the manner called 'shockingly unlady-like' of my early lessons in deportment. The flame flickers over the patent leather of her neat low-heeled boot, and strikes a spark from the pin in her tie. There is something manlike about her. I don't know where it lies, but it is there. Her hair curls in grey flecked rings about her head; it has not a cut look, seems rather to grow short naturally. She has a charming tubbed look. Of course every lady is alike clean, but some men and women have an individual look of sweet cleanness that is a beauty of itself. She feels my gaze and looks up and smiles. She has a rare smile, it shows her white teeth and softens her features:

'The fire is cosy, isn't it? I hope we shall have an easy passage, so that it can be kept in.'

I answer something in English.

She has a trick of wrinkling her brows, she does it now as she says:

'A-ah, I should have said you were Norsk. Are you not really? Surely you have a typical head, or eyes and hair at the least?'

'Half of me is Norsk, but I have lived a long time in England.'

'Father of course; case of "there was a sailor loved a lass," was it not?'

I smile an assent and add: 'I lost them both when I was very young.'

A reflective looks steals over her face. It is stern in repose; and as she seems lost in some train of thought of her own I go to my cabin and lie down; the rattling noises and the smell of paint makes me feel ill. I do not go out again. I wake next morning with a sense of fear at the stillness. There is no sound but a lapping wash of water at the side of the steamer, but it is delicious to lie quietly after the vibration of the screw and the sickening swing. I look at my watch; seven o'clock. I cannot make out why there is such a silence, as we only stop at Christiansand long enough to take cargo and passengers. I dress and go out. The saloon is empty but the fire is burning brightly. I go to the pantry and ask the stewardess when we arrived? Early, she says; all the passengers for here are already gone on shore; and there is a thick fog outside, goodness knows how long we'll be kept. I go to the top of the stairs and look out; the prospect is uninviting and I come down again and turn over some books on the table; in Russian, I think. I feel sure they are hers.

'Good-morning!' comes her pleasant voice. How alert and bright-eyed she is! It is a pick-me-up to look at her.

'You did not appear last night? Not given in already, I hope!'

She is kneeling on one knee before the fire, holding her palms to the glow, and with her figure hidden in her loose, fur-lined coat and the light showing up her strong face under the little tweed cap, she seems so like a clever-faced slight man, that I feel I am conventionally guilty in talking so freely to her. She looks at me with a deliberate critical air, and then springs up.

'Let me give you something for your head! Stewardess, a wine-glass!'

I should not dream of remonstrance – not if she were to command me to drink sea-water; and I am not complaisant as a rule.

When she comes back I swallow it bravely, but I leave some powder in the glass; she shakes her head, and I finish this too. We sat and talked, or at least she talked and I listened. I don't remember what she said, I only know that she was making clear to me most of the things that had puzzled me for a long time; questions that arise in silent hours; that one speculates over, and to which one finds no answer in text-books. How she knew just the subjects that worked in me I knew not; some subtle intuitive sympathy, I suppose, enabled her to find it out. It was the same at breakfast, she talked down to the level of the men present (of course they did not see that it might be possible for a woman to do that), and made it a very pleasant meal.

It was in the evening – we had the saloon to ourselves – when she told me about the white elf. I had been talking of myself and of Hans Jörgen.

'I like your Mr. Hans Jörgen,' she said, 'he has a strong nature and knows what he wants; there is reliability in him. They are rarer qualities than one thinks in men, I have found through life that the average man is weaker than we are. It must be a good thing to have a stronger nature to lean to. I have never had that.'

There is a want in the tone of her voice as she ends, and I feel inclined to put out my hand and stroke hers – she has beautiful long hands – but I am afraid to do so. I query shyly –

'Have you no little ones?'

'Children, you mean? No, I am one of the barren ones; they are less rare than they used to be. But I have a white elf at home and that makes up for it. Shall I tell you how the elf came? Well, its mother is a connection of mine, and she hates me with an honest hatred. It is the only honest feeling I ever discovered in her. It was about the time that she found the elf was to come that it broke out openly, but that was mere coincidence. How she detested me! Those narrow, poor natures are capable of an intensity of feeling concentrated on one object that larger natures can scarcely measure. Now I shall tell you something strange. I do not pretend to understand it, I may have my theory, but that is of no physiological value, I only tell it to you. Well, all the time she was carrying the elf she was full of simmering hatred and she wished me evil often enough. One feels those things in an odd way. Why did she? Oh, that . . . that was a family affair, with perhaps a thread of jealousy mixed up in the knot. Well, one day the climax came, and much was said, and I went away and married and got ill and the doctors said I would be childless. And in the meantime the little human soul – I thought about it so often – had fought its way out of the darkness. We childless women weave more fancies into the "mithering o' bairns" than the actual mothers themselves. The poetry of it is not spoilt by nettle-rash or chin-cough any more than our figures. I am a writer by profession – oh, you knew! No, hardly celebrated, but I put my little chips into the great mosaic as best I can. Positions are reversed, they often are now-a-days. My husband stays at home and grows good things to eat, and pretty things to look at, and I go out and win bread and butter. It is a matter not of who has most brains, but whose brains are most saleable. Fit in with the housekeeping? Oh yes. I have a treasure, too, in Belinda. She is one of those women who must have something to love. She used to love cats, birds, dogs, anything. She is one bump of philo-progenitiveness, but she hates men. She says: "If one could only have a child, ma'm, without a husband or the disgrace; ugh, the disgusting men!" Do you know I think that is not an uncommon feeling amongst a certain number of women. I have often drawn her out on the subject. It struck me, because I have often found it in other women. I have known many, particularly older women, who would give anything in God's world to have a child of "their own" if it could be got just as Belinda says, "without the horrid man or the shame." It seems congenital with some women to have deeply rooted in their innermost nature a smouldering enmity, ay, sometimes a physical disgust to men, it is a kind of kin-feeling to the race dislike of white men to black. Perhaps it explains why woman, where her own feelings are not concerned, will always make common cause with woman against him. I have often thought about it. You should hear Belinda's "serve him right" when some fellow comes to grief. I have a little of it myself (meditatively), but in a broader way, you know. I like to cut them out in their own province. Well, the elf was born, and now comes the singular part of it. It was a wretched, frail little being with a startling likeness to me. It was as if the evil the mother had wished me had worked on the child, and the constant thought of me stamped my features on its little face. I was working then on a Finland saga, and I do not know why it was, but the thought of that little being kept disturbing my work. It was worst in the afternoon time when the house seemed quietest; there is always a lull then outside and inside. Have you ever noticed that? The birds hush their singing and the work is done. Belinda used to sit sewing in the kitchen, and the words of a hymn she used to lilt in half tones, something about "joy bells ringing, children singing," floated in to me, and the very tick-tock of the old clock sounded like the rocking of wooden cradles. It made me think sometimes that it would be pleasant to hear small pattering feet and the call of voices through the silent house. And I suppose it acted as an irritant on my imaginative faculty, for the whole room seemed filled with the spirits of little children. They seemed to dance round me with uncertain, lightsome steps, waving tiny pink dimpled hands, shaking sunny flossy curls, and haunting me with their great innocent child-eyes; filled with the unconscious sadness and the infinite questioning that is oftenest seen in the gaze of children. I used to fancy something stirred in me, and the spirits of unborn little ones never to come to life in me troubled me. I was probably overworked at the time. How we women digress! I am telling you more about myself than my white elf. Well, trouble came to their home, and I went and offered to take it. It was an odd little thing, and when I looked at it I could see how like we were. My glasses dimmed somehow, and a lump kept rising in my throat, when it smiled up out of its great eyes and held out two bits of hands like shrivelled white rose leaves. Such a tiny scrap it was; it was not bigger, she said, than a baby of eleven months. I suppose they can tell that as I can the date of a dialect; but I am getting wiser,' with an emotional softening of her face and quite a proud look. 'A child is like one of those wonderful runic alphabets; the signs are simple but the lore they contain is marvellous. "She is very like you," said the mother. "Hold her." She was only beginning to walk. I did. You never saw such elfin ears with strands of silk floss ringing round them, and the quaintest, darlingest wrinkles in its forehead, two long, and one short, just as I have,' putting her head forward for me to see. 'The other children were strong, and the one on the road she hoped would be healthy. So I took it there and then, "clothes and baby, cradle and all." Yes, I have a collection of nursery rhymes from many nations; I was going to put them in a book, but I say them to the elf now. I wired to my husband. You should have seen me going home. I was so nervous, I was not half as nervous when I read my paper – it was rather a celebrated paper, perhaps you heard of it – to the Royal Geographical Society. It was on Esquimaux marriage songs, and the analogy between them and the Song of Solomon. She was so light, and so wrapped up, and my *pince-nez* kept dropping off when I stooped over her – I got spectacles after that – and I used to fancy I had dropped her out of the wrappings, and peep under the shawl to make sure – with a sick shiver – to find her sucking her thumb. And I nearly passed my station. And then a valuable book – indeed, it is really a case of MSS., and almost unique – I had borrowed for reference with some trouble, could not be found, and my husband roared with laughter when it turned up in the cradle. Belinda was at the gate anxious to take her, and he said I did not know how to hold her, that I was holding her like a book of notes at a lecture, and so I gave her to Belinda. I think the poor little thing found it all strange, and when she puckered up her face, and thrust out her under lip, and two great tears jumped off her lashes, we all felt ready for hanging. But Belinda, though she doesn't know one language, not even her own, for she sows her h's broadcast and picks them up at hazard, she *can* talk to a baby. I am so glad for that reason she is bigger now; I couldn't manage it, I could not reason out any system they go on in baby talk. I tried mixing up the tenses, but somehow it wasn't right. My husband says it is not more odd than salmon taking a fly that is certainly like nothing they ever see in nature. Anyway it answered splendidly. Belinda used to say – I made a note of some of them – "Didsum was denn? OO did! Was ums de prettiest itta sweetums den? oo was. An' did um put 'em in a nasty shawl an' joggle 'em in an ole puff-puff, um did, was a shame! Hitchy cum, hitchy cum, hitchy cum hi, Chinaman no likey me!" This always made her laugh, though in what connection the Chinaman came in I never *could* fathom. I was a little jealous of Belinda, but she knew how to undress her. George, that's my husband's name, said the bath water was too hot, and that the proper way to test it was to put one's elbow in. Belinda laughed, but I must confess it did feel too hot when I tried it that way; but how did he know? I got her such pretty clothes, I was going to buy a pragtbind of Nietzsche, but that must wait. George made her a cot with her name carved on the head of it, such a pretty one.'

'Did you find she made a change in your lives?' I asked.

'Oh, didn't she! Children are such funny things. I stole away to have a look at her later on, and did not hear him come after me. She looked so sweet, and she was smiling in her sleep. I believe the Irish peasantry say that an angel is whispering when a baby does that. I had given up all belief myself, except the belief in a Creator who is working out some system that is too infinite for our finite minds to grasp. If one looks round with seeing eyes one can't help thinking that after a run of 1893 years, Christianity is not very consoling in its results. But at that moment, kneeling next to the cradle, I felt a strange, solemn feeling stealing over me; one is conscious of the same effect in a grand cathedral filled with the peal of organ music and soaring voices. It was as if all the old, sweet, untroubled child-belief came back for a spell, and I wondered if far back in the Nazarene village Mary ever knelt and watched the Christ-child sleep; and the legend of how he was often seen to weep but never to smile came back to me, and I think the sorrow I felt as I thought was an act of contrition and faith. I could not teach a child scepticism, so I remembered my husband prayed, and I resolved to ask him to teach her. You see (half hesitatingly) I have more brains, or at least more intellectuality than my husband, and in that case one is apt to undervalue simpler, perhaps greater, qualities. That came home to me, and I began to cry, I don't know why, and he lifted me up, and I think I said something of the kind to him . . . We got nearer to one another someway. He said it was unlucky to cry over a child.

'It made such a difference in the evenings. I used to hurry home – I was on the staff of the *World's Review* just then – and it was so jolly to see the quaint little phiz smile up when I went in.

'Belinda was quite jealous of George. She said "Master worritted in an' out, an' interfered with everything, she never seen a man as knew so much about babies, not for one as never 'ad none of 'is own. Wot if he didn't go to Parkins hisself, an' say as how she was to have the milk of one cow, an' mind not mix it." I wish you could have seen the insinuating distrust on Belinda's face. I laughed. I believe we were all getting too serious, I know I felt years younger. I told George that it was really suspicious; how did he acquire such a stock of baby lore? *I* hadn't any. It was all very well to say Aunt Mary's kids. I should never be surprised if I saw a Zwazi woman appear with a lot of tawny pickaninnies in tow. George was shocked – I often shock him.

'She began to walk as soon as she got stronger. I never saw such an inquisitive mite. I had to rearrange all my bookshelves, change Le Nu de Rabelais, after Garnier, you know, and several others from the lower shelves to the top ones. One can't be so Bohemian when there is a little white soul like that playing about, can one? When we are alone she always comes in to say her prayers, and goodnight. Larry Moore of the *Vulture* – he is one of the most wickedly amusing of men, prides himself on being *fin de siècle* – don't you detest that word? – or nothing, raves about Dégas, and is a worshipper of the decadent school of verse, quotes Verlaine, you know – well, he came in one evening on his way to some music hall. She's a whimsical little thing, not without incipient coquetry either; well, she would say them to him. If you can imagine a masher of the Jan van Beer type bending his head to hear a child in a white "nighty" lisping prayers, you have an idea of the picture. She kissed him good-night too; she never would before; and he must have forgotten his engagement, for he stayed with us to supper. She rules us all with a touch of her little hands, and I fancy we are all the better for it. Would you like to see her?' She hands me a medallion, with a beautifully painted head in it. I can't say she is a pretty child, a weird, elf-like thing, with questioning, wistful eyes, and masses of dark hair; and yet as I look the little face draws me to it; and makes a kind of yearning in me; strikes me with a 'fairy blast' perhaps.

The journey was all too short, and when we got to Hull she saw me to my train. It was odd to see the quiet way in which she got everything she wanted. She put me into the carriage, got me a footwarmer and a magazine, kissed me and said as she held my hand, 'The world is small, we run in circles, perhaps we shall meet again, in any case I wish you a white elf.' I was sorry to part with her; I felt richer than before I knew her; I fancy she goes about the world giving graciously from her richer nature to the poorer-endowed folks she meets on her way.

Often since that night I have rounded my arm and bowed down my face and fancied I had a little human elf cuddled to my breast.

*

I am very busy just now getting everything ready; I had so much to buy. I don't like confessing it even to myself, but down in the bottom of my deepest trunk I have laid a parcel of things, such pretty tiny things. I saw them at a sale, I couldn't resist them, they were so cheap; even if one doesn't want the things, it seems a sin to let them go. Besides, there may be some poor woman out in Cincinnati. I wrote to Hans Jörgen, you know, back in spring, and . . . Du störer Gud! There is Hans Jörgen coming across the street.

EMILY HOLMES COLEMAN
INTERLUDE

She turned in the bed and tried to slide into the hollow on a conforming stomach. It happened then and she jumped out into the bathroom and listened. There were snow crystals outside dropping like petticoats on the brown ground. It had happened, and that would be the end of that. She stared at her body's profile in the door and put her hair behind her ears. She lifted her eyebrows and smiled.

Squirming down heavily under loaded sheets she lay on her back and closed her eyes. I will have a clinging chiffon dressing gown and wind it tight about my middle. I will leap into a treetop. And it came again and thrust through to her brain with small well-planed knives. Pleasant knives, cutting her away from imbecility.

It came again and she felt her warm cheeks with a cold hand. I had better go now. She collected things and put them in a half-packed bag. Three books she put in on top. Bending over to the window she saw the snow still floating. It would be easier the next time she looked out of that window. And her hands trembled like fresh-drawn water.

The street was covered with ice and there were wreaths hanging in many of the windows. Extravagant berries like blood drops in the green moons. I'll call a taxi of course. But the walking steadied her rolling legs and when it came again and she had to bend over to watch her breath she preferred being on the ground. The ice was in hard lumps like little knolls and her heels clicked against them. The bag was light and the snow squatted gently on her hat and vanished.

259

At the door a white person looked at her as if he had never seen her before. Haughtily she told him the number. There were wreaths hung in the windows here too. Wonder who does that. Mistake about the room, soon settled. She sat down and began to count seconds on the rigid face of her watch. No one, and the snow continued to drop.

There is really nothing. She pulled apart the sensation, holding her knees tight and bending forward above them. I have had this before, often. She held the watch.

Her husband came in, cheeks bright and fingers outstretched. He held her shoulders, smiling at the watch. Then you knew how did you know? His heavy hair was snowridden. His overcoat dripped. Put it on the chair.

You must get into bed, you must get undressed first. His lips shone at her. His eyes, cold behind thick glasses, warmed to her. Dear, he said. She laughed immoderately and put her fingers to her ears, looking out on the snow.

She was in bed, glistening under chilly sheets. The radiator hissed and he sat on it, putting a newspaper first, and continuing to look at her in the bed. He lit his pipe with deliberate smackings of his well-shaped lips until there was fire in the bowl. Then he began to read.

You don't care I don't care. It's coming now listen. She was on her back holding to the bars of the bed with taut wrists and counting. It comes four long and two shorts, she said. It's really nothing. But Jesus Christ, she said, that one hurt. He smiled for her.

Look out the window and tell me if you can see the Mosque from here. Yes with the lights on top. Are the telegraph wires frozen yet? Yes and they sing in the wind.

Please it's getting worse. It's long knives now all of them. No shorts. I don't really care except that I wonder where he is. He knows I'm here but I suppose he only delivered a dozen today. Dear, he said, don't cry. I'll go for the nurse. I'm not crying.

Brilliant blue stripes of nurse gliding into foreground. You need something? She is in great pain can't you do anything for her she is in great pain. I'm not I don't want anything thank you. You doctor will be here soon, Mrs. Temple. Don't worry about yourself. Pleasant retreat of nurse busying hands with apron tie.

Don't look at me impotently. Not your fault, my sweet, go on reading. Read out loud to me.

'And bountiful spilled tears
of living
and who know forgiving
only the vulture's hunch-ed shoulders . . .'

That's appropriate, she said, and twinkled a laugh. Her legs were strings. Don't look at me so or I'll have you sent home.

Please – don't – look – like that. She swayed in the bed and clutched the bars. She pulled viciously on them. Someone said to pull – God, the damn thing will be born this minute if somebody doesn't come. Goddam goddam goddam. Please dear you can't do anything at all nothing at all. Smoke your pipe and read some more poetry. I do love poetry. Jesus CHRIST! She reached up to clutch her hair. Her hands flew from side to side. I can't stand this. Only Jewish women scream good for them I should think they would. Dr. Rainer made fun of them everybody made fun of them. Screams of Jewish women when I went to see Marian Thomas and she said she only grunted a little. The ones who really suffer don't make a sound.

Don't come near me darling I'm sorry but go away. Muffled from the crazy pillow. Don't pick it up I want it there. Oh go away, my dearest I love you very much but please – PLEASE – don't stay in this room.

A great boulder, as large as Eagle Rock, was bursting from within her. Slowly, with the predestined drop of a hydraulic press it pushed downward. Her legs were strapped to wheels and the wheels began to roll relentlessly away from each other wrenching her limbs apart. She began to scream. She gripped the bedposts, and with all her throat, lungs and body she screamed.

This woman is having some pain. The doctor, thumping her body and noting that the snow was getting deep on the roof across the street. I think you had better get the ether and the cart. The head seems to be there. But doctor – it's – being – born – now, isn't it? Oh, no, my dear. We mustn't be impatient. Things are going very nicely. That's the head you feel. Yes, I didn't think it was the feet.

Bear down. Pull on the bars and bear down. That's the way. But – doctor – it – kills – me – to – do – that. Blue moons floated in seas of rich blood. Spirals of hot branding irons shot through her nerves and out her finger tips. Her fingers flew over her body. I can't keep them still doctor. Bear down, Mrs. Temple, it will make it easier for you.

'A steam roller chugged over her back, back and forth, crunching the boulder inside. Ether, ether! She sat up in bed swiftly, hair starting out, teeth champing. You get that ether, do you hear? Black impotent tears fell from her burning face into the dry bulbs of his inattention.

The cart rolled melodiously in on carressing rubber wheels. She clutched at the ether bag and thrust it violently to her face, breathing in the cool cessation of horror in tremendous gulps. The bag was patted into place, the assistant surgeon fussing in the rear. Did you ever see anything like that she almost broke the tube. Lifted in space legs hanging loose boulder diminishing in size hands drooping life beginning again not to die ignobly in childbirth lakes cool in summer fanshaped ducks swimming on glistening top ridges of circles from rounded pebbles thrown with loping arms blue blue lakes of gold – sky – of gold – summer – and gold.

...Take that and put it over there. The bichloride, Miss

Evans. What is this I'm awake again and no bump. My God no lump any more. Doctor is it really gone?

What did it turn out to be?

'And bid fair peace be to my sable shroud.' What is that she keeps saying? Have I been saying that? Yes and a lot more like it. Closed eyes again. She's not out of it yet. It's a boy, Mrs. Temple. Open again wide. Thank God for that. I'm awake. What does he look like? Strange I really want to know now that it's over. What are the nurses giggling at? Do you always swear so much Mrs. Temple? Yes always.

She was lifted to the cart again, after having had her legs taken out of the clamps that strung them up. Efficiency in hospitals. Deliveries every half hour. Mother sinks into calm sleep soon after. But she doesn't it still hurts. You were very brave, Mrs. Temple, the doctor said going down in the elevator. She tried to turn over. Doctor you don't have to lie to me I know you too well. You think I don't remember how I yelled? I may do it again this minute. Are you in pain now? Surprise. Of course I am but never mind.

She was lifted to the bed and fell back to the pillow. Her whole body throbbed. Flat stomach anyway. Strange little mound where the boulder had tried to get out. She felt it delicately. Bone . . . Ha, the median line, I am a mother now. She was pleased to discover it.

The nurse was in glowing white this time. How do you feel, said with the utmost sympathy. She doesn't give a damn. It aches still I can't move. Did I have what was considered a hard time? You had several stitches but the birth was quite normal. High forceps but that often happens. A beautiful baby, quite perfect.

Darling. There were little glittering drops in the corners of his eyes. He kissed her hands and put roses in them. You have a little boy what do you think of that? And you should see him said the nurse he is perfect. Can't I see him now? The nurse went to get him.

My darling little girl he said again and shook his head. Never again anything like this. They always say that. But he does love me. And I love him. And we have a beautiful baby. The nurse returned with a little bag of cotton and wool. Here he is. She laid him in the mother's crooked elbow.

But there's some mistake this isn't mine! Anxiously turned to him. He doesn't look like us he isn't mine. It's the wrong one. No dear see his name around his neck. TEMPLE. He isn't very goodlooking but he's ours.

That horrible little thing was her baby. His head went up to a peak like a Chinese pagoda. His claws wriggled slowly like snakes in a museum. He began to wail, thinly, eerily. She cried passionately into the pillow and crushed rose petals all over the bed.

You had better take it away, he said to the nurse. She is very tired and unstrung.

ANAÏS NIN
RAGTIME

The city was asleep on its right side and shaking with violent nightmares. Long puffs of snoring came out of the chimneys. Its feet were sticking out because the clouds did not cover it altogether. There was a hole in them and the white feathers were falling out. The city had untied all the bridges like so many buttons to feel at ease. Wherever there was a lamplight the city scratched itself until it went out.

Trees, houses, telegraph poles, lay on their side. The ragpicker walked among the roots, the cellars, the breathing sewers, the open pipe works, looking for odds and ends, for remnants, for rags, broken bottles, paper, tin and old bread. The ragpicker walked in and out of the pockets of the sleeping city with his ragpicker's pick. In and out of the pockets over the watch chain on its belly, in and out of the sleeves, around its dusty collar, through the wands of its hair, picking the broken strands. The broken strands to repair mandolins. The fringe on the sleeve, the crumbs of bread, the broken watch face, the grains of tobacco, the subway ticket, the string, the stamp. The ragpicker worked in silence among the stains and smells.

His bag was swelling.

The city turned slowly on its left side, but the eyes of the houses remained closed, and the bridges unclasped. The ragpicker worked in silence and never looked at anything that was whole. His eyes sought the broken, the worn, the faded, the fragmented. A complete object made him sad. What could one do with a complete object? Put it in a museum. Not touch it.

But a torn paper, a shoelace without its double, a cup without saucer, that was stirring. They could be transformed, melted into something else. A twisted piece of pipe. Wonderful, this basket without a handle. Wonderful, this bottle without a stopper. Wonderful, the box without a key. Wonderful, half a dress, the ribbon off a hat, a fan with a feather missing. Wonderful, the camera plate without the camera, the lone bicycle wheel, half a phonograph disk. Fragments, incompleted worlds, rags, detritus, the end of objects, and the beginning of transmutations.

The ragpicker shook his head with pleasure. He had found an object without a name. It shone. It was round. It was inexplicable. The ragpicker was happy. He would stop searching. The city would be waking up with the smell of bread. His bag was full. There were even fleas in it, pirouetting. The tail of a dead cat for luck.

His shadow walked after him, bent, twice as long. The bag on the shadow was the hump of a camel. The beard the camel's muzzle. The camel's walk, up and down the sand dunes. The camel's walk, up and down. I sat on the camel's hump.

It took me to the edge of the city. No trees. No bridge. No pavement. Earth. Plain earth trodden dead. Shacks of smoke-stained wood from demolished buildings. Between the shacks gypsy carts. Between the shacks and the carts a path so narrow that one must walk Indian file. Around the shacks palisades. Inside the shack rags. Rags for beds. Rags for chairs. Rags for tables. On the rags men, women, brats. Inside the women more brats. Fleas. Elbows resting on an old shoe. Head resting on a stuffed deer whose eyes hung loose on a string. The ragpicker gives the woman the object without a name. The woman picks it up and looks at the blank disk, then behind it. She hears tick, tick, tick, tick, tick. She says it is a clock. The ragpicker puts it to his ear and agrees it ticks like a clock but since its face is blank they will never know the time. Tick, tick, tick, the beat of time and no hour showing.

The tip of the shack is pointed like an Arab tent. The windows oblique like oriental eyes. On the sill a flower pot. Flowers made of beads and iron stems, which fell from a tomb. The woman waters them and the stems are rusty.

The brats sitting in the mud are trying to make an old shoe float like a boat. The woman cuts her thread with half a scissor. The ragpicker reads the newspaper with broken specs. The children go to the fountain with leaky pails. When they come back the pails are empty. The ragpickers crouch around the contents of their bags. Nails fall out. A roof tile. A signpost with letters missing.

Out of the gypsy cart behind them comes a torso. A torso on stilts, with his head twisted to one side. What had he done with his legs and arms? Were they under the pile of rags? Had he been thrown out of a window? A fragment of a man found at dawn.

Through the cracks in the shacks came the strum of a mandolin with one string.

The ragpicker looks at me with his one leaking eye. I pick a basket without bottom. The rim of a hat. The lining of a coat. Touch myself. Am I complete? Arms? Legs? Hair? Eyes? Where is the sole of my foot? I take off my shoe to see, to feel. Laugh. Glued to my sole is a blue rag. Ragged but blue like cobalt dust.

The rain falls. I pick up the skeleton of an umbrella. Sit on a hill of corks perfumed by the smell of wine. A ragpicker passes, the handle of a knife in his hand. With it he points to a path of dead oysters. At the end of the path is my blue dress. I had wept over its death. I had danced in it when I was seventeen, danced until it fell into pieces. I try to put it on and come out the other side. I cannot stay inside of it. Here I am, and there the dress, and I forever out of the blue dress I had loved, and I dance right through air, and fall on the floor because one of my heels came off, the heel I lost on a rainy night walking up a hill kissing my loved one deliriously.

Where are all the other things, I say, where are all the things I thought dead?

The ragpicker gave me a wisdom tooth, and my long hair which I had cut off. Then he sinks into a pile of rags and when I try to pick him up I find a scarecrow in my hands with sleeves full of straw and a high top hat with a bullet hole through it.

The ragpickers are sitting around a fire made of broken shutters, window frames, artificial beards, chestnuts, horse's tails, last year's holy palm leaves. The cripple sits on the stump of his torso, with his stilts beside him. Out of the shacks and the gypsy carts come the women and the brats.

Can't one throw anything away forever? I asked.

The ragpicker laughs out of the corner of his mouth, half a laugh, a fragment of a laugh, and they all begin to sing.

First came the breath of garlic which they hang like little red Chinese lanterns in their shacks, the breath of garlic followed by a serpentine song:

> Nothing is lost but it changes
> into the new string old string
> in the new bag old bag
> in the new pan old tin
> in the new shoe old leather
> in the new silk old hair
> in the new hat old straw
> in the new man the child
> and the new not new
> the new not new
> the new not new

All night the ragpicker sang the new not new the new not new until I fell asleep and they picked me up and put me in a bag.

NOTES ON THE AUTHORS

Djuna Barnes (1892–1982) was born in an artists' colony north of New York and educated by her English mother, a writer, and her American father, an artist. She had a career as a journalist and graphic artist before publishing *The Book of Repulsive Women*, a collection of poems and drawings, in 1915. After separating from her husband she left for Paris in 1919, where she was at the centre of the modernist movement. Her circle included Natalie Barney, Emily Holmes Coleman, Peggy Guggenheim, Kay Boyle, Gertrude Stein, Antonia White, James Joyce, Ezra Pound and T. S. Eliot. Famed for her wit and beauty, she became a cult figure with *Nightwood* (1936), written in the aftermath of her ten-year relationship with the American sculptor Thelma Wood. In 1940, her health damaged by bouts of alcoholism, illness and acute depression, she returned to Greenwich Village and lived as a recluse for the rest of her life. Her last major work was *The Antiphon* (1958), a dramatic poem inspired by her association with Eliot.

Kay Boyle was born in Minnesota in 1902 and studied music and architecture. Her first marriage to a Frenchman took her to Europe where she remained for thirty years. Much of that time was spent in Paris, where she knew Robert McAlmon, Bryher, Djuna Barnes, Mary Butts, James Joyce and Gertrude Stein. She published her first work in *Poetry* magazine and was interested in the movement for The Revolution of the Word promoted by Eugene Jolas and *transition* magazine. She returned to America in 1941 and embarked on a distinguished academic career. She has written, edited and translated more than thirty books; her first novel, *Plagued by the Nightingale*, appeared in 1930. Famous for her short stories, she won Guggenheim Fellowships in 1934 and 1961, and O. Henry Awards for the Best Story of 1934, 'The White Horses of Vienna' and of 1941, 'Defeat'. A member of the American Academy of Arts and Letters, she lives in California.

Mary Butts (1890–1937) was born in 1890 and grew up in Dorset. In 1911, when she was living in London, she became interested in socialism and knew Rebecca West, Wyndham Lewis and Roger Fry. Her work was known and praised by Gertrude Stein, Ford Madox Ford and Ezra Pound. She married John Rodker in 1918, but left him two years later for Cecil Maitland, with whom she shared a strong interest in magic, drugs and the occult. Her first book was a collection of stories, *Speed the Plough* (1923). In the 1920s Mary Butts travelled and lived in France, where she was a well-known figure in Paris. McAlmon's Contact Editions published her first novel, *Ashe of Rings*, in 1926. Though her output was small, her original writing made an important contribution to modernism. Her other books include short-story collections, *Several Occasions* (1932) and *Last Stories* (1938), and the novels *Armed with Madness* (1928) and *Scenes from the Life of Cleopatra* (1935). She died in Cornwall in 1937.

Winifred Bryher (1894–1983) was born Annie Winifred Ellermann in Kent and grew up in London in a wealthy family. At fifteen she went to boarding school, which she hated and later wrote about in her first novel, *Development* (1920). She was already interested in imagist poetry and modernist prose (including Dorothy Richardson's writing) when she met H.D. in 1918. Their close relationship lasted until H.D.'s death. From adolescence Bryher knew she was a lesbian and made a marriage of convenience with Robert McAlmon in 1921. Best known as a patron of writers, such as Barnes; of publishers, including McAlmon's Contact Editions; of psychoanalytic institutions, and of Sylvia Beach's famous bookshop, Bryher also published novels, poetry and criticism. She divorced McAlmon and in 1927 married H.D.'s lover Kenneth Macpherson, with whom she founded the film journal, *Close Up*, and made a film, *Borderline* (1930), starring H.D. and Paul Robeson. She is best known for *The Heart to Artemis: A Writer's Memoirs* (1962).

Leonora Carrington was born in 1917 and spent her childhood in a Lancashire mansion, the daughter of an Irish mother and an English textile tycoon. She was educated at convent schools, expelled from one, and 'finished' at Miss Penrose's Academy in Florence before being presented as a débutante in 1936. Rejecting the life for which she had been groomed, Carrington went to an influential art school the same year as the first surrealist exhibition in London, later meeting one of the movement's leaders, Max Ernst. They eloped to France; she was nineteen, he was forty-six and married. There, both painted, exhibiting in Paris, while she began writing. After his imprisonment as an enemy alien in 1939 she went mad, suffering horrific treatment in a Spanish mental asylum. Rescued, she went to Lisbon, met her first husband, a Mexican diplomat she had first encountered through Picasso, and went to New York. Later she moved to Mexico City with her second husband, the Hungarian photographer Imre Weisz, where she continued her work as a surrealist writer and painter. Disillusioned by reaction to student unrest, she left Mexico in 1968. Later she returned, and now lives in Mexico City. Most of her writings are collected in *The House of Fear* (1989) and *The Seventh Horse and Other Tales* (1989).

Sidonie Gabrielle Colette (1873–1954) was born and brought up in rural Burgundy, later fictionalised in her stories *La Maison de Claudine* (1922). She moved to Paris in 1893 with her first husband, Henri Gauthier-Villars – the notorious 'Willy' – and her first book appeared under his pseudonym. Through him she came to know Proust, Ravel (for who she wrote a libretto), Debussy, Fauré and many others. Willy profited from the *Claudine* novels (1900–3), while Colette remained economically dependent on him. Their unhappy marriage ended in 1906, the year of her début as a mime dancer. She also worked as a drama critic and stage actress, continuing to write. Her affair with Missy (the Marquise de Belbeuf) ended as Colette moved in with the editor of *Le Matin*, who was to become her second husband. Their daughter was born in 1913. Three years later Colette dropped the name 'Willy' and as 'Colette' established herself as a major talent with *Chéri* (1920) and *La Fin de Chéri* (1926). In 1935 she married Maurice Goudelet, with whom she remained for the rest of her life. One of the most admired writers in France, she was the first woman to become president of the Académie Goncourt.

Emily Holmes Coleman (1899–1974) was born in California and educated at a private school and at Wellesley College. At the age of twenty-five, having been married for three years, she gave birth to a son and subsequently suffered puerperal fever, which led to a mental breakdown and a period in an asylum. Her only published novel, *Shutter of Snow* (1930), is based on this experience. She published many poems in the influential and experimental magazine *transition*, after moving to Paris in 1925, where her closest friends included Djuna

Barnes (whose *Nightwood* she introduced to T. S. Eliot) and Peggy Guggenheim. She wrote prolifically throughout her life, producing reams of poetry and keeping a daily journal. In the 30s she lived in London, with George Barker, Dylan Thomas and Antonia White among her circle. Returning to America in 1939 she converted to Catholicism with typical energy and commitment. In 1953 she moved back to England, spending the years from 1957–68 on a Worcestershire retreat. Her last years were almost entirely occupied by painting, at the Catholic Workers Farm in New York State.

Hilda Doolittle (1882–1961) was born in Pennsylvania. She began university at Bryn Mawr College in 1905 but left after three terms. In 1910, when she was engaged to Ezra Pound, she met Frances Gregg, her first female lover and they travelled to Europe. She married the writer Richard Aldington, with whom she was at the centre of the London avant-garde. Her first poem appeared in 1913, under the name 'H.D., Imagiste'; her first collection of poetry, *Sea Garden*, followed in 1916. After her marriage collapsed, H.D. lived briefly with Cecil Gray, the father of her daughter, Perdita. She then began a lifelong relationship with Bryher. During the 1920s they travelled widely, with the mythology of Greece and Egypt providing inspiration for H.D.'s work. She was also interested in the unconscious and entered analysis with Freud in 1933. Although she is most famous as a poet, her prose is sometimes considered her most radical work. Her novels include *Her* (written in 1927, published in 1981) and *Bid Me to Live* (1960). 'Kora and Ka' was first published privately in *Vaud* (1930); the text here is from that edition, kindly supplied by Perdita Schaffner.

Dorothy Edwards (1903–1934) was born in Wales, and educated at University College, Cardiff, where she took a degree in Greek and Philosophy. Her parents were both schoolteachers, and her father, a socialist, brought her up as a strict vegetarian. A non-Welsh-speaking Welsh Nationalist and lifelong member of the Independent Labour Party, she read French, Italian, German, Norwegian and Russian, and was an accomplished singer, spending six months in Vienna. She also stayed in Florence for nine months before returning to Rhiwbina, on the outskirts of Cardiff, where she and her mother had moved after her father's death. The first story she tried to place appeared in Edward O'Brien's *Best Short Stories*; when her complete stories were published in *Rhapsody* (1927), she was heralded as a genius by the *Observer*'s

Gerald Gould. *Winter Sonata* (1928), her only novel, followed. Later she became friends with David and Ray Garnett, living with them in London in 1933, where she met Lytton Strachey, Virginia Woolf, Vanessa and Clive Bell, Roger Fry and Duncan Grant. She was not an unmitigated success in London and returned to Wales. On January 6 1934 she burnt all her papers and letters before throwing herself under a train.

George Egerton (1859–1945) was born Mary Chavelita Dunne in Australia and raised in Ireland. She worked briefly as a nurse in London, then went to New York. In the late 1880s she lived in Norway with her married lover, where she learnt Norwegian and was influenced by the writings of the Scandanavian Realists. She returned to London in 1890, translated *Hunger* by her friend Knut Hamsun and a year later married George Egerton Clairmonte, taking his first names as a pseudonym for her writing. Her friends in London included Havelock Ellis, Ellen Terry, George Bernard Shaw and the publisher John Lane.

She published two volumes of short stories, *Keynotes* (1893) and *Discords* (1894), which were republished in one volume in 1983. At times her interest in the 'New Woman', especially her relationship to sexuality and motherhood, was controversial. 'The Spell of the White Elf' (from *Discords*) is notable for depicting motherhood as a social rather than a biological function.

Janet Flanner (1892–1978) was born in Indianapolis. In 1922, with little income and no apparent profession, she left for Paris. From 1925, the year in which *The New Yorker* was founded, she produced its now famous 'Letters from Paris', under the pseudonym 'Genet'. Her closest male friend was Hemingway, and she knew – and wrote about – almost all of the famous members of the expatriate community, including Barnes, Colette and Stein as well as Sylvia Beach, Chanel, Picasso, Alice B. Toklas and Edith Wharton. Her only novel, *The Cubical City* (1926) describes the culture of 1920s New York, in particular the double standard of sexual behaviour for men and women. She was involved with Solita Solano for many years and, with her, appeared in Barnes' *Ladies Almanack*. In later years she felt embarrassed by the apparent frivolity of her early writings compared with her later more overtly political analyses. By 1933 her letters virtually formed a political record, exhibiting the intense French interest in Soviet Russia. One of the last to leave Paris, she fled to the

US on October 4 1939. The first volume of her *Paris Journal* (1965) won a National Book Award.

Charlotte Perkins Gilman (1860–1935), described as 'one of America's foremost feminists', was primarily a non-fiction writer. She was concerned with the historical and economic causes of women's oppression, and during her lifetime was perhaps most famous for her biting analysis, *Women and Economics* (1898), which was translated into seven languages and used as a college text in America in the 1920s. Born Charlotte Anna Perkins in Connecticut, she was brought up by her mother. After much deliberation, she married at the age of twenty-four, giving birth to her only child the following year. She then suffered the mental breakdown from which *The Yellow Wallpaper* (1892) arose. The effects of the breakdown plagued her for the rest of her life. Between 1895 and 1900 she lectured tirelessly and inspirationally, and produced the bulk of her work. During the years 1909–16 she single-handedly wrote and edited the monthly magazine *The Forerunner* from which four novels serialised in it were later published separately, including *Herland*. In 1900 she married George Gilman, who died in 1934. Suffering from terminal cancer, she committed suicide in 1935.

Susan Glaspell (1882–1948) was born in Iowa, and educated at Drake University and the University of Chicago. In 1915, in Massachusetts, she founded and later directed the Provincetown Players with her first husband, George Cram Cook. From its inception, the experimental company developed unknown actors, designers and writers, and offered roles to women. Most famous for producing Eugene O'Neill's early work, with which Glaspell's own plays are now favourably compared, the Players moved to Greenwich Village, where their productions included three one-act plays by Djuna Barnes. Although sometimes developing ideas at the expense of dramatic effectiveness, Glaspell's plays were in tune with the most advanced thinking of the time. *Trifles* (1916) dramatises the provocations that lead a farm wife to kill her husband; and *Alison's House* (1930), suggested by the life of Emily Dickinson, won the Pulitzer Prize. Despite its earlier success in Europe, *The Comic Artist*, a play written with her second husband Norman Matson, failed in America in 1933, and this prompted Glaspell to abandon the theatre. Her novels include *The Glory of the Conquered* (1909) and *The Visioning* (1911). Her short stories were collected in *Lifted Masks (1912)* and *A Jury of Her Peers* (1927).

Frances Gregg (1884–1941) was considered by Ezra Pound to be a fine poet; her work appeared in various magazines, including *Poetry* and *The New Freewoman*. In 1910, in Philadelphia, she was involved in an emotional and sexual triangle with H.D. and Pound, who were engaged at the time. She was to describe the events of this period in 'Male and Female', published here for the first time, and probably written in 1925. (H.D. also wrote about the relationship in *Her*.) Gregg's emotional life continued to be complicated; in 1912 John Cowper Powys, who was in love with Gregg, encouraged her to marry his friend Louis Wilkinson; Pound dissuaded H.D. from accompanying the couple on honeymoon. Gregg and Wilkinson co-authored a novel, *The Buffoon* (1916), satirising many of their friends, including H.D., Pound and Powys. Alistair Crowley (the Great Beast), also a friend of Wilkinson's, later tried to have Gregg certified as insane. After her marriage collapsed, Gregg spent the rest of life caring for her children and her mother, often in dire poverty. She had little time for writing, but produced further short stories and an unpublished memoir. She died in a Plymouth air raid.

Nella Larson (1891–1964) claimed to have been born in Chicago, but it may have been New York. Much uncertainty and error surrounds her life, but it has been established that she was born in 1891 and not 1893. Her mother was Danish, her father was probably West Indian. After his death, her mother married a white man, who seems to have disliked his step-daughter; the despair of middle-class Black American women, an important theme in Larsen's fiction, reflects aspects of her own displacement. A major figure in the Harlem Renaissance, Larsen won a literary prize for her novel *Quicksand* (1928); received excellent reviews for *Passing* (1929); and in 1930, as the first Black woman to be awarded a Guggenheim Fellowship, travelled through Europe. But success was not lasting: her story *Sanctuary* (1930) met with charges of plagiarism; her heavily publicised divorce from the Black physics professor Elmer Imes, became official in 1933, and two of her novels were rejected. Larsen was depressed for several years, and then returned to her former career of nursing. She became chief nurse at Gouveneur Hospital, New York, in 1944.

Vernon Lee (1856–1935) was born Violet Paget in France. She spent her childhood moving around Europe, educated by governesses and by her mother, and was extremely intellectual, if rather lonely. Her *Studies of* *the Eighteenth Century in Italy* (1880) met with acclaim; a large number of books and essays on aesthetics, philosophy and art history followed. Henry James numbered among Vernon Lee's admirers and she dedicated *Miss Brown* (1884), her first (unsuccessful) novel, to him, somewhat to his embarrassment. Success returned with her short stories, notably the collections, *Vanitas* (1892), *Pope Jacynth* (1904) and *For Maurice* which included 'The Doll' (1927). As a pacifist, she wrote the satire *Satan the Waster* (1920) in response to the First World War. Her 'decadent' writing, especially 'Prince Alberic and the Snake Lady' is also of interest. A lesbian, Vernon Lee spent some time in Paris, where she knew Edith Wharton, and lived in Italy for many years.

Mina Loy (1882–1966) was born Mina Gertrude Lowy in London. Originally a painter, she changed her name in 1903 after some success in exhibiting her work. She was one of the few women to be involved in Futurism, and the aggressive, polemical style of her 'Feminist Manifesto', written in 1914, bears its hallmarks. The first of her two volumes of poetry appeared in the same year; further poetry, as well as drawings, plays and manifestos, was published in experimental magazines, and by 1917 her reputation was such that a New York newspaper featured her as the prototype of the 'modern woman'. *Lunar Baedecker* (sic., 1923) was published by McAlmon; *Lunar Baedeker and Timetables* (1958) and *Last Lunar Baedeker* (1982) followed. The poet-pugilist Arthur Craven became Loy's second husband in 1918, but disappeared shortly afterwards. Gertrude Stein and Djuna Barnes were among her closest friends but, like Barnes, Loy became reclusive in later life. Her last thirty years were spent in America, mostly in New York, where, largely forgotten, she struggled to make a living and wrote some remarkable poetry. Her story, 'Street Sister', is published here for the first time.

Katherine Mansfield (1888–1923) was born Kathleen Mansfield Beauchamp in Wellington, New Zealand, and attended school in London 1903–6. She returned to London from Wellington in 1908. In 1909 she married, but left her husband after one night. In 1912 she met John Middleton Murry, whom she married in 1918. Their intense and stormy relationship lasted until her death, but was punctuated by separations. Their literary friends included D. H. and Frieda Lawrence and Virginia Woolf. In 1917 she contracted tuberculosis and, advised to avoid English winters, spent her remaining years between London and France, accompanied by her intimate friend Ida Baker (L.M.).

Mansfield was one of the most important practitioners of the short story of her time. Her first collection, *In a German Pension*, was published in 1911. Other collections include *Bliss* (1920) and *The Garden Party* (1922). She died at the age of thirty-four.

Anaïs Nin (1903–77), of French, Danish, Spanish and Cuban descent, was born in Neuilly, just outside Paris. She left with her mother for New York at the age of eleven and stayed there for twelve years before returning to Paris. A model, dancer, teacher and lecturer, she later became a practising psychoanalyst under Otto Rank. Her first book was the critical work, *D. H. Lawrence, an Unprofessional Study* (1932). She was encouraged to write by several of the 1920s' and 1930s' avant-garde, including Henry Miller and Antonin Artaud, as well as by her close friend, Laurence Durrell. Miller, as well as D. H. Lawrence and Djuna Barnes, all of whom she greatly admired, influenced her work. Returning to the U.S.A. at the beginning of World War II, she printed her own writings until Dutton published *Ladders of Fire* (1946), a stream of consciousness story about the amorous attachments among four women. Among many other works, she published several short story collections, including *Under a Glass Bell* (1948) and two volumes of erotica. Her prose poem *House of Incest* (1949) was set to music by Varese, and *A Spy in the House of Love* (1954) was filmed. Nin's *Diary* appeared in six volumes (1966–76), and in 1965 Henry Miller's letters to her were published.

Jean Rhys (1894–1979) was born Ella Gwendolen Rees Williams and brought up by her Creole mother and Welsh father. Coming to England at the age of sixteen, she drifted mainly between London and Paris in the 1920s and 1930s, employed variously as a singer and dancer in a chorus line, mannequin and artist's model. She began to write after the breakdown of her first marriage. Ford Madox Ford, with whom Rhys had an affair, wrote the introduction for the short story collection, *The Left Bank* (1927). The novels *Quartet* (1928) and *After Leaving Mr Mackenzie* (1930), *Voyage in the Dark* (1934) and *Good Morning, Midnight* (1939) followed. These semi-autobiographical works, concerned with women living on the margins of society, treat the issues of thwarted desire, social and sexual displacement and vulnerability. After the imprisonment of her third husband, Rhys disappeared for nearly thirty years, living with little money in Cornwall and Devonshire. In large part due to the enthusiasm of Francis Wyndham she was rediscovered, accumulating the stories for *Tigers are Better Looking* (1968) and working on *Wide Sargasso Sea* (1966), which won the Royal Society for Literature Award and the W.H. Smith Award. This was followed by the short story collection, *Sleep it Off, Lady* (1976) and the autobiographical *Smile Please* (1979).

Dorothy Richardson (1873–1957) was born in Berkshire, and went to Germany as an English teacher at the age of seventeen, when she realised her family was going bankrupt. In 1895, after a long period of depression, her mother committed suicide and Richardson moved to London. She worked as a teacher and then as a secretary-assistant to a dental practice and began to write articles, sketches and reviews for magazines. In 1913, during a long stay in Cornwall, she wrote *Pointed Roofs*, the first novel of *Pilgrimage*, lauded for its innovative technique and its exploration of gender, and published in twelve parts between 1915 and 1938. A thirteenth novel appeared in the posthumous 1967 edition. Richardson was poor all her adult life and supported herself, and sometimes her husband, Alan Odle, an artist, through her journalism and freelance editing. Her friends included H.D., Bryher, John Cowper Powys and H.G. Wells. She wrote only fifteen short stories, which were collected under the title *Journey to Paradise* (1989).

May Sinclair (1863–1946) was born in Cheshire and spent her early years in Liverpool. In 1881 her father died a bankrupt. Sinclair, the only daughter of six children, cared for her mother until her death in 1901 and nursed several of her brothers who had inherited heart disease. She was very interested in philosophy, psychoanalysis and classical literature, and began to publish poetry in 1887. Her first novel was *Audrey Craven* (1897); a novella, *The Divine Fire* (1904) was a bestseller. May Sinclair was one of the few writers here to make a good living from writing. Her other novels include *Mary Olivier: A Life* (1919) and *Life and Death of Harriett Frean* (1920). She was active in the suffrage movement and encouraged other writers, such as H.D. and Frances Gregg. An admirer of Dorothy Richardson, she reviewed the first three books of *Pilgrimage* in *The Egoist* and *The Little Review* in 1918.

Stevie Smith (1902–71) was born Florence Margaret, in Hull, acquiring the nickname Stevie one day when she was horse riding, after the jockey Steve Donoghue. She spent most of her life with her aunt in Palmer's

Green, North London. Her first book, *Novel on Yellow Paper* (1936), was mistakenly ascribed to Virginia Woolf by the poet Robert Nichols, who believed it to be her best novel. This and her first volume of poems, *A Good Time Was Had By All* (1937) established her reputation. She wrote only two more novels, *Over the Frontier* (1938) and *The Holiday* (1949), but produced seven further volumes of caustic and enigmatic verse, much of it illustrated with her comic drawings. Clive Bell wrote her a fan letter, as did Sylvia Plath, confessing herself to be 'an addict of your poetry, a desperate Smith addict'. A popular and accomplished reciter, both at poetry readings and on the radio, she won the Queen's Gold Medal for Poetry in 1969. Her *Collected Poems* appeared in 1978; *Me Again* (1981), her hitherto uncollected pieces, followed.

Gertrude Stein (1874–1946) was born in Pennsylvania. She spent her early years in Vienna and studied at the Harvard Annex and the Johns Hopkins School of Medicine. In 1902 she left the United States, and by the following year was living with her brother Leo at the legendary 27 rue de Fleurus in Paris. Together they bought work by Cézanne, Renoir, Matisse and Picasso, who became a lifelong friend. In 1907 Stein met Alice B. Toklas, with whom she was to live for more than forty years. During the First World War they worked for a hospital supply unit in France; on their return new painters and writers frequented Stein's salon, Gris, Picabia, Scott Fitzgerald and Hemingway among them. The author of over twenty books and one of the most avant-garde of the modernist writers, Stein's first published book was *Three Lives* (1909). The poem *Tender Buttons* (1914) won acclaim, but her first popular success came with *The Autobiography of Alice B. Toklas* in 1933. 'Miss Furr and Miss Skeene' was based upon two friends of Stein's.

Edith Wharton (1862–1937) was born in New York. In 1885 she married a Boston socialite and lived with him on Rhode Island, frequently travelling to Europe where she became friends with Henry James. Her first novel, *The Valley of Decision*, appeared in 1902. She went on to publish an average of more than a book a year for the rest of her life. Her first critical and popular success came with *The House of Mirth* (1905); a rich period of literary activity followed. Her husband's mental health declined, and in 1910, when they had moved permanently to France, the marriage broke up, ending in divorce in

1913. After an intense period of war work, Wharton moved north of Paris. *The Age of Innocence* (1920) followed, winning the Pulitzer Prize. One of America's greatest novelists, she was the first woman to receive a Doctorate of Letters from Yale University and was a member of the American Academy of Arts and Letters.

Virginia Woolf (1882–1941) is probably the most famous of the modernist women writers. Born Adeline Virginia Stephen and educated at home, she moved to Gordon Square, soon to become the centre of the Bloomsbury Group, with her sister and brothers in 1904. In 1912 she married Leonard Woolf. Her first novel, *The Voyage Out* (1915) appeared three years later. In 1917 the Woolfs founded the Hogarth Press, whose authors included Katherine Mansfield and T. S. Eliot. Virginia Woolf also made a name for herself as a literary critic. In 1927, her fifth novel, *To the Lighthouse*, was awarded the Prix Femina Vie Heureuse. She took a keen interest in women's writing and women's issues and her impassioned pleas are recorded in *A Room of One's Own* (1929), and *Three Guineas* (1938). She experienced several breakdowns, possibly stemming from childhood abuse, and committed suicide in 1941.

Also of interest

THE SHUTTER OF SNOW
Emily Holmes Coleman
Introduction by Carmen Callil and Mary Siepmann

After the birth of her child Marthe Gail spends two months in
an insane asylum with the fixed idea that she is God. Marthe,
something between Ophelia, Emily Dickinson and Lucille
Ball, transports us into that strange country of terror and
ecstasy we call madness. A twilit country where the objective
and the subjective are fused, where perspective is lost, logic
absent and only pain remains . . .

But Marthe is intelligent, witty and even in madness has her
wits about her. The doctors, the nurses, the other inmates
and the mad vision of her insane mind are revealed with
piercing insight and with immense verbal facility. In prose of
unusual beauty, Emily Coleman describes the borderlines of
sanity in a novel as hilarious and as moving as Ken Kesey's
One Flew Over The Cuckoo's Nest. This neglected masterpiece,
first published in 1930, was her only novel.
'An extraordinary, visionary book, written out of those edges
where madness and poetry meet' – *Fay Weldon*

ROMAN FEVER
Edith Wharton
New Introduction by Marilyn French

These elegant, finely-wrought stories by one of America's greatest writers are here published in Britain for the first time. Set in Italy, France and America they are powerful portraits of women who live in 'the world of propriety' at the turn of the century. They tell of the emotions women feel: in love, in jealousy, when they long for children or seek independence – and when their passions lead them to overstep the bounds laid down by exacting conventions. We see, too, what happens to those strong enough to break the rules, but rarely strong enough to live forever outside the pale of the society that has banished them. First published in America in 1964, this collection of beautifully-crafted stories contains some of Edith Wharton's finest writing.

Edith Wharton, the winner of two Pulitzer Prizes, best known for *The House of Mirth* and *The Age of Innocence*, was 'the most accomplished American novelist of her generation'
– Raymond Mortimer

HER
H.D.
New Introduction by Helen McNeil
Afterword by Perdita Schaffner

It is 1909 and Hermione Gart is in her early twenties – 'a disappointment to her father, an odd duckling to her mother, an importunate, overgrown, unincarnated entity that had no place.' Having just failed at her college, Bryn Mawr, she stays at home, stifled by her family, struggling for an identity, waiting for her life to begin. Then the wild poet George Lowndes returns from Europe, expanding her horizons, yet threatening her new, fragile sense of self. An intense and emotional friendship with another woman, Fayne Rabb, makes her hold on reality more tenuous. Inevitably Hermione is led to a mental breakdown that will become a turning point and a new beginning: as her own true self, as 'Her' – the poet H.D.

Recalling her brief, broken engagement to Ezra Pound (George Lowndes), and her relationship with Frances Josepha Gregg (Fayne Rabb), *Her* is both a fascinating record of a passage in H.D.'s life, and a novel written with the voice of one of America's greatest poets: at once evocative, witty and compelling, it puts her work alongside that of her friends and contemporaries – Ezra Pound, Amy Lowell, D.H. Lawrence, William Carlos Williams and her husband Richard Aldington.

'A rare talent' – *Denis Donoghue*

THE LIFE AND DEATH OF HARRIETT FREAN

May Sinclair

Introduction by Jean Radford

In this portrait of a perfect daughter of the Victorian Age we enter the consciousness of Harriett Frean from the day of her birth to the day of her death. Harriett is the embodiment of all those virtues then viewed as essential to the womanly ideal; a woman reared to love, honour and obey. Idolising her parents, she learns from childhood to equate love with self-sacrifice, so that when she falls in love with the fiancé of her closest friend, renunciation of this unworthy passion initially brings her a peculiar form of happiness. But the passing of time unveils a different truth . . .

In capturing the inner life of one ordinary woman, May Sinclair puts under the microscope a whole way of nineteenth century life. Ironic, brief, intensely realised, not one word is superfluous in this brilliant study of female virtue seen as vice. First published in 1922, it is May Sinclair's most perfect literary achievement and stands with the work of Dorothy Richardson and Virginia Woolf as one of the great innovatory novels of this century.

'A masterpiece' – *Walter Allen*

SMOKE AND OTHER EARLY STORIES
Djuna Barnes

Edited, with an Introduction by Douglas Messerli
Afterword by Kay Boyle

First published in New York newspapers between 1914 and
1916 these fourteen incisive tales wonderfully evoke
Greenwich Village Bohemia of that time. Sketched with an
exquisite and decadent pen are lovers and loners, schemers
and dreamers, terrorists and cowards, and many, many more.
There's the terrible 'Peacock', a 'slinky female with
electrifying eyes and red hair' whom all men pursue but
cannot entice; Paprika Johnson softly playing her pawnshop
banjo above Swingerhoger's Beer Garden and Mamie Saloam
the dancer who 'became fire and felt hell'. There's Clochette
Brin who 'knew that love and lottery went together', the silent
Lena whose stolid appearance disguised her animal spirit and
the cunning Madeleonette whose lovers enact the most
dramatic rite of all.

Written during her early career, and published in Britain for
the first time, these fourteen stories are 'startlingly strange,
cranky even, but also raw and exciting as swigs of poteen'
– *Times Literary Supplement*